Praise

"As Orwell knew, the best dystopias ... to make it scarily believable.... It's the ... ng debut *The Office of Mercy*.... At its he ... cary and realistic ... fast-paced ... exciting to ... ikian has crafted a hero who is memorable precisely because of her imperfections.... It's fascinating, and at times heartbreaking, to witness her incremental growth as she begins to question everything she's been taught. It takes a blend of intelligence and compassion to pull off that kind of convincing character arc, but it also takes great authorial skill.... *The Office of Mercy* is an indisputable page-turner with a surprising ending.... The stunning, willfully oblivious cruelty of America-Five is chilling because of its plausibility—you don't have to look past our own history for examples of mass slaughter, eugenics, and euphemized government propaganda. It's hard to miss the echoes of Orwell in Djanikian's dark vision of both the past and the future."

—Michael Schaub, NPR

"A cool and compelling dystopian bildungsroman from a debut author we imagine we'll be hearing a lot more from."   —Emily Temple, *Flavorwire*

"A remarkable coming-of-age dystopian novel, fast-paced and thought provoking throughout."   —*Largehearted Boy*

"A horrifically brutal, compelling debut ... A grim muse on a future with shades of *The Hunger Games*."   —*Booklist* (starred review)

"The title of Ariel Djanikian's first book, *The Office of Mercy*, is as disturbing as it is ironically fitting. Using a fresh, effortless descriptive style, Djanikian projects us into a futuristic world wiped clean by a man-made devastation called the Storm.... Djanikian puts us through the ethical ringer.... Which isn't to say there's not also a good deal of juice here, too—Natasha totally busts an actual move on her superior, as opposed to resorting to passive cybering."   —Whitney Dwire, *BUST*

"Ariel Djanikian has written a novel of strange and stirring passions. Her dystopia is familiar to us because it is the land of our nightmares, our myths, and histories—yet Djanikian infuses it with startling novelty. The writing is both languidly sensual and suspenseful. This novel ushers in an important new voice."   —Laura Kasischke, author of *In a Perfect World*

"A dark look at the extent of the sciences and a twisted form of ethics ... A story that has real legs throughout."   —Andrew Liptak, *Geek*

"Ariel Djanikian has crafted a suspenseful read that presents a fresh and provocative imagining of dystopian politics relevant to our own time."

—Alex Good, *Toronto Star*

"Fascinating . . . Djanikian's fictitious world combines both the horrifying consequences of ethnic cleansing with the bright new hope of how much one person can do to change history. Both believable and chilling, this tale transports readers to a futuristic utopic life where good and evil mingle with equal opportunity and are often indistinguishable to the characters. This intriguing slice of future drama ends much too soon and will leave readers begging for a sequel, if not a series."

—*Kirkus Reviews*

"A compelling story that goes beyond the typical dystopia by creating a world in which there are no clear distinctions between good and evil . . . A tightly written piece of speculative fiction."

—*School Library Journal*

"If you think a future world without suffering would be a good thing, Ariel Djanikian will convince you to reconsider in her impressive debut *The Office of Mercy*. Gripping, well-plotted, and boasting a fascinating setting, this utterly engrossing tale is thoughtful and surprising. Djanikian's adroit writing turns the elements of the dystopian novel on their head, and the central character's struggles in America-Five were, by turns, both starkly foreign and hauntingly familiar."

—Deborah Harkness, *New York Times* bestselling author of
A Discovery of Witches and *Shadow of Night*

"[Djanikian] truly shines by plunging her characters into existential crises as they question and finally confront the foundations on which their lives are built. Fans of sci-fi and speculative fiction will enjoy this adventurous exploration of human nature."

—Tobias Mutter, *Shelf Awareness*

"Intriguing premise . . . In this thoughtful debut, Djanikian explores the disconnect between a utopian vision and its dystopian implementation. . . . Natasha Wiley, a young citizen assigned to the Office of Mercy, knows empathy will only get in the way of her necessary work, but when she comes into close contact with one of the tribes, her reaction sets off world-changing events."

—*Publishers Weekly*

"*The Office of Mercy* confronts us with a portrait of a smoothly heartless world that's viscerally imagined, increasingly harrowing, and beautifully moving. As we continue to squander or destroy the finite resources our planet has remaining, and the gap between the elite and the trampled continues to widen, the heartbreaking and chilling vision that Ariel Djanikian outlines starts to seem like our most—if not our only—plausible future."

—Jim Shepard, author of *Like You'd Understand, Anyway*

PENGUIN BOOKS

THE OFFICE OF MERCY

Ariel Djanikian is a graduate of the University of Pennsylvania and the University of Michigan and is the recipient of a Fulbright grant. Born in Philadelphia, she currently lives in Chapel Hill, North Carolina, with her husband and daughter. *The Office of Mercy* is her first novel.

The
OFFICE
of
MERCY

Ariel Djanikian

PENGUIN BOOKS

PENGUIN BOOKS
Published by the Penguin Group
Penguin Group (USA) LLC
375 Hudson Street
New York, New York 10014

USA | Canada | UK | Ireland | Australia | New Zealand | India | South Africa | China
penguin.com
A Random House Company

First published in the United States of America by Viking Penguin,
a member of Penguin Group (USA) Inc., 2013
Published in Penguin Books 2014

THE LIBRARY OF CONGRESS HAS CATALOGED THE HARDCOVER EDITION AS FOLLOWS:
Djanikian, Ariel.
The Office of Mercy : a novel / Ariel Djanikian.
p. cm.
ISBN 978-0-670-02586-2 (hc.)
ISBN 978-0-14-312437-5 (pbk.)
1. Psychological fiction. I. Title.
PS3604.J36O34 2013
813'.6—dc23   2012015085

Printed in the United States of America
1   3   5   7   9   10   8   6   4   2

For Phil,
in every possible world

The

OFFICE

of

MERCY

PROLOGUE

The sun sank behind the trees, and the blue-black shadows of the forest encroached farther down the sloping beach. The younger children eyed the dark warily and pushed closer to the weak, gasping fire at their center; the babies rolled their heavy heads and fell into whimpering sleep against their mothers' necks. The mood among the women and the old men was tense and silent. Motionless they sat, kneeling against each other in the sand, backs against the ocean winds, gazes steadily fixed on the fire, while inside, their thoughts roiled and screamed:

Twelve, it was almost too much to believe, their twelve strongest hunters—their beloved sons, their adored husbands and fathers—were missing from the camp.

The hunters had set off into the forest on the morning of the last full moon, for what Roland, the leader among them, had announced during the prayers to Aliama would be a three-day hunt. The ocean had been greedy with her fish, and Roland and the other hunters believed they could do better venturing inland with their spears, following the rumor of deer, a scattering of split-toed tracks left in a slop of mud by the trees. They had crossed into the shadows of tangled vine and prowling beast with cheerful war cries and prideful hearts, the twelve. The clouds had made stripes in the sky, a sign from Aliama that

He would protect them. But on the fourth morning the hunters had failed to return, and on the eighth day of their absence the remaining young men had gone to look for them, fearing that the recent rain-storms had altered the forest somehow, causing the hunters to lose their way home.

Now they all were missing. Six more nights had passed and what could their families do but watch the swaying wall of forest with grow-ing dread?

Beneath the crackle and rushing gusts of the fire came the quiet sobs of a waiflike and darkly tanned little boy. He clutched at his stom-ach as if to catch in his fist and pull away the pain of his hunger, as one might remove a pinching crab. After a long, plaintive whine he was quickly silenced by his mother's sister with a sharp slap on his hand. It did no good to cry; everyone was hungry. They had found nothing to eat for many days but a half-dead bush bearing red sourberries and a few foul-tasting clams that two young mothers had dug up with sticks from the sand. The warm season would end; already the twilight air was crisp. If the hunters did not return soon, or if the terrible thing had happened and the forest had swallowed them all, then surely the women and the children and the old men left on the beach would starve.

Night crept in from the blank horizon and fell over them fully, and the children dropped off one by one into sleep. A pack of dogs howled in the distance, broadening the dark with their calls. The waves heaved and crashed, heaved and crashed, an endless song that had once brought comfort but now seemed like a terrible lullaby, their old friend the ocean saying goodbye. The older people rested their heads on mounds of damp beach. None had washed in many days, and the sand caked their hair and faces and gritted between their teeth; it settled in the crevices of their clothing and limbs, already laying claim to their flesh. Gradually the older people gave in to sleep too, though only the thin, reluctant dozes of those who are afraid.

It was from the deepest depths of this quiet, at the moment when despair had all but slipped to deadly acquiescence, when a strange noise suddenly reared from the forest. Instantly they were all awake, even the babies, who felt the rigid jolt of the bodies they clung to and screamed. Astonished eyes met with more astonishment around the circle. Then they were up on their feet, the women shrieking, the children clapping and darting like water bugs from one skirted hip to another, and the old men hollering prayers to Aliama, open-armed to the stars.

"Heey-yaa, hey-yaa-ho," came the swelling chant from the forest.

The hunters had returned! Their voices rang with triumph!

At last the chant crescendoed and the first faces sprang from the forest's grasp. They were all together, the twelve hunters and the ones who had gone after them. They were filthy and exhausted, in torn leathers and with matted hair and sliced, bleeding bare feet, but alive, truly alive, all of them.

Sobs of relief broke to the surface and hot tears washed many faces clean. The men's eyes glittered with merriment, for they had not returned empty-handed: slung up by the ankles hung one, two, three— four slain deer! "Oh!" cried the children, stretching up on their toes and rubbing their bellies. Now they would have a feast for their breakfast. The fire roared as if in anticipation and everyone laughed. Roland brandished a bloodstained spear in two strong fists over his head and led the reunion into the warm, happy light.

This was the last moment: the first sliver of sun appearing over the ocean, unfurling a shimmering, golden path across the dancing waves; the smell of meat filling the air; the boys and girls draping their long limbs over their fathers' shoulders; and the stories of trial and adventure still only at their beginning. Then from a high place in the nearby trees, a small red light flashed from the lens of a well-concealed camera, and a soaring bright object, like a giant spearhead, broke from the wisp of clouds above.

An instant later the sky exploded, and all existence turned to ash.

1

On floor six, the sixth level underground, Natasha Wiley shut her sleeproom door and stepped quickly down the narrow hall. She moved as people do when they sense danger directly behind them, though nothing pursued Natasha but her thoughts. She turned sharply past the faded orange doors of the laundry bank and past the entrance to the waste-release stalls. The air vents hissed on overhead, making her jump, though it was a familiar noise. At the far end of the corridor, near the elevator hub, two citizens, both holding briefcases, were speaking loudly of the alarm. Natasha knew them; they were Elliot Beckman, Gamma, from the Department of Research, and Roger Descartes, Beta, from Health. Everyone knew everyone in America-Five, though the settlement boasted one of the largest populations on the continent. Behind the men, the tall elevator doors were parting open, revealing a menagerie of faces that shined with alertness through their sallow, grayish complexions. They all seemed to be watching Natasha, who broke into an awkward jog.

"Natasha!" said Elliot, just noticing her and holding the door open as she squeezed inside. "Maybe you're the best one to tell us. Has it happened? Has there been a sweep?"

The other citizens stopped their chatter to listen. The doors thudded closed and the elevator (called the "elephant" by most for its silver massiveness, lumbering speed, and dank, vaguely animal smell) heaved them upward with a groan.

"They stationed me in the Dome," Natasha said a little defensively, holding a thick bundle of hair back from her face and straining her neck to look around at them all. "I don't know any more than you do."

"But it must have been a sweep!" came Anusha Jain's high voice from the corner. She rose on her tiptoes to find Natasha's eyes in the jumble of bodies. "There's never been a four-hour alarm that didn't end in a sweep. Why even the Palms—"

"Course we got 'em," cut in a gruff Beta whom Natasha disliked. "But was it Cranes or Pines, that's what I want to know."

Cries of agreement broke from the group, and Natasha bit her lip until they had quieted.

"I think—" Natasha began, but she stopped to correct herself. "I *hope* there was a sweep. But I can't say for sure till I get to the Office."

Two female generation Deltas joined them on level four, and a male Department of Agriculture Gamma elbowed in on level one, before they finally reached ground level, the Dome.

It was a relief, as it always was, to spill out from the cramped underground and into the light. The sky was especially clear this morning, and the sun touched the top of Natasha's head with its heat. The bright green treetops glistened and swayed on the other side of the arcing expanse of steel-framed, honeycomb windows; and the obscured figure of a blackbird traced easy loops in the empty, high beyond. Crowds of morningshift workers crisscrossed on the marble floor, dressed in blue coveralls, chem-repellent lab coats, medical scrubs, or second-skin shirts and tough synthetic-protein pants (Natasha's own outfit) as their jobs prescribed. As they walked, the citizens threw glances at the maincomputer, its eight-sided screen positioned atop the elevator hub. In the hum of talk, the word "sweep" echoed and bounced around the circular wall.

"Had to be a biggie," one medworker was saying to another, as they passed Natasha. "They wouldn't raise the alarm for a partial sweep."

"Oh, I don't know," answered his friend. "If a group got close enough to the settlement, it wouldn't matter if there were only three or four of them. . . ."

The mounting curiosity among the citizens only served to escalate Natasha's own, and she pursed her lips and stepped a bit quicker. For now, the citizens could do little more than guess at the details. The Alphas would not make the news public until they had verified the count and watched the sensor tapes for themselves. Of course, the wait was driving everyone else in the settlement into a state of frenzied anticipation. Natasha herself could not imagine waiting all afternoon to hear what had happened, and she counted herself lucky to be among the elite few headed to a back cubicle in the Office of Mercy, where she and her team had been tracking both the Crane and the Pine Tribes for weeks.

"It's an exciting day. . . ." Natasha overheard a Delta woman saying. And it was.

There had not been a full-Tribe sweep in more than two decades, since the nearly disastrous sweep of the Palms.

On most mornings as she crossed the Dome, Natasha would indulge in a private moment to gaze out at the world beyond the windows, to contemplate the movement of clouds or the particular shade of blue suffusing the atmosphere at this hour. Not today, though. Natasha told herself that she had no time to spare for distractions, and she determined it best to keep her thoughts as firmly as possible within the settlement's walls.

Besides, it wasn't as if Natasha had any lack of *inside* sights to admire. America-Five was the largest of its kind, and the Dome was the pride of the settlement: its apex soaring as high above the land as level three was deep. At evenly spaced intervals around the circular base (one precisely every sixty degrees) were six sets of large double doors—at this hour gaping open and closing with arrhythmic hurriedness—each set of doors leading into one of the wings: the

Department of the Exterior, which housed the Office of Mercy, where Natasha worked; the Department of Health; the Department of Research; the Department of Agriculture, comprising the Garden and the vast Farms; the Department of Living, where the citizens gathered for meals, recreation, or, in the Archives, for study; and finally, the Department of Government, which was the only wing that Natasha had never entered, partly on account of her age (she was a mere twenty-four, like every Epsilon).

Taken together, as Natasha and all the citizens had learned as tiny children, America-Five had the basic shape of a concrete- and lead-enforced flower, buried to its head: the column of underground levels made up the stem, the beautiful Dome that capped it was the bud, and the six wings were the flower's six petals, stretching out from the center.

Six wings now, Natasha thought, as an electron saw roared on to her left, but soon to be seven.

Between the Department of Living and the Department of Government doors, blue tarps covered a portion of the Dome's wall; and from beyond the temporary airlock there came the bangs and rumbles of construction. The New Wing would make room for the next generation, the Zetas, already wrinkled, funny-looking little creatures in the Office of Reproduction, and due to emerge from their liquid phase of development in less than five months. Natasha smiled just thinking about them. She couldn't help it; all the other citizens were like that too. Even the most cynical old Betas among them couldn't help but glow with cheerful pride at the mention of the Zeta generation.

The numbers on all eight sides of the maincomputer simultaneously flashed 0800, and the pace of the morning workers picked up a notch. The crowds split off and began disappearing into the wings. Natasha lined up at the Department of the Exterior doors, behind Joe McMahon from the Office of Air and Energy, who greeted her with a nod and who, as a Beta, Natasha knew would be too proud to search her for answers. Natasha took a deep breath and smoothed the front of her shirt; there was a small dot of gravy from yesterday's dinner, and she licked her finger and absentmindedly rubbed away at the porous material. Despite what she had told the group in the elephant, she was absolutely positive that there had been a sweep; with an unprecedented two Tribes in the area and Jeffrey Montague working the nightshift, she could not imagine otherwise.

While she waited in line, Natasha loosened her thoughts and allowed herself to remember last night. She had fallen asleep as soon as her head hit the pillow, full from one of her favorite dinners, roast chicken and peas. But her dreams had begun troubling her almost immediately: the dream of fire and smoke that had haunted her for years, which even the doctors in the Office of Psychotronomy had not been able to stamp out of her. She had just roused herself from the grips of imagined flame, as she had done a hundred times before, when the shrill cry of the alarm came over the speakers. The lights flashed three times quick and then blared on.

Min-he Fang, Natasha's roommate, cursed and tangled her legs in her sheets and half fell out of her bed. The two lockers containing their emergency biosuits burst open and their wallcomputers lit up with instructions: Min-he Fang, level two, main corridor, Ammunition Support. Natasha Wiley, Dome, outer circle position 270, Wave One Defense. Natasha retrieved her gun, a LUV-3, from its marked locker on the level six hall and boarded the first ride up to ground level. A lifetime of drills made it so that she hardly had to think as she took her assigned position, released the safety on her gun, and began scanning the night-blackened spread of honeycomb windows for movement. Around her, the ghostly figures of the other citizens on Wave One Defense did the same, and all together they made two concentric circles of resolute force around the Dome. During the early hours of the alarm, other citizens streamed through their formation, passing through to stations in various wings. The radio clipped to Natasha's ear buzzed with commands—"group eleven, fan the Garden," "rooftop group two, maintain current alignment." Yet as the night wore on and eventually began to tilt toward morning, all became silent. Natasha's biosuit clung to the sweat on her back and her LUV-3 grew heavy in her arms. The bodies of the other citizens swayed and seemed almost to sigh, though no one moved a step from their spot.

It came at 0548 hours, the low moan from the speakers that meant, by either success or failure, that the possibility of an attack had ended and all citizens could return to their beds.

What had made that surge of horror break across Natasha's mind? Suddenly her sight had changed—her imagination overthrowing the facts of the arcing Dome, the sky, the alarm—and the mundane dark had opened itself to her. The abyss where they had sent an entire Tribe of people (she had not doubted the fact of a sweep even then) had yawned at her like an open mouth.

Despite the warmth of morning sun through the glass, Natasha shuddered at the memory of it. "The Wall," she whispered to herself, as she did whenever she felt a primitive feeling or instinct interfering with her logical thoughts. And after some seconds of concentration, the Wall began rising block by block in her mind.

She took a deep breath and closed the gap that had opened between Joe McMahon and herself. This was no time to think of last night, she scolded herself. Later maybe, when she was alone.

"Climate control off again?" asked Joe McMahon, who had apparently noticed her discomfort. He sniffed the air to test it.

"No," said Natasha. "I was thinking of something."

"Now that's dangerous," he said with a friendly smile, before turning back toward the doors.

Natasha did not consider herself immune to the tricks of anachronistic emotions. She had to fight off her mind's irrationalities just like everyone else. Of course she knew that. Each generation was barely waddling around the nursery rooms on two feet before they had learned from their teachers that some of their deepest feelings were not to be trusted: that their fear of the dark, for instance, was a leftover fear from when their ancestors slept in the Outside with jaguars and poisonous spiders; or, likewise, that their greed for food persisted from a time when children did not always have enough to eat, and might have starved if they had not occasionally acted in pure self-interest.

Natasha remembered these lessons well. In the old Epsilon dormitory with its rows of bunk beds (that great room had since been transformed into a dozen couples' sleeprooms), Teacher Harriet had instructed the children to lie on their mattresses while she stood by the high control box. With the flip of a lever, she had plunged them into utter darkness, a dark so absolute that it made shapes and apparitions jump out before their uselessly opened eyes. During this exercise, in order to combat those shapes and apparitions, they were all to repeat the following mantra: *Nothing exists inside the settlement except the good things we have made. All bad things belong to Nature. All bad things live outside the walls. And they cannot come in, ever.*

Another time, a different teacher, Teacher Emmanuel, had taken their Epsilon group on a tour of the Farms and the silver kitchens. He had stood at the head of their cluster of child-sized tables and said: "Children, your greed for food is an instinct. It helped your great-great-great-great-great ancestors survive in the Pre-Storm times, and for that reason it became a behavior that is coded for in our genes. But we don't need that instinct anymore. Now we live in a settlement where everyone has enough to eat. You will never have to compete for food. It doesn't matter if you are unruly or sick or how many generations (Alpha willing) come after you. You will receive three nutritious meals a day, forever." And as the lessons continued, Natasha *did* learn that her fear of a snake under her bed and her desire to steal the dinner roll from her neighbor's plate were survival instincts, and she fought them down with reason.

Likewise, as she and the other Epsilons grew, they discovered that a great number of their feelings had, as their source, archaic situations in nature, situations that clearly had nothing to do with life today. For instance, in their adolescence, they learned that a preference for certain facial arrangements and body shapes held no rational meaning—that these predilections were a remnant of the animal drive for productive sexual selection, left over from a time when people needed to have sex to create new generations. On the same note, sexual drive in general (and in all its permutations) was essentially a manifestation of a vestigial need to continue the species, and should not be mistaken for mature, fully empathetic partnerships, which the Alphas did condone, though not encourage. Feelings of competition with other Departments or other generations had roots in bygone struggles for survival in the wild, and overdetermined urges of small-group pride and kinship were the same.

What Natasha had felt last night for the Tribe, that surge of horror, was a more subtle anachronism than any of those—though it was certainly not unheard of, especially among young Office of Mercy workers such as herself. It even had a name: Misplaced Empathy, a form of Psychological Projection. What Natasha had done during the alarm was to place *herself*, her level of awareness and expectation, onto the blank faces of the Tribe members. It was a very human, very natural thing to do. Psychological Projection in general—the understanding that other human beings have a mind that works more or less like your own—was a basic social necessity that allowed individuals to comprehend and to predict how people around them would act. The trouble came when one allowed this powerful but relatively crude mechanism of the mind to take over for reason. In the most mild cases of Misplaced Empathy, a person might project human faculties onto nonhuman minds: so that a child would think his doll capable of feeling pain, or a farmer would believe that the chickens she tended possessed special pangs of affection for her. But projection like what Natasha had done was not only wrong, it was immoral and dangerous. The Tribespeople did not have her life or a comparable life experience. They were starving and weak with disease; even if they burned with the animal will to live, they had no future to hope for (whether they knew it or not) except for further suffering and, soon, a painful death.

Last night, when the low alarm had sounded to signal a probable sweep, Natasha had mistakenly foisted onto the Tribe feelings that were, in this situation, simply beyond the capacity of their understanding. She had, more specifically, imagined for them the terror of imminent death that only a person who already *knew* about sweeps could possibly have experienced as they watched the round head of a nova rip toward them through the sky. But the Tribespeople—whether it was Cranes or Pines, Natasha would find out soon—could not have comprehended the meaning of the nova. They could not have felt dread. They could not have understood enough to mourn their own end. If all had gone right, they would have felt at most perhaps the briefest flicker of wonder; and Natasha could not expect to perform at her job in the Office of Mercy if she did not remember that most fundamental fact.

"You're up," said Maria Chávez, a fellow Epsilon who was standing in line behind her. Natasha thanked her a little breathlessly and stepped forward to tap her finger on the soft, rectangular reader, registering her unique genetic code.

The light flashed green and the tall doors smacked apart along their seal.

At least she was feeling a little better now, Natasha thought, as she entered the gleaming white hall of the Department of the Exterior. And as her hard-soled shoes rapped on the polished floor and fell into step with the steady stream of citizens moving toward their respective Offices, the values of the settlement—the values put into practice each day in the Office of Mercy—began to bloom and flourish again in her mind, so that she could almost forget last night, and forget the monsters of her imagination that lurked behind the Wall. The values of

America-Five, which Natasha lived by, were these: World Peace, Eternal Life, and All Suffering Ended.

The overhead screen in the Office of Mercy glowed above the jumble of four-person cubicles, rolling chairs, and arriving morningshift workers. It was so massive that it drew all attention toward itself as one entered the room; and its light reflected in glints of blue and gray off the silver desk legs, the idling computer screens, and the glass carafe of the coffee machine, which sat gurgling on the side table. Today the overhead screen showed a single feed from one of their easternmost sensors: a wasteland of beach and forest. There was nothing immediately remarkable about the image. One might have even thought it a still, except for the mute lapping of foamy waves and the occasional flutter of a bird on the periphery. But in the distance (it took a second to notice), about one mile from the camera eye, was a strange upset to the landscape. Here the trees lay split and tossed about—one ancient oak stripped of leaves and half immersed in the water—and the blackish wet sand from underground erupted to color the paler surface.

Despite the changes, Natasha recognized the place immediately: it was the same beach that she and the three other members of her team had been monitoring for the last fifteen days, only this image was from a sensor that she had never looked through before. Cranes, she thought, a tightness coming over her gut. True, she had already guessed that there had been a sweep, but it was different, so different, to see the proof before her. At that moment, the camera zoomed in to a spot of sand on the lower left side. At a detail of 500x magnification, Natasha could now make out the charred remains of a woman's bare torso draped backward over a thick, horizontal tree trunk and, a few feet away, what appeared to be the lower portion of a human jaw smiling full-toothed up from the sand.

She recoiled a step, knocking into her Director, who was just entering the Office; though luckily for Natasha, he did not seem to notice.

"We swept the Cranes," said Arthur Roosevelt, coming over to stand beside Natasha. Arthur was a broad-shouldered, round-bellied man of very dark complexion, except for a patch of unpigmented skin beneath his left eye, where he'd once had emergency bioreplacement. "But unless you're in system failure, you've probably figured that out already." He nodded toward Natasha's own four-person cubicle at the back of the room. "Jeffrey did it, he stayed up all night."

"Was it clean?" asked Natasha.

Arthur and Natasha began walking together through the rows of cubicles, Natasha now moving with the air of sharp watchfulness that the Office usually inspired within her, and her posture so straight that she stood almost as tall as hunched-over Arthur.

By this time, most of the morningshift workers were already at their computers. In the front of the room, the lower-ranking teams had satellite images up on their screens: it was their job to monitor weather patterns that might affect Tribe and animal migration. These workers seemed preoccupied with the sweep, though, as were the groups in the middle, who were looking at images of the Pine camp. At Natasha's cubicle, Jeffrey was talking into his audioset. He glanced furtively over his shoulder at her, then quickly away, and with a leap of feeling, Natasha wondered if Jeffrey had lingered past the end of his shift in order to see her. He had done so before, on several occasions in fact; it was by no means irrational for Natasha to hope that this was one of those times.

"The sweep was spotless," Arthur said, answering Natasha's question. "Not a single survivor from the whole Tribe. And it was overcast this morning so they probably never saw the nova coming. There they were, gathered around the fire, then, swish, nothingness. I only wish the men hadn't gone on that hunting trip," he added soberly. "That was fifteen days of terrible suffering that could have been preempted. Another week and I would've appealed to the Alphas to let us sweep the men and the camp separately."

They arrived at Natasha's desk and Jeffrey's eyes met hers, while he continued muttering coordinates into his speaker. His gaze was at once anxious and calm, curious and slightly aloof. Yes, Natasha was sure now that he had stayed for her. After all, a full-Tribe sweep within America-Five's perimeter, the fifty-mile radius of land that they monitored with sensors, didn't happen every day. This was by far the largest sweep since Natasha had joined the Office of Mercy, and Jeffrey probably wanted to hear her reaction.

"So now all we have is the Pines to deal with," Arthur was saying. "Speaking of which, there's a new group for you to follow. Yesterday the man we think is their chief broke off from the camp with two other guys. I'd like you to track them. Tell me if they get within ten miles of the Crane sweep site. That's the last thing we need after three months with these clever animals. I'd rather set off diversionary fires than be forced into a sweep that way."

"Of course," said Natasha.

For weeks in the Office of Mercy, they had worried about the complications of having two Tribes in the field (an unprecedented occurrence that promised to grow more common, with recent cold fronts pushing the Tribes south). The citizens' biggest fear had been that the Cranes and Pines would meet at some inopportune moment and incite a small but violent war between them. That would have caused multiple problems. For not only would the Tribes have suffered physically and emotionally from the warfare, but the fighting would have forced them to scatter—to run away from an attack, or to leave the weak in one place and march the strong to another—making a sweep of an entire group that much harder. But the worries in the Office of Mercy had not ended with the sweep of the Cranes. Now they had to make sure that the Pines did not find the Crane sweep site. This goal was in strict keeping with a principal rule in their ethical guidelines: namely, that no Tribe should ever be allowed to suspect that there was such a thing as sweeps. For if the Tribes ever did suspect that people like themselves were being systematically wiped from existence, they would feel dread, and dread was a particularly terrible form of suffering, worse even, as some had argued during the debates of Year 121 Post-Storm, than purely physical pain.

Jeffrey waited until Arthur had left for his office, behind a glass partition, before rolling around to Natasha's side of the cubicle. Natasha was already busy settling into her desk for the day, but she looked up, anticipating his movement. She was glad for his notice. It seemed that Jeffrey was as eager to speak to her as she was to him. And for the first time since she'd heard the blaring alarm in the night, Natasha's nerves relaxed.

Natasha trusted Jeffrey, far more than her Epsilon friends or even Arthur, to put the events of last night in perspective. Not that the others weren't helpful or wise, but Jeffrey alone had the power to speak precisely to her hidden troubles, like a sensor eye that infallibly finds the crouching, warm bodies in the teeming wild. For a long time (especially since beginning her career in the Office of Mercy), Natasha had felt a deep closeness with Jeffrey, a similarity between his mode of thinking and hers that she experienced with no one else. It was as if their thoughts existed on the same, flat plane of awareness: noting the same behaviors in other people, dismissing the same concerns as unimportant, and creating the landscape of their individual lives from a similar set of compulsions and worries.

Had Natasha vocalized this feeling of closeness between her and Jeffrey to other people in America-Five, they might have found it odd, given the outward differences between them. Jeffrey was a member of the Gamma generation, and one of the most advanced and accomplished Gammas at that. He was tall and pale with thin blond hair that he combed over the medical scars on his scalp; and a rashlike burn extended along his whole right side—a scar from when the Palm Tribe attacked the settlement, the only direct attack in the history of America-Five. He always wore long sleeves to cover the burn, but the top of it still showed on his neck, rising up from under his collar to the shadow of his ear. Back when the Epsilons were kids, some of the boys and girls used to cower from him and whisper about his strangeness when he happened to pass by their Dining Hall tables. But even then, Natasha had gotten the impression that Jeffrey was a kind person, and had found him more mysterious than scary. As for the burns from the Palm attack, she considered them the mark of a thrilling and adventurous past lived outside the settlement's enclosures.

"You look like you've seen better mornings," Jeffrey said to her now, his voice hoarse but upbeat. He moved his chair closer to hers, so that their thighs were only inches apart, causing a Gamma teamleader named Claudia Kim to glare at them from the adjacent cubicle. "What's the matter, didn't get much sleep last night?"

"Nice work," Natasha said with a smile. "You don't even need the rest of us. You could probably run this whole Office yourself."

"Well, I don't know about that," Jeffrey said, quick to temper the compliment. "Did Arthur tell you? It was pretty intense there at the end. The kids were so amped up about the deer and the men coming home. I kept thinking that a couple of them might run off into the water and I'd miss them and launch the nova too soon. That's my biggest fear. That one of them will survive the sweep and lie there mangled and terrified before we can get to them." He took off his glasses and rubbed his eyes, which were red and heavy-lidded with exhaustion. "You should see me, sometimes," he added with a short laugh. "I go a little nuts over it. I'm always calling it up in the Pretends."

"But it was clean," Natasha said reassuringly.

"It was clean." Jeffrey put his glasses back on. "Are you all right?" he asked more quietly, so that no one at the other cubicles would hear. "I've been thinking about you. Wondering what you make of all this."

For a moment, Natasha prepared to lie, to give him the easy answer she knew he hoped for instead of the truth. But then she stopped. If she had any desire to confess just a little of what she was feeling, her chance was now. Jeffrey would never report her to Arthur or to the Alphas. Unlike most people in the settlement, he did not consider the doctrines of the Ethical Code glaringly self-evident. He believed in them, of course, and lived by their word. But he also felt (and had told Natasha as much) that questioning and analyzing one's own ethical feelings were essential practices for understanding. Every great ethical thinker, he had told her once, has struggled with or even doubted the laws that the settlement holds most dear. Besides all this, Natasha simply felt good after talking to Jeffrey, and she was desperate for that reassurance now. He would listen to her. He would be curious to hear what she had to say. Not once in all of Natasha's life had Jeffrey ever judged her or reprimanded her for admitting her honest thoughts, no matter how silly those same ideas seemed to Natasha in retrospect, or how well they fit with the Ethical Code.

"I had this weird feeling last night," she said softly, the memory of the blacked-out Dome hovering in her mind. "Like I didn't want the sweep to happen."

"What do you mean?" Jeffrey asked. "You wanted the lives of the Tribespeople prolonged?"

"Yes, I guess so." She looked at him pleadingly. "It just feels so empty now, the place where they were all alive yesterday. I don't know how to describe it. It leaves a gap in my stomach. It makes me feel bad."

"You remember how they looked," Jeffrey urged. "Like corpses, practically."

"I know, I know." She could see them in her mind's eye: the skeletal faces, the backbones curved at awkward, uncomfortable angles as the women and old men shuffled through the sand, the babies who writhed and then went still from sheer lack of energy. They had been watching the Cranes for nearly a month now—from mid-June until this morning, the twelfth of July—watching their bodies shrink and their faces grow long and hollow.

"It's better now," Jeffrey said. "Better nonexistence than pain."

But it wasn't helping. Natasha was willing herself not to cry.

"What did they look like," she asked, to change the subject, "when they realized the men were alive?"

Jeffrey hesitated. "They were . . . overjoyed."

"And did they eat the deer?"

"No, we swept them while the first chunks of meat were still cooking."

"Oh."

Natasha could not help but feel disappointed. She and Jeffrey had been on shift together when the Crane hunters and the second group of young men had reunited and made the kills. They had watched the hunt play out on the sensors and it had given Natasha such a thrill to see it, she had almost forgotten to pity the deer.

"We couldn't have let it go a second longer, Natasha," Jeffrey said, as if reading her thoughts. "Besides, the food wouldn't have brought them as much enjoyment as you'd think. They probably would have gorged themselves. Their bodies wouldn't have been able to handle that much protein at once. They would have eaten too fast. It would have made them sick. In this case, anticipation of the meal was much preferable to the fulfillment itself. The smells, the sight. It shouldn't matter, ethically speaking, but the Cranes did leave existence at the moment of highest pleasure."

"I wish I could have been there for it," Natasha said. "Maybe seeing the sweep would have made it feel different."

"There's still the Pines."

"Yeah, right. We'll never get them. I bet they cross the southern perimeter by the end of the week and we never see them again."

The computer beeped and Natasha turned to enter her username and password: NWiley, Waverider4. She could feel Jeffrey's attention on her, a different kind of attention from what he'd showed her when she'd first walked in, and an attention that made her just slightly uncomfortable. Sometimes Min-he interrogated Natasha about Jeffrey, insisting that Jeffrey had lustful and maybe even fully empathetic and loving feelings for her, but Natasha would vehemently deny it. She and Jeffrey shared an interest in the Outside, she would tell Min-he. They worked on the same four-person team, and that was all. Privately, of course, if Natasha was being completely honest with herself, she did often feel something between her and Jeffrey: an attraction at once bodily and also deeply rooted in the mind, which Natasha had not experienced with any of her past Epsilon boyfriends when stealing kisses or sneaking quick embraces under the covers in their old dormitory. And yet, as all the citizens did with their feelings from time to time, Natasha forced her attraction to Jeffrey behind a Wall.

Even if Min-he was right, Natasha knew, even if Jeffrey *did* like her, he would never act on those feelings, not in the real world. Another man would have, perhaps, but not Jeffrey, who was always striving for a purely depersonalized, universal perspective, and who would never consciously allow the pursuit of his own happiness to interfere with the chance of living a fully ethical life. Because what were the fleeting highs of romance and love (Natasha could almost imagine him saying) compared with the exaltation of creating a pain-free and carefully maintained paradise here on Earth? What was an obsessive commitment to one individual compared with committing oneself to the whole of humankind? Jeffrey also took very seriously the Alphas' boast that all emotional and physical needs could be met within the bounds of a person's everyday work and leisure activities. For companionship, the citizens should find fulfillment among the members of their own generation and the people they worked with. For physical pleasure, they had the Pretends.

Of course, the majority of citizens did not follow the Alpha guidelines too strictly. People often met up for covert encounters with various favorites, and Natasha herself had never found such acts detrimental to a capacity for ethical thinking. Not that her opinion was based on any very recent experiences. For the last couple of years, Natasha had been slowly straying from these kinds of brief partnerings—with the exception of what she did in the Pretends. She attributed this change in herself to moving out of the old Epsilon living quarters and focusing on her career. And not, as Min-he would have done, to a preoccupation with a certain unobtainable coworker. As for actually romantically committing herself to one single person one day, even Natasha felt that was a long shot. Some people did it. There was an entire hallway of couples' sleeprooms on level one, with double-sized mattresses and bed frames and a table and lamp on each side. In general, though, those sleeprooms were never in high demand. Solitude was hard to come by in America-Five, and the citizens didn't relinquish it easily. The single rooms, for instance, had a waiting list of nine years.

At last, Natasha finished uploading the necessary coordinates and found the three Pine men whom she would track for the day. She could not get a good visual—only a limb here or there, the foliage was too dense—so she chose the infrared (or "IR") option. Three red streaks jumped out against the muted background. For now, at least, the men appeared to be stationary.

"You know," Jeffrey said, "as soon as we take care of the Pines, there's going to be a Crane Recovery mission. Arthur's put me in charge. I'm on my way to meet with the Alphas about it right now. They want me to assemble a team within the next few days. The mission can't happen for a while, of course, not with the Pines crawling all over the field . . ."

He trailed off as Natasha turned expectantly toward him. Could he be saying what she thought he was saying?

"I was planning to bring up your name at the meeting. The Alphas have the final say, but I can do my best to get you on the team. If you're interested."

"Are you serious?"

"Would you want that? This sweep has been hard on you." He paused, his brow wrinkled. "Maybe it's too much."

"But Jeffrey, you know," she could hardly get the words out. "You know I've been dying to see the Outside all my life!"

"Don't use that word." Jeffrey's face had turned as pink as the scars on his scalp. "Don't say you've been *dying*."

"Sorry, sorry, I'm just so excited."

"Well, don't get too excited. Remember, most people have ten years in the Office before they get assigned to a mission. I only wanted to tell you that I'd give it a try."

"Yeah, but it's different if you recommend me."

On the screen, the three red streaks billowed up and drifted like angry little clouds out of view.

"Mother," Natasha cursed. She quickly drew up the four sensors clustered in that area: MD19, MD20, MC19, and MC20. She found the Pines in the southeast corner of sensor MC20 and zeroed in on their location.

She turned the sensor to visual feed to confirm that the red streaks were indeed the men, a protocol move during sensor transfers ever since one now infamous Office of Mercy worker had inadvertently switched from tracking people to tracking a herd of wild cows. Through a triangular window in the spidery branches and vine, Natasha caught sight of a thickly muscled, bent human arm passing steadily through the forest. She was about to return to IR when a second movement caught her eye: appearing in the same spot, framed by a halo of jagged leaves, came the sudden and shocking profile of a man with a sharp nose and high, square cheeks. His thick mass of hair reached his shoulders and, as Natasha watched, he tucked one strand behind his ear. A beautiful man, Natasha thought, yes, *beautiful* was the only word to describe him. He took a step forward and, as he did, he carefully pushed aside a draping frond, almost as if he did not want the delicate thing to tickle his flesh. Maybe it was the lingering effect of having tracked the listless, withered Cranes for the last several weeks, but Natasha found herself stunned by this image of sensitivity and self-command and full-faced, full-muscled health.

"You should probably switch back to IR," Jeffrey said.

"Oh, right," said Natasha, flustered. She quickly changed the setting so that the three Pines transformed to red heat on the screen.

"Anyway, I should get going," said Jeffrey. "I wouldn't want to keep the Alphas waiting."

Jeffrey stood, pushing his chair away and stretching his elbows over his head. It was a marker of Jeffrey's status in the settlement that he did not appear a bit nervous. Anyone else on their way to meet the Alphas would be pacing trenches into the floor, or at least sweating under the arms a little. Jeffrey, however, wore the same cool expression as always. Of course, Natasha thought, as she had thought on many occasions, even the Alphas must respect his intelligence. Jeffrey had simply accomplished too much in the Office of Mercy—developed the new IR sensor technology when the Department of Research had failed, anticipated the mass Tribal migration of Year 278, and swept more Tribespeople than any individual in the settlement—not to be highly esteemed.

"Keep your eyes on those Pines, champ," Jeffrey said, touching Natasha's shoulder lightly as he passed behind her. "If they stumble on that Crane sweep site, no one's going anywhere."

2

The three Pines meandered through the lifeless gray background of the IR map, and Natasha—forgoing all previous avowals to stay focused on her work—allowed the dull screen to erupt into a world of colorful possibility: she and a team of citizens venturing to the Outside. If anything could distract her from her mixed feelings about the Crane sweep, or rather, if anything could further *complicate* those emotions, it was this. If Jeffrey could get her a spot on the team, if Natasha got to see the Outside, it would be the most amazing thing to ever happen to her—yes, she decided, even more amazing than receiving her position in the Office of Mercy. She imagined suiting up in a real, custom-fit biosuit, not the stiff, mass-produced versions they wore during alarms. She imagined passing through the airlock in the Office of Exit, the only passageway into or out of the settlement. All that *green*. All that *sky*. And miles and miles of fresh, Post-Storm wilderness to explore, and land that melted away into water, and the ocean that curved to infinity. There would be bumpy, gnarly forest ground beneath her feet, not marble; and wildly growing trees and wild animals and gusts of wind that did not come from a fan. Maybe a bluebird would come and land on her shoulder like they sometimes did in the Pretends. She would get to hike along the beach; sand intrigued her, how it was so soft and loose but sturdy too, when piled up; and waves, her heart fluttered at the thought of ocean waves, those little mountains rising up and disappearing indefatigably, with a calm vigor that put the monstrous backup generator on level nine to shame.

And Jeffrey would be there; Jeffrey would be leading the team. He was the only one in the settlement who talked openly about what the wilderness was like, and Natasha could never get enough of his stories. He had even been to the ocean once, on a sensor repair mission some time before the Epsilon birth, and he had told her (this was years ago, but Natasha remembered it well) that the waves made a sound like pulsing static on a dead sensor feed. He also said—not to be repeated to anyone from the Office of Recreation Engineering—that the Pretends were no substitution for the real sound and sight and full-flesh experience of the Outside.

For the chance to leave the settlement once, only once, and to live that dream with Jeffrey, Natasha was ready to trade two decades of cleanup duty in the Dining Hall. One mission, she was sure, would provide enough wonderment to replace the stuff of her nightmares for years.

Because there was another draw too; another facet of Natasha's desire to see the Outside that she revealed to no one, often including her own conscious self. Natasha believed—it made no logical sense but still she had believed ever since she was a small child in her upper bunk in the old Epsilon dormitory—that some burning curiosity within her might find relief if she could only get to the Outside. She could not explain *why* the Outside should have this effect or *what* exactly was so unsatisfactory about life lived entirely within the settlement. All Natasha could name was a vague feeling that despite the wisdom of the Alphas there yet remained some realm of being that they chose not to access, some ancient truth (*There is no truth but the truth that the human mind bestows,* the Alphas would say); no, no, but still some inchoate, natural understanding that only the wind could whisper in the listening ear, that only the leaves could describe in their rustling or the ocean waves convey in their white crash and backward swirl.

It was a ridiculous idea. People in ancient times had occasionally thought this way, had put their faith and hope in the natural world, and they had not arrived at any satisfactory method for living, and certainly nothing that rivaled the Ethical Code. Plus, what was of a more practical concern, if anyone knew that Natasha indulged such outrageous fantasies, they would never allow her to work in the Office of Mercy. Natasha, therefore, took care not to reveal the full depth of her unease—except occasionally to Jeffrey. She had extra reason to be glad about her caution now, if she wanted the Alphas to approve her for the mission. Especially (as Natasha thought, with a tinge of regret) given that there was enough in her permanent file working against her already.

Natasha felt confident, proud even, of the work she had done in the last six years in the Office of Mercy. Two awards had come her way, one group award for best four-person team, and one solo award for her work in mapping the migratory patterns of large game animals using data from the satellite sensors. But there were other things, incidents from Natasha's childhood that signaled a dangerous tendency for unethical thinking. From the ages of six through eleven—before she was old enough to hide it—Natasha had exhibited an overwhelming, even obsessive interest in the Outside; so much so that some of her fellow Epsilons still teased her about it when they got together in the Dining Hall to reminisce about old times.

It was normal, of course, for children to be curious about the Tribes, but Natasha had openly expressed empathetic feelings for them in a way that—in the words of her monthly school reports—completely disregarded historical contextualization, and disregarded the distinctions between her modes of thinking and theirs.

"Were the Tribes very frightened when the Storm came?" Natasha remembered asking in their Garden schoolroom, her knees tucked under her chin and her girls' uniform of pink shirt and white coveralls baggy around her waist.

"Most people did not have time to be afraid," Teacher Penelope answered. "Just like with the sweeps today, the Storm came too fast for anyone to realize what was happening. They saw the black clouds approaching, and that was it. There were survivors, of course, the ancestors of the people who make up the Tribes today. But even they could not have comprehended the enormity of what was happening. The survivors must have been in hiding already, most likely up in the mountains somewhere. Under no circumstances could they have perceived the full impact of the Storm on the world. But remember, everyone," Teacher Penelope told them firmly, "survivors of the Storm were a very, very rare exception. For the vast majority of people, the Storm was an instantaneous end to a lifetime of suffering. Really, to a whole history of suffering."

Teacher Penelope paused and looked down from her chair at the little Epsilons sprawled before her in the grass.

"There are some things, children, that even adults cannot imagine. I am a Beta and I cannot imagine it. In the dark times, when the Alphas were your age, before the Storm, there were fifty-nine billion living, breathing human beings inhabiting this tiny Earth."

"How did they fit in the Dining Halls?" Caroline Churchill whispered.

"There were no Dining Halls. There was not even food or clean water for many, many people. In order to have those things, you needed money. And some people had no money at all."

"What's money?" Preston King asked.

"Pieces of paper with faces drawn on them," Teacher Penelope said. "If you collected enough of them, you could own for yourself—for your own self and nobody else—anything in the world."

The children had laughed at this idea, but Natasha had not laughed. She was still imagining the black clouds covering the Earth during the

Storm and the thought of it had made her cry right there in the middle of the lesson. Teacher Penelope had scolded her and sent her away from the group, and Natasha had sat alone on a bench under the largest oak tree until she could calm down.

Surely Teacher Penelope's report of that day had found its way to the Alphas, and other incidents too: how Natasha used to have nightmares long after the other children had learned to banish strange visions from their unconscious mind, and how she used to draw pictures not of the beautiful, future Day of Expansion like most children did, but rather of wild animals and long-fanged monsters that positioned themselves just outside the settlement doors.

But even those were nothing compared with Natasha's worst transgression—the only thing she had ever done to seriously anger her elders. It had happened just weeks before the Epsilons' tenth birthday. The clock on the maincomputer read a few minutes past the twenty-third hour, and Natasha was being dragged by the elbow toward the Department of Health, on account of a bloody nose. Teacher Robyn was angry; she thought Natasha was guilty of "dirty picking," which Natasha should know better than to do at her age. Natasha, meanwhile, was holding a handkerchief to her face and doing her best not to fall. Teacher Robyn had not waited long enough for Natasha to find her rubber leisure shoes, and Natasha's socks kept slipping on the Dome's marble floor. Natasha would never have seen what she saw (or *thought* she saw) if not for two things. First, due to the presence of Tribes in the northern mountain ridge, the white floodlights were off in the Dome; leaving only the low, red floorlights to guide their way, and making the Dome windows transparent to the Outside. Second, in order to slow the drip of blood, Natasha had tilted her head way back, causing her to look not at the double doors to which she was headed, but at the first row of honeycomb windows just above the Dome's circular base.

She and Teacher Robyn were about twenty paces from the

Department of Health when Natasha saw them: three ghostly faces peering through the glass, two men and a woman, their pale heads floating like impossible little moons, swags of dirty fabric wrapped around their necks, and their eyes fixed directly on her. Natasha screamed. She screamed and threw her weight back, making Teacher Robyn trip to her knees and cry out in surprise. Blood poured over Natasha's lips and hotly to the bib of her nightgown. The faces disappeared but she screamed and thrashed to get away, back to the elephant, and eventually it took three full-grown Gamma men to restrain her.

In the following days, certain Betas and Gammas had given Natasha many logical explanations for the faces: that she, Natasha, had been semiconscious, still dreaming; that holding her head back too far had overstrained her windpipe, reducing the flow of oxygen into her bloodstream and making her brain go just a little foggy. They sat her down in the Archives and showed her surveillance images of the green inner lawn on that night. Nothing. No one. But Natasha would not change her story, and her elders went from being sympathetic to being annoyed. They suspended her for three days from her Epsilon group on account of her promoting illogic, and her teachers told her how disappointed they were until Natasha's anger had transformed to a dull ache in her chest.

Eight years later, when Natasha applied to work in the Office of Mercy, her past came back to haunt her. The Department of Government had held her application five days past the usual timeline, despite Natasha's ranking third in her class and scoring a 97 percent on the Office of Mercy entrance exam. She could not be sure, but she believed that Jeffrey had vouched for her. He had visited their Epsilon group a few times as a volunteer teacher, and he had always paid a little extra attention to her. Not overtly, nothing that the other children would notice, but in the way he stood still and listened to her when she gave an answer and how once, when she was very little, he had put his hand on top of her head and kept it there, as if to say, *Out of all the sixty-two Epsilons, you are special.*

The metallic clang of a chair leg striking the cubicle announced the arrival of Natasha's fellow Epsilon team member—twelve minutes late for his afternoonshift. As a conciliatory gesture, he had brought Natasha a mug of coffee, which he set down beside the feeler-cube in which Natasha's fingers danced, controlling the computer.

"You should see it out there in the Dome," Eric said, looping his audioset around his neck and rolling back in his chair. "The Alphas finally posted the sweep. Everyone's cheering around the maincomputer. Hey, you weren't in the Office for it, were you?"

"Nope," said Natasha, taking a break to sip the hot coffee. "Wave One Defense in the Dome. Jeffrey did the sweep himself."

"Well, that's still better than me. I was on ammo support with your roommate."

"We're back to tracking Pines, did you check your instructions yet?"

"I am right now. Mother, I was hoping to monitor the Crane sweep site."

"Claudia's team got the assignment, I think," said Natasha, savoring a few more sips, then setting the mug aside. "But Arthur says it's clean. There's nothing to see."

"Exactly," said Eric, letting forth a mighty yawn. "By the way, I was browsing the America Boards this morning. Did you know we're ahead of America-Forty-seven now? Way ahead of America-Six."

"Are we really?"

Natasha flicked her pinky finger in the feeler cube, drawing up the Extra-Settlement connection. This was the single feed used for communication with the other American settlements, the 158 Dome-capped structures stretching from ocean to ocean, all along latitude 39 degrees North. Besides weather warnings and announcements of new generations, the America Boards served almost exclusively to keep track of the sweeps. One of the programmers in a central settlement had set up a ranking system, where settlements could self-report the number of Tribespeople swept. Officially, the Alphas in America-Five did not approve of this program—though they had never made a rule against it either. America-Five usually ranked very high, in part because they were the easternmost settlement (Americas One through Four had been tragically lost during the Storm, when the ocean surged miles inland, in defiance of all computer models and calculations). America-Five, therefore, intercepted most of the fishing Tribes traveling down the coast. Tribes, in other words, like the Cranes.

The top rankings on the board read as follows:

America-158	147,011
America-5	146,987
America-47	146,935
America-6	143,002

"Check out the total count now," Eric said, looking over Natasha's shoulder.

Natasha scrolled down. The total count, the number of human beings on the North American continent granted mercy since the Storm, was 8,300,019.

"That's something, isn't it?" Eric said. "We're the ones to push it over 8.3 million. Mother," he said in a hushed voice, "all those people."

There was something in Eric's tone that Natasha had detected before, a note of giddy self-satisfaction that Jeffrey would have reprimanded him for, had he been here.

"I saw Jeffrey this morning," Natasha said, reminded of her earlier conversation. "He's meeting with the Alphas right now about putting together a Recovery team. It's supposed to go out as soon as we sweep the Pines. Or at least as soon as the Pines are out of the field."

"I wouldn't mind being a part of that. Too bad we're Epsilons."

"Actually, Jeffrey said he'd bring my name up to the Alphas."

"What?" Eric cried. A few people glanced over from nearby cubicles, though when they saw it was only Eric talking, they quickly lost interest. "I logged just as many hours as you this quarter," he continued. "Plus I was the one to correct the count to 437 when that female gave birth. If you're getting on that team, then so am I."

"The Alphas probably won't clear it. Like you said, we're Epsilons." Natasha was backtracking quickly, but Eric waved her off, shaking his head. "Take it up with Jeffrey then," Natasha said, very sorry that she had confided in him. She should have known better. Eric was quick and smart at his work, but famously immature.

"You bet I will. And Arthur too. How come you were on Wave One Defense last night and I got supplies? Playing favorites."

"Eric," she snapped. "We rotate through those positions. Next alarm, I'll probably be four levels underground—"

A new shape on the screen caught Natasha's eye while, at the same time, Eric's face widened from an expression of self-absorbed petulance to one of genuine shock.

"Oh, no," Natasha moaned.

The IR map burned with a fourth orb of radiating life, one much larger than the men. Natasha knew at once what she was seeing: bear. So that's what the three Pines had been after. Natasha switched to visual. The men stood on a rocky patch of ground, partly walled off by a sharp rise of stone. They looked terrified, taut and still to the point of being inhuman. Their shoulders tilted toward the same shadowy place, and then the bear came into view—its big round body half obscured by a leafy tree in the foreground. The beast got up on its two hind legs, snapped its jaw, and fell heavily down again with a soundless bellow. The tallest of the men, the beautiful one, stood before the animal, his spear raised and his sandaled feet shuffling as if searching out some magical position that would give him the strength to make his kill. To his right was a round-faced curly-haired man and, to his left, a man with narrow features and spiraling black tattoos up each arm. Natasha fumbled for the switch on her audioset. She inhaled a breath. The Wall rose up in her mind, blocking interfering feelings of Misplaced Empathy behind it.

"What is it?" sounded Arthur's voice in her ear. "They're nearing the Crane sweep site?"

"No. Bring up sensor MC30."

"Ah," said Arthur, with dawning understanding. "They must have gotten desperate. Or arrogant. They're hard to understand, these guys."

"Look!" Natasha interrupted.

The beautiful man had launched himself forward and pierced the bear through the thick fur of its shoulder. Soundlessly, the beast roared, rolling its head on its muscular neck. "Poor bear," whispered Natasha, recognizing the perversity of the kill-or-be-killed Outside in a distant sort of way. But then—two seconds later—it was not "poor bear" at all. The blow did not have enough force behind it; the spear unstuck from the flesh as the bear lashed out, enraged. With one sudden swipe, the bear caught the tattooed man in the chest. The man's face turned to the side and he staggered. His legs crossed over themselves and he fell.

"Arthur!" Natasha said. She could feel Eric breathing hard at her side. She was already drawing up the command box for launching a nova. Her thoughts from that morning, her doubt about the goodness of sweeps, dissolved in the face of this singular instance of terrible suffering. "We have to do something. A G4. They're twenty miles from camp. No one would see."

In certain, very rare situations, when the suffering was especially awful, the Office of Mercy broke its own rules: it allowed for one group to be swept separately from the rest of their Tribe. In a case like this, it would only take a tiny, compact explosion. Four bodies, all within a radius of ten feet. The yellow box flashed before her, asking for the clearance code to access the nova launch program. She waited, wishing that Jeffrey were here to watch for mistakes, to make sure that their next moves proceeded correctly. She could do no more herself. Only Arthur and certain teamleaders had access to the nova controls. On the screen, the tattooed man twitched once, as if wanting to bring his knees to his chest. The curly-haired man was waving his arms and jumping, trying to scare the bear away. The beautiful man lurched forward ineffectually, reaching for his spear. It could not be allowed to continue, no, they must wipe it out now.

"Father of races, put them out of their misery," whispered Eric.

The audioset crackled. "We can't sweep," Arthur said, with an air of finality.

"But they're far enough from the camp!" Natasha cried. "I'm looking at the map right now!"

An echoing in her ear signaled to Natasha that their feed was now public. Likely her computer images were public too, up on the big screen. The Office of Mercy had become very quiet.

"It's not an issue of other Pines observing the blast," Arthur said. "We believe that the curly-haired man is their chief. The other two men are leaders in the Tribe. If we sweep them, the rest of the Tribe will go nuts. They'll fan out looking for them, a worse scatter than what we observed with the Cranes." He paused, breathing heavily into the speaker. "If you think the Pines are hard to sweep now, well, annihilating these three would make it impossible."

A flash came in Natasha's mind: the Wall disappeared and in its place was a bright conflagration, her own dread and terror at the sight before her. This evil, this death. Her feelings for the tattooed man and the two hunters forced to witness his pain reached such a state of intensity that Natasha was no longer feeling *for* them but *with* them. Suffering what they suffered. Only another small but well-trained part of her mind comprehended that she was being unethical; that she must overcome this passionate burst of Misplaced Empathy in order to do what was right. Natasha was good at controlling her thoughts, when she chose to. She had turned on and off, at will, whole regions of her brain during the Office of Mercy entrance exam, and she had the bioscans that proved it. Natasha gripped the edge of the desk. She looked at the man again, only now with the tether of instinct-driven feeling cut off. Then the tattooed man was receding from her, and existing, now, at a faraway distance. Instead of seeing a reflection of her own fears and her own sadness in his image, Natasha saw a stark human figure, solitary and small in the universe. The Wall had returned, and Natasha's mind was clear to make the most rational decision. She would, as Arthur was urging, act in such a way as to ensure the greatest good for the greatest number of people.

"Got it," she said. She closed the program, her hand trembling ever so slightly as she did.

Out in the forest, forty miles from the Office of Mercy, the Pines fought for their lives. The beautiful man retrieved his spear, and they battled the bear over the body of the tattooed man until their legs moved sluggishly and their weapons circled in tired arcs. The bear was injured, but angry too. The tattooed man lay still. His lacerations were not visible to them in the settlement, but a pool of dark blood was thickening beneath his body, seeping slowly into the earth.

"It's horrible," said Eric.

Natasha understood his revulsion but understood better the necessity of their restraint. Her mind remained focused; her years of training were serving her well. Instead of wishing for Jeffrey's help, she thought now that he would be proud of her for keeping so calm.

Arthur was addressing the group: "This is one of those unfortunate cases in which deferring the present suffering would lead to more pain in the future. . . ."

With a click, Natasha switched from visible to IR feed. The red streak of life that had once marked the tattooed man had lightened to pink. The other two men began creeping away from the bear, into the forest. Twice they made quick changes of direction, last-ditch efforts to retrieve their third, but soon they retreated and took off at a jog. Meanwhile the pink gave way to orangey-yellow and the fringes softened. By the time the bear returned to inspect and gnaw at its kill, the smear of life was a warm tan. Then the only color was the burning red orb of the bear; the tattooed man had faded into the grayscale shapes of the forest.

"He's dead," said Natasha, aware that everyone in the Office and maybe even the Alphas could hear her. "Permission to change the count?"

"Permission granted," said Arthur.

She pulled up the Pines' profile and deleted the count of the living. Then she reentered the number: 436.

3

Night settled over America-Five, tumbling in its quiet way to those dark, inscrutable hours deep within the nebulous middle between lights out and the underground dawn. The morning and afternoonshift workers from all five departments (only the Alphas in Government kept to their own mysterious schedules) had long retired from their dinnerhour in the Dining Hall—baked apples and sausages tonight, a special treat; they had enjoyed their evening recreation in the Pretends or socializing in the Garden, and had filtered down the elephant in groups of fifteen or twenty to their respective sleeprooms. The current group of nightshift workers were now in the Department of Health, monitoring those citizens who had recently undergone bioreplacement. Two or three agriculture workers lethargically patrolled the cow pastures and pigpens in the Farms, sweeping dim spotlights across the chicken coops and net-enclosed beehives, their steps soft on the dirt and grass ground. There were at least a dozen scientists propped on high stools in the circuitous labs of the Department of Research, attending to the vats of replacement cells and the molecular splicing experiments. Yasmine Gulsvig (a bland but agreeable woman, and the fourth member of Jeffrey, Eric, and Natasha's four-person team) was working tonight in the back cubicle of the Office of Mercy and, at other workstations, Rachael Kaminski and

Vincent St. Peter with her. One door down the hall, a lone citizen operated the panel of blue and yellow controls in the Office of Air and Energy, while outside, beyond the honeycomb, polycarbonate-enforced windows, the half orb of America-Five was shining in the black forest like a star that had fallen and lodged itself there.

Below all this, in the calm, cool depths of the settlement, Natasha lay fitfully in her narrow bed, in the ten-by-ten-foot room that she shared with Min-he. Her face burrowed into the pillow and she clutched a synthetic-protein wool (or prote-wool) blanket close to her neck. For several minutes now a panic had been growing within her and forcing her, against her will, awake. Her heart bumped loudly in her chest, rebelliously even, as if it were being squeezed between the fingers of a ghostly hand.

She opened her eyes with a sharp gasp and rolled onto her back. But vision could not pull her out of her head. The dark consumed every detail of the room, save for the two dim squares of the wallcomputers, hovering on either side of the black gulf where the door would be. A soft hiss of air whirled through the ceiling vent and, shivering, Natasha grabbed a pair of thick socks from under her pillow and pulled them over her feet. She huddled under the blanket again and scooted closer into the corner. She could hear Min-he's gentle snores two arm-lengths away and feel the low vibrations of the level-nine generator traveling up through the floor.

If she wanted to, Natasha could build a Wall right now; she could barricade her mind against her present feelings and try again for dull, easy, thoughtless sleep. Earlier today that had been right; but not now, not when she had the luxury of open, empty night before her. Hadn't she promised herself standing in line yesterday morning that she would confront these terrors? That she would face them head-on?

Natasha squeezed her eyes shut, giving herself back to the horrific landscape of her semisubconscious. Then she was here but she was not here; the concrete column of underground levels could not contain her; her thoughts burst out in all directions, expanding like a super-nova through time and space. She allowed it to be so. More, her release was a testament to her faith in the Ethical Code. For Natasha knew, in the Office of Mercy, in the blacked-out Dome during the alarm, that she had acted rightly only because she had forcibly used the Wall to block out her true feelings. That was okay for a child, for an Epsilon, but a mature, enlightened citizen of the world should not require such crude techniques. Faced with the merciful destruction of life, an enlightened person would be capable of perceiving all the goodness in that annihilation, and afterward, after a sweep for example, would feel only the firm satisfaction of having, by the power of human action, increased the pleasure and lessened the pain in the universe. If Natasha ever grew to be as wise as an Alpha, she would not need to correct her mind to fit the Ethical Code at all, because living ethically would be as obvious to her as putting one foot in front of the other in order to walk across the room.

Black blood seeped through the crevices of her imagination, like creeks within the darkness, distinguishable for its stickiness and its heat. He must have died slowly, the man with the spiral tattoos up his arms, and known as he lay on the ground that he was dying. Was there some fantastical place he believed he was headed? Had his last thoughts blossomed with the expectation of some miraculous world of sweetness and light; a wondrous unreality constructed stone by stone by the labor of one generation after another, and perfected only finally in the last moments of the mind's eye? For his sake, Natasha wished that it was so, though she suspected a different end. Because there had been no peace in his movements and no calm resignation, no willingness to die, in that last twitch of his legs. More likely, his last thoughts had raged out against his fate: I will not fall like this, we will murder the beast, they will save me. . . . Until the fight had collapsed with his body into the dust. Impossible, impossible, I will stand up and walk home again, impossible. . . .

If only Arthur had allowed a partial-Tribe sweep. But how many more deaths would that have led to? Natasha closed her eyes tightly, thinking it through. The total suffering must be kept to a minimum; that was the essence of the Ethical Code.

As her mind relaxed deeper into these dreams, her fingers uncurling from the edge of the blanket, Natasha's thoughts reached back to the Cranes, and how it had made her sick to see their empty, obliterated camp on the Office of Mercy's overhead screen. But hadn't it been just as bad, she asked herself—no, worse—watching them suffer? Even before the Crane men had taken off from the camp on their final hunt, the members of the Tribe had been starving. Residual weather patterns from the Storm, the citizens knew from the satellite feeds, had made the ocean temperatures inconsistent, leading to an instability of fish populations all along the eastern coastline. Recently the fluctuations had been so pronounced that Tribes like the Cranes could not adapt quickly enough to the changes. In fact, just days after the Cranes had crossed the perimeter, Natasha had watched from the Office of Mercy as they launched their final boat into the waves. The boat was a flimsy thing, a skeleton of rounded riblike wood, with a flesh of stretched, dried hide. Two lanky, thin-faced boys sat at the bow, holding paddles over their laps (brothers, maybe, they looked so alike), while two men with fishing nets draped over their shoulders shot the vessel powerfully out from the shore.

In the wild, Jeffrey had told her once, hunger is an inexhaustible source of illogical choices.

Is that why, when the sky closed over with dense, silver clouds, the four Cranes had not returned to land? Did they think the first drops of rain would bait the nonexistent fish to the surface? And did they hang on to this hope even while sprays of chilly water filled their boat and turned their limbs to ice? They capsized at 1512 hours, in the high corner of sensor W13: four dark heads disappearing and reappearing, their bodies breaking over the water clean through to the waist, then melding into the waves again. The black silhouettes of their twiglike arms thrashed and tried to climb above the ocean's plane, but there was nothing to call brave, as Pre-Storm fairy tales about heroes battling the natural elements would have one believe. There was nothing permanent or noble, no shining of the human soul. And when the water sucked them down at last (they were so weak and diminished already), they must have clawed against their death until the very last current of thought had drowned too.

A muffled sob broke from Natasha's chest into the hard mattress. Poor people. Poor creatures of Earth. It was terrible. A terrible design that would allow suffering to flourish, and make pain and dying essential gears in the machine of life. To imagine that a benevolent God had made such a world! (Because for centuries their ancestors had all thought so.) Once Natasha had asked Jeffrey about it, about religion, and according to Jeffrey, the pervasive belief in God actually revealed a great deal about Pre-Storm times. The religions of that era, Jeffrey had said, were almost always concessions that pointed directly to the violent nature of living itself; and concessions that exposed more than anything else the defeat that once had lived in every human heart. Their poor ancestors, much like the Tribes, had not wielded a power even remotely comparable to the power of the settlements to put an end to suffering and death. And so, Jeffrey had explained (he explained now, his voice soft and soporific in Natasha's mind), their ancestors had done the next best thing, they had colored their doom with a sense of purpose. They gave to suffering the aura of the divine; they gave it a witness and a reward; and to death, they granted a nature inverse of truth—calling the end a beginning.

Natasha sat up, pushing her hair back from where it stuck to her cheeks. She wanted out of these thoughts; she could not lie still anymore. She groped for the switch of the small table lamp and turned it. For a second, she held her breath, looking at the other bed. But the sprawling black mop of Min-he's head was still, and her breathing did

not falter. Natasha smiled. This was one of Min-he's many good qual-
ities as a roommate: she was unfailingly an extremely sound sleeper.
Natasha felt a little better in the light (no matter what they had learned
as children, the light always helped), but not good enough to try sleeping again. Quietly, Natasha pulled out the drawer of the table between
their beds and removed their copy of the book that was present in
every sleeproom and office of America-Five, and present (though no
one could verify this directly) in every room of every settlement across
the whole continent and in the other Alpha-inhabited continents too:
the Ethical Code.

Their copy, according to Min-he, was from the fifth printing, published thirty-one years ago in honor of the Deltas' birth and revised to
fit the conclusions of both the Year 251 and the Year 267 debates. It was
a heavy book with a navy cover that had frayed to white at its edges.
Natasha ran her fingers over the simple black letters on the front and
felt a kind of warmth travel up through her arms. She stood her pillow
up against the wall and lay back again, propping the book open on her
stomach, and allowing its comforting weight to forcibly slow her
breathing. She was not in search of any one particular section; what she
needed was a reminder that the chaos of questions that haunted her
this night was not hers alone; that these were the same terrors that the
Alphas had known since the Pre-Storm times, and the same that the
Alphas had pledged to end and *would* have ended, had it not been for
the extra-settlement survivors of the Storm. But one beautiful day—
and this was the promise of the Ethical Code, of all labor within the
settlement—they would make the world clean of horror Outside while,
at the same time, their bioreplacement programs would absolutely
guarantee eternal life, cell by cell with no end. Then, according to the
Alphas, the Day of Expansion would come. And human beings all over
the planet would break free from the self-created confines of the settlements, and live again in the open air. Only this time, in this society,
human life would look much different than it had before. Because *this*

civilization would not have come about by the haphazard forces of nature and Pre-Storm political history, but rather by the grace of reason, ethics, and science alone. That was the dream, the achievable paradise. Of course, for Natasha, especially in this moment, it felt a long way off.

Natasha turned to the chapter titled "The Last Unmade Generation," the history of the Earth in the years before the Storm, and she began to read at random, near the middle of the second page of the chapter.

In the century leading up to the Storm, the human population had experienced an inflationary rate of growth. The rapid downfall of economic infrastructure across Western Europe, the unification and expansion of central African cities, as well as the organized rejection of fertility regulation policies, all contributed to this effect. In the Americas and eastern European countries, a steady average of 4.28 children per woman during the preceding New Jacobean Era resulted in a population boom concomitant with the first reported losses in worldwide food production, as well as the first criminal reconfigurations of the energy grid. The Era culminated in massive shortages of fresh water and energy, which in turn caused not the dip in population that one might expect, but instead ten years of unprecedented surge. In the year preceding the Storm, 39 percent of the population was under the age of twelve.

The effects were staggering: men, women, and children starving with no means of bettering their situation, women dying in childbirth at rates unheard of since the beginning of surgical and sterilized medicine, and vast living complexes so unsound in their construction that one in every one hundred deaths was thought to be the result of a building collapse. After millennia of slow improvement, sanitation conditions eroded. Sewage systems backed up and leaked into the already

precarious soil and local water sources—leading to the
return of many bacterial and viral diseases thought to have
disappeared two centuries prior.

Natasha stopped. Min-he rolled over, still asleep. With a restless
flick, Natasha jumped ahead several pages and began reading again.

A senseless, unethical jungle, that is what the inhabited
Earth had become. As unrest and fighting spread, only the
extremely resourceful were able to find isolated spots of ref-
uge in what remained of the wild. (Eventually those hideaways
would be compromised too, and what survived of them purged
with the cities during the Storm.) The farming and ranching
industries still produced enough to keep their ventures active,
but the food did not travel far, and was heavily guarded. Every
storehouse on the continent posted ten armed guards at each
door. As for the cities, no outside food ever reached them, the
tunnels, bridges, and major arteries having fallen to the
power of highly sophisticated pirates.

By this time, we should remind ourselves, any hope of
reviving the Yang political system had gone. And the peaceful
society of shared prosperity and shared labor that the Yangs
had imagined was irrevocably out of reach. Without communication, without basic infrastructure, the transformations in
societal organization could not occur, and everyone felt it.
Chaos, fear, and suffering reigned, and the law of violence and
strength took over as it had not since pre-Modern times. The
Yang members refused to acknowledge their own defeat, a
failure which only worsened the already immense suffering of
that time and delayed its relief. But change did come, despite
the terrible odds against it. Change arrived as an act of will,
from people who could not stand by any longer.

For when the bunkers that housed the Yang political

leaders—as well as the power that was synonymous with
those bunkers—at last fell into the hands of their natural children, we knew better than to repeat the mistakes of our natural parents. We converted these bunkers into settlements,
sealing ourselves off from the death outside. Within this self-
destructing world, only your Alphas harbored any positive
plans for the future. Only your Alphas did not partake in this
terrible march toward extinction. Only your Alphas asked
instead: How can we start over? How can we live better than
the way we are living now?

The heaviness in Natasha's chest gave way a bit. She had always
found the Alphas' tone in this section jarringly and almost humorously
self-aggrandizing. They gave scant information about the Yang political group, and yet still managed for several pages to assert their supe-
riority over their predecessors. (On page 284, for example, the Alphas
dismissed the Yangs as "fumbling moral philosophers, who, if they
were to spot a venomous spider perched on the shoulder of their dearest friend, would not know which creature to save.") Granted, the
Alphas had good reason to feel proud. The members of the Yang party
had all died around the time of the Storm, back in Year 0 (the current
date in the settlements was Year 305), while the Alphas, who were in
many cases the biological children of leading Yang members, had preserved themselves through those dangerous times and, subsequently,
had kept themselves alive century after century with the bioreplacement programs of their own invention. The Alphas had also remained
overseers of the old Yang bunkers, rescuing the structures from decay
and transforming them into the brilliant homes they all lived in today.

A click came from high over the foot of Natasha's bed: the circular
light above the door was glowing weakly, the first phase in five of the
underground dawn. By 0700, it would be shining across the full solar
spectrum brightly enough to illuminate every nook and cranny in the

room, and with a high-intensity spike at 297 nanometers, enough to warm the flesh and activate a morning burst of vitamin D in the system. Natasha replaced the Ethical Code to its spot in the drawer and crawled out from under her blanket. From the basket beneath her bed she fetched her robe and pulled it snugly over her nightclothes. She tore off her socks, tossing them onto the bed, and slipped her feet into a pair of rubber leisure shoes.

The hall was empty, as she'd expected, and only one of the ten stalls in the women's shower room was in use. A warm white steam hung in the air, and the hot damp smell carried with it just a tinge of lavender shampoo. Natasha pushed open the creaky cedar door to the changing stall, and closed the latch behind her. She removed her robe and nightclothes and hung them neatly on the metal hooks. Then she stepped behind the curtain and gave the water some seconds to heat up before moving under it, her chestnut brown hair darkening a shade and becoming wet and heavy on her back.

As she washed—the pounding warmth relaxing her muscles and sliding down the length of her body—Natasha was careful to keep her lips tightly closed. The water, which came from underground streams and rainwater gathered on the roof, was treated and purified of course, though not with the same attention as the water that went to the kitchens. She turned her face to the spigot and scrubbed her cheeks, nose, and forehead with rapid motions, at last feeling fully awake.

After Natasha had wrapped herself in her robe again, she left the changing room, expecting to find the shower room empty. The sight of a second reflection in the mirror took her slightly by surprise: the intelligent eyes and black bangs that made a severe line across the forehead, a perfect and striking contrast to the pale, oval face beneath. It was Claudia Kim, the Gamma who worked at the adjacent back cubicle in the Office of Mercy—and one of the last people Natasha felt like seeing right now.

"Oh," said Natasha, "I didn't realize there was still someone here."

Claudia sniffed; she laid her hairbrush aside, meeting Natasha's gaze in the foggy reflection.

"What did you expect, Alpha treatment? Are we supposed to defer to you, give you privacy?"

"I'm sorry—what?"

Claudia turned to face her.

"Look, we all know that Jeffrey adores you. He'd probably drain his arteries into your bloodstorage banks if you asked him to. But you should know that whatever special advantages he's managed to wrangle for you, you haven't earned them. You're a rookie. Your record is average. You've done nothing to distinguish yourself among your peers. If it was up to me, you never would have been permitted—" Claudia stopped and shook her head, too full of loathing to continue.

Been permitted into the Office of Mercy, Natasha was sure she had wanted to say.

As far as Natasha knew, she and Claudia were not enemies, exactly, but the older woman had made it obvious early on in Natasha's career that she did not care much for Natasha at all. In general, Natasha tried to ignore it. From what she could tell, Claudia didn't like anyone who was close with Jeffrey—and so, logically speaking, there hadn't been any reason for Natasha to take Claudia's feelings too much to heart. It still hurt Natasha's confidence, though, and on some days made her more nervous and unhappy at work than she would have been otherwise. But what could Natasha do about that? As for the nature of the *original* antagonism, the one between Jeffrey and Claudia, Natasha had virtually no understanding of it at all. Both Jeffrey and Claudia were Gammas; they had a history within their own generation that was beyond Natasha's awareness and general interest. It was not strange that it should be like that. Each generation contained its own nuances of relationships and hierarchies and rivalries that remained largely invisible to those outside—and especially to those farthest removed by age. The Gamma generation had eleven and a half years on the Deltas, and a full nineteen years on the Epsilons.

"I don't know what special advantages you're talking about," said Natasha, growing more curious by the second to know the cause of Claudia's anger. "Unless you mean tracking a poor, suffering Tribe man for five hours and watching him die."

"Check your mail then." Claudia sneered. "I hope you'll be satisfied."

Natasha stood rooted in place as the shower room door banged shut. Could this mean what she thought it meant? Had Jeffrey done it? Had he actually done this for her? The Alphas held him in such high esteem, and if he had fought for her, he may have been able to get her through. Her body, damp and steaming from the heat, tingled with excitement. Out of love, he would have made it happen, a quieter voice within her said, because Jeffrey understood her, because her happiness brought him happiness too. Several seconds had passed now, enough to ensure that Claudia would be gone from the hall, and Natasha burst out of the shower room and rushed to her sleeproom, the tie of her robe dragging behind her and her feet sloshing in her shoes.

Min-he was dressed for work; she was hurriedly making her bed and stuffing papers into a file.

"There you are," said Min-he. "I didn't think you'd gone up to the Dome already. You missed Eric. He came around looking for you."

"Did he seem upset?"

"Actually, he seemed kind of giddy. Smug too, but that's just Eric."

"You didn't see a message come in for me, did you?"

"I hadn't noticed—"

But at that moment, Natasha's wallcomputer began to flash blue. Only once had it done that before: when Natasha had received her assignment in the Office of Mercy.

"Natasha," Min-he whispered, her eyes widening with alarm. "A personal message from the Alphas."

"I know." Natasha quickly entered her password. The text filled the screen, overriding the usual arrangement of icons. Min-he rushed to her side, reading over her shoulder.

Natasha Wiley,

You have been selected to serve as one of the six members of the Crane Recovery team. The object of your mission is to (1) ensure the cleanliness and efficiency of the Crane sweep, (2) replace the sensors destroyed by the blast, and (3) document the site of the sweep for the Archives. As you know, a Recovery team would usually deploy within a week of the sweep. However, given the presence of the Pine Tribe in the field, this is impossible. The team will therefore await deployment until after the Pines have left the area, either by the Tribe's own volition or, we hope, by the force of a sweep.

Beginning tomorrow morning, you will stop your regular shifts in the Office of Mercy and report instead to Pod G11 in the Pretends for group training, both morning and afternoon-shifts.

The members of the team are: Jeffrey Montague, Office of Mercy; Eric Johansson, Office of Mercy; Natasha Wiley, Office of Mercy; Alejandra Rodriguez, Extra-Settlement Engineering; Nolan al-Rashid, Extra-Settlement Engineering; and Douglas Truman, Office of Land and Water Management.

Eternally Yours, Alphas/deptofgov

"I'm going Outside," said Natasha.

"I can't believe it," said Min-he. "You and Eric too. You're only Epsilons."

"I wonder if it posted to the maincomputer yet."

"Only one way to find out."

Natasha had just pinched the last fastening of her shirt when a knock thudded at the door.

"Finally!" Eric said, with a grin that threatened to leap from his face. "You saw the message then? Alpha believe it, I don't regret the day we got assigned to Jeffrey's team. Poor Yasmine, though, she always seems to get the short end of the deal. It's her fault, I think. She doesn't show the same dedication as you and me. Remember the time Jeffrey caught her playing Monkey-Go-Huntin' during the nightshift?"

"So I guess we're friends again," Natasha said. She laughed, genuinely happy that she and Eric had made the team together, and not only because it meant that she was spared his indignation.

"When weren't we friends?" Eric asked. "Come on, I think I hear the elephant. They're going to post upstairs any minute."

A small crowd had gathered in the Dome, drawn there by the rumor of an Alpha announcement. "I hear they're upping the meat serving to three times a week," Maria Chávez was telling a suspicious-looking Tom Doncaster, who headed the Farms. A huddled group of doctors were shooting meaningful looks at one another, as if they suspected the announcement indubitably had to do with their Department. The clock switched to 0730 and the morning bulletins came up on the screen. For a moment it was quiet while the citizens read an abbreviated version of what had appeared on Natasha's wallcomputer—and then Natasha and Eric were being jostled from every direction; a swarm of their fellow Epsilons having converged upon them.

"It's about time they gave us important assignments!" someone was saying near Natasha's ear.

"Not the babies anymore, are we? What with the Zetas coming—"

"You deserve it," said Min-he, her round, friendly face flushed with excitement. She squeezed Natasha's arm, and Natasha gave her a grateful smile.

The anxious and jubilant faces parted to let someone through: Jeffrey. He looked both happy and complacent and Natasha beamed at him. He was the one to thank for all of this. For one wild moment, Natasha imagined taking a running step forward and throwing herself into his arms and telling him, really telling him, how it meant everything to her that he had brought this dream to life.

"Good luck," Jeffrey said, shaking Eric's hand first. "The Alphas are behind you."

"Thanks, Jeffrey," Eric said. "Thanks a lot."

Jeffrey turned next to Natasha. He took her hand and she stepped as close to him as she dared, with so many people watching. As their touch loosened, though, Natasha noticed that his smile was a little strained.

"Don't tell me you regret this," she said quietly. "It's too late for that."

"Not at all, not at all. Who am I to argue with the choice of our superiors? You should be proud of yourself, Natasha," he added in a more serious tone. "The Alphas do not take these matters lightly, and neither do I. You would not be on this mission if anyone doubted your potential in the field."

"I don't know, I bet I can name a few," said Eric, nudging Natasha in the ribs.

Natasha looked, expecting to see Claudia Kim. But instead, she followed Eric's gaze to a tight group of Deltas standing to the side of the elephant doors. At the center of the group was Raj Radhakrishnan, a lean man with deeply set eyes and caramel skin so smooth that it seemed untouched by bioreplacement. Natasha had never spoken to Raj in any meaningful way, but she did know a little about him. Raj had served as Min-he's director in the Archives until the Alphas had abruptly transferred him to level nine—to the Electricity and Piping crews. His name came up now and then in the Office of Mercy, though never in a very friendly light. Raj was one of the only citizens in America-Five who openly objected to the existence of sweeps. Natasha did not know the details of his views, only that he had called for the abolition of the Office of Mercy on several occasions. She had heard similar rumors about the Delta men and women surrounding him now, though nothing so extreme. From across the room, Natasha picked out their faces: Mercedes Laplace, Eduardo Castilla, Benjamin Rook, and Sarah O'Keefe. She thought that Mercedes and Sarah both worked in Health. Eduardo's winning smile she recognized from one of the current construction teams, and also from when he'd had a long-standing romantic relationship with her favorite childhood doctor, a man named Malcolm Finn. Ben Rook was a nervous, small-boned man who tended the beehives and vegetable gardens in the Department of Agriculture, and who rarely spoke more than five words together. He and Sarah were a couple, Natasha did know that for sure, one of the eccentric few who had a sleeproom together.

As Raj finished speaking, he rubbed his hand slowly over his mouth, a sad, serious gesture strikingly at odds with the mirthful crowd around him. Raj was a distinctive man, most people agreed, even outside his views on the Office of Mercy. He had a quiet, appraising way about him that made him seem too intelligent to laugh at, yet too reserved to merit much in the way of kindness or general cordiality.

"Try not to worry about them," Jeffrey told Eric and Natasha, shaking his head. "There's always going to be dissent in a free society. But they'll get over their petty selfishness soon enough. A couple of nights looking over the Ethical Code wouldn't harm them either. *Be conscious of the universe and let it overwhelm the personal and the particular*," he added, quoting from the final chapter.

The tide of people was moving toward the Dining Hall, and Natasha, Eric, and Jeffrey moved with it. The new team had converged at one of the tables, their trays of biscuits and gravy and coffee growing cold as they stood at their seats shaking hands all around. Natasha did not know Douglas Truman or Nolan Al-Rashid very well, but she liked them both immediately. Alejandra was an outspoken, gregarious woman and, true to her reputation, within minutes she was laughing loudly and cracking jokes with Eric.

"And what about our precocious Epsilons, eh?" Douglas said, giving Natasha's shoulder a hearty pat. "Makes me reevaluate the successes of my own youth, I'll tell you that. If I remember right, at age twenty-four, my greatest responsibility was tallying chicken-to-egg ratios in Agriculture at the end of each month."

"Maybe Eric and Natasha work harder than you did," Nolan suggested.

"Not like we have a choice," said Eric good-naturedly, piping up from across the table, "working for Jeffrey."

Jeffrey, who had been standing off to the side, gave a quick retort, though not before Natasha had noticed again the concern weighing down the lines of his face, and his hand rubbing the crisp sleeve of his opposite arm.

4

The training took place in the Pretends, in the third of the three great spaces that made up the Department of Living, just behind the Dining Hall and below the Archives, where Min-he worked. Developed by Alpha engineers in the first century after the Storm, the early Pretends had originally served to supplement the education of the Beta generation: to show them the world and grant them the experiences that reading and study alone could not re-create in so visceral a way. Soon, though, only a few years into their use, the young Betas had also found in the Pretends an alternate and much superior means of entertainment and exercise as compared with the Alpha-built baseball diamond, soccer field, and basketball court that shared the great room with the Pretends today. (Those games had long gone out of style, though the courts, synthetic grass fields, and equipment remained in pristine condition, ready for use.)

The basic experience that defined the Pretends, that of complete and artificial sensory immersion, had been present in the Pre-Storm times. However, the technology was very new then, and had never gotten past its early limitations before scientific work in such matters ceased. The America-Five engineers had managed to pick up where history had left off. They perfected and mastered the technique of using highly accurate nanomagnetic fields to alternately activate and suppress trigger regions in the brain, ultimately gaining control over the sensations of touch, sight, smell, sound, and taste to a degree never achieved before. What was more, the technology in the Pretends, like the technology in every field, was always advancing. The Betas had improved on the Alphas' model and, since then, younger generations had implemented their own new ideas. Just in the last decades, for instance, the engineers had discovered how, instead of allowing only for prewritten or prescripted experiences, the computer could essentially *read* the imagination of the player and, by working one nanosecond behind the player's thoughts and desires, simulate in "real life" the fantasies of the mind. This type of simulation was called "Free Play," but it was only just emerging into general use.

Natasha herself, like every citizen, had spent countless hours in the small Pods where these experiences took place. It was no secret to anyone that the confined space of the settlement could not accommodate every human need. And the Epsilons had been encouraged all their lives to run and play and act out violently or in any way they felt inclined within the private world of the Pretends. The simulations served more straightforward, educational purposes as well. During school, for example, all their exams were held here. And Natasha could remember with crisp feeling acting out virtual lab experiments and very basic bioreplacement tasks, translating by sight Latin, Chinese, and Spanish from a scrolling screen, and pontificating on computer-selected passages of the Ethical Code before a simulated audience of her teachers and hooded Alpha elders.

Natasha and Eric passed together through the back doors of the Dining Hall promptly at 0754 on Monday morning and walked across the bare expanse of the soccer field, baseball diamond, and parquet basketball court. Five levels of identical white doors, accessible by a metal scaffold of stairs and wraparound balconies, rose up on all four walls. Beside each door was an occupancy light, so that the entire room was dotted with little pricks of green and red. The vast majority of

Pods held only single players, but there was also a row of group training rooms on the ground level. The two Epsilons found Pod G11; the
light at the door glowed green.

"You ready for this?" Eric asked.

"They wouldn't have picked us if we couldn't handle it," answered
Natasha.

He raised his eyebrows, no more convinced of her fearlessness than
she was of his.

"Too late to turn back now," he said. And with a last little pang of
trepidation, Natasha followed Eric inside.

Jeffrey was already there, strapping himself into the center harness,
and the others arrived within minutes. Jeffrey greeted them and
directed each person to one of the stations. He was all business; there
were no special glances for Natasha today—a relief to Natasha. She
had enough pressure on her already.

Like the individual Pods, Pod G11 had an interior of gray-blue rug
that rose up the walls and onto the ceiling, and a very sedate blue light
that glowed upward from a panel near the floor. The team members
strapped elaborate harnesses around their middles; the apparatus
would keep them safely in place while their bodies acted out in whatever world they would soon find themselves. They pulled down their
helmets, which also hung from the ceiling, and fastened them over
their heads—the helmet flaps making them blind to the "actual" world
around them.

"All right," Jeffrey said, "as long as everyone's feeling good, I'm
going to throw us right into our first simulation. In this one, we walk
straight to the Crane sweep site. I want you to look for identifying
landmarks as we go, start familiarizing yourself with the route."

The effect came gradually, as the simulators touching Natasha's
head began to warm. At first, Natasha saw only the black helmet flap.
But then she allowed her eyes to flutter closed and, as she did, the
sensation of the harness where it crossed her legs and torso

disappeared; the weight of the helmet dissolved. She opened her eyes—whether she had opened her eyes in the real world as well as in the Pretend world, Natasha could not say. She sensed the presence of a cool, light, stretchy material just grazing her skin. She ran her hands down her thighs, touching through thin gloves the biosuit that covered her body. The air tasted cool and clean, and she became aware of the lightweight airfilter strapped to her back.

Darkness gave way to looming forms, and these forms steadily coalesced into a forest of thick trees, about thirty paces away. The other members of her team were standing beside her, in the same arrangement as they had stood in the Pod: Douglas, Nolan, and Jeffrey to her right, and Eric and Alejandra to her left. They too were testing the feel of their biosuits, stretching their limbs and feeling over their shoulders for their airfilters. The biosuits were light gray in color, with bright red stitching. Stiff, protective helmets covered their heads, and clear visors covered their faces.

Natasha turned in a circle and recognized their location immediately. They stood on the green, the large circle of lawn that surrounded America-Five. Two steel wings branched out on either side of them: each wing a series of massive rectangular structures sunk into the earth. The nearer one had the long, thin configuration of the Department of the Exterior. That would make the adjacent, shorter wing the Department of Government. Each of the steel structures connected back to the high Dome, its concrete base stained in yellowish ribbons from dampness and weather, and the honeycomb windows opaque in the noontime sun.

"Welcome to your first training session," said Jeffrey's voice in her ear. "As I said, the purpose of this exercise is to familiarize yourself with the route to the Crane sweep site. Douglas has our navigation tools. I've kept the obstacles to a minimum for now."

"What, no lion attacks?" Eric asked.

"Don't expect this kind of treatment to continue," Jeffrey responded.

The air shimmered once and then was still. "Douglas, we'll go on your word."

When the Alphas had first announced the team, Natasha had only felt excited—the fear had not set in until that night. Then she had realized what she was up against: that, immersed in simulations of the Outside, her feelings of Misplaced Empathy might break through the Wall—as they had on the night of the Crane sweep—only this time, her lapse would be visible to more minds than her own. Natasha need not have worried at all, though. From the very first training session, Natasha surpassed herself in the Pretends. In an odd way, she actually found it *easier* to maintain the Wall, knowing that her efforts were all in service of getting to see the Outside. She had a goal—an end result strong enough to focus her thoughts. In fact, during some of the simulations, Natasha almost felt like she was seventeen again, training for the Office of Mercy entrance exams. She had a knack for mental geography and for orienting herself in the field. She was alert to her surroundings, the first to catch an animal sneaking up on them, especially when their tracking devices had failed. Douglas, the most senior member of the team except for Jeffrey, took to calling her "quick-draw" in deference to her speedy reflexes. Even Eric acknowledged Natasha's skill a few days into their training, if only with a grudging regard. And more—what was of a much higher importance to Natasha—she could not detect in Jeffrey any of the anxiety that he had tried to hide from her just after the Alphas' announcement. He complimented her only sparingly, but each compliment was sincere; he seemed genuinely impressed with her performance. Natasha was glad about that. The last thing she wanted was for Jeffrey to regret recommending her for the team.

The simulations in the Pretends got progressively harder as the days went on. They practiced traveling through violent weather systems and negotiating catastrophic equipment failures. They fought off wolves and mountain lions, occasionally losing limbs in the process and rushing each other back to the green for emergency bioreplacement. Their mapping systems failed a dozen times over, leaving them to navigate their way back to the settlement using the sun and the stars as their guide. In one Pretend, a forest fire spread through the trees in a mission already plagued by a communications breakdown. The team neglected to keep watch on their air quality meters and missed the spike in CO_2 levels that would have clued them in to the danger. The last thing Natasha saw was black, billowing smoke lacing through the trees before Jeffrey (who controlled the sessions) abruptly ended the simulation and spent ten minutes upbraiding them for their inattention.

But they all feared the dirty sweeps the most—when, at the sweep site, they came across half-alive Tribespeople tossed into the trees or sand, their hearts still incomprehensibly beating and their skin open with sour and rot. Once a man rolled down from a pile of toppled trees and took hold of Alejandra around the neck, crying and begging through cracked lips for what could only be water, before Eric wrestled him to the ground and Natasha delivered the merciful shot to the head.

"What do you think of our progress?" Jeffrey asked Natasha one evening as the two of them followed the others out of the Pod. "Think we'd be ready to go Outside, if it wasn't for the Pines?"

It was the conclusion of the afternoonshift, and the team had just completed their fourth full week of training. Natasha's shirt radiated the heat and sweat of her body, and she was looking forward to a quick shower before the dinnerhour began.

"We're definitely close, I think," Natasha said. "It feels good, it feels like you've had us work through every possible disaster."

"That's the idea," Jeffrey said. "Actually, for next week I was thinking of rotating responsibilities—"

But Jeffrey did not finish his thought. As the Pod door slid closed behind them, Jeffrey and Natasha found themselves standing on one side of a strange confrontation. Facing Douglas, Nolan, Eric, and

Alejandra—and now Natasha and Jeffrey too—was Raj Radhakrish-nan and the four others who had been talking with him on the morn-ing the team was announced.

Raj stood at the edge of the deserted soccer field, his arms folded. Flanking him on one side, leaning against the netted goal, was Mer-cedes Laplace, her bright hair haloing her face in a frame of tight curls. Eduardo Castilla perched atop the rolled, never-used stretching mats, and beneath him, almost touching, stood Sarah O'Keefe and Ben Rook, both ashen-faced and scowling.

"Finally," Raj said. His dark eyes swept over their sweaty, dishev-eled bodies. "We couldn't believe it when we realized you were still running a simulation. I have to say, as a settlement citizen, the idea of a last-minute cram session doesn't fill me with confidence."

"What do you want?" asked Jeffrey, looking from one to the other. "Raj, what's the meaning of all this?"

"Do you really have to ask?" Raj said. He seemed genuinely sur-prised, but Natasha knew better than to take any performance of his at face value. She couldn't trust anyone so hateful of the Office of Mercy, no matter her own occasional uneasiness about the sweeps. "We came here," Raj continued, "because we want to know your plans for the mission. We would have asked Arthur Roosevelt directly, but none of us have clearance for the Department of the Exterior."

"You know our plans," Jeffrey answered curtly. "It's a standard Recovery mission. We're going to fix the sensors, document the sweep site, and check for survivors. That's public information."

"That's all?"

"Yes, that's all. And now I don't feel that I owe you any more of my time. Come on, everyone."

But no one moved.

"You're telling me the plan from a month ago," Raj said, glaring at them. "I want to know what the Office of Mercy is thinking *now*."

Jeffrey repeated his previous answer, with even less of an effort for civility. "Anyway," Jeffrey added, "why should it make any difference to you?"

Raj's eyes hardened; Ben and Sarah laughed disdainfully.

"I don't think you're being totally honest," Raj said. "But that won't keep *me* from being honest with *you*. It makes a difference to me because I have spent most of my working life as an archivist, and I suspect that you are, at this present moment, acting in a way to repeat the wrongs of the past. I want to know, we all want to know, do you intend to enact a manual sweep on the Pines?"

Natasha relaxed a little at these last words and, beside her, Eric did too. So it was only a misunderstanding. Raj and the others did not realize that of course Arthur would not send them into the field until the Office of Mercy had swept the Pines in the usual way, with a nova, or else until the Pines had slipped across the perimeter. That was the plan since the beginning.

But Jeffrey had become disconcerted. "Why would you think that?" he asked.

"Ben saw the engineers bringing your biosuits to the Office of Exit," said Raj. "We could only assume that you intend to leave the settlement in the morning."

"If that's true," Jeffrey said, "then you know more than us."

"Why sweep the Tribes at all?" Mercedes said, stepping forward to stand beside Raj, her cheeks and eyes alight with the force of her own accusation. "Why not let them pass through our area and travel south like they're trying to do? There are inhabitable places there. We've seen them on your own satellite feeds. Why can't you let them be, let them live and grow and reproduce themselves? And then, at the time of Expansion, we could incorporate them. Welcome them as our brothers and sisters of the human race!"

"That's a conversation for another time, perhaps," Jeffrey said with mounting impatience. "I would respectfully suggest that you're ignoring the immense suffering and loss of life that would take place within that timeframe. Not to mention that you are greatly oversimplifying the difficulties of blending ourselves and the Tribes in that way—even in some distant future."

"You of all people should know best, shouldn't you, Jeffrey?" said Eduardo, hopping down from the mats. "You've killed more Tribes-people than anyone."

"Enough," Jeffrey said. "If you don't get out of my way this instant, I will file a charge with the Alphas for disrupting Department business. If what you say about the mission leaving tomorrow is true, then your interference is all the more serious."

"Murderers," Ben spat. But it was an insult made in desperation, Jeffrey was moving past them already.

With a word from Raj, the group pulled away, and the team crossed the playing fields without further harassment, moving quickly toward the Office of Mercy.

"Useless people," Alejandra huffed. "All talk and no solutions."

Douglas, Nolan, and Eric quickly agreed, adding their own remonstrations.

"I can't believe that Eduardo guy would speak to you like that," said Natasha, catching up to Jeffrey. "We *should* file a charge."

Jeffrey shook his head, waving it off, but his mouth and cheeks remained tight, his blue eyes cold.

"No," he said, "it wouldn't make any difference. If they're that elementary in their ethical thinking, then only a solid course of reeducation would correct their minds. I'm more worried about what's going on in the Office of Mercy right now." But a second later he muttered, speaking to himself, "Unethical, instinct-driven people. As if the Alphas hadn't thought through everything. As if I hadn't."

Natasha could not think how to respond, but she respected him so much in this moment. More than he could know.

They reached the Office of Mercy minutes later, and Arthur met them at the door.

"I was just coming to get you," he said. "There's something you have to see."

"Are the Pines attacking?" Alejandra cried.

"No, they've left the perimeter. They just picked up and left a couple of hours ago. But—"

"But what?" Jeffrey cut in.

"Well, here, we're playing the sensor recordings back on the big screen."

On the overhead screen appeared the image of the Pine camp. Around the room, the current shift workers rolled back from their computers to look. At first, the image of the camp appeared unexceptional, if somewhat more active than usual. The men, women, and children milled around the plateau, near the gaping mouth of the cave that had served as their shelter for the last ninety-four days. Many warmed their hands at the leaping fire outside the cave entrance.

"Watch the group on the far right," Arthur said.

Three men off to the side—one of whom Natasha recognized as the curly-haired chief—suddenly looked at them, *directly* at them, their gazes piercing and aware. Eric cursed; Alejandra gasped. An iciness shot through Natasha's core, her body perceiving the threat almost before she understood it herself. The men's eyes moved away quickly, but the sensation remained.

"What was that?" Natasha asked.

"You saw it," said Arthur.

"Hard to miss," Douglas muttered under his breath.

"Well," Arthur said, "it gets worse."

Beside Natasha, Jeffrey seemed stuck in place; his face was absolutely still and his fingers bent awkwardly together. Natasha wished that he would say something, but apparently he was as shocked as the rest of them. The image jumped and now the chief was saying something to the other men. In seconds, his words seemed to spread across the crowd, awakening the bodies into agitation. Natasha noticed that many of the Tribe, even the children, carried woven sacks or other small objects, blankets or tools. The chief looked at the sensor again, only this time the others followed his lead. The screen filled with their hard eyes, and their stares seemed to burn through the cable that connected the sensor receivers to the Office of Mercy, and burn through the screen itself. The curly-haired chief jerked away from the group, approaching the sensor, and others took cautious steps forward. Natasha could see the pockets and wrinkles in their skin, the stubble on their cheeks.

"Great Alpha," Eric said from behind her.

The chief lingered directly under the tree that held the sensor. Then he disappeared from view. An instant later, the image began to shake; the faces hopped and blurred, until the final blow came and the screen went to static.

"Why didn't you sweep?" Jeffrey said. He had not spoken till now; everyone turned to look at him. "Right then, before they had the chance to move."

"We didn't have a count," Arthur said. "I didn't know how fast they'd start moving. We couldn't see anything."

"Why not later, then, once you caught them on a different sensor?"

Natasha glanced between Jeffrey and Arthur; she hoped that Arthur would miss the obvious tone of accusation in Jeffrey's voice.

"There were no other sensors," Arthur said. "They disabled two more, two on the north mountain ridge, smashed them apart just like the first. Here, we can play it for you."

They all looked again at the overhead screen and watched as the Pines overwhelmed the images and went behind the sensors, and screens RN22 and RN28 went to static.

"It's wild," Douglas said, "a Tribe that knows about our sensors."

"It's more than wild," Alejandra whispered. "It's terrifying."

"As long as we're blind in those areas," Arthur said, speaking over them, "I consider the settlement in imminent danger of attack. We're going to have to change our plans. The Recovery team is now strictly a Repair team. Forget about checking the Crane sweep site. The work there will have to wait. Our priority is to repair the three sensors that the Pines destroyed. They're closer to the settlement." He tore his attention from the overhead screen and looked at the team. "Unless anyone has questions, you're all dismissed. We'll move you out in the morning."

A cry of surprise rose from the group, Natasha included, and Douglas, Nolan, and Alejandra left the Office of Mercy almost immediately, talking excitedly among themselves. But Eric and Natasha lingered, determined to stay as long as Jeffrey showed no signs of abandoning the Office. Eric kept trying to catch Natasha's eye, but Natasha would not let him, afraid of responding inappropriately to the news. It was clear that Jeffrey did not share their exhilaration. And indeed, as soon as the others had gone, he turned toward Arthur.

"You can't be serious about this," Jeffrey said.

"Of course I'm serious," Arthur answered.

"But you said you never got an accurate count. What if part of the group stayed behind? Besides, the Tribe's hardly over the perimeter. They might be planning to double back any minute!"

"If so, then we'd see them coming. Your team would have more than enough time to return to the settlement."

"Natasha and Eric should stay behind," Jeffrey said, with an air of decisiveness. "They're too young for a mission like this. I never would have recommended them for anything but a basic Recovery job. They don't have the same maturity of judgment. It's too dangerous."

The two Epsilons had only just opened their mouths to protest when Arthur spoke for them.

"Natasha and Eric are a part of this mission."

"The mission has changed."

"We need everyone, Jeffrey," Arthur said. "The Alphas agree."

Arthur dismissed Natasha and Eric again, in more certain terms than before, and this time they cleared out right away, terrified of giving their Director the chance to change his mind.

"We're going Outside," Eric said, as soon as they had gotten halfway down the Department hall.

"I know," said Natasha. "I can't believe that Jeffrey tried to kick us off the team, though."

"Who cares? We're going *Outside*."

"Yeah," said Natasha. "Outside."

They stared at each other in wonder, and Natasha almost felt like they were kids again, the way they reveled in the confusion and danger of what lay before them. Anything was possible, it seemed, and the expectation of tomorrow swelled and shined like new.

That night Natasha could not sleep, however hard she tried. While Min-he slumbered with her head buried in her pillow, Natasha read two chapters in the Ethical Code, curled up under her blanket and seeing by the soft glow of the pages after the underground nightfall. Entering the field would be a shock, and she wanted to keep her thoughts in the right state to receive it—to maintain within herself a calm and ethical steadfastness. She had performed well in the Pretends and that was good, but the real thing would be another story. As far as upholding the Wall, well, it had occurred to her that this sudden change in the mission's objective had eased the demands on her behavior. She had prepared herself to confront the Crane sweep site, the place of so much death, but now they would not see it. Instead they would be repairing sensors in the forest and investigating the abandoned, not decimated, Pine camp. Natasha skimmed the text, opening herself to the teachings of the Ethical Code. Perhaps it was the effect of her nerves, but reading the book filled her with a sadness and pride and hopefulness that she had not felt in years: the beauty of human intelligence poured into these words, the enlightenment of the Alphas, and the transcendence of nature's false laws that the settlements had at last achieved.

5

"Arms out at your sides, please."

Two long, thin gloves slipped over Natasha's hands and over her elbows.

"Now lift your right foot. These might feel tight at first, but you'll get used to it. We wouldn't want your socks falling down fifteen miles from home."

White socks of the same synthetic fabric reached halfway up Natasha's calves.

"We only have the medreaders left. Veronica, if you will?"

Natasha stood very still while a petite Beta woman from the Department of Research began fixing cold, plastic circles, the size of thumbnails, across her bare abdomen, over her heart, and down the length of her spine.

The team was in the Office of Exit, suiting up under the direction of the settlement's top engineers. They were all naked—the biosuits had to be worn directly against the flesh—and Natasha's skin was shivery and goose-bumped despite the warm air coming through the vents. Eric and Alejandra were laughing nervously together, while Douglas and Nolan were asking one of the engineers about the particulars of the biosuits' self-replicating material. Arthur stood in the far corner, his arms folded over his chest, wordlessly evaluating every preparation, ready to jump if he suspected an error.

Across the room, a male engineer was attaching medreaders to Jeffrey's back. From this angle, Natasha could see the burn that covered Jeffrey's whole right side, creeping rashlike over his back and stomach and up to his ear. She could not help but stare. Both because she had never seen Jeffrey without clothing before, and because she could hardly imagine the pain of a fire that would leave such a mark. Jeffrey rarely spoke about it, even when Natasha asked directly. "When the Palms attacked, they torched half the forest," he would say with a shake of his head. "They tricked me into getting too close. But I was making the choices that day, and I have only myself to blame."

Jeffrey took his glasses off and handed them to one of the engineers. His vision problems, Natasha knew, were a result of the fire too: a slight melting of the cornea, pupil, and retina. One day the doctors would need to bring him into the medical wing and give him new eyes and new optic nerves; though, in the meantime, Jeffrey seemed to be doing okay with the special lenses constructed for him in the Office of Dry Engineering.

A woman from Research slipped a pair of lensed goggles over Jeffrey's head and Jeffrey looked around the room, testing them. Natasha noticed how the muscles in his shoulders and back stood out in the bright overhead light. Judging from his body alone, one would never guess that Jeffrey was a Gamma; in fact, he appeared in better physical shape than most of the Delta men in the settlement.

Jeffrey's gaze caught Natasha's and he smiled. She blushed but did not look away. It was not supposed to be such a big deal to see someone naked; bodies were bodies, cells were cells. Plenty of medworkers had seen Natasha without her clothes and she had never cared. But then again, the rules were different where Jeffrey was concerned.

An engineer approached Jeffrey with a biosuit, and the private moment between Natasha and Jeffrey ended. At least, Natasha thought—while the engineers tested her own medreaders—at least Jeffrey's mood had changed since last night. He had not said anything more about leaving Natasha and Eric behind. Probably he felt reassured (as they all did, if by varying degrees) by the elapse of so many hours with no further sign of danger. Last night, the Office of Mercy had drafted twenty people for the nightshift. The teams had watched every sensor, searching for any sign of human movement. But the night had passed as an unbroken calm, and the Tribe had remained tucked behind the mountains, beyond the perimeter and out of sight. They could not say for sure, of course, but it was possible that the Tribe had continued traveling at the same speed with which they had fled their camp. If so, then the Pines were far away by now, twenty miles north of the perimeter's end.

"Ready for your biosuit?" asked Lewis Matsuki, who was supervising the outfitting of the team.

"All set," Natasha answered.

Two engineers brought Natasha's biosuit over from the rack. It looked identical to the others, except for the modifications in size and her two initials *NW* stamped onto the upper arm. Just as in the training sessions, the suit was gray with red stitching and made of a stretchy but very impenetrable-seeming material.

"It's perfect," said Natasha, reaching out to touch one of the arms.

The engineers were pleased, and they helped Natasha step carefully into the legs, then pushed her hands through the armholes. The biosuit enclosed her entire body up to the neck. She bent her arms, testing its movement, and was glad to discover that the fabric flexed easily.

"I doubt you'll experience any damage to the suit," Lewis said. "But if a rip does occur, just pinch the fabric together and hold for sixty seconds. The fibers will regenerate."

"I know," Natasha assured him. "We practiced it lots of times in the Pretends."

Veronica strapped an airfilter to Natasha's back and a small tracking device to her wrist.

"Ready for the helmet?" she asked.

"Yes."

Natasha tried her best to breathe evenly as the engineers screwed the helmet into the thin metal ring of the biosuit collar. For a moment she experienced a suffocating feeling, but then the air began to blow in from the filter tube. The air had a sharp, cool taste, with just a tinge of plastic.

"Okay?" Lewis asked, his voice muffled in Natasha's ears.

Natasha gave a thumbs-up.

They were all ready now, the members of the team; and they converged at the doors of the airlock. The engineers made a flurry of final adjustments to the six biosuits. They were nervous too, Natasha realized. If the biosuits did not perform as expected, it would be their years of work on the line.

"We'll be watching every sensor we've got," Arthur said. "If the Pines double back over the perimeter, we'll give an emergency call for return. If that happens, you drop everything and come home as quickly as possible. Leave any tools if you have to. The most important thing is your safety."

"We'll be fine," Douglas said. "You worry too much."

Eric smiled in nervous agreement, but Jeffrey was nodding.

"Good luck," Arthur said. "I'll see you in seventeen hours."

They stepped into the airlock. Natasha took one last, long look at the room: Arthur's heavy countenance, Lewis's anxious expression, and the exhilarated faces of the engineers lined up in front of the metal racks of extra airfilters, clothing, radios, and imaging devices. Then, as Veronica raised one hand in farewell, the doors closed on the Inside.

It was very quiet. The team was alone.

"We'll just walk through the airlock on this end," Jeffrey said. "The acid bath and UV lamps are only necessary coming the other way."

They passed into a second, white cube-shaped room, and then Jeffrey hit the control for the last set of doors.

"Here we go," Jeffrey said. "Take your last breath of settlement air."

They exited the airlock into a large but low-ceilinged storehouse lined with overstuffed shelves. On the walls hung at least fifty guns, all LUV-3s, and four electron saws that appeared untouched for decades. Boxes on the floor held everything from ammunition to plastic tubing, screwdrivers and metal parts for sensors. The space most closely resembled one of the storagerooms on level eight, except for one important fact: everything here was filthy. A fine coat of dust gave the entire room, even the floor, a monochromatic brown color. Natasha took a deep breath. The air tasted different, its plasticky coolness now seeming to mask a musky, thicker air beneath, and a scent like what one might experience in a fallow pasture room in the Farms.

Eric went to the nearest shelf and ran one gloved hand over the surface. He held up the circle of dirt on his finger for show.

"This is gross," he said.

"We're technically in the Outside now, Eric," Jeffrey said. "The environment rules here. Dirt, leaf, microbes, mammals. Our control ended at the airlock."

Jeffrey took a gun off the rack, loaded it, and handed it to Natasha; the dust had settled in the grooves along the barrel and in the curve of the trigger.

"Don't worry," Douglas said. "We tested them pretty recently, they're clean where it matters."

"I'll take your word for it," Natasha said.

She holstered the gun at her waist and waited while the others did the same. They had gone through this process in the Pretends, but the reality of it was different. Her body felt clumsier, and her fingers thicker, in a way she could not blame on the biosuit.

They were ready now. They gathered at the far end of the storehouse. Sunlight leaked in from beyond the door, interrupted by two rusty hinges. A spider with white markings scuttled above the knob and disappeared into the shadows. There was no genetic code reader here, only a series of deadbolts. Douglas opened the door.

Four sun-drenched steps led up to a verdant shock of grass. The trees towered in a ring beyond, ancient, intricate, and majestic, their sharp tops pointing to the bright blue infinity of the sky, the white puffs of cloud and the too-powerful, blinding sun: the universe. They climbed the steps. Natasha ran her hand along the sunken, moss-covered stone wall at her side. She felt slightly dizzy, as if the first strong gust of air might scoop her up and carry her off the curve of the planet. Was gravity really enough to secure one's feet to the earth? No walls, she thought. No walls to hold them in. She climbed the last step, following Jeffrey, Douglas, and Alejandra onto the circle of short grass that surrounded the settlement. She squinted against the light; it was too bright, it hurt her head. Colors exploded before her eyes: not only the blue but the deep green of the pine needles and the rippling green-yellow-white of the leaves, the textured browns of bark and the outlines of the dark, inscrutable shadows pocketing the woods before them.

"Team out," said Douglas, over the comm-link.

"What do you think?" Jeffrey asked.

Instead of looking around at the forest and sky like the rest of the team, his squinting, smiling eyes were on her, as if he cared more about Natasha's reaction to the Outside than about the whole Outside itself. Though of course, Natasha thought, this wasn't his first mission.

"It's—" she started to say.

Before she could finish, she caught sight of them: black and soaring from above. Novas, she thought, adrenaline rushing through her body. But then she heard them caw.

Jeffrey was laughing. "Crows," he said. "It's only crows. Eric?"

Eric removed his arms slowly from over his head, looking abashed.

The birds swooped up, changing direction, but gracefully, as if without effort. Their black wings shone in the sun. They cawed.

"It's amazing," Natasha said, laughing with Jeffrey, watching the birds disappear to specks.

Truly, the Pretends did not do the Outside justice. Now that Natasha was seeing it with her own eyes, the simulations became in retrospect like block-color outlines of the real objects they aimed to represent. In the Pretends, the grass was green, yes, but it had no definition, the blades did not distinguish themselves as they did in real life; the simulations had not captured the variation, the scattered patches of yellow, or the matted spots where, as Alejandra said, either deer or wild pigs had rested. Natasha leaned down and ran her gloved hand over the grass, feeling its soft resistance; she picked up a leaf and looked at it closely. The pale skeleton on its underside was blemished by disease, and yet it was beautiful in its imperfection. She looked again at the random growth of the woods. She thought it was wonderful. She could have stared at the same spot for hours and not comprehended the whole of it—so detailed and intricate and unique was every square inch of the Outside.

But their time for enjoying the green was soon over; they had to get moving. One by one, the team passed into the trees.

"Abandon all hope," Jeffrey said, as he stooped below a pine branch, "ye who enter here."

"What's that supposed to mean?" Eric asked, hesitating at the edge of the lawn.

"It's just an old quote from the Archives," Alejandra assured him, nudging Eric's shoulder. "He's joking."

Natasha looked back at the settlement. The sunken metal, joined boxes of the wings were such dull, lifeless objects. It felt impossible to believe they contained well-stocked, cheerful rooms full of busy citizens. Above the wings peaked the Dome, as still and faceless as its adjacent structures. The Dome was the bud of the flower and the wings were its petals, Natasha thought. Though the analogy did not seem so apt from this perspective—except for how it cast America-Five as a tiny thing glued to the Earth. Three stories the honeycomb windows rose over the grass, and yet, compared with the sky, it was nothing. In fact, even taking into account the column of nine underground levels, it seemed suddenly absurd to Natasha that they kept all that life squeezed into so small a space, when the rest of the land was so empty.

The way through the forest was rough and slow, and they were forced to move single file: first, Douglas, who held the title of navigator, though they all knew the way, then Alejandra, Eric, Natasha, Nolan, and finally Jeffrey. Natasha's energy was largely spent keeping her footing, pushing the small springy twigs out of her way and releasing them gently, so they did not snap back against Nolan's visor. They saw animals, creatures so alert and perfect it seemed bizarre that they had come into existence without any help: a brown tuft-tailed rabbit, pretty little birds with iridescent wings, a squirrel, spread-limbed, climbing a tree, and little flying specks called gnats that would have nibbled their flesh, if not for the biosuits.

Of course, not all of it was pleasant. A few hours into their hike, Eric stuck his foot into what turned out to be the open and maggot-infested carcass of a raccoon. The rancid pink and white inside was enough to make Natasha gag. And she could hardly pay attention while Eric wiped his boot against a tree and Jeffrey explained that the death was probably the work of another male of that species.

"See the gash here?" he asked them. "Right across its middle? It probably took him a long time to die. Nature at its finest . . ."

The bright spots of sun grew brighter and the woods took on the glow of a full-fledged mid-August day. Soon, through her helmet, Natasha could hear a new sound: like water gushing from a sink but magnified by a thousand. Eventually, the trees thinned and the land curved downward, sloping into a bank of rock and mud, identical to the one opposite. A fast path of dark water ran in between. A river.

"Amazing," rang Alejandra's voice in her ear. "It's like it has its own life."

"I wish we had one of these in the settlement," Eric added. "Do the Tribes actually drink from this?"

"Of course they do," Nolan answered. "And so did a lot of other people too, before the Storm."

"Didn't work out well for them, though," Jeffrey said. "That water may look pretty, but it sickened thousands. In Pre-Storm times, it was flowing with toxins. People would drink and then their stomachs would puff out like balloons."

"And worse things that we won't mention," Douglas added.

"But it's clean now?" Natasha asked. The water was so clear and bright, she could not imagine it making anyone sick.

"Clean enough for the animals, and for the Tribes," Jeffrey said. "But not for us."

They veered off from the river, toward the northern mountain ridge, approaching the place of the first downed sensor. They were in a deadzone now. The Office of Mercy could not see them, and would not be able to catch sight of a bear approaching or a dead branch swaying dangerously in the wind. The team reached the ridge and began to climb. The ground became loose and dry. They ascended higher than the sprawling tops of trees, keeping to a natural pathway along the mountain edge. The cliffs bordered them on one side, and their other side was wide open to the valley beneath. The sun beat down, making Natasha sweat.

"Don't look right at it," Jeffrey kept reminding them. "Unless you want a very unpleasant few hours in the Office of Bioreplacement."

At a place where the path momentarily widened and flattened, Douglas and Nolan broke off from the group to find sensor RN22, while Jeffrey, Alejandra, Eric, and Natasha continued on to the Pine camp. They followed a declivity into a low, isolated area of thick trees, before climbing a second mountain path, this one a little less steep than the first. They had not walked long before they entered onto a rocky plateau that was bordered by pocketed cliffs.

Initially the place did not strike Natasha as familiar, but then she saw: the gaping mouth of the cave where the Pines had kept disappearing, and the black smudge at its entrance where their fire had burned. Scattered on the dry ground were the jagged shards of a clay pot, and at the opposite end of the plateau lay the rotting and discarded bones of animal carcasses, buzzing with flies. The brush that grew along the cliff sides had been trampled and ravaged for kindling; and the loose ground had been scuffed smooth by milling life.

"The camp," Eric said, seeing it too. They had arrived at last.

They found the silver and white ruins of sensor RN59 by a group of tall birch trees. Jeffrey took a collapsible ladder from his pack and extended it against the trunk of the tree where the sensor had been.

"They unscrewed the bolts," Jeffrey called down, once he had reached the top. "Except for a couple of scratches, the base is completely unscathed."

A chill ran through Natasha, despite the glare of the afternoon sun.

"How did they?" she asked. "It's not like they have tools."

"Maybe they do, maybe they stole stuff from America-Six," Eric said. "What if they don't lock their storehouse like we do?"

Alejandra glanced behind them, suddenly jumpy.

Jeffrey descended the ladder. "It's possible they used a spearhead. They're not bad at crafting tools. They're just as ingenious as we are, only with different starting materials. The good news is that it won't take long to repair."

While Alejandra began photographing the shattered sensor, Jeffrey moved to examine the trash heap, and Eric and Natasha returned to the circle of charred wood outside the cave. They sifted through it with their hands. The blackened wood splintered at a touch and the soft ash billowed up with every disturbance. Natasha knew it was safe. The fire had been out for nearly a day and could not spontaneously ignite, but she still recoiled from the puffs of ash, imagining that it would.

They moved into the cave, passing through the arched opening that Natasha had spent hours observing from the settlement. The roof of the cave was low, and they put their hands up to keep from bumping their heads. Jeffrey followed them in with a flashlight and swept the beam across the interior: a dank-looking fur, a pile of stones, a stack of dry twigs and leaves, two pieces of a snapped bow, still connected by sinew, and a lump of leaves that must have served as a bed.

"It's so much smaller than I thought it would be," Natasha said. "They must've really squeezed in here."

"Didn't leave much behind either, did they?" Alejandra said.

"They're pretty thorough that way," Eric agreed. He sounded disappointed. "I'm going back outside." But as Eric turned to go, he stopped just before the archway. "Hey Alejandra, take a photo of this."

They all looked. Jeffrey moved the flashlight. Within the circle of light to the right of the cave's opening blazed the brown-red imprint of a human hand. Blood, Natasha thought, and shuddered.

"That's creepy," Alejandra said.

The circle of light wavered and Natasha looked over at Jeffrey.

"Have you seen anything like this before?" she asked.

"No," he said, then adding, as if to temper his quick response, "But it's not all that strange. Most Tribes decorate their habitats in some way. It's art."

"Not to me, it's not," Alejandra said. "The Dome is art. This is just sick."

Jeffrey shrugged. He ran the light once more along the cave walls; yet except for the long striations and pockets in the stone, the rest of the cave bore no markings.

Natasha walked over to the print.

"You don't think it's *human* blood, do you?" she asked.

"No," Jeffrey said. "I'm sure it's animal."

Natasha held her hand over the print; they were almost exactly the same size, accounting for the added bulk of the biosuit. She spread her fingers so that she matched its position.

"What are you doing?" Jeffrey asked.

"Nothing." She took her hand away. "I think it might be a woman's hand."

"Maybe," he said. "Or a teenage male's. The young make most of the markings."

They had just set to work fixing the sensor when Arthur radioed. Douglas and Nolan needed an extra person back at sensor RN22, and Arthur wanted Natasha to go. Natasha didn't mind at all; she had already seen everything at the camp. But Jeffrey, who had up until this moment treated Natasha and Eric as competent and equally qualified members of the team, rejected Arthur's order outright. Before Natasha could respond to Arthur, Jeffrey came in over the comm-link. He told Arthur that he would send Alejandra instead, as she was a Delta, and experienced enough to go off on her own. But that was no good. Alejandra was an engineer, and Jeffrey would need her help for the sensor repair. In response, Jeffrey said that he would go himself. But by then, Natasha had heard enough; she could not let Jeffrey continue speaking for her. Arthur had assigned her a job, and she had no problem getting it done.

"I'll be fine," Natasha said. "Arthur has my position."

"I don't want you walking alone."

"It's a mile back the same way we came. I'll radio if I see anything out of the ordinary." She started across the plateau.

"Or *hear* anything. Or *sense* anything," Jeffrey said after her.

"Okay. Got it."

"And if suddenly things don't look familiar to you—"

She gave him a small smile that he did not return, and as she crossed the plateau, returning to the mountain path, she could feel the pressure of his gaze at her back. As she walked farther, though, his presence thinned, and the brush and the cliff edge came between them.

6

I n a settlement, you never got to be far away from everyone. Even when you were by yourself in a sleeproom or Pod, there were always other people stacked in nearly identical rooms above and below and at each side. Cry out in your sleep, and someone would call the Department of Health; tap on the wall, and they'd hear you. What a strange feeling, Natasha thought as she descended the mountain path into the valley. How strange to be alone, absolutely alone in the folds of this insentient, nonhuman world. She took several more strides, breathing hard. She had never been more removed from human company in all her life. One third of a mile separated her from the plateau; two thirds of a mile from the RN22 sensor. A flock of birds flew overhead in a V formation and she stopped to watch them pass. She had to; she was the only person in the world to see it. When she started walking again, she stepped more slowly, eager to savor these moments. She was experiencing a liberating sensation, like some immaterial part of her was at last expanding, like souls in old religious texts connecting to a universal spirit, breaking free from the body. Was this how the Tribespeople felt? Full and large and continuous with everything between the sky and the ground under their feet? Or was it not? (Natasha frowned, considering this.) Because without a settlement to go home to at night, and with the possibility of injury and death waking with them at every dawn, the Tribespeople must constantly feel fear; and perhaps fear made the world feel, *not* continuous, but divided and small. Natasha regarded again the intricacy of the spreading treetops and the effortless scatter of dry leaves across the orange pine needles of the forest floor, only this time with a more ethical understanding. A life in nature was a life that rushed toward death, without relief, without the possibility of resistance, without the pity of the blue-faced mountains or the monstrous sky. Dwelling upon the prettiness of the wild, as Natasha was doing, was as reprehensible as admiring the beauty of cancer cells on a slide.

Amid these thoughts, Natasha had become somewhat careless in monitoring her surroundings. And only several meters before reaching the rise of land which led to where Douglas and Nolan were working, she saw a bright streak of close movement in her peripheral vision. Her muscles tensed. She threw herself into a defensive position, just as she'd practiced a hundred times in the Pretends: her back up against the trunk of a large, half-dead sycamore tree, her gun unholstered and thrust forward in both hands.

"Natasha, what's the matter? You're nervous—"

Arthur's voice from the Office of Mercy. She had forgotten; they could see her heart beating.

"There's something. An animal."

"You're loaded?"

"Yes."

The flash of pale movement appeared again through the bushes. It could not be a bear, unless it was a very small bear. She had once seen a mountain lion on the sensors here. What if a mountain lion had slipped into the deadzone without anyone noticing? Or what if it had lived here for months, and just emerged from hiding now that the Pines had gone? It barked. Natasha raised her head from the crosshairs. The animal bounded out of the bushes, its pink tongue hanging to one side and its ears down, its coat bright in the sun.

"A dog," said Natasha. She could have cried with relief. They had studied dog breeds in their fifth year of school, a very popular lesson. "Part golden retriever, I think."

The dog wagged its tail and barked again, then leapt up against Natasha with its front paws on her stomach.

"Whoa," she said, and staggered back, laughing.

"Take care of it then," Arthur said. "Quickly." Then he began talking to Nolan.

But Natasha, instead of following Arthur's orders right away, turned off her speaker. She wouldn't get a chance like this again, a couple of minutes wouldn't hurt the mission. She put her hand out and the dog sniffed. She wished she wasn't wearing gloves.

"Poor thing," Natasha said. "The Pines must've forgotten you, didn't they? You're not part of a pack."

Then, amazed at her own daring, Natasha reached down and scratched its head; a gesture remembered from some Pre-Storm book she had read long ago. The dog leaned into her hands. Then it barked and pulled away, not in a threatening motion, but like it wanted Natasha to play.

"Sorry, buddy, I've got to go."

She took a deep breath and hoisted up her LUV-3.

"Stay still, this is for your own good."

The dog stared, panting, its black lips pulled back, as if to smile. The gun drifted a little in Natasha's hands. She stopped and took another long breath and repositioned her grip.

"Good dog," she said.

Now was the moment to shoot, but something was wrong. She could not disengage from the immediate and see the dog's life from a universal perspective. She could not build the Wall.

The dog barked and wagged its tail; its ears perked up and it turned, bounding back toward the bushes. With a cry, Natasha dropped her arms; she could hear it barking, chasing a rodent or squirrel maybe.

She started running after it. She had to. She could sweep the dog and get back to the route before Arthur or anyone else noticed that she was taking too long. Natasha plunged through the branches. The dog's golden back caught the light. Luckily it was moving toward the mountain, only a little farther north from where she needed to be. A bark sounded ahead and she ran forward. Her heart beat hard, too hard, they would notice in the Office of Mercy. She moved quickly, tripping and stumbling on the rough ground, holding back tears of frustration. How would she be able to return to the settlement knowing the dog was out here? It could starve or freeze to death in the winter, all because she had failed to hold her stupid feelings behind the Wall for one eighth of a second.

But her anguish did not torment her for long. As the trees began to give way to the rise of rock, she saw the dog near the edge of the mountain. She stopped and reached for her gun. Her hand had only just touched the metal when a branch cracked directly behind her. Before Natasha had time to react, a blow to the back of her head launched her entire body forward. She landed on her side, with her right arm tucked under her. A foggy darkness rose before her eyes. And the last thing Natasha saw was the golden dog a little way up the rocks, smiling and wagging its tail and leaning against a pair of human legs, while a human hand, streaked with grime, petted and ruffled its ears.

In her dreams, Natasha was a child again, clasping her teacher's hand and circling the Dome to walk off a stomachache while the noise of a boisterous celebration echoed from one of the wings. Natasha was groaning and holding her middle while her teacher said *step breathe step breathe or else we'll have to take you to the medical wing with the other children who ate too many sweets*. Then the noise was gone and Natasha was watching herself from above, as one can choose to watch a prescribed drama play out in the Pretends. She stood all alone in the black Dome, and the glass of one of the honeycomb windows was missing. Natasha watched herself watch in horror as one, two, three yellow jaguars slunk in from the Outside. . . .

A pain from the back of her head rushed over her skull and the ground pressing against her cheek felt unsteady, swaying. From far away in the darkness came two voices, dreamlike and strange.

"Her?"

"Yes."

"Are you certain?"

"I was sure then and I'm sure now."

"We should call . . ."

But then the world lapsed into silence again and when Natasha woke, the voices were gone.

It was the dry air that had roused her: it caught in her throat and made her cough. And the heat too, the flesh of her face stung with heat. When she unstuck her eyes, she found herself on a floor of gravel, and staring into a fire. Instinctively, she recoiled from it, her back hitting a rough wall. The light was too much, it burned her eyeballs and she squinted against it with a cry. Where were the overhead lights? But then with a sickening feeling she remembered the mission, the dog, the naked limbs, and the blow that had come from behind. She cried out again, this time with dread. Her eyes opened wide. She had no helmet and the pressure of her biosuit had deflated to nothing, the fabric limp against her skin. She held her breath. Frantically she looked around, registering vaguely that she was in a cave, that she saw no exit. Her helmet sat on its side several feet away. But when she reached for it, she realized her wrists were tied together at her stomach. She jerked one leg; her ankles were tied together too. A low groan escaped her lips. They would kill her, whoever they were. They might return to do it themselves or they might leave her here to die of thirst; either way, whoever had brought her here would kill her.

Her mind drifted again, and the next time her vision cleared, she was no longer alone. A shape moved in the dark behind the fire, rising up to full height. A man. He moved above the flames and the light revealed a weathered, round face, a head of curly hair, and an expression of gruesome expectation.

"Who are you?" Natasha said, kicking herself backward against the stone.

Her legs were shaking, her teeth knocked against each other. It was like her body already knew. I'll die here, Natasha thought, I'm going to die. She wished to be anywhere in the world but here. She wished that some force, anything, would come and take her away from this place. She could see Jeffrey as he watched her leave the Pine camp; she could feel his face close to her own. I'm sorry, I'm sorry, her lips whispered in a rush. A low rumble reverberated around her, shaking the walls of the cave. Natasha didn't know what it was, maybe the noise of the universe ending.

The man stepped around the fire. His ragged, animal clothes smelled of earth and sweat; a string of long, curving teeth hung from around his neck. He grinned, making his cheeks fat and dimpled. Suddenly Natasha recognized him: he was a Pine, the chief, one of the two hunters who had survived when the tattooed man died. This was the man who had looked into the sensor eye.

"Let me go!" Natasha screamed, her fear bursting forth as rage. "You let me go right now."

To her surprise, the man stopped and frowned, and a flicker of near-comprehension lit his face, like he had understood her words and was contemplating how to respond. But that was impossible. Her outburst must have only startled him. He moved toward her again.

"Let me go," she sobbed, knowing that he could not understand. "I'm not anything to you."

"You are!" the man said. The sounds emerged rough and gravelly through his lips, caught up with bits of phlegm, but they were unmistakable.

He was standing directly over her now. Had she not seen his lips move, she would not have believed that the words came from him. For a moment, Natasha's shock caused her to forget her own situation. She stared at him, her mouth open, her eyes dry.

"How—how can you speak?"

"Speak? Why shouldn't I speak?"

Suspicion flared within Natasha anew. "Who are you?" she demanded. "You can't be a Tribesperson. You're from another America. A spy!"

But then she remembered again how this man had fought the bear. No settlement citizens would ever risk so much for a disguise, just to get a peek at their neighbors. He breathed in, unhurried, smelling her as if she were a Garden plant.

"We are the People," he said at last. "My name is Axel. I am the chief."

"What are you doing here? What do you want?"

It was terrifying, the way he stared.

"We live in the forest near the water. When the cold comes, we travel south. We always have."

"What do you want?" Natasha demanded again.

He paused for a long moment, entranced by the look of her, her face, her body, her biosuit. Then the rumbling came again, like thunder.

"I am not the one to explain," he said.

"You said you're the chief."

He seemed amused; two boyish dimples showed in his cheeks. He found a long stick on the ground and poked at the fire. "Yes, and as chief, I have promised the job to a different person."

The sound of other voices came from the dark recesses beyond the fire, echoing and full, and approaching at an urgent pace. Axel looked around. From a thin break in the rocks—Natasha's vision had adjusted enough to see it now—entered two Pine men and a woman. The first man had a shiny ponytail, and the second carried a bow and arrow. The woman had strings of red beads stacked up her neck.

Behind them by several paces arrived a second, younger woman with two tiny people at her sides: children, a boy and a girl, each clinging to the woman's skirt. They all stared at Natasha, the children too.

"Axel," said the ponytailed man, the first to break his gaze. "They've found the area. They're attacking from above."

"They have fire weapons!" the man with arrows added. "We should have had more people stay behind. Who will fight with us now? Them?" He threw a dismissive gesture toward the woman and her children, but the ponytailed man caught his arm.

"Don't mention my family."

The woman with red beads jumped between them, then looked to Axel for help.

"Enough, Raul," Axel said, addressing the ponytailed man. "How did they find us? They followed us?"

"No," said the woman, still eyeing the two men. "I circled the area. She was alone. The others didn't come till much later."

"It's her." The man with arrows pointed at Natasha. "She's calling them. Right now, you're calling them!"

More rumbles came from overhead and rock and dust showered down on the fire. In the midst of everyone coughing, a new noise came: rhythmic cracks from high above, *tkk-et-koom tkk-et-koom*, what could only be the shots of a gun. Her team, Natasha realized, a thrill of relief running through her. Jeffrey. Her team. They were trying to find her.

"We can watch them better from above. Mattias, Hesma."

Axel left the cave, followed by the man with arrows and the woman wearing red beads. The ponytailed man, the one called Raul, began to follow. But he stopped when the little boy began to cry.

"Papia," the boy said.

Raul froze, then doubled back and knelt down beside the boy. He kissed the boy's forehead, and then the girl's, as she had started to cry as well. Natasha stared at the children's large, smooth faces and giant eyes. Had she and the other Epsilons really looked like that once? They were captivating and beautiful, these children.

"Stay here," Raul said. "And listen to your mother."

He stood, and then he kissed the woman on the lips. But instead of kissing him back, the woman grabbed onto his neck and clutched her fingers into his hair, with violence.

"We were supposed to stay together," she said.

"I'm only going to look. You'll be safer here."

"I want us all to be safe."

"I'll be back soon," Raul said. "Sit against the stone and cover your heads if the earth shakes again."

The woman looked at Natasha.

"She won't bother you," Raul said in a hushed voice. "She can't get free."

Raul removed the woman's hands from his neck and disappeared through the break in the rock. The woman pressed against the wall, clutching the children at her sides.

The fire crackled and Natasha closed her eyes, the terrible pain in her head briefly overtaking her body. At least she had time; instinctively, Natasha knew that this woman would do nothing to harm her; she could rest until the others returned. The man with arrows and the woman with red beads—Mattias and Hesma—if these people did want to kill her, they would be the ones to do it.

An explosion sounded from overhead and the floor rattled in a rain of pebbles. The children shrieked and, in the quiet aftermath, began to sob. When Natasha opened her eyes, the woman was pulling the children up from the ground, dragging them toward the exit. The boy screamed and wrestled under her hold.

"But Papia said to stay," the girl protested.

"We have to go outside. It's dangerous."

"Wait!" said Natasha.

The woman froze.

"If you go out and they see you," Natasha continued with deliberation, speaking over the pounding in her head, "they'll sweep you, shoot you."

"Why should I believe you?" the woman spat. "I know what you do. Your glasshouse is the most evil thing on this planet."

The abrupt change in the woman's manner startled Natasha.

"I don't—" Natasha fumbled. "We're not evil. We try to do the right thing."

"You kill," she said.

"Not killing." Natasha felt dizzy. She couldn't remember the most simple goal of the Office of Mercy. What was it? "We end suffering. Sweep. We don't kill."

The earth shook and a piece of rock rolled down the wall and struck Natasha's back, making her scream.

The woman stared. She had her children securely at her sides again.

"The rope is brittle," she said. "There's a sharp edge behind you. Rub the rope and it will snap. I've seen caves fall before, and this one is going to fall."

With the sound of gunfire echoing through the earth, the woman fled out of sight with her children. A minute passed. Another explosion burst forth and the fire toppled with a crack of splintering wood; the air filled with smoke and Natasha coughed chokingly, trying to heave the stuff from her lungs. The woman was right; she had to get out of here. Natasha struggled into a sitting position, her vision swaying as if she had just finished a round of bioreplacement. The cave wall sloped to a sharp edge about waist high. Grunting, Natasha scooted over to it and began to rub the rope binding her wrists against the stone. She could feel the rope getting hot with friction; the fibers weakened, weakened and finally snapped. She fumbled and yanked at the ties on her ankles and, seconds later, they gave. She lunged for her helmet and tried to fit it back on her collar, but the blow must have damaged the metal somehow; it wouldn't screw on; she would have to try it again in the light.

The yellow and orange flames of the fiery logs grabbed at the air, and a spray of glowing embers covered the floor. Natasha was afraid to go around the fire, but she had to. She stepped slowly with her back scraping against the curving stone, terrified of losing her balance, until at last she reached the opening where the Pines had gone. The tunnel arced low over her head; it was dark and narrow. If the Pines came back now, they would crash right into her, but she had to try; trying was better than waiting to die in that cave.

She fell several times, rubbing her palms raw on the pebbled ground. The tunnel split into two paths and she chose the way that inclined slightly upward. She saw a suffused glow of white light ahead, a light so placid and strong that it could only be sunlight. She threw her body toward it, stumbling up the incline. A large flat boulder, chiseled with pictures of birds and fish, was blocking the way. Natasha screamed in agony. But then, dropping her helmet, she dug her fingers around its edge and pulled, and the boulder slid so easily that it could only have been designed for that purpose. She grabbed her helmet and ran. When she saw the broken bow with its sinew, she knew where she was. She was in the cave of the old Pine camp that she had explored with Eric, Jeffrey, and Alejandra. She saw the decaying furs and the bed of leaves and the brown-red hand that she had touched with her own. She ran into the light, but the plateau was empty.

Near the shattered sensor, tools lay on the ground. Her team must have left them. Natasha ran, gulping the fresh sweet air until her senses kicked in and she choked on it. She ran toward the path, toward the settlement. Her vision blurred but she did not have to think of the route; her legs knew it from the Pretends. She was halfway down the mountain path when a wave of pain came over her and she fell. She tried to get up again but her arms had no strength. She lay with her bare face in the dirt while gingerly, with one hand, she reached to touch the pain at the back of her head. Her fingers met a warm, sticky clump of hair. Blood. Her skull was bleeding. She drew her hand back and saw the brilliant red of her own body. Only once in her life had her flesh split open before, when as a child she'd suffered the quick, even slice of a paper cut. She remembered how she had stared at the white line of flesh and the rising blood, mesmerized, until a Beta had scolded her and sent her to the Department of Health. Natasha tried to get up, pushing herself to her knees this time, until her muscles went slack. Her lips touched the ground, dirt sticking to her mouth. She groaned. I'm sorry, Jeffrey, she thought, the words drifting by as if they existed apart from her, apart from the mind that had thought them. I'm sorry, I'm sorry.

A powerful defeat washed through her limbs, her eyes were closing but from the wrong direction, the dark creeping upward. She heard familiar voices from far away, calling her name, or maybe not, maybe only the birds. Her mind went dizzy until, all of a sudden, the voices were loud, right over her head.

"Get her helmet on!"

"I've got to stop the bleeding first."

"Is she breathing?"

"Yes. Shallow, but yes."

"All right. Get it on now."

"I'm trying, I'm trying."

"Here, let me."

"No. It's broken. Dented."

"Leave it then. Hurry."

"I've got her."

Natasha felt herself being hoisted up in sturdy arms, her hot wound touching cool fabric. Her head throbbed at every jostling step of the body holding her. She drifted in and out of consciousness like during a long bad night when sleep only comes in shallow undulations. At one point she was falling, her body instinctively tightening for impact. But then, before the impact could come, she was swinging up again and the voices were saying, "Alpha be it," and "No, no, I have her." At last, with the pain becoming almost unbearable, she felt the unmistakable drops of a careful descent, stair by stair. The brightness beyond the lids of her eyes dissolved and a sudden coolness chilled her flesh, and Natasha knew in a burst of clear thought that she was with her team and that they had reached the Inside.

7

I n the Office of Mercy, all was chaos. The wallphone rang shrilly with calls from the Department of Government; the audiosets crowded with voices; the overhead screen flashed with sensor images of the deadzone perimeter; and huddles of people argued over field maps and coordinate figures at various computers throughout the floor. Claudia Kim ripped off her audioset and pushed back in her chair.

"They're here," she said to Arthur, who had just heard the same news over the comm-link from Douglas.

They rose together, and Arthur followed Claudia around the cubicles, across the hall to the Office of Exit.

Claudia tugged at the base of her shirt and tapped her finger to enter the room. She could not wait to see what kind of shape they were in, the Office of Mercy team members: Natasha, abducted and battered around; Eric, broken by the mere sight of a flesh-and-blood Pine; and Jeffrey—well, Claudia was sure that Jeffrey would be in worse shape than any of them. This whole disaster was his fault; it was always his fault. At least it satisfied Claudia to know that *he* must understand his own culpability better than anyone.

Claudia and Arthur entered the Office of Exit, where several Department of Health workers, dressed in full biosuits, were waiting with stretchers—each bed enclosed with plastic and exhaling through its own independent air system.

"I told Douglas to disable the acid bath," Arthur said, explaining these extra measures. "It's too dangerous with Natasha's biosuit damaged."

"You'll risk contaminating the entire settlement," Claudia replied. "The UV only kills the weaker bacteria."

"It's unlikely that they're carrying anything."

"The Alphas have been nothing but cautious for the last three hundred years. It's amazing to me that you would find *your* circumstances as Director so special as to disregard all precedent—"

"Please, Claudia," Arthur stopped her. "I have enough to worry about. We don't even know how badly she's hurt."

A low hum sounded from the airlock, and the medworkers began readying the stretchers. Claudia could not wait to see their faces. She had predicted this from the beginning, from when Jeffrey had first broached the subject of allowing Natasha Wiley to join the team, that the mission would end in disaster. Earlier, in the Office of Mercy, Claudia had been the first to notice that Natasha was gone. She had watched Natasha veer from the route, and she had heard her blow off her Director when he asked for an explanation. She had watched, too, as Natasha's medreaders suddenly went flat, and the tracking signal— a green dot on the map—went soaring through the coordinates at a speed that implied it was no longer attached to her body, that someone had taken it from her wrist and thrown it into the trees. At 1010, they declared Natasha missing and put the entire settlement on high alert.

Even Arthur could not prevent Jeffrey from abandoning the plateau when he heard. Jeffrey bolted down the mountain by himself, leaving Eric and Alejandra to trail behind.

"You've seen nothing, absolutely nothing, enter the deadzone since we left?" Jeffrey demanded.

"Nothing but jackrabbits," Arthur told him.

"You're sure they were jackrabbits, not wolves or bears?"

Claudia rolled her eyes; why Arthur allowed Jeffrey to take control of every situation was beyond her. He should pull rank and tell Jeffrey to shut his mouth and follow orders for once.

"You said Natasha saw a dog," Jeffrey continued.

"A golden retriever," Arthur said. "A Tribe dog, it sounds like."

"The perimeter?" Jeffrey asked. His voice had become tense and, despite herself, Claudia got a chill imagining Jeffrey out there on the mountainside, wholly exposed to the wild.

"The Tribe hasn't moved," Arthur said. "Whatever's out there, it isn't them."

But so much for that. Two minutes later, Eric and Alejandra came off the mountain path and ran straight into a Tribe man.

"What should we do?" Eric said.

"What should you do?" Claudia repeated, wrestling communication from Arthur. "You sweep them, Eric. What do you think we armed you for?"

But they had waited too long, and the man escaped into the trees. In her dreams, Claudia could not have envisioned a more incompetent group of people. Between the five of them—Douglas, Nolan, Jeffrey, Eric, and Alejandra—they reported seeing as many as twenty different Tribespeople. At the end of the manual sweep, they'd only managed to eliminate three.

Their efforts came to a halt when they found Natasha. Jeffrey and Nolan were chasing a male back toward the plateau when they came upon her sprawled out in the middle of the path. Over the comm-link, the voices of the team arrived in jarring spats.

"We're evacuating the area now," Douglas shouted.

In the background, Claudia could hear the popping of rapid-fire LUV-3s. She sighed. They had panicked; they were firing blindly into the trees, trying to clear a way home. They had dropped even the vaguest semblance of ethical thinking. She rose from her chair, went to the wallphone and dialed 999 for a direct line to the Alphas.

"Yes," Claudia said, when the Mother answered. "Natasha Wiley. We have her."

Now, in the Office of Exit, the light beside the airlock began to flash, and the doors were parting open. Jeffrey stood at the center of the group, holding Natasha clutched to his chest. Her helmet had fallen, and there was a bright red stain on his biosuit where the gash on her head had touched. As soon as the door had opened wide enough, the team rushed forward, as if they were still fleeing the Pines. Nolan dropped his airfilter and Eric's gun swept over the crowd, eliciting screams from the approaching medworkers.

"Whoa there, Epsi," Claudia said, catching Eric's arm and forcing it down. "You're supposed to leave the guns in the storehouse."

No one heard her. The medworkers came forward and took Natasha's limp body from Jeffrey's grasp. Jeffrey held on to her some seconds too long, completely dazed, like he had left his mind in the field and didn't understand what they wanted. Or perhaps, Claudia thought, he believed that Natasha was already dead, that this was his final moment with her.

At last, the medworkers got Natasha onto a stretcher and wheeled her out. Meanwhile, the engineers could hardly extract Jeffrey from his biosuit and throw him a fresh pair of prote-pants before he'd gone after her. Claudia followed with Arthur and the members of the team. The citizens on Wave One Defense jumped aside to let the party through. There were cries of horror and amazement as people caught sight of Natasha's injured body through the plastic enclosure of the stretcher. One citizen, unidentifiable in the biosuit, bumped into Arthur while trying to get a better view.

"We're on high alert, people!" Claudia shouted.

Once again, the citizens resumed their positions and the guns trained back to the glass.

They passed through the doors of the medical wing, and a team of new doctors descended upon them. They took Natasha straight to

Bioreplacement, while the others they herded to the high-frequency electroimaging bank for complete brain and body evaluations. Jeffrey wouldn't go. Two Delta doctors had to block him from following Natasha into the preproom.

"You have to give her blood, she's lost so much," he shouted after them. "And check for viruses, she breathed unfiltered air for over two hours."

Claudia felt the rage build up inside her. The others had all left now; it was only Jeffrey and the two Delta doctors in the corridor. She reached out and grabbed Jeffrey's face, squeezing his cheeks.

"How dare you," she said. The three men looked at her, astonished. "Your fascination with that girl almost cost us our peace. You'd have us die for her, would you? You'd have us suffer? Why the Alphas support you—"

"But they do support me, Claudia." His shock worn off, Jeffrey shook out of her grasp. "They always have."

"Not after this."

"We'll see."

His blue eyes radiated disdain, but Claudia met them. He could not scare her. Ever since she and Jeffrey were children, there had been an intensity of feeling between them. They had been the two top-ranked students in the Gamma generation, and even back then they used to fight. They had once gotten into a punching match over the issue of a stolen pillow; and in classes they had vied for the teachers' attention and battled for the highest scores on tests. Later, in their adolescence, their feelings for each other had briefly flared into love. Claudia would never admit it to anyone, but those days spent studying together for the Office of Mercy entrance exam, sneaking kisses in deserted corners of the Archives, were some of the best of her life. The nights they used to crawl into each other's beds she still relived in the Pretends. But that was years ago. Before Jeffrey had become so unrecognizable, wholly different from the rule-breaking, spontaneous, confident person whom she had known in their youth. She had never been able to forgive him for changing; and working together had kept Claudia's feelings fresh. Especially given that in the last several years (adding insult to injury, as they said in Pre-Storm texts), Jeffrey had managed to pull ahead of her in the Office of Mercy, rising up through the ranks to become Arthur's right-hand man. Claudia could not comprehend how Jeffrey maintained so much prestige among their peers and elders. She certainly saw him for what he was today: a man who, despite his hard exterior, had only doubt and fear in his heart.

"Get out of my way," Jeffrey growled.

Before the doctors could stop him, he'd thundered through the windowed doors to the Office of Bioreplacement, holding his arms high and already making demands, as if he held the status of an Alpha.

What a mess, Claudia thought, while the doctors went chasing after him, shouting about contamination. Attacked by the Tribes, outsmarted by savages. They should have swept the Pines when they'd had the chance, before the Tribe had messed with the sensors. And Mother forget the possibility of a dirty sweep. Arthur had been too careful, and all his carefulness had led them here.

Disgusted by the whole situation, Claudia started back toward the Office of Mercy.

Jeffrey must be punished for this, she thought. Surely the Alphas would see it her way now.

When Natasha woke, she found herself lying naked on a long, high table. Thousands of hair-thin needles covered her body like a fine, stiff fur, and from these needles rose ultrafine transparent fibers, which met in a large tangle of crystal opalescence at the ceiling. Startled, Natasha tried to raise her head. But she couldn't move; she couldn't even wiggle her fingers. A soft blue light poured down on her, ubiquitous and familiar. Slowly the realization came over her that she knew this room.

It was a cell injection room in the Department of Health, part of the Office of Bioreplacement. She blinked, searching for some sign of life within her limited periphery of vision. She did not like the silence; she found it unnerving, and a heavy anxiety began to build in her chest. Finally she heard the sound of a door whooshing open and, seconds later, a masked female face appeared hoveringly over her own.

"You surfaced a little early. How are you feeling?"

"Fine," Natasha said, her voice cracking. "I don't feel anything."

"Well, that's good news, isn't it? We did a nice job on your head, if I say so myself. We transferred forty billion cells fresh from Bioproduction and two dozen bundles of neurotransmitters. You're as good as new. Better than new."

"Where's the rest of my team?" Natasha asked. Her mind didn't feel quick at all. She was straining to remember something, something about the Tribes . . .

"Asleep, I would think," answered the doctor. Then she added hesitantly, as if afraid of taking Natasha too much by surprise, "It's been six days since the mission."

"Six days?" Natasha tried to sit up, forgetting her earlier attempt.

"This will help you sleep a little while longer," the doctor said, touching a screen on a panel near Natasha's feet. "You need to give your body time to recover."

When Natasha woke a second time, the needles were gone. She was on a stretcher, moving down the central hallway. She could shift her arms around, and she wore one of the crinkly, purple nightshirts standard in the Department of Health.

"We've been waiting for you to get up all morning," a new face said, leaning over her own. This time Natasha recognized the speaker immediately. It was Roy Heaney, an Epsilon nurse. "Any pain?"

"No," Natasha answered. "How many days—"

"Two days since you last woke up. Eight since the mission. We have just one more scan to run."

They were wheeling her into the electroimaging room, the same room where all the citizens of America-Five received routine evaluations for natural cell decay. The high bank of hexagonal openings rose up the far wall, one into which her own stretcher would slide. A feeling of urgency flared in Natasha.

"Wait!" she said. They were lifting her, transferring her into the tubelike imaging machine. She grabbed the sides of the stretcher.

"Don't do that," a man's voice said. "Your fingers."

"I want to talk to Jeffrey. Jeffrey and Arthur. You have to tell them not to sweep. I saw the Tribe. The Tribe spoke English. I talked to them. There was a woman with children. They're scared that the cave will collapse."

"You'll see them soon," Roy said. "From what we hear, the Office of Mercy is proceeding with caution."

Alone in the narrow, bright tube, Natasha's fear returned. How did she get here? How had she escaped from the cave? For a moment, she tried to remember. But when she did, when she remembered moving around the fire and seeing the sunlight at the top of the tunnel, she could not figure out how her team had found her. Had they intercepted her on the plateau? No, she thought, she had made it farther, she had seen the trees in the valley before she fell.

When they brought her out, her cheeks were slick with tears. Roy wiped them away with the sleeve of his scrubs.

"Don't worry," he said. "The meds will be out of your system soon. You'll feel more like yourself."

"I want to talk to my team."

"We told them, they're on their way."

As the nurse had promised, Natasha had just finished dressing in one of the small recovery rooms when a knock came at the door.

"Natasha," Arthur said, walking into the room with Douglas and Alejandra. Natasha looked past them, expecting Jeffrey—Jeffrey whose face had come to her during what she had believed were the final moments of her life. But Alejandra closed the door behind her, and Natasha forced herself to suppress her disappointment. "We're glad to see you well," Arthur continued. "The doctor said your results came back fine. Not a molecule out of place."

But Natasha had no interest in her own health. When Arthur outstretched his hand to her, she gripped it in both of hers.

"Tell me you haven't swept," she said.

"No."

Natasha released him. "Thank the Alphas. Listen to me, you have to let the Pines go. They're not the kind of people we thought."

Arthur's expression was one of consternation. Douglas and Alejandra both glanced at him.

"Please, Natasha, relax for a second," Arthur said. He led her to the edge of the bed and sat down beside her. "Whatever you've been through, I know it's been a lot. And I have to apologize to you for everything that happened. If I had guessed that there was even the slightest possibility of Tribespeople still in the field, I never would have let anyone out of this settlement."

"I know, it doesn't matter. I'm glad they took me."

"So they did take you?"

"Yes. And Arthur, you have to stop the sweeps. I talked to them. Actually *talked* to them. Just like we're talking now." But her team did not seem to understand, and so Natasha, forcing herself to be patient, started from the beginning. She told them how she had encountered the Tribe dog and how she had chased after it, running blindly into the woods. She openly took the blame for the capture, despite her shame in her own decisions. She told them about the Pines in the cave, even recalling the names she had heard: Axel, Raul, Hesma, Mattias. "The curly-haired man said that he was the chief. Like we thought. And then two men and a woman came and said you were sweeping. And there was another woman too, and she had two children. She was the one who told me how to escape." But they seemed to be missing her point;

and Natasha could not quite manage to capture the essence of her meaning in words. How could she explain the effect of seeing the Pines face-to-face? The way they had ceased to exist for her as desperate animals in want of relief? No matter that they had no settlement and no bioreplacement. No matter how futilely brief their lives were. "I talked to them," she said, though lamely, understanding that language was only part of it. "I talked to them just like we're talking now."

"We know they speak English," Arthur said.

"You do?"

"We heard a couple of them shouting to each other. Right before we found you." Arthur sighed, he seemed very worried. "You must have been surprised, on top of everything else. But it's not the first time we've engaged with a Tribe that retained the original English language. The vast majority of these people descended from the North American survivors of the Storm. The same group of people who once begot our Alphas. The survivors spoke English and they passed it on, generation to generation."

"You knew that the Pines spoke English this whole time?"

"No." Arthur shook his head. "There are hundreds of new dialects. A Tribe that has fully maintained a recognizable grammar and vocabulary is extremely rare. We didn't know until you did."

"But it was a possibility."

"That's not a secret, Natasha. Granted we don't generally emphasize it in our education programs, at least not until you've reached advanced standing in the Office of Mercy. We find that an awareness of language overlap makes it more difficult to maintain the Wall."

Natasha felt the implication of his words, but allowed his reproach to pass her by. The Wall; she could not worry about that now. She felt too confused.

"Do you know what happened to them?" she asked.

"Only the three that Nolan swept," answered Douglas.

"You did sweep?" Natasha cried.

"If you can call it that," Arthur said apologetically, misunderstanding her sudden excitement. "Only three. A woman and two juveniles."

"I told that woman to stay in the caves!" Natasha said. "I didn't want you to hurt her!"

"They won't suffer anymore."

"I didn't want you to kill them!"

Natasha knew how infantile she sounded, how unethical, but she didn't care. She thought of the man, Raul, who had kissed them goodbye; all she wanted was for it not to be true. Tears came to her eyes, and Douglas and Alejandra both looked away.

"Where's Jeffrey?" Natasha asked. "I want to talk to Jeffrey. He'll understand."

Was it her imagination, or did all three of them cringe at her words?

"He's busy in the Office right now," Arthur said. "I'm sure he'll stop by later."

"Those children had a father," Natasha said. "You broke up a family."

"I know how bad it was, Natasha. You don't have to tell me. The whole situation was very, very far from ideal. But at least, in the end, the pain of one human being is preferable to the pain of four. As bad as it was, it could have been worse."

"You're wrong," said Natasha. A heaving, wet breath racked her body.

"You've been through too much," Arthur said, reaching out to touch her hand. "None of us could have maintained the Wall during such close contact, especially without proper training. But give yourself time to confront your feelings, and I promise you, once the shock has worn off, your perspective will broaden and your ethical understanding will come back to you."

• • •

They did not release her for several more days, and in those days, Natasha found herself subjected to countless physical and psychological evaluations. The doctors finally told her the details of her injuries. She had suffered an eight-centimeter laceration across the back of her head. Apparently, the blow from behind, when the Pines attacked her, had unlocked her helmet and forced the metal ring upward. The fall gave her a slight concussion, hence the necessity of the neurotransmitter replacements. She had also come in with bruises and cuts all over her body, but those they had healed within the first days of her return. Her psychological state they could not describe in such certain terms. Ultimately, they pronounced her brain "Feignimic"—unable to fully process that she had escaped the possibility of further danger—and they gave her a small vial of orange pills that would serve to quiet her anxiety. They had it wrong, though. Or at least Natasha's anxiety had an additional source other than the one they had named. She could not believe, she could not understand, why Jeffrey had not come to see her.

As Natasha had feared, her arrival in the Dining Hall that afternoon caused a bit of a stir. Min-he came sprinting from the serving line and embraced her at the door.

"I've missed you!" she cried. "You have no idea how terrified I was."

"Everyone's looking at me," Natasha said quietly.

"Well, of course they are. It's not every day that one of us gets carried off by a herd of Tribespeople."

"It wasn't a *herd*."

"I know," said Min-he, immediately contrite. "We're just happy to have you back, okay?"

Natasha nodded and felt stupid for snapping at Min-he. Especially given how grateful she was that Min-he wasn't fussing over her or acting standoffish.

The two roommates heaped hot sandwiches and salad onto their plates and joined a table of Epsilons. Natasha told the group right away that she was not permitted to give details of the mission, though neither her words nor her persistent evasions dissuaded them from bombarding her with questions. In the breaks in conversation, Natasha had the chance to look around at the other tables. The Betas and Gammas appeared to be avoiding any notice of her, all except for Claudia, who scowled from over an untouched bowl of steaming mushroom soup. At the far corner of the Dining Hall, near the swinging doors to the kitchen, Raj leaned over his table, talking quickly to his group of Delta friends. As she looked at them, feeling that she must be the subject of their conversation, Raj glanced suddenly at her, catching her eye and making her face flush with heat. Several minutes passed before Natasha had the courage to give the Dining Hall another wide look. It was enough to confirm what she had guessed already—that Jeffrey was not here.

She arrived at the Office of Mercy eight minutes before the thirteenth hour, only to face a worse disappointment. At the back cubicle sat Eric and Yasmine, and Natasha would be the third for the day. As Natasha made her way to her computer, a sinking sensation in her middle made her feel both hollow and queasy at once, and the unease she had been suffering from since the mission morphed swiftly into dread. Jeffrey planned out the shifts for their Office team. He must have deliberately taken himself off the afternoonshift. Natasha could not hide from the truth any longer: Jeffrey did not want to see her.

Yasmine seemed pretty happy about getting bumped from the nightshift, and she greeted Natasha warmly. Eric politely acknowledged her return too, though not with his usual cheerfulness. Arthur had asked Yasmine to get Natasha up to speed on their progress with the Pines, and so Natasha drew her chair around to Yasmine's computer.

"They opened up the deadzone since the mission," Yasmine said. "We didn't see them do it. But we lost sensor RN49 and the next night they took out RN50."

"They might be moving underground," Natasha said.

"Yes, we considered that. It's also conceivable that they're using the river to hide, and staying within the most treacherous areas."

"Our sensors are positioned along the main travel routes—"

"That's right," Yasmine said. "They weren't built to catch human beings deliberately working to avoid us."

From around the corner of the cubicle, Eric put on his audioset and Natasha could hear the faint murmurs of music. Was it possible that Eric was mad at her too? Her actions had cut the mission short, after all, and—though she had not thought about it till now—likely the Alphas would not send Epsilons back into the field until well past their thirtieth birthday.

"So what's our assignment?" Natasha asked. "Are we watching the deadzone perimeter?"

"Ahh—no," Yasmine said, shifting her gaze. "We're on satellite duty. Weather patterns in the northeast quadrant."

The sinking feeling in Natasha's middle reached a new depth.

"It's because of me, isn't it?" she asked. "Arthur doesn't trust me to maintain the Wall."

"Not only you," Yasmine said. Her eyes flickered over to Eric, and for a moment Natasha dared to wonder if Eric's sour mood had nothing at all to do with her.

The afternoon passed with no sign of the Pines, not at the outer perimeter or at the edges of the deadzone. Wherever they were, whatever they were planning, at least they weren't doing it yet. When Natasha's shift ended, she ate a hurried dinner in the Dining Hall, sitting with a still-subdued Eric and some other Epsilons. Then, instead of spending her leisure hours above ground, she boarded the elephant. She did not return to her own floor, but touched the command for level three, which housed the sleeprooms occupied mostly by generations Gamma and Delta. When the elephant opened, she walked to the outermost of the three concentric hallways, tracing the curving wall until she found Jeffrey's door.

8

Her heart thudded as she knocked, and louder in the pause that followed. A yellow line of light glowed from under the door and a shadow crossed it; he could not pretend to be sleeping. Part of Natasha wanted to dash away while she still had the chance, but no, she had to at least try to figure out what was going on with him. Whatever Jeffrey had to say to her, it was better than the torture of his silence. Besides, she did not think she could stand it for one more day, this not-knowing. I'm sorry, Natasha thought, as she had thought in the Pines' cave. And now Natasha would tell him in person; she was clinging to the hazy idea that these simple words could set everything right.

She knocked again, only this time the door flew open. Jeffrey stood before her, his mouth firm, his shirt only partly fastened into his protepants. Red veins shot through his eyes and the pink burn climbing his neck seemed inflamed, bright and prickling over his flesh. In her surprise, Natasha took a step back.

"What are you doing here?" He had not spoken the words harshly, but the absence of his usual warmth brought a thickness to Natasha's throat. For a moment, she gaped at him, and then he seemed to realize her agony, because he added next, "It's wonderful to see you healed, Natasha. We were all so worried about you."

He looked away as he spoke, at the row of sleeproom doors behind her. *We were worried*, Natasha thought. He would not say *I was worried*, but only *we*. She forgot about the Pines; she forgot about the mission. She tried to cover up her distress, especially when the noise of two people approaching became audible from around the bend of the circular hall. Jeffrey started to speak, then seemed to change his mind. With a heavy sigh, and with a glance in the direction of the nearing voices, he stood aside, waving Natasha into the room.

Natasha had not seen the inside of Jeffrey's sleeproom before, or any of the sleeprooms on level three. Its dimensions were only slightly grander than what she and Min-he had, though without a second bed and second wallcomputer, the area felt much larger. The furniture was similar to what she was used to, only a little nicer. The bedframe and table were not made of metal, but of a deep brown, sturdy-looking wood. The lamp had a thick brass base and a glass shade, as opposed to ceramic and paper. The only item that was identical to the one in Natasha and Min-he's sleeproom was Jeffrey's copy of the Ethical Code, which lay open under the light.

Jeffrey sat down on a worn upholstered chair in the corner, which occupied the space where a second bed would have gone in a double. Natasha hesitated, unsure of what to do next, and only finally sat down at the very edge of Jeffrey's bed.

"I'm sorry to bother you like this," Natasha said, even though she wasn't sorry at all, only desperate to break Jeffrey's silence.

"I understand you're upset," he replied. "But that can only be expected. You experienced a terrible trauma. Maybe it was a mistake for you to come back to work so soon. To have Tribes on the monitors all around you. I imagine that might be rather frightening."

Natasha's face burned at his words; they were cold and formal and distant from his true thoughts, whatever those were. Was he really going to pretend that her only problem was the Pines? That he had not been cruelly ignoring her for days?

"It doesn't bother me to see the Tribes," she said, her voice sharp.

"Really?" His eyebrows peeked over the frame of his glasses, as if she were some mildly interesting puzzle, put forward for his observation.

"No," she insisted. "And if it did, it wouldn't be because I'm scared. I tried to explain it to Arthur when he came to see me in the medical wing. I told him how the Pines spoke English but that didn't surprise him. Only it wasn't just that. Their speaking English only made it easier to see."

"See what?"

"That they're *like* us. The Pines are *like* us. I never expected that, but it's true." She spoke in an angry rush. His questions felt unfair; he was doubting her without listening first. But if he wanted to discuss the Tribe then, fine, that's what they'd do. She wanted to shock him. "I was scared in the cave," she said, "I was. But now I don't believe that they ever wanted to hurt me. Because they had the chance and they didn't. They left me alone in the cave rather than kill me."

"You're projecting. You mean that if *you* had been in *their* situation, *you* would not have caused purposeless harm to another human being."

"I'm not projecting. I was there. I'm telling you what I saw."

"Okay, then how about abducting you and terrifying you beyond belief? Is that like us?"

"Oh, I don't know," Natasha faltered, her voice rising with irritation. "But at least you have to agree that the Pines aren't in the same situation that the Cranes were in. The Cranes were suffering. I can see how they needed our mercy. But these people—I saw it with my own eyes, Jeffrey. They're healthy and strong and they want to keep living."

"But they can't keep living," Jeffrey said. "Surely you see that. They don't have bioreplacement. Their bodies decay with no intervention. You've stopped thinking clearly, Natasha. Healthy and strong *now*, for a moment. But it won't last. The human body wasn't built to last—not until our technology changed that."

"Well, maybe the people outside aren't so obsessed with eternity. Maybe the moment's good enough for them."

"So what's your point?" Jeffrey asked, suddenly sounding fatigued.

"That we change things!" Natasha said. "That we stop what we're doing in the Office of Mercy."

There was a crack in his demeanor, a subtle twitch of his mouth. She could see that she was finally getting through to him. At the same time, the Wall had disappeared in her mind, letting forth a wave of other thoughts, new thoughts. Natasha didn't care. She didn't want the Wall. She'd rather remember everything that had happened to her, unfiltered by the Ethical Code.

Jeffrey rubbed the fabric of the chair with his thumbs. He grunted and then he stood and opened a door in the base of his bedside table, removing a green bottle and two waterglasses. He poured a clear, strong-smelling liquid from the bottle, only filling each cup a quarter full.

"That's alcohol," Natasha said, recognizing the sting of its aroma. "How did you get that?"

"The rules are somewhat more lenient for the older generations," Jeffrey said. "Try some if you'd like. You've never had this kind before."

He returned to his seat, taking slow sips. Natasha took the waterglass and brought it to her lips. The liquid burned in her throat but she drank it all. She returned the empty glass to the table with the tingling, grassy taste still in her mouth. Jeffrey's eyes remained fixed on her through all this, though he did not speak.

Natasha glared at him, wiped her mouth with deliberate force, and stood. There were three pictures hanging in a line near the door, and a polished piece of wood, a flute, resting on two large nails above them. On closer inspection, Natasha saw that the pictures were photographs of Outside things: one was of a valley of leaning trees, their branches weighted by ice; the second showed a human shelter of animal skin and sturdy sticks, propped against the base of a vertical cliff; and the third was of the river. Natasha reached up and touched the flute, understanding now that it was not some relic of a childhood pastime, but a genuine artifact from the Outside.

Jeffrey rose from his chair and walked over.

"I don't know why I still have those things," he said, a note of annoyance in his voice. "I've been meaning to move them to the Archives for years."

He was close to her, only inches away. The familiar smell of his body, the familiar, low tenor of his voice, the hard symmetry of his muscular shoulders and handsome features, all except—no, *including*—the furious burn—these sensations of his presence impressed themselves upon Natasha with a power that blocked out all the world but him.

He looked down at her and before she could consider the magnitude of what she was doing, Natasha raised one hand and cupped his neck over his scarred flesh, her fingers reaching to trace where the mark rose to a gathering point, the way fire would, just below his ear.

His steady expression gave her no permission, no response, but driven by the momentum of her own mounting passion, Natasha lifted her face to his and kissed him on the mouth. His lips yielded, though he did not make a move to touch her. Her arms wrapped over his shoulders, clasping at the back of his neck. She kissed him hard, determined beyond all else to break through the barricade he had made to keep her out; she kissed him so that he could not ignore her, so as to force his feelings to come raging to the surface.

Their mouths pressed together, and now Jeffrey did touch her, holding her waist, taking against himself the weight of her body. Natasha's hands traveled down to find the first fastening on his second-skin shirt. She removed one and then the other, down to the base, where she fumbled to release his prote-pants too.

He stopped her then—an abrupt and startling halt—releasing her body so that she stumbled. He turned away and quickly redid the fastenings, leaving her stunned and staring at the large square of his back.

When she finally spoke, her voice was hoarse.

"You didn't want that to happen?" she asked.

He was silent.

"Well?" she asked, more forcibly now.

"This is not appropriate, Natasha. You know as well as I do what the Alphas advise. A well thought-out, committed partnership is one thing. But for lustful feelings, there are other ways, the Pretends—"

He turned around, striving to appear tidy and put together, like nothing had happened.

"I don't care," she said loudly, as if to drown out her own embarrassment. "It's not like other people follow those ridiculous rules."

"Well, I do care. And as your teamleader, I cannot in good conscience engage in this type of action with you. My work means too much to me. I know the Office of Mercy means a great deal to you too. Besides," he said, with a small and infuriating smile, "we're not even of the same generation. You'd be better off with someone like Eric, or one of the other Epsilon men—"

"Oh, stop it, Jeffrey," Natasha said, cutting him off. "I'm really sick of how you've been treating me. You've been a real jerk and it's just getting worse."

He paused, considering this accusation. "You mean since the mission."

"Of course that's what I mean," Natasha answered, completely exasperated. "What else would I be talking about?"

He retrieved his waterglass from the bedside table, his expression thoughtful and cold. In the course of just minutes, he had managed to banish the whole, amazing moment of their kiss and return them right back to where they'd been before, when Natasha had first entered his sleeproom. He took a sip, regarding her from over the top of the glass.

"I'm extremely disappointed in you, Natasha. You're aware of that, right?"

Of all the terrible things she had imagined him saying, she had not prepared herself for this. The words hit her with material force.

"What do you mean?"

"Not, not this." He waved his hand at where they'd been standing. "I'm talking about the mission."

Natasha shook her head, unable to speak.

"I went to the Alphas," he continued. "I vouched for you. I put my own reputation on the line. I told them that I'd never seen a young member of the Office of Mercy with more promise. That you had more than lived up to your scores on the Office of Mercy entrance exam. So how do you thank me? First you refused to listen to me—everyone refused to listen to me—when I said that the mission had changed. Then in the field you go gallivanting off on your own despite my warnings. And then . . . then you fail to maintain the Wall at the most crucial moment. And not even in the face of a human being, but for a dog! Never consulting with me or Arthur, never stopping to think how suspicious it was, that a Tribe dog just happened to find you. You ran right into their trap!"

"Fine." Natasha blinked, fighting to hide her emotion. "Fine, I understand."

"I'm not done yet," Jeffrey said. "At the very least, you could try to make up for it now. Instead, you go spouting nonsense to Arthur, the head of your Office. You come running to me in my sleeproom during my leisure hours. . . . Did you know I have Claudia going behind my back, talking to the Alphas? If it were up to her, she'd get both of us transferred."

His tirade seemed to exhaust itself here, but it was too late, because Natasha felt she would collapse if he made her listen to more. Amazed that her legs could carry her, she got up and walked out of the room. Three people passed her in the corridor but she did not dare look up or return their singsong hellos. She jammed the button for the elephant until the slow, stupid thing arrived; and, by the power of will alone, she managed to keep the explosion of tears at bay until the doors had closed.

Her own sleeproom was mercifully empty. On her bed, someone had left a bag of freshly laundered clothes, the clothes that she had worn on the morning of the mission. Beside the lamp on the bedside table stood a waterglass with three daisies and, tucked beneath the glass, a note from Min-he: *Welcome home!* Natasha sniffed and inhaled a shuddering breath. That was kind. Min-he must have snatched the daisies from the Garden when no one was looking, as the private use of Department of Agriculture flowers was not allowed. Natasha pulled off her shoes and lay facedown on her bed, letting her own misery overwhelm her as Jeffrey's terrible words echoed through her body in painful waves. Was it possible? Natasha wondered. Had she really misunderstood him so completely? All her life, Jeffrey had distinguished her from the group, had made her his confidante, his apprentice, his favorite. It was simply impossible to believe his indifference. She could not believe it! And yet. The facts spoke for themselves: she had kissed him and he had stopped her. The memory of it was excruciating, and Natasha pressed her face down until the air was hot and she could hardly breathe. She felt humiliated and she sobbed, hating Jeffrey and hating the world.

Because then, on top of everything, there was the mission, his disappointment in her over the mission. (Or maybe the two were intertwined, Natasha thought—he decided he liked her less when he realized what an idiot she was.) It hadn't occurred to Natasha to regret what she had said to Arthur until Jeffrey had cast this new light on her actions. She realized only now how ridiculous it was to have thrown a fit over the Tribe's speaking English. She should have perceived that possibility herself, simply from knowing the basic history of the Storm, and knowing that once, the Alphas and the other human beings on this continent had shared a common language. She thought about chasing after the Tribe dog and her self-hatred plunged a notch lower. Of course she knew how stupid she'd been, of course everything Jeffrey had said about her mistake was true—but hadn't she suffered enough for it yet? She certainly didn't deserve to have people like Claudia gloating over her failures. Natasha pressed her cheek into the pillow, wishing for a thing that she had never wanted before: that she did not have to go to work tomorrow, that she could spend her Alpha-given eternity in bed.

The evening deepened and the lights began to dim automatically. Natasha felt too tired to get up and hit the override switch by the door, and she was about to change into her nightclothes when a noise from the hallway caught her by surprise. She lay there for some seconds, listening. Then it came again, someone tapping lightly at her door. Thinking it must be Jeffrey coming to apologize, Natasha jumped out of bed. She wiped her face with her sleeve and turned on the lamp, catching sight of her own reflection in the small oval mirror by her wallcomputer. She pinched her cheeks to redden them but it was a losing battle; she was a frightful mess. The tapping sounded again and she leapt across the room and opened the door. But she had guessed wrong: it was not Jeffrey, but Eric who stood in the hallway, hands in his pockets, looking weary and afraid. The hopeful glow in Natasha's chest snuffed itself out at once; she had never been so disappointed to see anyone in all her life. She remembered what Jeffrey had said about her being better suited for Eric and she almost slammed the door in Eric's face.

"Your roommate here?" Eric whispered, noticing nothing of Natasha's distress.

"She's working late, I think."

"Good, that's what I heard. Can I come in? I need to talk to you."

Natasha sighed heavily, but she stood aside and let Eric past her. Citizens rarely visited one another in their sleeprooms. To have two visits in one night—first Natasha to Jeffrey's and now Eric to hers—was unheard of. Natasha gestured to Min-he's bed and Eric sat down, still nervous.

"What's the matter?" Natasha asked. "Did something happen in the Office?"

"No. At least, not yet."

"Not yet?"

"Listen," he burst out, "I want to know what they said about me, what Arthur said. I heard he came to visit you in the medical wing."

"We didn't talk about you," Natasha said, completely bewildered.

"But they told you about the manual sweep?"

"They said Nolan did it. Eric, what's this about? I was almost asleep." Natasha was getting annoyed; she didn't feel like talking about the Pines right now.

But then, to Natasha's astonishment, Eric dropped his face into his hands and groaned.

"I messed up, Natasha. I totally froze out there."

"What? What are you talking about?"

"Twenty minutes after you left," Eric said, still refusing to look up, "they told us you were missing. Jeffrey took off. Alejandra was ten feet ahead of me when I heard something behind us. I knew it couldn't be Douglas or Nolan, because they were coming from the other direction. It was a Pine. A man."

"Who?" Natasha asked.

"I don't know *who*," Eric said. "But he spoke to me."

"In English."

"Arthur gave the order for a manual sweep," Eric continued, "but I just stood there. And then when I finally thought I could do it, the man dropped to his knees. He begged me to let him go. He swore he wouldn't come back here again. I couldn't do it. I couldn't sweep him. It didn't seem right. I know it was the ethical thing to do, but it didn't seem *right*. And then he ran away and everyone yelled at me."

"Maybe it wasn't right," Natasha said. Suddenly Eric's presence was not so unwelcome, perhaps someone in the settlement did understand her after all. She walked over and sat beside him on Min-he's bed. "The same thing happened to me when I tried to sweep one of their dogs. I hesitated and it got away and I followed it. That's how they got me. But the thing is, I don't feel sorry I let the dog live." Natasha wasn't totally sure how safe it was to confess the full truth of her feelings to Eric, but she pressed on. "I'm glad it lived, no matter what the Alphas say." She put a hand on Eric's shoulder. "Aren't you glad you let the man live?"

"He won't live long," he answered. "And I wasn't strong enough to give him a peaceful end. Stupid, embracive thinking. I let down my Wall."

"But it's more complicated than that," Natasha urged. "And I bet other people would agree with us too, if they'd seen the Pines like we had."

"There was something different about them, wasn't there?" Eric said. "They didn't act like the Cranes. Or the Larks or the Wolves," he added, naming two partial sweeps from when they were children. "I tried to explain that to Arthur, but he didn't get it."

"Jeffrey wouldn't listen to me either."

As Natasha spoke, trying to keep the hurt out of her voice, her gaze drifted to her wallcomputer, which was glowing with an announcement. She walked over to turn off the screen, her eyes scanning the Alpha bulletin regarding progress on the New Wing.

Eighteen members of the Office of Material Science and the Office of Agricultural Maintenance have been transferred to the Construction team. We hope that these new additions will hasten work on the exterior paneling, as well as free up our electrical engineers to work exclusively on the phase-three and postliquid incuvat environs. As for our eighty-three generation Zetas, they continue to develop in the Office of Reproduction. Their liquid-emergence date remains December 10th, and not even we, as Alphas, can request that they push it back.

Eternally Yours, Alphas/deptofgov

Natasha circled the sender address with her finger. She had an idea. It was risky; it would probably get them in trouble with Arthur. But given that he had already demoted their team to satellite watch, she figured they didn't have much to lose.

"Eric, do you think you could write down what you just told me, about the man begging for his life?"

"Why would I write it down?"

"Because I want to send a message to the Alphas. I want to tell them what happened to us in the field. Both of us."

Eric shot her a dubious look.

"Wait, think about it. Who knows what Arthur's telling them? What he's censoring from his reports? He's already made up his mind about the Pines. Why would he bother making a case for them to the Alphas?"

"And you'll message them?" he asked. "Message the Alphas? You realize what you're saying, right?"

"Yes, I do. We should explain what really happened and request a meeting with them. A meeting in the Department of Government. No Epsilon has ever contacted them directly before, as far as I know. At least they won't be able to ignore us."

To Natasha's surprise, Eric did not immediately dismiss the idea. In fact, he agreed to the plan with seemingly more conviction than what she herself felt. They spent the next hour writing their message, thinking over every aspect of the mission and refusing to leave out a single detail. They signed it *Natasha Wiley and Eric Johansson, Epsilons, Office of Mercy*, and on Eric's final okay, Natasha sent the message to America-Five's highest authority.

No response came, not the next day or the day after that. Probably Natasha would not have been able to hide the turmoil she felt over the message or, what was worse, the shaky agitation that gripped her at any mention of Jeffrey's name, except that everyone in America-Five was anxious these days, and so Natasha fit right in.

Ready or not, the Zetas were nearing their sixth month of gestation, and would soon grow too large for their current phase-two incuvats in the Office of Reproduction. The scientists wanted to transfer them soon, but construction continued to fall behind schedule in the New Wing. The parties in charge had considered transferring the Zetas *before* the construction had concluded, but no one liked the idea of laser drills and electron saws flashing and roaring around the developing babies. Anyway, it seemed a dark, inauspicious beginning if it did come to that. Conversations from last year were slowly cropping up again: doubts about the prudence of creating a new generation when the underground levels were already filled to capacity, and when they were forced to build a whole new wing just to make room for the phase-three incuvats. (To say nothing yet of the dormitories and schoolrooms that the Zetas would eventually require.) The Alphas had waited more than two hundred years after the Storm before creating the Betas; and, in turn, the Alphas and Betas had waited another sixty years after that before considering themselves fit to receive a generation of Gammas. Because of course, as the Ethical Code directed, no new life should ever be brought into existence without the settlement's first proving to itself that it had triple the energy, space, and resources to sustain the new additions. With this truth in mind, a few citizens were going so far as to wonder if the Alphas would choose to destroy the Zetas. But according to Cameron Pacheco, who was heading the project, however unhappy the old ones were, the Alphas did not view the situation as dire as that.

Meanwhile, in the Office of Mercy, the Pines continued to elude detection, and the stress was wearing away at them all. Arthur lapsed into periodic fits of faultfinding, accusing one team or another of missing a flicker of human migration over the deadzone perimeter. But he was always wrong. Nothing tripped the sensors but birds, rabbits, deer, and the occasional fluffy-tailed squirrel. The Alphas called at regular intervals now, and Natasha had learned to recognize the drawn, despondent expression that came over Arthur's face when he spoke directly to the Mother or Father. The whole settlement felt their failure, and shared in their fear. Even Min-he began asking Natasha for updates, though she hadn't shown much interest in the Office of Mercy before, and had once even dismissively dubbed the sweeps "janitorial work," cleanup from the Storm.

For most citizens, the only thing that made these setbacks bearable was the promise of the Crane Celebration, scheduled for the first week of September. The settlement held a celebration for any large sweep; and they were among the most extravagant and unique days in America-Five. According to a short section in the Ethical Code, such celebrations served to remind the citizens of their higher purpose on Earth: namely, not only to create peaceful, happy, and long lives within the settlement (as described the work of most citizens), but also to supplement this *positive* work with the work of *negating* what life was not peaceful and happy and long. The Epsilons especially were looking forward to the holiday, since they had only attended a handful of celebrations before, and most as children. Also at the Crane Celebration, the citizen whose labor had most directly contributed to the success of the sweep received a medal of service. In the case of the Crane sweep—as was announced on the maincomputer, and to no one's surprise—that citizen was Jeffrey.

As for Natasha, she wanted absolutely nothing to do with the preparations for the Crane Celebration. Work was bad enough, with Eric a nervous wreck and Yasmine a total dolt—always going on about how proud they should be about Jeffrey's medal—and Claudia Kim sneering at Natasha whenever she had the chance. So far, the only real mercy (as far as Natasha's life was concerned) was that Jeffrey seemed to be consciously staying away from the dayshifts, and steering clear of the shift changes too.

Natasha had no desire to put an accidental end to this deliberate estrangement, and no desire, either, to put herself in the company of those citizens who still liked to ask her questions about the ill-fated mission. So in order to avoid the volunteer committees that gathered in the evenings—the Menu Committee, the Garden Committee, the Agriculture Beautification Committee, and the Committee for Music and Entertainment—Natasha took to returning to her sleeproom directly after dinner. These long evening hours would have been unbearable, she could not have endured them, except that lately Min-he had been borrowing stacks of Pre-Storm books to look over during her leisure hours. While the Ethical Code sat cold and foreboding in the table drawer, no longer holding for Natasha the promise of comfort, she would instead leaf through these strange manuscripts, printed on delicate, musty-smelling paper: stories of people living in cities and wars between nations and other strange subjects like slavery and marriage and ocean voyages. She could barely comprehend the concepts, or the finer details of the texts. But the stories sparked Natasha's interest and allowed her, at times, to forget herself and her own situation, and made her wonder, too, at the variety of experiences possible within far-flung, individual lives of the same human species.

One night, though, while poring over the fantastic tale of a man who fights off a fire-breathing dragon to save his home village (a place of thatched-roof houses, no less), Natasha began feeling restless. Eventually, she closed the book and returned it to the top of Min-he's stack.

She threw on a fuzzy second-skin top and, for the first time since before the mission, she headed to the Pretends.

The gray-blue walls of the Pod curved around her, nestling her in its cocoon. On the virtual menu hovering before her eyes, the computer presented three options: Experience, Game, Free Play. On a whim, Natasha chose Free Play. The neurotranslation technology specific to Free Play still had a few glitches, being so new. Last time, when Natasha had tried to evoke the scene of a Pre-Storm, black-tie dance, it had thrown her into an aviary with ostriches and cockatoos and Natasha had ended the simulation only just in time to avoid being pecked and squawked at to oblivion. But Natasha did not really care what the computer did. All she wanted was something new, some escape from her messed-up life. She wouldn't mind if it sent her skateboarding with baby antelope or whatever else. The Pod faded from blue to black; her eyes closed and then, a second later, the world lighted to reveal the Dome on a usual morning at 0800 hours.

She wore her regular office clothes: a cream-colored, second-skin shirt fastened into a pair of brown prote-pants. Her hair draped over her shoulders and carried with it the faint smell of shampoo, as if she had just showered that morning. Weaving through the crowd of morningshift workers, she made her way to the doors of the Department of the Exterior and down the white hall to the Office of Mercy. In every way, the day suggested business as usual: the regular crew sat hunched over their keyboards, the coffee machine gurgled on the side table beneath the wallphone, and Natasha's own station appeared orderly and waiting, her audioset neat in its holder and her desk chair tucked in the way she always left it. And yet. Despite all this, the air felt charged, ready to snap with a bolt of energy. She slipped into her seat and logged in, and a moment later, Jeffrey arrived, his eyes on her as he dropped a stack of binders on his desk.

"You look very pretty today," Jeffrey said.

A tickle of heat came over her flesh. "Thank you."

His attention stayed on her and she typed commands slowly, drawing up the coordinates for the Crane Tribe. Her fingers felt thick; it took her two tries to get the coordinates right. Jeffrey walked over to stand behind her, his hand on the back of her chair.

"Are you bringing up the W13 shoreline?"

"Yes, here it is."

"Oh, good, we've had a few disturbances in that area. Why don't you put together a seven-day data chart and we'll look at it together."

But Natasha was only half listening. While he was speaking, Jeffrey's hand had eased its way from the chair to her shoulder, and then slipped lower, below her arm and to her side. He held her across the narrow curve of her ribs. She stiffened, but the hand did not move.

"Shh," he whispered. "No one can see. Draw up the visuals."

Natasha typed the commands, feeling the warmth of his palm through the second-skin of her shirt. Her body tingled under his touch; he wanted her, Jeffrey wanted her. His hand slipped lower and she could feel his need in the sliding, gripping movement of his fingers. The computer screen flashed and her eyes drifted to where the count glowed in the upper-right portion of the screen: 138, the Crane count. What did that number mean? Were the Cranes alive or swept? Jeffrey's hand moved down to cradle her thigh but she couldn't concentrate because she couldn't remember. The number was reminding her of something, something bad. . . .

She tried to hold on but she couldn't. The Office was fading before her eyes and with it the pressure of Jeffrey's hand on her body, the smell of coffee, the clicking of keys. . . .

The world shifted.

Bright and bland to dark with an upward bleeding of color—red.

Red lights skimmed across the marble floor, the emergency lights. Natasha was alone, stepping quickly across the blacked-out Dome, under the watch of a streak of stars. Her clothes had changed. Now she wore a blue silk-skin dress that gathered in tight, horizontal folds over her chest and then fell gracefully down to her ankles. The heels of her shoes clicked determinedly while at the same time she realized her destination: the south-facing doors of the Department of Agriculture, the wing where the Crane Celebration would take place, the wing that she had avoided for weeks.

The doors parted for her, she did not need to touch the reader, and then before her lay the vast Garden, the broad strip of lush grass bordered on each side by giant maple, oak, poplar, and cherry trees. Around the base of the trunks bloomed flowers of every shape and color, though Natasha could barely make them out in the dimness. Here the entire settlement would gather for the Crane Celebration, here they would acknowledge their own success and their own benevolent power, and renew their sense of shared purpose.

Instead of continuing farther down the lawn, Natasha turned through a large archway to her right. Again she had access, only this time it was because someone had left the doors open. The ragged silhouette of this year's wheat crop stretched expansively, black and still in the blue nightlights that replaced the bright, high-energy spectrum of the day. The ceiling hung low overhead, and a spiral staircase in the corner passed through spherical cuts in the ceiling and floor, each of which led to near-identical fields above and below. It was one of America-Five's early feats in agricultural engineering: to stack the crops one on top of the other like reams of paper. Natasha breathed in the cool, sweet air; she ran her hand over the tips of the rough stalks. Then she took off her shoes and started down one of the footpaths, the dirt cool and pleasant and squishy under her feet. She had walked deep into the crop when a rustle of movement came from behind her and before she could turn around, Jeffrey was there, speaking hot words against her neck.

"You couldn't stay away, could you?"

His arms clasped around her middle, and he held her while kissing her neck up to her ear.

"Jeffrey," she said.

A shiver ran through her and she turned, her front now pressed against his and her arms thrown over his shoulders. She could not see his face in the blue shadow, but his mouth found its way to hers and he kissed her deeply. His hands crept to her waist, running smoothly over the thin, slippery skin of her dress. He grabbed the skirt, bunching it in his fists, and yanked the whole dress up and over her head so that now Natasha stood naked before him. With sudden force he lifted her into his arms, and then they were moving deeper into the high wheat, his mouth never breaking from hers.

"Wait," said Natasha. She pushed against him. There was something wrong with the way he was holding her. She did not like how it felt. His grip was too tight. "Wait, put me down."

The room flickered, and the blue deepened to the true dark of a night sky. She was losing her hold on the dream; she was remembering. Then, before she could stop it, the Tribespeople broke through.

Natasha stood among the trees, before a raging fire. The ground pressed coldly under her feet, not the soil of crops but a drier, older, rougher ground; stiff rags and strings of beads draped over her body. She was singing—a song she both knew and did not know—she was singing with the Tribespeople who stood in a ring around the flames, all half-naked and jumbled together and dancing. Natasha felt exhilarated, triumphant. Atop her mess of hair she wore a crown of ivy leaves and red berries; she could smell the rich earth emanating from her own flesh. A man with a wrinkled, leathery face and blackened teeth threw a stream of water from a clay pot onto the fire; a pillar of thick smoke poured toward the sky with a hiss. He looked at Natasha, they all did. They were honoring her, welcoming her.

"Is that her?"

Yes.

"Is that her?"

Yes.

"Is that her?"

They were closing in around her, the circle constricting.

"Is that her?"

Yes, yes, she's come at last—

"Stop!"

Natasha ripped off her helmet without properly ending the simulation. A sharp pain erupted in the front region of her brain and her vision went black. She writhed, not knowing where she was until the harness caught her halfway to the floor; the straps held her there, her body limp and suspended and trembling. She breathed jaggedly, clutching her head while the pain began to subside and her mind began to recover its orientation, her cheeks matted with sweat and tears.

9

On the morning of the Crane Celebration, the citizens of
America-Five stepped out of the elephant to behold a crystal clear blue sky. The clouds and drizzle of the last several
days had suddenly departed, and this abrupt change in the weather
only further boosted their spirits. The floor of the Dome was also
transformed: around the outer wall, little makeshift stands stood piled
with new second-skin clothing, each stand attended by a very proud-
looking member of the Office of Biotextiles. Over the course of the
day, the citizens were invited to pick out five new items to wear for that
night. The new clothing and accessories—all in the earthy colors of
yellow, blue, green, and brown—represented (according to tradition,
and as the older generations were constantly reminding the Epsilons)
the human power the citizens wielded over the unethical forces of the
world: their ability to excise, with the snip of a sweep, the evil that
nature's laws commanded.

For the first time since the failed mission, people stopped to chat
with their friends as they crossed the floor to their respective Departments; they gathered in clumps around the tables of second-skin
dresses and shirts and other new things. Their smiles were small, but
hopeful; their laughter strained, but genuine. No one spoke now of
the bitter ideas that had begun to circulate after a few posts to the

intergenerational boards—about the inappropriateness of any celebration given the disastrous situation with the Pines. Such denounce-
ments felt overly self-punitive in the gentle light of day, and overly
brutal amid thoughts of newly potted flowers and tables dressed with
colored cloths and candles. Anyway, the Mother herself had conde-
scended to publicly address these concerns. In the early morning, she
had posted a long and eloquent letter, addressed to all the generations
below her, reminding them that the suffering of one group should
never negate the happy salvation of another, just as the reverse would
always be true.

Of course, as was inevitable in any free human society, there was
one group that did not agree: near the Department of the Exterior
doors stood a huddle of silent protesters, Raj Radhakrishnan and his
team of eccentrics.

Their solemnly held signs said enough about their lunacy: SWEEPS
END NOW and THE GREAT EXPANSION IS FOR ALL and, most inane of any
of them, SAVE THE TRIBES.

Save the Tribes! Isn't that what they were trying to do?

If anything, the protesters' presence, by a simple logic of opposites,
only furthered the other citizens' conviction that a Crane Celebration
was right and in order.

When Jeffrey entered the Office of Mercy that morning, many
people briefly abandoned their cubicles to push forward and shake his
hand. For them, the Crane Celebration was a reminder of how much
their work mattered both within the settlement and to humanity as a
whole. To end suffering. To bring peace to the world. No one said the
job would be easy, but at least it was work they could believe in. And
someday soon, once they did manage to sweep the Pines, they would
be able to look back at these hours of labor and know that they were all
in service of a great and necessary end.

At 2030 hours, the hallways began to crowd with people waiting to
ride up to the Dome. Natasha and Min-he stood in the middle of the

line on level six. Natasha wore a green, textured dress that shimmered with a silvery glow, like high grass tossing about in the wind; and Min-he had picked out a short-skirted outfit with a yellow and brown leopard print design. (Only Min-he, who had a small, compact physique, could have made it look good.) A long, lifelike snake wrapped around Min-he's neck, and its red mouth snapped open and hissed any time a person patted its head—which Min-he convinced many of their unsuspecting hallmates to do. By the time the roommates crossed through the open doors to the Department of Agriculture, the Garden was already swarming with people gasping and admiring its beautiful transformation.

"Oh, Natasha," Min-he squealed. "Have you ever seen anything like it?"

Natasha shook her head, staring around in wonder.

The Garden looked stunning: crepe paper streamers of blue and yellow draped between opposite rows of trees; flowers so bright with color that they seemed ready to burst reached from their beds; and all the trees were trimmed and pruned to perfection. At the back of the room, several rows of white chairs faced a high platform, built for the occasion. On the far wall, behind the platform, towers of colored blooms made a picture of a yellow sun with bright, reaching beams.

Most amazing of all, though, the thing that captured Natasha's attention and would not let go was the two rows of thin, tall torches lining the edge of the Garden's lawn: each erupting at its tip with identical, dancing flames.

As they passed between the first set of torches, Min-he gripped Natasha's arm in fear and excitement. The smell of the burning oil mixed with the strong perfume of the flowers, and the heat of the nearer torch touched the side of Natasha's face, making her shudder and steer Min-he to the center of the lawn. Fire was a great rarity in the settlement, not only because of its inherent danger, but also because of its wasteful consumption of purified breathing air. Natasha had only seen the torches once before, at the party commemorating the three hundredth anniversary of the Storm. She was sure they had not had fire at the Wolf Celebration, the year her generation turned eight, perhaps because that sweep was so small.

The roommates walked together toward the neat rows of white chairs; here, though, Min-he broke off to join a group of other archivists, while Natasha continued to the front, where the members of the Office of Mercy had gathered. She took a seat in the second row, next to Eric. Jeffrey sat on the opposite side of the aisle, directly facing the platform and talking with some Betas. He looked both nervous and resigned, as if being publicly honored by the Alphas was some slightly unpleasant task that he had to go through now and then. Natasha stared. A female Beta was saying something to Jeffrey and he laughed. Natasha quickly looked away, the air catching in her throat. Her hurt was still raw and it made her shaky with jealousy to see him interacting so casually with other people.

Once they had all found their places, a hush fell over the crowd. The first notes of a familiar melody sounded from four Beta violinists, who stood in the shadow of trees. Then the citizens rose as a line of hooded men and women entered through the Department doors, some as upright and sturdy as the Epsilons, others walking on wobbly legs and hanging their weight on Beta escorts. The Alphas. In all, there were forty-one people in the Alpha generation. Not every Alpha had come, though. It looked like only ten or twelve at most. That was expected; most Alphas preferred not to leave the Department of Government. As two men stepped gingerly by, Natasha wondered who among them had read the message that she and Eric had sent. What had they thought? If any of them noticed her and Eric standing together near the aisle, they gave no distinct sign of recognition. Natasha could just make out the ashen skin and deep wrinkles beneath their hoods. Their features were sharp, and their cheeks heavy and sunken. The last two people to pass were a woman and a man: the Mother and

Father. The positions were not permanent ones; the Alphas elected their leaders every fourth decade. But for Natasha, as for all the Epsilons, the Mother and Father had been the same two Alphas all her life.

The Alphas arranged themselves in a section of roped-off seats to one side, except for the Mother, whom a Beta man escorted to the podium at the center of the platform. She was the only Alpha who did not wear a hood, and Natasha guessed that the expressive features of her broad, pale face were visible even to those citizens seated in the very last row. The Epsilons had only laid eyes on her eight times before—at Celebrations and on a few special days when she had visited them at school—but Natasha knew her face well. The Mother's real name was Elsie Miller, but as long as she held the highest leadership position in the settlement, everyone called her Mother.

"What pleasure it brings me," the Mother began, her gaze falling lovingly over the crowd, "to see our children gathered here before us in good health and happy spirits. These have been difficult times for us all, and it is very fortunate that we should have this opportunity to recognize the good in our continued state of peace and vitality, the peace and vitality of our fellow citizens all over the world and—what brings us here tonight—to recognize and celebrate the peacefulness in death of the one hundred and thirty-eight members of the Crane Tribe."

Here the Mother's voice expanded with the fullness of her compassion and, among the citizens, there was a collective rise of emotion.

"This work is the same work that we began three hundred and five years ago, when the Alphas from every settlement in the world launched the simultaneous sweeps that eliminated from existence fifty-nine billion suffering souls. When, by the power of our own intelligence and will, we prevented what would have been the end of worthwhile human life on earth. This is the work that continued when we realized, with deep regret and agitation, that the Storm, despite its grandness and its power, had failed a scattered population in the northern regions. Failed them by letting them live. Since those first

reports, and the sweeps that swiftly followed, we have brought an additional 8,300,019 lives to permanent relief on this continent alone. It is
a number that includes this most recent annihilation, which we have
gathered to honor tonight."

She cast a warm look upon those from the Office of Mercy.

"In the second week of June, a Tribe we had never observed before
entered from the north into our field. We called this Tribe the Cranes
after the sandhill cranes that once populated this area, and for the
Tribe's practice of building camps by the water. Our hard workers in
the Office of Mercy watched them for many weeks, waiting until the
group assembled in one place, until they could confirm the count. . . ."

As the Mother talked on, a feeling of pride now swelled from the
citizens, a recognition of their own goodness growing within them all.
Only Natasha did not feel this. And as the Mother expounded upon
the particulars leading up to the Crane sweep, which every Office of
Mercy worker knew already, Natasha's eyes fixed on the orange flame
of the torch closest to her. Fire like the fire that the Pines had: hot,
dangerous, unbridled energy, and beautiful too, the most beautiful
thing in the Garden by far. Did the others feel that way too? Did the
Alphas know the beauty in danger, even while they stamped it out of
existence? They must.

Looking at the flame, feeling its heat on her eyes, made Natasha
remember the children she had seen down in the cave, how the mother
had clutched the boy's arm so hard he'd cried out. Mother and mother,
she thought, Father and father; the same words but not the same meaning. She remembered the man named Raul. How had he learned of his
family's death? Did he see their bodies? Had he put the woman and
boy and girl in the ground as people did in the Pre-Storm books? But
bodies meant nothing, Natasha knew, once the force that kept the parts
connected had gone. Those people no longer existed; those disklike
eyes of the boy and girl had gone to nothing, and the world was emp-
tier than it had been before. Natasha took in a sharp gasp of breath, but

the Mother had just said something amusing and, in the ripple of laughter that followed, no one noticed Natasha's distress. To end suffering, Natasha's education reminded, but that reminder was weak and pleading, and it paled against the fire and the will to live.

Natasha missed hearing the moment when the Mother called Jeffrey's name. Only the startling burst of applause (not to mention Eric's whistle right near her ear) forced her attention back to the Ceremony.

". . . for one hundred and thirty-eight lives delivered to peace," the Mother was saying.

Jeffrey stood on the platform, his face bright pink with embarrassment. He bowed as the Mother lifted over his head the red ribbon that supported his gleaming gold medal of service.

The entire crowd rose to give Jeffrey a standing ovation; the noise grew deafening and chaotic, and Natasha felt like she was going to be sick. From the podium, Jeffrey's eyes met hers and a shadow of unease crossed his face. Only then did Natasha realize that, though she'd managed to stand, she was neither smiling nor applauding for her beloved Jeffrey like everyone else. The heat of the crowd became unbearable; she had to get out of here right away.

The Mother had hardly left the podium before Natasha was pushing to move past Eric.

"What are you doing?" he hissed, purposefully blocking the way with his elbow while he continued to clap.

"I'm tired. I want to go to my sleeproom."

"But we still have dinner and the party after!" he said, shocked by the mere idea of leaving. "Hey, this isn't about the message, is it?"

"What message?"

"The Alphas. You didn't check?"

"No, what? I was getting ready with Min-he. They wrote back? What did they say?"

"What we expected. They're definitely not going to meet with us.

Actually, they're kind of put out. Told us, in the future, to report our problems to Arthur."

At that moment, both Natasha and Eric realized that the Mother herself had paused in the aisle right near them, and they turned to face her, stunned.

"I hope you enjoyed the ceremony, children," she said.

Natasha waited for Eric to answer, but in vain. "Yes," Natasha whispered, at last.

"Good," said the Mother. "Then perhaps we can put that other nonsense behind us."

She continued on, the applause still loud around them, while Natasha's face grew hot.

"Well," Eric said, slowly coming back to life. "I guess we know where they stand."

Without responding, Natasha ducked past Eric's arm and into the aisle. By now, the rows at the back had begun to empty, and only after some effort did Natasha escape to the open lawn. Volunteer teams were rolling out buffet spreads from the Dome and assembling the tables for dinner. Natasha rushed by them and hit the control for the first door past the trees.

The metal door rose and then sank down with a whoosh behind her. A loud sob broke from Natasha's lips. She collapsed against a wooden fence built to keep the livestock away from the exit: forty dairy cows grazing in an open pasture.

She did not know how long she stayed there. She had draped herself over the wooden beam, in a position to vomit, though the sickness never came. The cows observed her with their large, stupid eyes, their jaws patiently churning the warm-smelling grass and their chins dripping with greenish saliva.

There were no skylights in this room, only the vast brightness of long, low-energy bulbs. The cows must have only recently entered this pasture, as the grass stood high and lush. Along the two side walls, narrow troughs ran with fresh, clear water. At the far end of the pasture, beyond another wooden fence, Natasha could see the door to the stalls where the cows went for milking. She could also hear the distant squawking of chickens from that direction, though she could not see the coop. When the sound of new music came muffled from the Garden, Natasha's tears fell harder, blurring her sight. Her misery had forced her to feel so alone that, despite her proximity to the celebration, when the door rose behind her, she whirled around in surprise.

"What's going on?" Jeffrey asked, walking into the room. The door fell closed. "Natasha?"

The glow of merriment still showed in his cheeks, despite his obvious concern. Natasha turned back to the cows, furious that he had found her here.

"Hey, are you all right?" he asked. "I've been looking everywhere for you."

Natasha sniffed and tried to wipe her face dry.

"I realized that I don't like Celebrations very much," she said. "You should get back, though. They'll notice you're gone."

But, amazingly, he did not go away. He was already walking over to her; and then (though Natasha could hardly believe it) he was pushing the damp strands of hair out of her face. He looked so confused, so worried. The mask of anger he had worn since the mission, and since she had kissed him, had disappeared from his face. The sincerity of his concern disarmed her. Suddenly it was impossible to pretend, impossible to hide her anguish.

"I don't know what's wrong with me," she said. "Ever since the mission, since the Pines . . . it's like I never came home. I'm sorry for what happened in your sleeproom, but you have to understand, I'm all messed up. I don't know if I'll ever go back to just living *normally* again."

"No, Natasha. Don't say that."

His hands stroked firmly through her hair.

"It's my fault," he said. "I'm sorry I was hard on you. So sorry. I don't know what I was thinking."

"You shouldn't be sorry, though. You're angry that I screwed up the mission."

"No."

"You are! You told me! I was in the medical wing for a week and you didn't even come to see me."

"I was upset, deeply upset, that the mission failed. And it terrified me, having things get so out of control like that. Having you disappear. I've never been so scared in my life. But I didn't mean to put the blame on you."

Natasha shrugged. What would it matter to the dead who took the blame for the manual sweep? And who cared what Jeffrey said to her now? His words could not temper her pain. She had thought he felt one way when in fact he felt something different. No words could take away that sting.

"Forgive me, please," Jeffrey said. "This is my responsibility. I'm angry with myself."

"I was the one who kissed you," Natasha reminded.

She blushed and looked at the cows; for the first time in her life, she was beginning to understand why the Alphas recommended that all sexual play take place in the Pretends. It wasn't worth the pain, the disruption to the peacefulness of one's work and well-being, just to satisfy the body in situations where close friendship would suffice. And yet. As Jeffrey looked at her, her heart beat harder and, in the rush, she forgot it all again; she would not trade her feelings for anything.

"I did visit you in the medical wing," he said, bending to rest his arms on the fence, so that his face was level with hers. "I came after my shifts, in the evenings. You were sleeping, but I was there. I thought you knew. I thought one of the nurses would have told you."

"Stop," she said, briefly closing her eyes. "We don't have to talk about it. It doesn't help anything."

"Then tell me," his voice was strangely desperate, "tell me what will help."

In response to his movement, she leaned into him, allowing her cheek to press against his shirt. She breathed his smell, feeling how it mingled with the smell of the cows and the sweet grass and the warm stench of manure. Thoughts of her Free Play in the Pretends came creeping into her mind, but she pushed them back, embarrassed. She was just glad to have Jeffrey. He squeezed her close, crushing her chest against something cold and hard. She drew away; she hadn't noticed the gold medal.

She let go of him and turned back to the pasture, her weight resting against the fence. The bad feelings that Jeffrey's appearance had pushed away were drifting slowly back.

"Eric and I wrote to the Alphas," she said. "We requested a meeting."

"I know."

"You do?"

"Yes, they told Arthur and me. It's best that we have a complete understanding of what's going on in the Office."

"Did they tell you they denied our request?"

"No. But I figured they would."

Natasha bent down and grabbed a handful of untouched grass growing near the fence post. She held it out to the nearest cow who, after contemplating the offer for some long moments, lumbered one step forward. And yet, still as Natasha remained, the beast would not eat from her hand. It huffed hot breath through its nostrils; and, eventually, Natasha dropped the grass to the ground.

"Can I ask you something?" Natasha said.

"You can ask me anything."

He leaned against the rail beside her.

"Instead of growing new babies for the next generation, why don't we take in Tribal children?"

"What made you think of that?" He was trying to sound casual, but his whole body had stiffened.

"It's just . . . seeing them up close. That boy and girl. It seems like the most ethical thing would be to make use of the life that's already here."

"And what about those eighty-three Zetas in the Office of Reproduction?"

"I know it's too late *now*. I was thinking for next time."

"The Wall, Natasha," he said with quiet urgency.

She nodded vaguely.

"You're letting your fear get to you," he said, speaking the way a teacher or a teamleader would. "It's impeding your abilities. It's giving you tunnel vision, as fear often will. Right now, you are making conclusions based on the particulars of one, isolated situation—in this case, a very brief interaction with a forest-dwelling Tribe—instead of seeing from a universal perspective. Plus, you're doing something very dangerous. You are trying to bend ethical thinking into a form that will help you cope with the horror you perceived in the field. I want you to build a Wall right now."

He was no longer leaning on the rail; he had turned to face her, waiting. Natasha closed her eyes, but she was not concentrating on the Wall, not really.

"How do you think *they* do it?" she said at length, opening her eyes.

"Who?"

"The Pines, the Tribes. How can they see from a universal perspective? Do you think they build Walls in their minds?"

"I wouldn't consider it likely," Jeffrey said, an expression of grim amusement touching his face. "It's not necessary for them to perceive the world in that way because they're not making decisions for vast numbers of people like we are. They worry about themselves, their children, occasionally their immediate relations and allies. For a Tribesperson, tunnel vision, or a nonuniversal perspective, actually helps them survive."

"What about fear, then? If they don't have Walls, they must live in a constant state of fear."

"Yes and no," Jeffrey answered. "Certainly fear is a driving force in their lives, but they've found ways of pushing it into the background, covering it over with other ideas. Ultimately, they don't experience fear in the same way we do because they don't have the same *object* of fear. Or if they did once, it's been morphed beyond recognition."

"What object?"

"The same as always," Jeffrey said darkly. "Suffering. Death. In the settlement, we never mess around with the truth of those terrifying realities. We let them stand—cold and vast and undeniable. That recognition, that acknowledgment, is an extremely difficult thing. You don't always realize, because you grew up with this system of thinking. But no human society before the Alphas ever structured itself in stark opposition to these absolutes the way we have. Dared to look them in the eye. It's what defines us. It's what makes this the modern age. And it has—this recognition—it's what allowed us to make such leaps in medical technology and ethics. The sweeps were a revolutionary idea when they came about. So was bioreplacement, the unapologetic pursuit of eternal life. Only by feeling the full force of suffering and death were we able to usher in this world of peace and life. It's astounding," he said in a faraway voice. He seemed to be losing himself in his own meditations. "Truly remarkable what the Alphas did."

"But we need the Wall," Natasha prompted.

"The Wall tames us, for starters," Jeffrey said, returning from his thoughts. "It blocks out the irrational instincts that nature built into the structure of our brains. Modes of thinking that, after two hundred million years of evolution, are too enmeshed in our genes to cut out. That's the usage you learned first, what we teach in school. It's what happened to you after this mission, if you don't mind my saying. You are perfectly safe in this settlement, and yet some prerational part of your brain is holding on to the sense of danger you felt in the field. In ancient times, this behavior would have been advantageous. It might have kept you from putting yourself in danger again, in the future. You can see, though, how in your situation it's merely an inconvenience."

Natasha nodded.

"The Wall has an even greater importance in the field of ethics," Jeffrey continued. "It keeps us from projecting ourselves onto others, as in cases of Misplaced Empathy. Other times it helps us in situations in which the most ethical decision does not match our natural inclination. Like when the tattooed man was killed by the bear. We were forced to allow suffering in the moment in order to prevent greater suffering in the future. Our minds tend to rebel against those sorts of decisions. Or at least they do without learned intervention. We're evolved to react to immediate harm rather than the harm in some hypothetical, even an extremely *likely* hypothetical, future."

"And sometimes the Wall shuts down all thought," added Natasha.

"Our recognition of horror can be overpowering," Jeffrey agreed. "So much so that it dissolves our capacity for a universal perspective. A single man or woman cannot save ten others from drowning. The drowning ones would pull that person down."

"And the Tribes?" Natasha asked, after a pause. "How do they manage?"

"For them, the horror of existence is inevitable. Like I said, they're not able to fight it and so they deal with it in other, nonproductive or indirect ways. They think of their existence as extending through the lives of their children, their children's children. They have religion, legends. Ways of thinking that glorify suffering, or at least transform it from pure horror into something that has the sheen of godliness, or purpose. In many of their stories, suffering and death are the very gates that lead to eternal peace."

"I feel sorry for them."

"You should. We all do, that's why we're trying to help them." He looked at her, searchingly. "If I tell you something, Natasha, will you keep it to yourself? Not mention anything to Eric or Yasmine, or even your roommate?"

"Sure, of course."

"Well, we're going to step things up with the Pines. The Alphas have planned another mission. Only Gammas on this one," he added quickly, "Arthur, Claudia, Douglas, and myself. We didn't announce it on the maincomputer because the Alphas don't want to cause unnecessary worry. But we're going to attempt a manual sweep of the Pines who are still within the perimeter. Soon you won't have to worry about their pain."

"Another mission?"

Forty large heads rose up from the grass, startled and staring with big, round eyes.

"I thought you'd be relieved," Jeffrey said.

"When are you doing this?"

"Tomorrow, in the morning. We'll be back before lunch."

"You can't!"

"Of course we can. We have to." He was getting flustered. "Look— I thought you were coming around. I was trying to put your mind at ease. If I'd any idea you'd react like this, I wouldn't have told you."

"You can't sweep them, Jeffrey! We should wait. We need to learn more about them at least, that's what I've been trying to tell you. I'll go right now and tell that to the Alphas!"

A whoosh interrupted their talk, and the door opened to reveal a chatting, jolly party of seven Gammas and Deltas. At the front of the group stood Tom Doncaster, Director of the Department of Agriculture, wearing his usual blue coveralls. Unlike everyone else, he had apparently decided to forgo the chance to dress up in new clothes.

"Oh. Hello, Jeffrey, Natasha. Hope we're not interrupting anything. I was just leading a tour of the Farms."

An awkward moment followed as the others poured in, their talk dying down as they noticed Natasha's distress. Natasha didn't care, though; she didn't care what they thought of her, she was too busy fighting the desire to scream. Sweep the Pines. Tomorrow. A manual sweep with the best in the Office. And this time, the citizens would be prepared, they would know where to look, thanks to her.

"No problem, Tom," Jeffrey said. "We were just admiring the herd here. Wonderful work you've been doing." As he spoke, Jeffrey's hand closed forcefully over Natasha's arm and he began leading her past the group. "Anyway, we were about to head back to dinner."

In the Garden, the white chairs had been dispersed around the circular tables, and the tables themselves glittered with silver utensils and white china; sparkling candles scattered across sky-blue table-cloths. The Alphas had left, though that was expected. Even the more socially inclined among them never remained outside the Department of Government for more than a few hours. In their absence, the formal feeling of the Ceremony had given way to the thrill of a festive reception. Groups sat talking around plates of roast lamb and glasses of wine, while others gathered around the musicians, dancing in slow circles or laughing conspiratorially at some private joke. Still others wandered in groups of two or three under the canopy of branches, admiring the recent bloom of the magnolias or orchids or stargazing lilies. Jeffrey led Natasha firmly through the Department doors and into the Dome.

Raj and his friends were still standing near the elephant with their signs, and an argument was brewing between Raj's group and a hand-ful of Epsilons. No one noticed as Jeffrey tapped his finger at the Department of Research doors and hurried Natasha inside. The cir-cular lobby was empty.

"Since when do you have access to Research?" Natasha asked.

"There are certain perks to being a Gamma."

"Where are we going?"

He tapped his finger again, this time at the door labeled OFFICE OF BIOPRODUCTION.

"Somewhere private," he said.

They passed through the doorway and it closed behind them. There were no overhead lights in this room; instead, row upon row of bluish, glowing vats lit their way, each vat containing a pale, growing organ. The sight did not help Natasha's already weak stomach, and she told Jeffrey as much. But not until they had come halfway down the aisle of replacement hearts, each one thumping mutedly in its liquid home, did Jeffrey stop and look at her.

"All right, this is it," he said. "I want to know the truth. The whole truth. Your behavior has gone far beyond a normal response to a traumatic event. You need to tell me why you're acting like this."

"I want to come on the mission," she said, almost wildly. She was desperately thinking of some way she could warn the Tribe before the team got to them. Once she got Outside, she could break off from the others and run ahead, or else make so much noise that the Pines would hear them coming and flee. "Please, Jeffrey, get me on this team."

"Don't be ridiculous."

"You got me on the last one. And it wasn't my fault they took me. Why should I be punished for it? I should've been Arthur's first pick. I understand the Pines better than anyone."

"There, like that." Jeffrey's face was livid. "What do you mean by that?"

"Nothing," Natasha said. Her mind was reeling; she was making things worse. "Just that I'm the only one who saw their cave and actually talked to them. You might not know they spoke English if it wasn't for me."

"How many times do we have to tell you, it doesn't matter what they speak?"

Natasha shrugged with feigned nonchalance, but her heart was beating fast, twice as fast as the replacement hearts around them. A kind of violent awareness was coming into Jeffrey's eyes.

"Was there anything you left out of your report to Arthur?" He regarded her closely. "You've been a terrible liar ever since you were a kid. Remember how they'd catch you sneaking chocolate squares out of the Dining Hall?"

"I'd never lie about this," Natasha shot back, furious.

"I hope not, considering that you're a member of *my* team in the Office of Mercy, who was given the extraordinarily misguided privilege of leaving this settlement."

In a sudden, violent gesture, Jeffrey yanked the sleeve up his right arm. The bright burn raged over his flesh, pink even in the blue dim. For the first time in her life, it made Natasha flinch.

"There is no one in this settlement who understands the capabilities of the Tribes better than I do. I know their tricks. I feel the consequence of their trickery in a way that—Alpha willing—no other citizen ever will. Now I want you to look me in the eye and swear that you will never speak of leaving this settlement again."

"Why are you doing this?" she asked.

His eyes seemed filled with an answer he could not express. His hand remained on his sleeve and his whole being insisted on her response more vehemently than if he'd been shouting.

"I swear," she gave in. "I swear not to go on a mission again."

"Good. That's good."

He rolled down his sleeve in a gesture that seemed almost embarrassed, and with a sudden calm that made Natasha regret her acquiescence almost immediately. He reached out to touch her shoulder, but withdrew just as soon. The blue light from the vats reflected off his glasses.

"Let me walk you back to the party," he said, acting as if nothing unusual had happened between them.

"I'm not really in the mood to mingle."

"To your sleeproom, then."

"I think I can find it."

"Okay," he said, showing his empty hands in defeat. "I'll give you some space to calm down. See you at the afternoonshift tomorrow."

Natasha remained rooted in place as Jeffrey's footsteps echoed down the long aisle and the door fell closed behind him. In the quiet, the low, deep thuds of the replacement hearts seemed louder, and the glow of the vats dreamlike and menacing. The array of floating organs cast strange, odd-shaped shadows on the ceiling, within the rippling patterns of light.

She knew what she had to do, though she could hardly think it. But she knew, as absolutely as if it were the single possibility, a future laid out before her like a walled Garden path. While she waited for the minutes to pass, for Jeffrey to be absorbed back into the crowds at the party, she took measured steps farther down the aisle, gliding one hand along the counter and absentmindedly reading a label here or there.

Most of the hearts in this row were full-grown and ready for transplant; and a plate at the base of each vat gave the name and generation of the intended host. She paused at one vat that held a bit of pulsing biomatter much smaller than the rest, about the size of a grape, floating above a mesh of thin, stringy veins. KENNETH MARIO, GENERATION BETA, the plate read. That made sense. Kenneth had just received a new heart early last month; the bioengineers must have only recently started his next one.

Several minutes had passed; it would be safe now. Natasha reached the far wall, turned the corner, and began walking back through the purplish kidneys. She shuddered, knowing that one of them belonged to her and that, elsewhere in the room, dispersed among the different rows, were the replacements for every vital system in her body, waiting to find their home in her flesh. But she shouldn't have to worry about transplants yet; she still had time. The rounds never began before the half-century mark. Unless, of course, Natasha thought cringingly, as she entered into the deserted lobby, unless a citizen was brash or crazy enough to risk the body premature damage.

10

The party had spilled out into the Dome, creating a scene of unusual havoc. The din of human voices echoed off the circular wall, mingling with the music and joyous singing emanating from the open Department of Agriculture doors. The flora and animal-themed dresses and wraps had begun to slip from women's shoulders; and most of the men had their jackets off, the top fastenings undone on their shirts. Near the Department of Research, a group of Epsilons and Deltas, the most gregarious from their respective generations, were laughing loudly and throwing extra rolls of streamers toward the hub, so that the colors unfurled gracefully in the air before the spools clunked to the floor. It took Natasha a moment to realize they were not just horsing around, but very deliberately antagonizing Raj and his group, who remained near the elephant doors with their signs, looking just as menacing as ever.

"Hey, Maria," Mercedes called, breaking the protesters' silence, "throw another one of those and I'll stuff it down your throat. Give everyone's ears a break."

Maria, known for her distinctly shrill voice, flushed pink from her neck to her forehead. But her outraged response was overpowered by one of her friends.

"That's some mouth you've got," Jared Sullivan shouted to

Mercedes, "for a traitor. No one wants you here. You're ungrateful for what the Alphas give you and you disrespect the suffering of the Crane Tribe."

Mercedes rejoined with her own ideas about respect and suffering, but Raj, calm and aloof as ever, stopped her with a small gesture of his arm. The damage was already done, though. The wall of silence had disappeared and the two groups were shouting and taking steps toward each other. The crowd in the Dome was noticing, straining to see who had finally done the inevitable and told the protesters exactly what they all thought of them.

Natasha spotted Eric standing with a few other Epsilons, holding a bottle of wine by its neck and looking ready to launch himself into the center of the action. Natasha went to him quickly and grabbed his arm.

"I need to talk to you," she said.

"Hold on, I want to see how this turns out." But one look at her face must have changed his mind. "What is it?" He allowed her to guide him toward the Dome wall, away from the others.

"Did you know that the Office of Mercy is sending a team out in the morning?" she said.

"Who told you that?"

For a moment she considered lying, and keeping her promise to Jeffrey, but given what she wanted from Eric, she figured she owed him the truth.

"Jeffrey told me," she said. "Just now. He said they're planning a manual sweep."

"They can't," Eric said simply. "We don't even understand how the Pines have been hiding from us, or how they're destroying the sensors. And it was awful last time. It wasn't even close to ethical."

"That's why we have to stop it."

"How?" He was looking over her head, through the open doors to the Garden.

"We can't convince them. I tried already, with Jeffrey. They have

Alpha approval and nothing we do will change their minds. You heard the Mother. No one is listening to us." She took a breath. She had just caught sight of Jeffrey, well inside the Department of Agriculture, picking at the tables of food. "We have to warn the Tribe," she said. "Suit up and find them, and tell them to leave the perimeter if they want to live."

"You're promoting irrationalities," Eric said. But Natasha could see that she had roused his interest. This is what she had counted on: Eric's history of breaking the rules. Back when they were kids, he had held the record for sneaking out of bed at night; and in school, he had always been the one goofing off during lessons, the one whom the teachers had to move to the front. Now he was thinking fast, running through the logistics as Natasha had done just minutes ago.

"The sensors are off on the green," Natasha said, "for construction. That means no one will see us leave. As long as we keep near the riverbank, we won't set off any alarms. Once we hit the ridge, we're in the deadzone that the Pines created."

"How do you expect to find them?"

"Jeffrey thinks they stayed near their old camp, hiding in the caves. I bet you he's right. Where else can they go? Anyway, if they're not there—"

"If they're not there, then they've already left the area and the team won't find them either."

Eric set the wine bottle carefully against the wall. With the argument continuing near the hub, no one was paying any attention to them.

"Okay," he said. "Let's do it."

Until this moment, the idea of leaving the settlement had felt wild, locked within an aura of impossibility. But now, she and Eric were walking through the groups of people toward the Department of the Exterior doors. They were going to do it; they were going to walk right out of America-Five.

Just as they were entering the hall, a shout sounded from behind them and Natasha looked back. She could not see through the crowd to the center of the activity, but what she did see, Natasha found startling: Raj Radhakrishnan, standing slightly apart from the others, his placard dropped to his side, watching Natasha and Eric with steady and curious eyes.

But then he was gone. The doors closed, and Natasha hurried to catch up with Eric, who was already a little way down the hall. They were lucky; with only a scattering of people working tonight, the hall remained deserted as they slipped into the Office of Exit. A row of biosuits hung on a rack near the wall, ready for tomorrow's team. Wordlessly, they stripped down and each found the best fit—Natasha took Claudia's biosuit and Eric took the one made for Douglas.

"We're really going out there," said Eric.

"Yeah, we are."

"I don't think the Alphas even have a reeducation plan for something like this."

"Hopefully," said Natasha, "they won't need to write one."

They put on their helmets and entered the airlock. Then, as they had done on their mission, they passed through the two white cube-shaped rooms and into the supplyhouse. Natasha kept thinking that someone would stop them, that, at any moment, the door behind them would open and a clamor of furious and incredulous citizens would arrive to drag them back Inside. But no one came. The supplyhouse was pitch black and silent until, with a click, Eric flipped the lever for light. The dust kicked up from under their feet and hung lazily in the glow.

"What should we take?" he asked, eyeing the guns.

Natasha had thought about this already. "Nothing," she answered firmly. "They've seen what our weapons can do. If we walk into their camp with a couple of LUV-3s, there's no chance they'll stick around long enough to hear us out."

The light from the Dome cast a warm glow across the green and the inner circle of trees. They found that their helmets had lights, and they switched them on. Even in the dark, they knew the way. They had practiced navigating this area hundreds of times in the Pretends. What a strange way for their vigilance to pay off, Natasha thought. *They* made it possible for us to do this; *they* taught us everything we know.

Neither Eric nor Natasha had brought a tracking device, which served a secondary purpose of showing the time, but they guessed they had reached the plateau in just under three hours. The beams of light from their helmets swept across the empty camp as they examined the scattered, ash remains of the old fire and the bits of sensor parts abandoned near the birch trees. All was still. An owl hooted from one of the branches behind them. The lights reached into the large, curving dark of the cave, hitting the far stone in two circles made jagged by the uneven surface.

"They're not here," Eric said.

"They're probably still underground." Natasha started for the cave's mouth. "One of those rocks has a tunnel behind it, that's how I escaped."

Something moved, cutting the beam of light in half. Then a shout. People running from the trees.

Within seconds, Natasha and Eric were stumbling backward, standing on the charcoal remains of the fire, with five people coming at them, the shiny points of their spearheads thrust menacingly out.

Natasha saw Hesma and Mattias. The violent ones whom she had feared in the cave. Hesma wore the same red beads. Mattias's chest was bare and his skin was painted with thick white lines over each rib.

"Hesma," Mattias said, "take away their weapons. London, go tell Axel."

The smallest Tribesperson, a skinny boy years from being full-grown, sprinted into the cave, while Hesma, the only woman in this group, came forward and began pulling at Eric's airfilter.

"Hey, come on!" Eric protested. "We didn't bring any weapons. No guns."

"We came to warn you," Natasha said, as the woman's tugs now threatened to dislodge her own airfilter. "The people—the same people who swept, I mean, attacked you before—they're coming back."

"Quiet!" Mattias said. While Natasha had been talking, she had turned to him, and the beam of light from her helmet glowed in his face. He put his hand up, squinting against it. Natasha turned off the light and told Eric to do the same, but he shook his head. Natasha could hear a quiet stream of curses from behind his visor.

The boy emerged from underground.

"Axel says to bring her down," he said, pointing to Natasha. "But not the other one. He doesn't want him to see where we live."

The boy beckoned to her, maybe even smiled a little. Resigned to do anything to make their warning known, Natasha started to follow—until Eric stopped her.

"You're not going down there," he said.

"Yes, I am. I have to. Listen, I know that name. Axel. He's their chief. If we want to save these people, we need to tell him directly."

"No way. They're going to kill you, and kill me too. This was stupid. Really, really stupid. No one knows we're here. No one's coming to help us."

"We won't need help."

Though even as she said it, she had doubts. Since the mission, Natasha had convinced herself that the Pines had never intended to harm her, not when they abducted her and not even when they had her bound in the cave. And yet, even if she was right about that, it was no guarantee that they wouldn't hurt her now. She remembered one of their units in school on primitive ethics: Revenge. An eye for an eye. A life for a life. The most rudimentary idea in all justice-based social systems. If the Pines trusted their human instincts, which they almost certainly did, then murdering Natasha would be a perfectly fair, if not lenient, response to the death of three of their own. She paused a moment, looking at the boy, who was scratching a red welt on his calf while he waited. Then she squeezed Eric's arm and spoke some hushed instructions about not scaring the Tribespeople and, before Eric could stop her, she walked between two spear-holding men and into the cave.

The boy—London, they had called him—led her through the same opening in the rock from which she had escaped weeks before. He carried a bit of fire (a candle, Natasha thought, remembering the name), though even with that light and the calm motions of the boy's bare shoulders to guide her movement, Natasha still had trouble on the tilting, bumpy ground. They took two turns where the tunnel split, both turns to the left, and then the path began to level and smooth. London put the candle forward to reveal a strange sight: the cave wall did not seem to be of rough, mountain stone, but of smooth concrete. In the concrete was a large square of glass, like the windowpanes in the settlement but smaller and, as Natasha saw in a moment, movable too. London raised the glass and pushed aside a hanging piece of blue-and-green checkered fabric. He stepped through the opening and Natasha, because she had come this far already, followed boldly behind.

She did not know how many she had expected, but it certainly was not the number that greeted her on the other side of the glass. They rose to their feet as she entered—forty or fifty of them in all. Their eyes fixed on her and did not look away. They wore dark, earth-soiled fabrics, and the space smelled foul. A bright energy showed in their movements, which gave Natasha a chill.

"You don't have to wear that, you know." It was Axel. Natasha recognized his round, open face and dimpled cheeks. He indicated her helmet.

"We don't wear them," a second man added, "and we're all perfectly healthy."

As the man emerged from the shadows, Natasha was surprised to find herself face-to-face with the beautiful man she had spotted on the sensors. She stared at him a moment, transfixed by his perfect arrangement of features. In return, his expression showed a mixture of hopefulness and welcome that made her inexplicably glad.

Natasha had a feeling the Tribe's standards of health did not quite match the cell-by-cell perfectionism of the settlement doctors. But figuring that she had already breathed the Outside air once before, and had come out all right, she unclasped the helmet from the biosuit collar and lifted it over her head.

As she looked around, the Tribespeople showed no signs of aggression; in fact, they seemed positively happy to see her. She could observe the room better now too: a small fire crackled at its center, the smoke rising up through a hole in the ceiling and drifting through a rectangular opening in the far wall, too perfect to be natural, and with the unmistakable dimensions of a manmade door. The floor was littered with a patchwork of trampled furs, clay jugs, and baskets. It seemed that the Pines had set up a semipermanent home here, though why they would resort to such measures, why they would stay close to America-Five when they had the whole forest at their disposal, Natasha could not imagine. The cave itself was strange, the walls not rough but square and smooth, with sharp corners that formed near-perfect rectangles. But Natasha had no time to reflect on this strangeness because they were all staring at her, waiting for her to speak.

"My name is Natasha Wiley," she said. "The man who I'm with is Eric Johansson. We came back Outside by our own choice. No one else from our settlement knows that we're here. We came to warn you. The people—the people where we're from—they plan to nova these caves in the morning. I guess you don't know what that means. But it's bad. Like fire, but worse. You have to know, you'll die if you stay here."

Axel, far from being startled by her words, remained impassive. And seeing his reaction, the others took on a similar countenance.

"The weapons we used to attack you last time," Natasha pressed on, "those were guns and thermo-grenades. Those are *nothing* compared with a nova. You can't outrun a nova, and you can't hide from it. This whole underground place will collapse. Most of the time, we don't find a single body. You have to run away. Go over the mountains like the rest of your Tribe. Go as far south as you can and never come back here."

But at this, there was an unhappy murmur, and a shaking of heads.

"Sit with me, Natasha Wiley," Axel said.

He knelt on a clean-looking pelt of fur and indicated the place between the beautiful man and himself. Natasha knelt. The other men and women squatted down where they stood—all except for London, who, at a motion of the chief, handed over a small wooden box of what looked like rolled papers. Axel took one of these papers, lit it in the fire, and somehow sucked the smoke into his mouth from the opposite end. He then handed it to the beautiful man, whom he called "Tezo."

"We do not plan on going anywhere," Axel said. "We made the decision to stay and that will not change." Natasha began to protest, but he went on. "We know about your fire weapons, and the power they have. It is an old story, all the people know it. How the god-people who live underground brought night and death to the earth. Many generations considered the god-people the stuff of legends only, but not us. We knew that the god-people who made the skies black still dwelled here."

Natasha was disturbed by what he was saying, and a moment later she realized why: this group had memory of the Storm, however hazy it was. That wasn't accounted for in the ethical practices of the Office of Mercy; the Tribes weren't supposed to have any notion of past anni-hilations.

"We know that you still use these fire weapons," Axel continued. "And that you send them from your glasshouse. We know about your eyes in the trees. How do you think we survived these last two seasons without knowing?"

"But how?" Natasha asked, curiosity fully overtaking the last remnants of fear. "You never entered our field before April, but you came knowing exactly how to evade us. You must have seen other settlements before, haven't you? America-Six or America-Seven?

They made some mistake and you figured out the Alpha system of observation. . . ."

Axel seemed, if anything, amused by Natasha's assumptions. He also seemed ready to satisfy her curiosity, and would have done so had it not been for the low growl of another person sitting near him: Raul, the man who had lost his children and their mother in the manual sweep.

"Tell her nothing."

"But my friend, didn't we all agree? We could tell by the look of her, by the way she came to us in the woods. She was the god-person sent to help us, just as fate intended. And look! She understood by the grace of the divine that we only meant to keep her safe when we restrained her in our home. Isn't that right? Didn't you understand?" Axel was suddenly prompting Natasha, who nodded despite her confusion. "And now," Axel continued to Raul, "look how much she has risked in coming back to us. Why would she lie?"

"How can we know what she risked?" Raul asked. "By what she told us? She could be lying about that too. Who knows if there will be an attack if they can't drive us into the open first? Like Ollea, like my children."

"*She* didn't kill your family," Tezo interjected. "That was the others." He looked appraisingly at Natasha. "She is the one who will help us. I'm sure of it, and I trust her."

Axel seemed to weigh both men's words, and said, at last, "How about this, Natasha Wiley? If you are telling the truth about the attack tomorrow, then we will meet you again in the place of your last murder, at the next full moon, and I will give you the answers you want. If you are lying . . . well, your people will suffer for it. We know our way around this land."

"I know you do," said Natasha. "That's partly what made me see things differently—your intelligence. No other Tribe is like you, except maybe the Palms."

"The Palms?"

"I don't know what they called themselves," Natasha said, "but they were a Tribe that entered this area a couple of decades ago. The settlement swept, I mean, killed them. But only just barely. They got within a quarter-mile of our home before we even saw them. No one's threatened us like that before."

"Twenty-two years ago," said Axel.

"What?"

"The attack on your settlement, the murder of those people, it happened twenty-two years ago."

"How did you know that? Were you here, underground? Did you see it happen somehow?"

"I know because we are them."

"Axel!" Raul said, horrified. And even Tezo looked shocked.

But this time, Axel ignored them.

"We were children then," Axel said, indicating the faces around him. "All the people here. I was very small. Tezo and Raul were a few years older, but not the age of a fighter." The mood among the Pines had changed, a tense stillness descending over them. "We lost our parents, our siblings. Tezo here watched as his dearest friend was crushed by a burning tree."

"That can't be the same attack, though," Natasha said. "The Tribe I'm talking about all died."

"Don't you remember the deaths, the fire weapons?" Axel asked Natasha, intently.

"No, no," Natasha said, "I was too young. But it can't be you," she repeated, her head still reeling from his claim. "We swept the Palms. It was clean. The Office would never have left survivors. . . ."

No one was listening to her. Axel, Tezo, and Raul were rising to their feet, and the others too. Then Natasha heard what they heard: a voice calling her name from a near distance. Eric was somewhere inside the cave, he must have broken free of the others. Before she had fully processed this fact, there came the sound of a small metal object clanking onto stone and rolling down the passage outside. A fine white mist began leaking through the checkered fabric that covered the window. Everyone began to cough, deep hacking coughs. Natasha's eyes streamed with tears; her throat was closing up. It was dispersion gas, it had to be; a gas designed to drive Tribespeople out of closed areas before a sweep. Eric must have taken a canister from the supplyhouse when she wasn't looking. The men and women scattered, pushing through the doorlike opening on the other side of the room. Natasha managed to put on her helmet. She could still hear Eric calling for her and, furious, she went to find him. The dispersion gas would not harm the Pines, though Natasha guessed it would damage her cause. She should not have asked Eric to come. She would have been better off alone. But there was nothing more she could do now: the Pines would have to decide their fate for themselves.

Was it possible they had gotten away with such a blatant act of treason? Natasha could only wonder, awestruck by what she and Eric had done. Of course they had left the settlement at a time when the sensors were off on the green, and Natasha's and Eric's knowledge of the field had allowed them to keep securely within the deadzone. And yet, it still seemed as if they had done what should have existed only outside the realm of the actual; as if they had acted out in real life an experience that belonged to a fantasy world in the Pretends. When they returned to the Office of Exit, they found the room as empty as they had left it. The chemical bath and UV lamps had cleaned and dried their borrowed biosuits, and so they were able to restore them to the rack seemingly as good as new. They slipped into the Department hall unseen and, first Eric and then Natasha, joined the late-night stragglers in the Dome. The clock on the maincomputer read 0326 as Natasha boarded the elephant in the company of a male Delta and a female Gamma, both looking ready to collapse with exhaustion. (The Department of Health, Natasha thought, will have their hands full tomorrow.) She found Min-he sprawled over the covers, still dressed with only her shoes kicked off, her snake necklace coiled at the foot of her bed.

Natasha changed into her nightclothes, threw back the covers and got into bed, her thoughts screaming with the fact that the people Outside had talked to her, and that they had wanted to meet her again. The leader of the Pines knew her name; and the beautiful man whom she'd watched on the sensors was a real person who actually seemed to like her. As she lay on her mattress, staring up at the ceiling, the secrets burned in her core. Happy secrets and disturbing ones too: the Tribe's claim about the Palms, their understanding of the sweeps, and their apparent belief that her helpfulness fit some supernatural prediction about a "god-person" doing them good. At least we warned them, Natasha thought as her tiredness took over, we gave them a chance. As for the rest, she and Eric had no choice but to keep what they'd learned about the Tribe to themselves.

Now it was morning, and Natasha sat at her desk in the Office of Mercy, her mind still raging with the memory of the Outside. She was not exactly sure how Eric was feeling today. Their trip back to the settlement had left little time to discuss more than the basics: that the Tribe would not leave the area, and that they claimed to be the same group as the Palms. He had told Natasha that he was furious with her for going into the caves, and that he did not share her trust in the Tribe. Apparently, when he broke away from the group with spears, they had poked him several times in the sides. The spear points did not penetrate the fabric of the biosuit, or even damage it in any way, but the affront was enough to dispel much of Eric's sympathy.

Meanwhile, the news of Jeffrey's team and the intended manual sweep became public, and, in the hour after lunch, the updated news that the mission had failed. According to Arthur, the Pines had deserted the cave area and left no trace of their presence and no trail to a new camp. Eric, as soon as he had an opportunity, caught Natasha's eye from around the side of the cubicle wall and glared at her with such alarm that (though she had no regrets) Natasha's stomach tightened with fear. The full consequence of their actions must have sunk in for him at this moment, as it had for Natasha. The Pines had listened to them after all. They had moved before the team could get them and now they were somewhere out in the forest, and it was all Natasha and Eric's fault.

As the days passed, Natasha's fear only grew. She was afraid that someone (particularly Raj) would come forward, claiming to have seen her and Eric leaving the settlement; she was afraid that the Pines would try to attack; she was afraid that they would stay in the area as they had promised and get themselves killed. Plus Natasha had Jeffrey to deal with. It seemed that their talk on the night of the Crane Celebration had made him nervous about leaving his team alone all day. He did not return to the morning or afternoonshifts, but he began checking on them in the Office of Mercy at random hours—on Natasha especially. She could not really blame him, given all the blatantly unethical things she had said. But his attention, his calm, stony way of standing over her desk or listening in on her conversations with Yasmine made her jumpy and distracted. She could not believe how desperately she had craved his notice just days ago, when all she wanted now was to slip through the tasks of her shifts ignored.

During the long, idle moments—watching the cumulus clouds drift by on her screen while Jeffrey watched her—Natasha could not help but wonder how Jeffrey would react if he found out that she had left the settlement. Would he keep her secret? Or would he turn her over to Arthur? To the Alphas? After the way he'd treated her since the mission, Natasha could only fear the worst, that one more tug would snap the already tenuous bond between them. Despite how angry she was with Jeffrey right now, it still hurt Natasha to think that her actions within a mere cluster of hours could destroy what remained of his affection for her, for herself as a whole person. Could his regard for her—could the years of history between two people—crumble as easily as that?

Unfortunately, Natasha could not dismiss these as idle worries because she was constantly and increasingly aware of the possibility that Eric might give them away. In the last minutes of one otherwise uneventful afternoonshift, Arthur sent Natasha and Eric to wheel two faulty memory cubes (which together backed up three hundred years of sensor data) to the Office of Dry Engineering, and Eric seized upon this chance to once again make his opinions clear.

"You know I don't like this," he said, as soon as they were out of hearing range of the Office. "I mean I really, really don't like this."

"They haven't caught us yet."

"I'm not worried about getting caught, Natasha. I'm afraid we made the wrong decision. Going out and telling some random Tribe to disappear is one thing. But they're not leaving the perimeter. Apparently they have no intention of leaving. And according to you, they're not random at all." They pulled the cart to a screeching halt while they waited for the Department doors to open. "According to you, they're the *Palms*."

"That's what they said. But maybe they're lying. Or misrepresenting themselves, you know? Like how we would call ourselves citizens like the citizens of other Americas, even though we're not really the same group."

"Then how do they know about the sweep?" Eric challenged. "There was no one left to tell them."

The doors opened and they passed into the Dome. The other citizens hopped out of the way of the cart and veered sharply along different paths. The din from the construction site was deafening; Natasha had heard that the workers were pulling double shifts this week.

"The thing is," Eric continued, "if they really are the Palms, then we're not dealing with just any Tribe. The Palms were the smartest, most aggressive Tribe that this America has ever seen. Even more dangerous than we thought, if they managed to hide the existence of a dirty sweep."

They arrived at the Department of Research, and Natasha tapped her finger; Arthur had temporarily granted her genetic code access to the wing. They maneuvered the cart in a clumsy arc across the circular lobby, toward the door marked OFFICE OF DRY ENGINEERING.

"We shouldn't keep this secret, Natasha."

"If you tell Arthur or Jeffrey what we did," Natasha said, "we're both getting eternal bans from the Department of the Exterior. And I can't even imagine what the Alphas would say." Eric only shrugged but, sensing a weakness, Natasha pressed on. "Look, I'm not crazy, okay? I don't want to put the settlement in danger any more than you do. But we have to be smart about this. Jeffrey has always told us that the Tribes are tricky, so before we throw away our careers, let's figure out if they're telling the truth."

"How do you expect to do that?"

Natasha tapped her finger once again, and they wheeled the memory cube into the Office of Dry Engineering. The room contained a series of long, high metal tables with men and women in white lab coats and goggles tinkering with small instruments. A contained wreckage of computer and electrical boards lay scattered before them. At the back of the room, a few stooped and very still bodies peered into the eyeholes of compact u-quark microscopes, which, according to a recent bulletin, the scientists were using to investigate new subatomic energy sources.

Upon seeing Eric and Natasha, two of the engineers stepped stiffly down from their stools.

"Just leave it to me," Natasha said. "My free day is coming up soon. I'll go to the Archives and have Min-he dig up everything there is about the Palm attack. If the sweep looks as clean as we've always been told, then we'll assume they were lying. If not, then I agree with you. We have to tell someone."

Eric was already nodding hello to the engineers.

"Fine," he said, under his breath. "Do what you have to do. But I don't want it to be 'we' anymore. I shouldn't have let you convince me to leave the settlement in the first place. They could've killed us, easily. I mean, Alpha, we're lucky the Office didn't sweep us by accident. I'm out, okay? I'm wiping my hands clean of this mess."

11

The Archives were one of the great feats of America-Five. In the time before the Storm, when other Alphas had put all their energy into transforming the Yangs' underground bunkers into suitable homes, shoring up their Domes, and gathering enough seed, animals, scientific equipment, and raw DNA supplies to last them until the Day of Expansion, the America-Five Alphas had also had the foresight to gather information. For the first two hundred years after the Storm, the piles of books, digital files, and paper records had lain fallow in one dehumidified room on level eight. Later, though, sometime just before the Gamma birth, the Alphas and Betas had decided to siphon off the top story of the Department of Living and make this area into a reading room and library. At first no one saw much use in it, since they already had the Pretends for entertainment and schooling, and the Ethical Code for moral grounding. But as the years went on, interest in Pre-Storm documents grew and, eventually, added to that interest, there arose a desire to keep detailed histories of the happenings within the settlement itself, records beyond what individual memory could retain. Now, as had been the case since the first professional assignments of the Gamma generation, the Archives maintained a healthy staff of twelve to fifteen citizens. Their work consisted of recoding the old, Pre-Storm documents and books, maintaining the living record and the yearly biosnapshots of each America-Five citizen, and—though Natasha would never say as much to Min-he—endlessly shifting information from one organizational system to another.

After breakfast, Natasha climbed the spiral staircase to the top floor of the wing. Today was her first free day in weeks, and she was all too happy to spend it away from the Office of Mercy and the dull, streaming data from the satellite feeds. She cleaned her hands in the decontamination sink at the landing and pushed through the handsome, Pre-Storm–style glass doors that led to the Archives. The air in this room was cool from the dehumidifying vents and smelled of old paper. Towering shelves cut narrow rows along each side of the aisle leading to the archivists' stations, and each shelf boasted a tightly stacked row of faded book spines. Except for the printings of the Ethical Code, these were all Pre-Storm books—really, the only sentimental relics that the Alphas had preserved from that previous world.

Tucked off to one side of the room was the reading area: a comfortable nook of plush armchairs with ottomans and little tables that one could draw up and over the armrests. Along the opposite wall were seven windowed conference rooms that citizens could sign out for private meetings. Arthur met here sometimes with the heads of the Department of the Exterior offices; and often, a handful of citizens would organize discussion clubs that gathered in the evenings. Natasha herself had attended a few meetings of the Moral Principles Discussion Group in her first year out of school, and Min-he had once dragged her to a culinary club responsible for providing the kitchens with innovative menu ideas. Just now, there were five Betas talking animatedly (though silently, to Natasha's ears, since the rooms were soundproof) around one of the tables. They were not volunteering, though. A sign on the door identified them as the Reeducation Committee, a subgroup from the Department of Government. These men and women helped the Alphas organize specific behavioral and psychological goals for citizens who had acted against the common good, against the Ethical Code. Natasha looked away; she could not worry about them right now.

Natasha found Min-he at a large desk in the back corner of the room. A giant book was propped open on a wooden stand, and loose papers were scattered across the desk and floor. Min-he sat hunched over a small computer, typing rapidly. Wisps of black hair had escaped from her usually neat ponytail, and her eyes exhibited a wide, slightly crazed look.

"Hey," Natasha whispered, "can I bother you for a second?"

Min-he's head shot up from the screen, but she smiled when she saw Natasha.

"I forgot it was your free day! Sure, I was about to take a break anyway." She closed the massive book gingerly, so all the pages lined up straight, then laid it down on its side.

"What are you working on?"

"A new index of the Bible. My Director gave me the assignment this morning."

"Didn't someone just finish a new index last year?"

"Yes." Min-he sighed. "But this one will cross-reference thematically parallel passages in the Ethical Code. Anyway, were you looking for something? Leisure reading?"

"No, something for work, actually." It was harder to lie to Min-he than Natasha had anticipated. "Well, you know we're still having trouble with the Pines. Our tracking methods haven't been working, and we need some new ideas." Natasha faltered a moment, looking up as one of the archivists coughed. "A few of us have been talking about the Palm attack," she continued. "Just to see—behaviorally, I mean—what we might be up against."

"Does Jeffrey know you're here?" Min-he asked, with some suspicion.

"Of course," Natasha said, "it was practically his idea."

Min-he frowned, and Natasha was pretty sure that her roommate guessed there was more to the story. And yet, without further questioning, Min-he set Natasha up at one of the viewing consoles in a dimly lit corner of the room, with a list of video codes from Year 283, on the day of the Palm attack. With a last glance at the archivists, Natasha typed in the first code and tapped her finger on *Play*.

The recording came from one of the sensors on the green, and began seconds before the alarm sounded. Natasha watched, captivated, as teams of suited citizens jogged up from the stone steps and fanned out into different positions, their weapons snug under their arms. Some climbed ladders to the roofs of the wings, while others knelt on the green, with still others standing behind them. One team of four vanished around the side of the settlement and into the trees, perhaps hooking through the forest to keep the Palms from retreating.

When the manual sweep happened, it happened fast. The Tribe burst onto the green; they emerged running from the trees amid a flurry of arrows and spears aimed for the hearts of the citizens on the ground. But the Tribe's weapons could not stop the quicker and sharper spray of bullets from the citizens' guns, and the Palms fell, if not all at once, then in very quick succession. Natasha leaned in toward the screen, searching for any clue that the Palms and the Pines were connected, as Axel had claimed, or else searching for some great discrepancy that would make a connection unlikely. But it was too hard to say. Many Tribes had overlaps in appearance and dress, and any difference Natasha noticed could easily be attributed to the elapse of twenty-two years. Now on the recording, medworkers were rushing up the stone stairs, and Natasha saw with horror that at least five citizens had arrows sticking straight up from the tough fabric of their biosuits. Then, while the others were stowing their weapons, a group of three citizens went from body to body, guaranteeing with precise, single shots to the back of the head, which made the bodies jump as if shocked by live wire, that no human being of the Palm Tribe would continue to suffer.

The video was in its last minute when Natasha noticed, in the sliver of sky above the tree line, a column of dark smoke dividing the screen in two. That must have been the fire that the Palms had set in their wake, the fire that had caused Jeffrey's burns and, if Axel was telling the truth, that had killed many Tribespeople too. Jeffrey must have been among the four who had left the green before the attack. Natasha watched anxiously for his return, but before anything more could happen—and to Natasha's frustration—the recording ended.

Natasha hurriedly selected the next code. She wondered if there was footage of the Palms actually starting the fire, or a record of whatever tricks they'd performed to trap Jeffrey in the flames. But this next video showed a similar location as the first, only from a different angle on the green; and it cut off even earlier. The third recording was from Inside, when the archivists used to keep a camera in the Dome, attached to the maincomputer. (They had since dismantled it, after too many complaints from the citizens about being treated like Tribes in the field.) By the time Natasha entered the code for the fourth and final recording, she had remembered something important. There probably would be no documentation of the Palms in the forest because the Office of Mercy didn't have as many sensors back then—hence the Palms' success in reaching America-Five undetected.

Indeed, the last video again showed the attack on the green, though at least this one was a little more interesting. Here, Natasha could better make out the faces of the team of four who had gone into the forest before the Palms arrived.

As she had suspected, one in the party was Jeffrey. A second was definitely Claudia. As for the identities of the other two, though, Natasha could not tell. She wondered if the team had inadvertently startled the Palms with a covert approach—and in that way had instigated the Tribe's violent and sudden retaliation—or if the Palms had seen the team coming from a long way off and had set the fire deliberately in their path. She wished that Jeffrey wasn't already watching her for signs of unethical thinking, or that she didn't have so much to hide; otherwise she would have tried again to get him to talk about that day. For now, though, she decided she could not risk it.

This last recording, once again, ended abruptly, and Natasha turned off the console and went to find her roommate.

"Hey," she said, squatting down beside Min-he's desk. "Do you have any more information from that day? Audios or logbooks or anything?"

"Nope, that's it," Min-he replied. "Why? Didn't find what you were looking for?"

"No, it was helpful," Natasha said evasively. "It's just that all the records stop right after the sweep is over."

"Well, we can't keep *everything*. If the records stop, then probably not much happened afterward. You saw the whole sweep, didn't you?"

"Yes."

Min-he tore her attention away from her computer to gaze at Natasha. "I promise I gave you everything we have. The Archives are open to everyone. I'm not allowed to keep things back. I'd lose my position here if I did."

Not wanting to raise Min-he's suspicions any further, or attract the attention of the archivists seated nearby, Natasha hastily thanked Min-he and went back to the console.

She watched the recordings again and again. The lunch hour came and went, and the dark of the room and the glow of the screen tired her eyes and made them dry.

The Tribespeople were falling to the ground again, hit by a field of invisible bullets, when a light touch on Natasha's shoulder made her jump.

"You won't find anything useful there," came a smooth, confident voice. "You're not the first to try."

Raj was leaning over her, one hand on the back of her chair, his delicate features and clear skin illuminated by the glow of the screen.

"What really makes me curious, though," he continued, "is what prompted you to dig up these records in the first place. If, of course, you're willing to tell."

"It's no secret," Natasha said, willfully returning her eyes to the screen. "We're having trouble with the Pines. I thought that looking at the Palms might give me some new ideas."

"*You* thought? Didn't you tell Min-he this was Jeffrey's idea?"

"It's not polite to eavesdrop."

"I agree. But I wasn't eavesdropping. I asked Min-he what you were up to and she told me. We go way back," he said, sensing Natasha's surprise. "I used to be her Director."

"Until the Alphas transferred you to sewage," Natasha said. She wasn't trying to be mean, but Raj was making her nervous.

"Electricity and Piping," he said, "but close enough." He shrugged. "It was a punishment for lesser offenses than the ones you've committed."

She would not allow him to see her fear. He had spoken the words casually, but the meaning was not lost on Natasha. She vividly remembered how he had watched her and Eric leave the Dome on the night of the Crane Celebration. Well, whatever he suspected, he would receive neither denials nor confirmations from her.

He drew up a chair from another console.

"I've gone through all these recordings," he said, "and many others that Min-he didn't give you because they're so peripheral to the attack. I'm guessing you've noticed by now that there are gaps in the record. Well, I was Director of the Archives for five years and I can tell you that those gaps are real, and were created by someone in this settlement. I don't know who did it, or why, but they're definitely covering up something. And I'm sure that it goes all the way to the top. The Alphas know. When I was Director, I filed several appeals for more information."

"Did they tell you anything?"

"Only a little. And nothing on purpose. Eventually, they got tired of my curiosity. Hence my abrupt career change."

The reference to his transfer stirred Natasha to recall that, officially, she stood in harsh disapproval of Raj. Only a month ago, he had harassed her and her team outside the training Pods and had addressed them with loathing and total disrespect. Apparently, though, Raj felt no antagonism for her now. And Natasha wondered if he was even more perceptive than she'd thought, if he'd noticed a change in her since the mission.

"Why don't you come to our meeting on Sunday?" he asked.

"What meeting?"

"Me and some other Deltas. Mercedes, Eduardo, Sarah, and Ben. We meet at twenty hundred hours on Sundays in conference room A, just around the corner. We discuss the murder of the Tribe populations."

"You're allowed to do that?"

"Of course," he said. "It's still a free America."

He stood and looked quickly over the codes that Min-he had given Natasha. "Like I said, you won't find anything useful in these, or anywhere else in the Archives for that matter. But if you are truly curious about the Palms, you might look someplace else."

Natasha said nothing, but her eagerness showed.

"The Pretends," Raj said quietly, "are not as completely imaginary as most people assume. You can discover quite a bit about the past in there, if you know how to look."

"What do you mean?"

"This new program they've developed, Free Play—officially it takes thoughts out of the player's mind and forms that dream into reality. Except, as you might remember from the trial runs, that's a difficult thing to do, even for our brilliant engineers. Human thoughts, human dreams, they're too vague and fragmented to translate into the solid literal worlds we expect of our Pretends. So in the newest version of Free Play, the engineers allowed the computer more versatility. They allowed it to combine the current player's dream with the dreams of previous players. This way, the creative integrity and adaptability of

Free Play would not be compromised, since the engineers still would not be scripting the sensory world. But at the same time, we would all get the immersive, convincing experiences that we citizens seem to enjoy."

"So we can see other people's thoughts during Free Play?"

"Their thoughts, their fantasies, but especially those moments that have taken the deepest hold of their minds. The moments they try to suppress."

"Are you saying that the missing hours in the record play out in the Pretends?" Natasha asked. "No offense, but I think that's a little far-fetched."

"It's impossible even for players themselves to distinguish completely between their own dream and the dreams of others. But yes, if you start down the right path, if you clear your mind of expectation and force the computer to fill in as many gaps as possible, I do think you might stumble upon thoughts that are recognizably not your own." He leaned down and spoke close to her ear. "It's probable that the citizens who experienced the entire Palm attack haven't forgotten about it. Whoever they are, my guess is that they choose to relive it in the Pretends."

Natasha thought a great deal about what Raj had told her, even though the possibility of learning anything hard and true about the Palms in Free Play still struck her as unlikely. However, no matter what she believed at the moment, she couldn't go rushing off to the Pretends right away. The next day, the Zetas reached their sixth month of gestation, the time for them to receive their names. A special, cross-generational committee had been working on the project for months. They had looked closely at each Zeta's DNA package, itself a blend of what the Alphas had gathered in Pre-Storm times. Then, in an exercise at once historical, scientific, and artistic, they pinpointed the

Pre-Storm culture associated with the fetus's dominant genetic patterns and assigned a name that bore some relevance to that bygone
nation or community.

Usually the naming celebration (this was according to the older
generations) took place in the completed nursery, with all the Alphas
present and as many citizens as could squeeze in around the incuvats.
For the Zetas, however, it was a much more subdued affair. The equipment in the Office of Reproduction was too delicate to risk the presence of a crowd, and the aisles were too narrow to accommodate a
number of people with any comfort. Instead, the citizens packed into
the Dome and watched each name appear one by one on the maincomputer. The situation was not ideal. They should have been together in
a freshly painted, freshly furnished New Wing. And yet, at the
announcement of the first name, Charlie Abraham, all concern and
worry and bad feeling dissolved in a bright surge of hopefulness and
love. Nisha Adante, Leah Broussard, Magdalena Chang, Asumana
Donovan. Tears gathered in the otherwise steady, dry eyes of the older
generations, while the younger ones squeezed hands and cheered till
they were pink in the face. Each new name roused a fresh tumult of
feeling, especially for the Epsilons. So excited and proud they were to
welcome their little brothers and sisters. Christine Engle, Ali Fuhad,
Yael Glassman, Takumi Goto.

The names went on and Natasha wanted, she yearned, to love the
Zetas too. She *did* love them, for their innocence and their potential,
for whatever absolutely unique combination of aptitudes and failings
and predilections and aversions each Zeta child would possess. She
loved them simply because they were *here*, because she and every other
citizen had labored to make their existence possible, and because it
would be her responsibility, as it was every person's responsibility, to
share in the work of raising them right. The Zetas were each wholly
and irreplaceably themselves; and yet, at the same time, though they
could not know it, they already belonged to the citizens of

America-Five, just as the citizens of America-Five belonged to them, and the Zetas, in their uniqueness, would become essential and indispensable parts of the vibrant and unified whole. Everyone in the Dome could feel it, feel the specialness of the coming of a new generation. Harold Wyeth. Su Young. Natasha loved them, she did, but her love had a bitterness to it. Because how was it fair? With the Pines and all the Tribes on the continent, how was it fair for the Zetas to force themselves into the world? By the time the announcements concluded with the naming of Frederic Ziblenski, the swelling feeling of pride in Natasha pressed with a jagged, sharp edge.

Her doubts about Raj's advice persisted, yes, but with no other places to go for information, she eventually found herself turning to the Pretends. The night of the next full moon was fast approaching, and she was seriously considering going back to meet the Pines, and trying again to get them to leave the perimeter, unless she uncovered some clear reason not to.

Eric had not spoken to her again about the Tribes. But it seemed that, despite his unease, he was willing to leave the next move to her. At the very least, Natasha felt sure he would not turn them in without warning her first.

It was after dinner, and the Pretends were crowded. Natasha had to climb up to the third level before she found an open Pod. She selected Free Play and, as Raj had suggested, she tried to clear her mind of any direct want or expectation—that wasn't too hard, because she did not really believe this would work. Vaguely, with a light probing of thought, she evoked the day of the Palm attack, of that calm summertime afternoon twenty-two years ago. And soon, only a second later, the glow of sunlight beyond her eyelids told her that she was there.

The birds shrieked from the trees and the orange sun watched like a massive eye from the cloudless sky above. The air was dank and humid and thick in Natasha's throat, even though it passed through an airfilter strapped to her back. She lay belly down on the low metal roof of one of the America-Five wings—the Department of Government— as she quickly surmised from its northwest orientation. She wore a bulky, old-model biosuit and her finger hovered over the trigger of an early-generation LUV-2. The gun balanced on a mount between two turrets, aimed at the forest beyond. The sunlight reflected off the metal roof, roasting her in its heat. A man's voice spoke to her through an earpiece.

"Aggressive Tribe approaching from due north. All citizens on high alert. Maintain camouflage."

Natasha checked that she was fully hidden behind the turrets. From her vantage point, she could see the citizens on the ground shift slightly, no doubt nervous in their more exposed positions. At the tree line, citizens on well-concealed platforms cocked their necks to peer through the eyepieces of their weapons.

They heard the drums several minutes before they saw them. *Brrum-ta-ta-ta-brrum.* A sound in rhythm, Natasha was sure, with the marching of the warriors' feet. The noise grew louder, closer, until right when Natasha thought she would explode with anticipation, the Tribe broke from the forest and into the ring of green lawn. Two arrows whizzed over her head. A hundred Tribespeople, many armed with bows, approached the Dome. The drumbeat came to a sputtering halt, the arrows flying faster now. But the Tribe's awe at the enormous structure before them was apparent by their break in formation: some charged awkwardly forward while others stumbled back.

"They've cleared the forest," said the voice in Natasha's earpiece. "Prepare to sweep in four, three . . ."

The Tribespeople spoke to one another, *weesh ar haar,* words that Natasha could not make out. They were naked except for loincloths tied at their hips and strings of animal teeth hung around their necks.

They had wide, dirty faces and wild hair. A rock soared from the center of the group and hit the windows of the Dome with a clang. Another ricocheted across the metal roof near Natasha.

"Two, one, fire."

The shots came from every direction, the ground and the sky, the forest and the roof where Natasha's whole body was shaking with the power of lit ammunition. In seconds, it was over. Silent, unknowing, and unrecognizable they lay, and the brassy smell of blood and dirt leaked into Natasha's airfilter.

The citizens emerged from their positions, examining the bodies. No Tribesperson had escaped this; if this indeed was the real Palm sweep, then the Pines must have been lying—no one could have survived to continue their lineage. Natasha stood up on the roof, surveying the scene below. Still, something was bothering her. She watched as the citizens began dragging and stacking the bodies and then she realized: there were no children, no old people, no one outside the range of late adolescence to full, adult strength. She hadn't noticed at first because children in the Americas were such a rare phenomenon. But not for the Tribes; they reproduced one by one, without care or planning. Their populations spread evenly over the ages and yet— She looked again. No, there were no bodies short of full-grown, and none with wrinkled faces or thin white hair.

And where was Jeffrey and the rest of that team? The manual sweep was long over now, and still they had not returned. . . .

The image of Jeffrey's face, squared by a biosuit visor, hovered before her: his shocking blue eyes, his look of grim consternation. A feeling of love and longing shot through Natasha and, as it did, the image brightened and became more solid and sharpened into a form so vivid that she was there.

Or not there. Because she was only watching. Her vision was pure and hovering and free of body. She could see the others running with Jeffrey now too. Beside him came Claudia and then Arthur and then a

Beta named Gaurav Gandhi who had directed the Department of the Exterior for three decades in the mid-200s. They moved swiftly through the trees, their motions panicked, twice halting and shouting to one another and abruptly changing direction. The branches and sharp arms of the forest brush snapped at their visors and ripped across the fronts of their biosuits, but they didn't care. They kept running. They had gone many miles away from the settlement when Claudia looked at her tracking device and pointed their way, a hard left through the trees.

The team's shouts and trampling steps roused the forest to life: and their sounds were answered by terrified screams. Natasha's vision would not stay steady. The deep greens of the forest swirled and the too-blue sky tilted and dipped. The noise of destruction raged in her ears, and she could not block it out because she was not really there; she was watching but she had no eyes to close. The world exploded in fire. The flames surged up the trunks of trees, sparking the pine needles and felling the trees to the ground where the fire writhed and spread. From out of the chaos, Claudia, Arthur, and Gaurav emerged at a sprint. But no Jeffrey. Where was Jeffrey? The smoke swirled, allowing for a dark tunnel of sight into a cliff-bordered valley, and he was there. Run, thought Natasha. He wasn't hurt but he refused to run from the fire. He stood facing the flames, reaching for something he could not quite grasp. He made a final lurch and his face lightened with joy, but just as he did so, the flame licked his side and he was on fire. The screams came from everywhere; the whole universe screamed and would not stop and the fire that scorched Jeffrey's flesh enveloped all in its murderous heat.

The dream world of the Pretends would not let Natasha go—not as the hours passed, not as the days passed—and still very much within its grip Natasha found herself walking, sleepwalking almost, to conference room A that Sunday evening at 2000 hours.

They were overjoyed to see her, Raj and the others. Raj jumped to shake her hand. Eduardo drew up a chair for her at the table, Sarah waved, Ben nodded a nervous hello, and Mercedes, who never looked anything but angry and scornful, bestowed on Natasha a lovely, radiant smile. Raj made it clear within minutes that he suspected Natasha of holding, as the Alphas would call it, "unethical" views. He openly confessed to spying on her and Eric the night of the Crane Celebration. He had watched them disappear into the Department of the Exterior and, when they did not reemerge, had followed on the heels of a tipsy Department worker and gone looking for them. When it turned out that no one had seen them in the Office of Mercy, the Office of Air and Energy, the Office of Land and Water Management, or anywhere else, Raj concluded that they had done it—had walked out of America-Five.

Natasha refused to respond to these suspicions, though her silence immediately led the whole group to assume what they wished to believe—and what was, in this case, the truth.

"Tell me, though," Raj continued, "there is one thing I can't figure out. Are you and Eric responsible for the failure of the manual sweep?"

"Eric wants nothing to do with helping the Tribes," Natasha said quickly.

"Okay," Raj said. "Are you responsible?"

Again Natasha refused to answer, and again they guessed the truth. They praised her for her ingenuity and bravery. Raj said she had accomplished just the type of action that they had been discussing for years.

"Exactly *what* do you discuss, though?" Natasha asked, seizing on the chance to move the subject away from herself. "What do you want for the Tribes?"

They could not get the words out fast enough, as if they had been waiting years for someone to ask precisely this.

Mercedes wanted to hasten the Day of Expansion and, as soon as possible, to absorb the Tribes into settlement society. "Before the

Storm," Mercedes said, "when the Yang group had control of the continents, the world was on a better path. The Yangs wanted to make it so that every person on Earth had a proper share of food and drink and their own portion of land to live on. They built these settlements—or I guess they were called bunkers then—not for their own well-being, but as places to serve the people who once lived in this area. The Yangs would manufacture food and medicine, stuff like that. They considered it their duty to give every person on Earth a fair shot at happiness and health. Back then there wasn't any forest. There were cities and workhouses that had garden courtyards and pumps for water. It could have been good. It *would* have been good. Except that the Yangs never had the chance to see their vision through. The Alphas came into power next and blew it all up. But we could do like the Yangs imagined. We could build outside the settlement and make peace with the Tribes and have them live with us, as equals."

Eduardo said that if they could only stop the sweeps, the Tribespeople could live rich, fulfilling, and independent lives—lives that would inevitably last under a century—but that would still probably rival the citizens' own in excitement and depth of experience. He and Mercedes had spent a good deal of time looking over the Office of Mercy's own satellite data, and they had noticed for themselves the large animal migrations of last year.

"Why can't we allow the Tribes to continue in that direction?" Eduardo asked. "Right now there's a huge gathering of animal species due south of this settlement, five degrees down longitude seventy-five. If the large mammals are thriving in that area, then it follows that the Tribes would do well there too. What makes us think that the people Outside wouldn't be happy in a place like that? The problem is that we're so demeaning to them. We act like the suffering they endure robs the rest of their life of any meaning or profundity, and that's a mistake. Look at what we call them, even. Cranes. Pines. Obviously that's not what they call themselves. Language like that is designed to keep up the Wall. It's an attempt to position ourselves above them. Keep us from misplacing our empathy, or whatever the Alphas call it."

Ben, his voice trembling slightly with so much eager attention on him, turned his large brown eyes to Natasha and said, speaking for himself and Sarah both, for she had taken his hand in silent encouragement, "If we only shared a little of what we have with the Tribes, it would do so much good. Seeds from our gardens, medicine from the Department of Health, or simply knowledge about our world. Anything that could help them build permanent homes and food supplies of their own. Just little things would help so many."

Raj spoke the most passionately of all.

"We think," he said to Natasha, "that because the Alphas wield control over death, because they have stolen that control from nature, they also in some way have a *right* to it. But they don't. To me, they are nothing but overgrown children. Control does not give the *right* to control, and it certainly does not grant understanding. Our lives are mysteries, Natasha. Yours, mine, the Alphas', every one of the Tribespeople's. And just because we've figured out how to keep rearranging our cells to force our bodies to go on century after century doesn't mean we've gotten one nanometer closer to the true nature of our existence. What is life? What is that spark of consciousness that makes you more than a collection of material stuff? What is that whole universe of thoughts and memories that exists for you? That exists for each of us? Doesn't it bother you, for instance, that the nature of your thoughts as you think them and the flicker of chemicals between neurons in your brain bear so little resemblance to one another—and yet we say they are the same phenomenon? The Alphas don't have answers. None of us do. We can't begin to explain it." Raj shook his head. Then he folded his hands before him and looked deeply into Natasha's eyes. "We do not know what life is, and so we cannot know what death is. And if we cannot know, then we should never, no matter our earthly justifications, kill."

They had plans, too. Or rather, they had plans to make plans. They wanted to do what Natasha had done, to sneak out of the settlement and talk to the Pines. They got it out of her that she knew where to find them, and that she was considering going to meet them six days from now, on the night of the next full moon. With their rapid talk and zealous scheming, they convinced her that any such action would require their help. Eduardo, who held a high position in Construction, could schedule maintenance work on the exterior of the New Wing, thus ensuring the shutoff of the sensors on the green. Ben and Sarah could linger in the Dome, keeping their eyes and ears open for anything out of the ordinary—signs that a citizen suspected a breach, or worse, signs that the Office of Mercy had found the Tribe too, and was preparing to sweep. Mercedes could wait in the hall of the Department of the Exterior, ensuring that Natasha would not need to reenter the settlement blind. And Raj. Raj wanted to go with Natasha. The Outside was a dangerous place and she could not possibly go alone. Besides, he had devoted his whole adult life to fighting for the rights of the Tribes. He wanted to meet them. He needed to see them with his own eyes and touch the hot flesh of their hands and know that the people he fought for, the people for whom he had already sacrificed so much, were more than just numbers on the maincomputer or grainy sensor images—that they were more than dreams.

Oh, it was happening too fast. They invented schemes with such optimistic hurriedness, a hurriedness that pushed aside the horror that lived in every blade of grass and every molecule of air in the Outside. Natasha had to interrupt the rhythm of conversation several times to remind them how quickly safety and danger and life and death could interchange once a person exited the sturdy enclosures of America-Five. She left the conference room in a turbulent state, with too many voices and possibilities swirling around in her head: the chief, Axel; the beautiful Tezo; and Raul, whose family had died; Jeffrey and his recent reprimands, his sincere and heartfelt warnings, but the fire too, the orange flames and heat of the past that hid a truth she could not begin to name; and Arthur and Eric and all that she had worked for in the Office of Mercy; the Wall and the Ethical Code and the Alphas, those three pillars that had supported her life for as long as she could remember. And now Raj, Mercedes, Eduardo, Sarah, and Ben—their voices rang in her ears as if she were still in the room with them, their words about life and justice and death and consciousness echoing within her skull until, late that night, she moaned into her pillow to shut them up, waking Min-he, whose startled cry, "What is it, Natasha? What is it?" disturbed her as much as her own thoughts.

The next morning, Natasha made a decision. She typed in a request at her wallcomputer (not even minding when Min-he peeked at the screen), and within minutes she had an appointment at 0800 hours with Neil Gershman in the Office of Psychotronomy, a place she had not gone since her childhood. Instead of continuing down the central hallway to the Bioreplacement offices, as she usually would when visiting this Department, Natasha entered through the first door on her left. The Psychotronomy office had a small, comfortable waiting room with dark maroon walls and two threadbare but still very plush couches. Neil's office too had a warm, cozy feel, so different from the sterile coldness that characterized the rest of the Department of Health. He offered her a seat in a large prote-velvet armchair while he brought up her file on his wallcomputer. Once she was settled, he uncapped a pen and reclined in his own high-backed chair.

"Let's begin with your feelings about the Office of Mercy," he said. "When did you first make the decision to work there? According to your records, you passed the entrance exam with very high marks at age seventeen, within just a month of finishing school. . . ."

Neil Gershman was the senior psychotronomist. He was a Beta and he had held this position twice as long as the vast majority of citizens remained in any one Office: an uninterrupted seventy-one years. He was a handsome man with a head of thick brown hair that was famously his own—not transplants like most Betas wore.

His expertise showed. His kind, pointed questions had the power to shed light on the strangest corners of Natasha's mind, and coax answers out of her that she hardly knew were there.

"I guess I only felt curious about the Tribes at first," she found herself saying. "It wasn't until a year or two into working at the Office of Mercy that I sometimes wouldn't build the Wall when I knew I should. But I *liked* to think about them. And then there was Jeffrey. I knew he couldn't keep the Wall up all the time because he understood the Tribes so well. He could predict what they'd do better than anyone. He's always been the best in the Office, everyone knows that. I thought maybe I could be like him . . ."

"But there are consequences to letting the Wall down, aren't there?"

Tears rose in Natasha's eyes. "When you don't build a Wall, you start to project yourself onto them. And then, when it's time to sweep, the ethical thing doesn't feel right anymore." Natasha exhaled a deep breath. "I've realized something, though," she said.

"What's that?"

"I've realized there's a whole history behind our dealings with the Tribes that I've only just begun to learn. And also that, well, other people, especially *older* people, must have felt the way I do sometimes, and asked the same questions. The Alphas have lived through all these changes. If they believe the sweeps are ethical, that this is the best possible action, then maybe I should trust them. And as I get older, maybe I'll begin to understand it better too."

Neil smiled. "That's very sensible of you, Natasha, very thoughtful. I've had Gammas and Betas in here who aren't capable of that kind of maturity."

At the end of the session, Neil had her schedule an appointment for the following week, this time on her free day, so that she wouldn't have to miss work again. He also gave her a bottle of small orange pills.

"I happen to know that these were prescribed to you after the mission. But this time, maybe you'll take them?"

Natasha nodded and promised she would, tucking them into her pocket.

Outside the Department doors, a lone figure was pacing up and down the marble floor of the sun-drenched Dome. It was Jeffrey. When he saw her, he came to her and drew her into a tight hug. Natasha did not resist.

"How did you know I was here?" she asked. But she was not at all surprised. She had guessed that when she failed to show up for work, he would come looking. She had counted on it in fact.

"When the maincomputer canceled your shift, I got worried. I thought maybe one of your injuries had healed improperly. So I called the Department of Health and kept them on the line until they gave me answers. I'm sorry, you don't mind that they told me, do you? I know the sessions are supposed to be private. I didn't give them much choice in the matter."

"No," Natasha said. "I don't mind."

She pressed her face against his chest.

"I'm proud of you," he said. "You're going to be just fine from now on."

12

"She's not coming."

"She will," answered Tezo.

"She's not coming, and we'll be dead if we stay here!"

Mattias rose to his feet, his bare chest, which he had painted that morning, thrust out as if ready to fight.

Axel glared from where he knelt in the cold sand. He did not like Mattias's temper. He would have sent the young man off to the mountains with the children and old ones, if not for his unparalleled strength.

"We should go on without her," Mattias continued. "We'd be better for it. Besides, the risk is too great. If she's told them already—"

This time, Tezo did not respond. Instead, he unsheathed the knife that hung at his right hip and began to sharpen the blade against a palm-sized rock.

"I agree with Mattias," spoke up Hesma, the most skilled of their female hunters and, recently, their new leader of prayers. She snapped a bundle of kindling over her knee. "I'd rather risk blood than let years of preparation go to waste because of one god-person girl."

"Then let it be your blood, not mine," growled yet another voice from near the fire. Raul.

Hesma met this challenge with excited resolve. "You're upset about your family," she said. "But they never should have been here. Ollea, maybe, but not the children. Why you allowed them to stay—"

Raul suddenly grabbed a copper-tipped arrow from where it lay on the ground. He held it gleaming over his head, his mouth open, threatening not only Hesma but also some pervasive and unseen enemy of his mind, the whole vast darkness beyond the shallow light of their fire.

This would not do.

Axel rose and stood before Raul; he laid a hand on his shoulder while the others looked on. He whispered words for only Raul to hear, words of comfort, of understanding.

Tezo walked over too. He urged Raul to put the arrow down and, in its place, to take his last handful of grain, as Raul had eaten little in days. Axel stepped away. He could count on Tezo. Of course, he used to be able to count on Raul too, before they had lost Ollea and the children.

"Do you think she's really coming?" a boy asked hesitantly from beside the wind-whipped flames, interrupting Axel's thoughts. "Nassia?"

Now it was London who had spoken, Axel's half-brother who, at fourteen, was the youngest person allowed to stay for the fight. Too young, that was obvious now.

"Yes," assured Axel. "As soon as she can, she will be here. She warned us about the attack on our caves, didn't she? If it wasn't for her, we might have been dead. Those were strong weapons, like she told us."

London nodded and, moving out of the shadows, stoked the fire with a stick, his solemn face bronze in the orange radiance of heat, his eyes squinting against the ash.

"But for tonight," Axel continued, now openly addressing the group, "we need to forget about ourselves. We came here to honor the sea-fishing people who died in this place, who were killed by the same murderers who tried to destroy us. Their bodies are scattered here, with no one left to remember them but us. Let us pray and ask God to accept their souls into the land hereafter."

At this reminder, the people stifled their own impatience and fear and returned to the task before them: preparing a funeral for the sea-fishing people. They had not known this group well, only traded with them once or twice in the North. But they had witnessed the cloud of black smoke that had signaled their annihilation; and, in death, these strangers had become dear to them, like distant family.

As soon as the fire grew strong enough, they lit four torches and carried them to the four points that marked the corners of the wreckage. Two torches burned where the ocean foam broke across the sand, and two others at the edge of the toppled, singed expanse of forest. Usually during a funeral, these four points of light would mark the area of the deceased person's body: two torches at the head and two at the feet. Arranged in this manner, the light allowed God to look down from His place in the afterworld and see the soul that was ready for Him to free from the shallow dwelling called Earth. Here, however, because the bodies of the sea-fishing people had gone to dust, and had mingled with the particles of sand and dirt and water up and down this beach, the best they could do was to mark off the whole spread of death. They imagined the souls lingering just above the sand, in the exact place of the body's death, waiting, however the dead may wait, for God to call them home.

Once they had secured the torches, Axel ordered the fire at their camp built higher. Then, in the orange heat, with the circular dark of forest at their backs and the depthless dark of ocean before them (*fushh-ahhh*, the ocean breathed, sighing cold gusts that made their ears and noses go numb), the group began the funeral prayers.

They appealed to God for forgiveness, their voices gathered together in song: forgiveness because they themselves had not done more to warn the sea-fishing people of the danger here, forgiveness for the humbleness and hurriedness of these funeral rites, and, most of all, they asked forgiveness on behalf of the dead. For though it was probable that the sea-fishing people had not worshipped the true God in life, surely it was only ignorance of His presence, and not pride or evilness, that had prevented them from a holy existence.

Hesma, the leader of prayers, began the concluding calls, and the rest of the Tribe gave answer:

"Who is gathered here?" Hesma sang.

"We, the children of God."

"God in His mercy will bring these souls to Him."

"We trust in God. He who gave us life, who lifts our souls at death, who promises life forever in His grace."

"We trust in Him."

"We trust in You, God."

"The Sun and the Moon are Him."

"Lead us, God, our lives are lived for You. Accept us at death into Your kingdom."

Their voices converged to one and then dispersed, leaving behind the climactic silence of sixty-four desirous souls. Because now God would come, if He had deemed their prayers worthy. The people fell to their knees, digging ruts into the sand, their arms outstretched to the sky and their wrists and fingers stiff with reaching, their heads thrown back. Oh, and now God was close, they could feel His invisible presence against their flesh, filling their hearts. He had come to carry those poor souls away; the air rang with cries to Him.

"O God, I love you. Forgive me," cried London, with the heartfelt sincerity of youth, and who would have fumbled to name his offenses if pressed.

"Watch over my family," said Tezo, thinking of his mother and his little brothers and sisters. "They are with the others in the North Mountains. The children, please, the children. They are so afraid."

"Save us," said Mattias, who had only weeks ago promised himself to the most beautiful woman on Earth. "Let me return to Nona. It will kill her if she hears I have died."

"O God," cried Raul. "I have said bad things against You. I have been angry. But I will be better, the best, if You will see us through this fight."

"Fight with us, God," said Axel, his voice full and assured. "I beg you, I beg you."

The forest and the sky absorbed their calls. The torch at the north corner, near the water, blew out in a gust of wind. The fire at their side shrank low, drawing its heat into itself and returning the air to the ocean's chill. The prayers were quieting when a crunching noise came from the forest, the deliberate rhythm of human steps making a slow approach.

At first, only Axel and Hesma heard it, as they were standing closest to the trees.

"I told you," said Axel, his dimples showing. "She is with us. God has provided."

"You are too eager," said Hesma, fingering the red beads on her neck. "Too optimistic, like always."

"But she's here."

"Yes, and that's good. So far, we have everything in place. Without her, there can be no attack. But it's going to take some careful talking to get her to do what we want."

The oldest of all the women, Sonlow, raised her chin, her glassy eyes bright in the firelight.

"You know your part, dear one," said Axel.

"Yes, boy," the old woman answered. "I have prepared myself."

The crunching noises grew closer; a twig snapped. Now the others heard it too.

"Look!" cried London, pointing at two bobbing white lights in the forest, broken and then unbroken by trees. "It's Nassia. She's come back!"

The reason for the travelers' laborious movement became clear as soon as they had reached the sand. Natasha and Raj carried four giant bags between them, each one stuffed with food that Ben had marked spoiled from the Department of Agriculture inventory. The Pines approached cautiously at first, and then with glee. Natasha quickly introduced Raj as a friend, a person who had been fighting for years to end the sweeps. The Tribe regarded him curiously, though they seemed even more intrigued by the bags he held out in timid offering. At the first revelation of fresh fruit and meat packed in paper, the Tribe crowded in. The skinny boy, London, and the younger ones began to eat first, then Raul and others whom Natasha could not name. Mattias, the violent man with angry eyes, pushed forward only when the food began to disappear. He grabbed one of the plucked, raw chickens, speared it, and began to roast it over the fire, looking warningly at Natasha and Raj, as if daring them to take it back. Only the chief, Axel, stood back, rubbing his hands together and grinning almost foolishly, his dimples deep pockets in each of his cheeks.

"You came back," he said, moving to stand beside Natasha and Raj. "I knew you would. Some of the others weren't so sure. But I didn't worry. And you brought a new friend. I think we frightened the last one."

"He wasn't ready," said Raj. "I'm not accustomed to being out of the settlement either, but I'll tell you that I've been dreaming of this. Dreaming of being out here with people like you for as long as I can remember."

Axel was satisfied with this answer, though as Natasha was beginning to notice, the chief seemed predisposed for contentment.

The threat of the meeting now behind them, Natasha realized how exhausted she was. While Raj questioned Axel on the Tribe's numbers and their hunting practices, she crouched down in the sand, the forest behind her. She was still a bit shocked they had made it to the beach this quickly, and with no interference. In fact, the break from the settlement had happened so easily and so precisely according to plan that, more than relief, Natasha was beginning to feel open scorn toward the Alphas and the dutiful citizens of America-Five. She had given the

Office of Psychotronomy a final chance to sway her mind, and they had failed to convince her. Jeffrey had simply assumed her opinion of the Tribes reformed, and Eric and Min-he had followed his lead. Presumably, not even the Alphas could begin to guess her true thoughts.

Natasha watched with satisfaction while the Pines gnawed into the plums, spilling juice down their chests, and bit straight into the orange rinds. The beef shoulder and chickens they had speared began to cook over the fire. Then to Natasha's surprise, Tezo, the beautiful man, came and sat beside her. He touched one finger to the visor of her biosuit, right at the nose.

"You wore your mask again," he said. "Like you don't want one grain of sand to touch you."

"It's not the sand," Natasha said. "We're trying to avoid viruses, germs. . . ."

Tezo's quizzical look made her smile, while a different, bitter thought turned within her. How could she be sure the air was dangerous at all, just because the Alphas said so?

She hit the release on her biosuit and took off her helmet, and immediately the smoke of charring meat and the fresh saltiness of the ocean winds and the warm rank smell of human bodies awakened her senses in a way she had never experienced before.

Tezo handed her a chicken leg, scalding hot and dripping, and Natasha bit in, burning her lips.

It was a beautiful, joyous moment and one that filled Natasha with reassurance. Once again she had wagered her safety and her future to come here, but it was not a mistake. This was real. This was human. Not the high philosophies of America-Five, not their computer programs, not their counts, not their cube-shaped sleeprooms and suffocating enclosures, not the *mercy* she had always believed in. No, she was done with that fakery. From this moment on, she would believe that other voice inside her. The one that loved the core things, like earth and fire and sky and hunger and desire and grief and the want to live.

Raj was staring at her, slightly alarmed. But then, without saying a word, he took off his helmet too. He breathed in long and deep, making his nostrils flare.

"Amazing," he said, and the peace and fulfillment that showed in his face and body reflected what Natasha felt in her own being. And she was glad, so glad, that they felt the same, that they were united in this experience.

"This meal is a very kind gift," said Axel, as the Tribe passed around the last cuts of meat. "We think we can call you our friends."

"We are your friends," Raj said earnestly. "We hope you can believe that. We risked everything to come and warn you. I know Natasha has told you already, but you need to leave this place. We can't stop the people in our home from trying to kill you. It's the most we can do to tell you the truth and have you spread the word to others. There are still hospitable lands due south of here, away from our settlement. Natasha knows them. She could give you a map, show you the way."

But Axel only shook his head, looking a bit disappointed, as if he had expected to hear this warning again, though he had hoped against it.

"No," he said. "We have suffered under the power of the god-people for too long. We refuse to leave."

"Natasha said you've been to this area before," Raj said, changing course. "She said your people are the same ones who attacked the Dome twenty-two years ago."

"That's right."

"But we don't understand," said Natasha, rising to her feet. "Every one of those people died. The citizens didn't leave a single survivor."

Axel looked searchingly at Natasha. Several Pines were listening now: Raul, Hesma, Mattias, and Tezo. They seemed terrified by what Axel might say next, but they remained silent and still, their jaws making circles as they chewed. An old woman, by far the oldest person here, was the only one who seemed eager for the conversation to continue. She nodded along every time either Axel or Natasha spoke.

"No one survived the attack on your glasshouse," Axel said. "But people survived."

"There was another group, wasn't there?" Natasha asked. She was remembering the Pretends, and the conformity in age among the Palm attackers. Her voice rose with realization. "Because you wouldn't have brought everyone. You must have left behind the people too young or too weak to fight. Just like you did this time. How you sent that group past the perimeter on the night you took down our sensors."

"Yes," Axel said. "But the chief of that time didn't send them far enough. Many from that group died too. Terrible deaths. The fire was everywhere. No one knew where to run, and the smoke made it like night. The grown ones among us today, we escaped, many of us as children. As did our very eldest." He nodded to the old woman. "But you must know this already. Your people are the ones who started the fire."

"Our people started the fire?" Raj asked.

"Of course," said Axel, annoyed. "Why would we harm our own families?"

"The citizens would never do something like that," Natasha protested. But then she wavered and did not say more; she wasn't sure.

"Natasha and I were only children then too," Raj quickly reminded Axel. "No one has ever told us the details of that day."

Axel nodded and seemed to require no further explanation. Their stomachs now satisfied, the Pines again had grown slightly wary of these strangers in their camp. And as they wiped the juices of fruit and meat from their lips, their eyes stayed on Natasha and Raj.

"We have suffered," Axel said. "We have lost our families and been pushed to the edges of livable land, but we refuse to stand by any longer." The Tribespeople were shuffling around the fire; they seemed energized by the meal. "You came back to us," said Axel, turning suddenly to Natasha. "And if you came back, we knew that you would be loyal to us. That you would help us."

"I *am* trying to help you," Natasha insisted. "That's why I'm telling you to go."

"We're not leaving," said Axel.

"Then you'll die."

"We are prepared for that."

"But what's the purpose?" Raj intervened. "Just to keep jumping around from camp to camp, knocking out sensors until eventually our people catch up to you?"

"No," Axel said. "We do not plan to keep living like this."

"Then what do you want?" asked Natasha.

"The same thing we wanted before. We want to get inside the glass-house. We want to take away your power."

Natasha shook her head, any thought of saving the Tribe flying out of reach at these words. She looked to Raj and saw his hopefulness disappear.

"It's impossible," Natasha said.

"If you say so, then you say our death is certain, and soon."

The sixty-four faces held Natasha pinned in a confluence of expectation. Even Tezo was alert, demanding. For the first time since arriving here with Raj, Natasha felt afraid.

"Think of what you're asking," she protested. "I can't do it. I know what they're doing is wrong, but I can't help you harm the citizens."

"We are not like the ones you live with, who raised you," Axel said furiously. "We do not want to murder your people the way they murdered ours. Our beliefs do not permit it. Judgment is for God alone to dispense. All we want is to live in peace. To live without hiding, to live without the constant fear that some little mistake we made yesterday is going to send our deaths screaming down from the sky. We know how to get to the glasshouse without detection. We know where the Eyes are and how to take them down. And the door, the way in, it's the silver door at the base of the stone steps, isn't it? If you could open it for us, let us inside—"

"What would you do?" Raj asked.

"We want to steal the weapons. Show us where you keep the Birds of Fire, and we will take them. We will destroy them."

"Destroy them?" asked Natasha.

"Yes," said Axel. "Show us the place and we will take them away one by one. We have a boat, a good and sturdy boat. We will carry each weapon across the forest to the beach, and row them out to where the water is deep. We will drop them into the ocean."

Natasha's mind was racing, the ocean was deep off this shore. Even the A1 novas, the largest of all, would not cause destruction to the land if they were to detonate on the ocean floor, within several cubic meters of water. Only Raj's words brought her back to her senses.

"They'd kill you before you ever got inside," he said.

"That's why you need to bring us a Bird," Axel said. "Bring it to us and we will carry it with us. Your people will not attack then. If they did, it would mean the end of us all—us, them, you. And we will tell them that. They will stay away and we will win peace with the threat of death."

Natasha shook her head.

"Bring us a Bird," repeated Hesma.

"We will end this," said Mattias. "You must do this."

"No," said Natasha. She looked to Raj and she could see in his face that he agreed with her, that he too perceived the promise of disaster here. "We will help you in any way we can," she continued. "We'll help you escape this area but we can't—"

The rest of her explanation was drowned out by a surge of furious cries. Then all Natasha could see was a crush of heads and arms and eyes. They closed in on them, the whole Tribe, even Axel's shouts could not stop it. Suddenly she could not find Raj anywhere. The Tribe had pulled him out of view.

"Tezo," Natasha screamed in panic. He was standing a little beyond the clawing arms yet he too seemed drunk on the moment, just like the rest of them. His eyes caught hers.

"You were born to do this," Tezo said.

She was moving. Their hands hooked into the collar of her biosuit and they grabbed and pulled her arms. They were reproaching her, specks of dampness from their wet lips touched her face and she yelled out in disgust at their closeness. A voice rose above the others, and through the mesh of bodies Natasha saw the old woman commanding even Axel.

"It is time. It is time that she knows."

Before she could stop them, Natasha was rushing with the group through the trees. She could not tell who was touching her. Their hands grasped all over her body. She could not see and when she stumbled and began to fall, her feet would leave the ground and they would carry her onward until she found her footing again. Raj called from behind her, whether they were forcing him along or whether he followed her freely, Natasha did not know. The trees blocked the moon and the night was close at her eyes. They were not gentle. Their hands dug firmly into her sides and they did not slow down even when unseen vines or branches lashed across her cheek or struck her middle. At last they reached an open plain that sat beneath the silhouette of towering mountains, and suddenly they released her, catching her again only when she began to fall forward.

The gray moonlight revealed a deathly, chilling scene: an open expanse of naked ground and decaying, strong-smelling rot. Trunks reached sharply upward though they were leafless and dead and stopped abruptly, as if beheaded. The place looked familiar, but Natasha was sure she had never seen this area on the sensor feeds. It looked like the landscape of one of her nightmares—or no, she *had* been here before, in the Pretends. Jeffrey and his team had come to this place during the Palm attack. She recognized the jagged cliffs and the basinlike curve of the valley. The fire had burned here. Raj was right; it must have been real, what she saw during Free Play, a real memory fragmented and distorted, yes, but still connected by a thread to a true, actual past. As she kicked, her boot sent up a cloud of soft dirt. The rest of the Tribe poured into the clearing and Raj was with them, breathing hard.

"God," said the old woman, her arms outstretched in a V to the sky. "You have delivered our daughter, now help us open her eyes." Her hands made fists and she beat them, horrifyingly, at the moon-washed stars above. "Open her eyes and let her see."

"But Sonlow," said Axel, coming up beside her, his jocular tone returned and his white grin a gleam in the dimness. "Her eyes *are* open. They must be. Why else would she return to us?"

It was worse than a nightmare, worse than any horror of the Pretends. Axel charged her, and Natasha screamed. But then he caught her shoulders, holding her in what appeared to be an affectionate embrace. "Our little Nassia."

"Nassia, Nassia," the Tribe echoed in a dancing hiss.

"Look," he said, throwing his arm back to gesture at the old woman. "There is your Sonlow. Your mother's mother. Your own flesh and blood!"

"Stop," said Natasha. Fear was building in her, gathering in her gut and rising, rising until it burned her throat and made her head pound.

"Here is Tezo, the best friend of your oldest brother who died. Your handsome Tezo, who doted on you when you were a tiny girl. You might have committed yourself to him—eh, Tezo?—if you had stayed. Both of your mothers hoped for it. Here is London and myself, our mother was your father's sister. Here are your cousins," he said, pointing to two sallow-faced women about Natasha's age, and who had Natasha's same shade of chestnut brown hair. "Here is your auntie, here are your babyhood friends. . . ."

"Don't listen to them," came Raj's low, smooth voice from behind her. "They're just trying to trick you into changing your mind. It's okay."

Axel heard too.

"You are *ours*," he cried, grabbing Natasha's arms. "You belong to us. This is the place where they came with their fire. They killed so many. They killed your mother and father and your brothers and sisters. But not you." His voice was rich with awe—anger and awe. The world tilted and Natasha fought the urge to be sick. "After they killed hundreds, thousands, they took you alive."

"Nassia has come home," the voices of the Tribe sang. Their bodies were merging into one mass, then splintering in the dim gray. Tezo grinned, his expression bashful and happy. London took hold of Hesma's arm and playfully spun her in a circle.

"Let me go!" Natasha screamed. "I'm going back to the settlement."

"Oh, no, don't say that." Sudden hurt showed in Axel's eyes. "We have put so much faith in you. Ever since we first suspected what they had done. We trusted that you would lead our triumph over the god-people. You remember when we found you, don't you? We've been exploring this area for a long time. One night, fourteen years ago, Sonlow, Mattias, and myself were searching the walls around your glasshouse. We were able to climb a ladder on one side and look in. Sonlow saw you. You were covering your face, bleeding from the nose, but Sonlow recognized you still. She said you looked like your older sister who died at that age. And now you look like your mother."

"You're imagining things," Raj said. But Natasha was distressed. Of course she remembered seeing the faces.

"God led us to you, just as He led you to us two moons ago, when you walked right to the edge of our camp, alone and unguarded. It's amazing," he said. "Only the most amazing occurrences we say are God's work."

Sonlow had fallen to her knees and other women joined her, holding her shoulders and sobbing into her ragged dress.

"You must bring us a Bird," said Axel. "You must save us."

"You must."

"Our Nassia."

"Stop."

"Our Nassia, Nassia."

For a long time, they would not release her. They touched their cold palms to her cheeks, they pulled her one way and then another, trying to move her unyielding body into their dance. Sonlow hung on her arms, the tears gone now, rasping that this was God's plan for Natasha, that the hand of the divine had brought them together at last. Tezo kissed Natasha's cheek, rousing hoots of coarse, hideous laughter. Only when Raj convinced them, in shouts, that his and Natasha's absence from the settlement would be noticed if they did not leave immediately did the Pines finally let them go.

They moved together through the forest, alone at last. Raj gripped Natasha's hand in his. He told her where to step and where the ground became suddenly steep. She was badly shaken and she could tell that Raj was trying to suppress his own panic for her sake.

They had reached the river before Natasha got her bearings again. As far as she could tell, Raj had kept them away from the Office of Mercy's sensors. Natasha shivered; the air near the water was fast and cool and she could feel the cold dampness touching the still-exposed flesh of her face. Her legs ached with exhaustion; the adrenaline had receded from her muscles, leaving them limp. They stopped and Natasha dropped to the ground. For a moment she felt destined to remain there forever, silent and still, a collapsed person among the rocks, but the fresh air strengthened her body.

"Raj," she said. But she could not even speak, she was too terrified. He knelt beside her on the damp ground.

"I'm sorry," he said. "Are you okay?"

"Why would they do that?"

"I don't know. I guess they really can be tricky, these Tribes. I'm sure you've heard that before. And the Pines, the Palms, whatever you want to call them, they may be the trickiest ones of all."

"But I remember," Natasha said, the words bursting forth. "I did see them. I was nine. I had a bloody nose. They were taking me to the Department of Health, and I saw three faces looking into the Dome."

"Well," Raj replied slowly, with some concern, "maybe you did. Maybe they did find our settlement. But that doesn't prove the rest of their story. That only shows how adept they are at manipulating a set of circumstances for their advantage. They're not unthinking, these people. You told them before that you can't remember the Palm sweep, and apparently they've seized on that fact as a way to draw you in."

The roar of the water rose from the ravine below, the river itself perceptible only as glints of moonlight.

"But Natasha," said Raj, his voice rising with a faint note of curiosity, "you don't actually believe them, do you?"

"You don't?"

"At first I did—or at least I wasn't sure. But as soon as I had a second to think about it, I realized that it wasn't likely. I know the Archives and I've searched the Pretends, and I've never come across anything that would corroborate a story like that. A dirty sweep is one thing. I believe they're telling the truth about that. But the idea of a Tribe child getting Inside rings of wish fulfillment on their part. As I said, I've put countless hours into studying our settlement's past. And I can assure you that for three hundred years the Alphas have been, if nothing else, consistent in their ethical practices. If Tribe children ever did survive a sweep, then saving those children would have meant killing them, not bringing them Inside. Probably the Tribes can't wrap their minds around an idea like that. But I'm afraid that's the society we come from."

"I don't know," Natasha protested. "People break the rules. We're breaking the rules right now."

"Not like that, though. Our leaving the settlement wasn't condoned by the other citizens, as an open interaction with a Tribesperson would need to be."

"They hid the footage," Natasha pressed. "The footage of the Palm attack."

"And now we've uncovered the reason," Raj answered soberly. "Our people started the fire that burned hundreds of Tribespeople alive and injured our own people too. The Alphas are probably protecting someone, someone who made a mistake. Likely they're protecting their own pride too, though they'd never admit it."

They were quiet again, then Raj smiled a small smile. "It honestly never occurred to me that you'd accept their word as truth, considering your background in the Office of Mercy. Actually, I've only been worried—I'm *still* worried—that you might be so angry with the Pines for making up such wild lies that you've lost your desire to help them. It was foolish, what they did. They're very desperate to secure you as a friend."

"What about you?" Natasha asked. "Are you angry?"

They were sitting side by side now on a narrow, moss-covered stone. Their biosuits were filthy; they would have to run the acid bath twice just to wash the dirt away. The moon had dropped out of sight, all but for a shimmering glow at the tops of the trees. Natasha could barely make out Raj's profile beside her.

"I don't like it," he said. "I wish they could have just trusted us. But even with the mistakes they made, that doesn't change my commitment to saving their lives. They're victims, not angels. We can't expect them to always do the right thing. And really, it's hard to blame them for attempting everything within their power to get what they need."

"I guess our people would do the same in their situation," Natasha said.

"That's right. Look how far we go to create the world that the Ethical Code tells us is best. You know," Raj said, after a pause, "it's also possible that they truly believe their own story. Maybe they did lose a little girl in that fire. Maybe that old woman really has convinced herself you're her kin. They don't have the same education that we do. They may not be able to separate emotional desire from empirical fact. They have no psychotronomy. They have no Ethical Code. The concept of projection probably doesn't even exist for them."

"So this doesn't change how you feel about the Tribes?"

"No, I don't think so. It was an unfortunate choice to put on that charade. But I'm still committed to stopping the sweeps. It's interesting, isn't it? Their idea for destroying the novas. Ingenious, really."

"Are you actually thinking of helping them?" Natasha asked. "Giving them a nova?"

Raj rubbed his cheeks, contemplative.

"We've had the novas for the last three hundred years and we've killed more than one hundred and forty thousand people, and that's not even counting the Storm. They say they'll destroy the weapons in an effort toward peace, maybe they deserve a try."

Natasha shivered again, though this time it was not the river air that chilled her. She was still angry with the Tribe for what they had done, how they had scared her, twice now. But there was truth to what Raj was saying. After all, what terrors had America-Five heaped on the Pines, on all the Tribes? In the night, outside the settlement and its protection, the memories of the ones who had died rose to vivid life in Natasha's mind: the woman and her two children, the Palms on the green, and the Cranes, all of the Cranes. She remembered them, starving but resolved, about to feast with their families when their future was sliced from existence with the sharp, exacting blade of a nova. Could she really say that nonexistence was better for them? Could she possibly make herself believe that those on the Inside had sufficient information to judge the ideal moment for those Outside to die?

"You're right," Natasha said at length. "Anyway, I don't know how else to stop the sweeps. We'll bring them a nova, and we'll end it together."

Raj did not answer right away, but he put one arm around Natasha, tilting her against his side; it was a friendly, warm gesture that took Natasha by surprise.

"You're pretty amazing, Natasha."

"You don't have to say that," she quickly assured him. "I'm fine now. It was just scary in the moment, having them surround me like that."

"I'm serious. I never imagined that I'd find a person in the settlement who cared about the Tribes as much as I do."

"What about Mercedes and Sarah, and Ben and Eduardo?"

"They're great. I love my friends. They're all really smart people. But it's not the same thing. You came to your conclusions about the settlement's ethical practices independently. Without my influence, without my prodding. It gives me hope that we're onto something here."

"Maybe we're both out of our minds."

"Maybe we're both right."

The moon had set and the dark took over except for the dizzying array of stars. Natasha breathed more evenly now, though her mind was grappling to make sense of all that she had seen and heard. Certain moments kept flashing before her eyes: the jumble of angry faces, Sonlow's embrace, Axel's fiery demands, and Tezo's planting a kiss on her cheek. Raj rubbed her neck above the collar of her biosuit, under her hair. They stayed like that, determined to use up the precious moments outside the settlement before the approach of the morning alarms. There was a deep closeness growing between them, and both of them felt it. Together they had made a decision that no Alpha had imagined possible and that, until now, they could not have imagined themselves. But Natasha, peering into the morphing shapes of the dark forest, was thinking other, private thoughts too, ones that even Raj would find shocking. Because now that the danger had passed, Natasha could sense again those unsettling feelings that defied all reason, and that had, on this night, disrupted even her own understanding of herself: first, a bursting sense of joy when Axel told her she belonged to them, and second, the crushing loneliness when Raj had said (as Jeffrey had said so many times before) that the Tribespeople were tricksters, and that their claim on her could not possibly be true.

13

I f Mercedes experienced any of the fears that Natasha and Raj had felt when Axel first demanded a nova, she did not show it.

"It's brilliant," she said, as she yanked the helmet from Raj's bio-suit in the Office of Exit. "We talked about ways to destroy the novas but we never came up with much, did we? Nothing that didn't involve blowing up the whole settlement. We didn't have the courage to think of smuggling the novas Outside."

"You never had the means either," Natasha pointed out, dropping her airfilter and shimmying out of her biosuit with Mercedes's help. "We'll have fifty Pines carrying the novas to the ocean, and we'll have their boat. Plus I'm the only one with access to the Exit."

That evening, Natasha learned that Ben, Eduardo, and Sarah were equally committed to helping the Tribe. The six of them met in Mercedes's sleeproom, a single on level five. Now that Natasha was part of their group, and actively conspiring against the Office of Mercy, they all had thought it too risky to continue meeting in the conference rooms. They needed to prevent a transfer—something along the lines of what had happened to Raj—from happening to Natasha. Besides, as Ben had informed them, for he was the one responsible for planning their meetings, the conference rooms were too crowded these days. A new volunteer committee had begun planning a two-year education program for the Zetas. The Governing Club was drafting a new set of addenda to the Ethical Code for submission to the Alphas. And, on top of all that, the Philosophers were working double-time, believing themselves tantalizingly close to a new p's and q's logic proof that would ensure once and for all the rationality of the Post-Storm sweeps. ("I'd like to see that one," said Sarah.)

Mercedes's sleeproom was barely large enough to hold them. Mercedes and Eduardo sat on the floor, Raj stood leaning against the door, and Sarah, Ben, and Natasha sat squeezed together on the bed, their heads resting against the wall. They were exhausted, none of them had slept in the last twenty hours, but still, the talk was lively. Natasha explained to the group how the Tribe had attempted to trick her. She was glad she did; none of them made her feel embarrassed, not even when she confessed the degree to which they had convinced her.

"Isn't the rumor that Jeffrey Montague got tricked by the Palms?" Eduardo asked, once Natasha had finished her story.

"Yes," she answered. "But he's never told me more than that. It's not even clear anymore who started that fire."

Natasha rubbed her hands over her knees. The mention of Jeffrey's name made her anxious, though no one seemed to notice but Raj, who regarded her with curiosity.

"But still," Eduardo said, "the point is, it just goes to show you how good they are, if they managed to trick the best in your Office."

"That's true," Natasha said slowly. She had not made that connection till now. Jeffrey was a hero in the Office of Mercy, and *he* was not above the trickery of the Tribes. Plus he never acted ashamed about what had happened—secretive, yes, but not embarrassed.

The talk moved to their more immediate problems: whether the Tribe could be trusted, and, if so, how to go about sneaking a nova out of the settlement. On this first point, Raj once again managed to make the whole situation cogent and clear. The Pines claimed they did not believe in murder, and to date they had killed zero people. They had not killed when they had come as the "Palms," and they had not harmed Natasha even when they had her bound and weaponless, deep in the caves. The citizens, on the other hand, both openly professed themselves to be "mercy killers" and, true to their word, had murdered 146,990 people, on top of the millions they took responsibility for during the Storm.

"The Alphas teach us to see from a depersonalized perspective," Raj said. "Well, from that vantage point, if *our* goal is to preserve human life, I think it's clear who we should trust."

The second point, however, how to physically deliver a nova to the Tribe, had no easy answer. The Tribe wanted to meet them again, but exterior work on the New Wing would be finished soon, and the sensors would be back on in the green. Presumably Natasha, though she could not disable the alarms entirely, could at least silence them from the Office of Mercy. But this plan itself had two problems: first, it would mean Natasha would have to stay back, and no one liked that, considering she was their main liaison to the Pines; and, second, Natasha worked only the morning- and afternoonshifts, and there was no way for the others to go strolling down the Department of the Exterior hall in the middle of the day with a nova in their arms. Finally, there was the issue of getting into the Strongroom—a thick-walled room at the very tip of the Department of the Exterior, geographically the farthest point from the Dome—where the novas were locked away. Natasha did not have access, and she knew of only four people who did: Arthur, Jeffrey, Claudia, and one man from the Maintenance Office who handled the upkeep of the launchpad. Probably a whole host of engineers had access, but that group was constantly changing as people moved from project to project.

"So much secrecy," Mercedes said with a sigh, once they had talked themselves into circles. "But secrecy can only last so long. As soon as the Pines come into the settlement with a nova, that's it. We'll have to let them through the Office of Exit, and show them the way down the hall—"

"You're saying we might be conspicuous?" Ben asked.

"Think about it," Mercedes said. "Even if we pull it off perfectly, even if we manage to get the novas out of the Strongroom and all the way to the ocean without anything going wrong—"

"No one blowing up, you mean," said Eduardo.

"Well, then what?" Mercedes continued. "What's going to happen to us? The other citizens will despise us. They'll turn on us for good. And the Alphas—"

"The Alphas don't believe in punishment," said Sarah. "Only reeducation."

"For willing members of the social group," added Natasha, finishing the full quotation from the Ethical Code.

"Exactly," said Mercedes. "Look, I'm still in. I believe in putting an end to murder and I'm willing to risk everything for it. But this could be it for us. They could throw us out of the settlement."

After a long quiet, Raj looked at Natasha and then at the others, a gleam in his eye.

"The Pines already consider Natasha a member of the Tribe," he said. "Maybe they'll extend the invitation to the rest of us."

They all had to laugh at this, covering their mouths and ducking their heads to muffle the noise. The absurdity was almost too much to bear: not only the absurdity of an America-Five citizen joining a Tribe, but more, the absurdity that such a future actually existed within the realm of the possible.

In contrast to the complete upheaval of Natasha's life during her leisure hours, her shifts in the Office of Mercy could not have been going more smoothly. Ever since Jeffrey had found out about her continued sessions with Neil Gershman, his behavior toward her had totally changed. Their team had returned to searching for Pines, and satellite duty had shifted back to one of the lesser-ranked teams near the front of the room. Once again, just like before the mission, Jeffrey arranged the schedule so that he and Natasha had most of their shifts together. He would often find excuses to roll around to Natasha's side of the cubicle, and together they would compare notes about a fuzzy image the sensor had caught, or discuss (as everyone did in the Office these days) the impossibility of the Pines' remaining hidden much longer. But it was different between them too. The events of the last three months seemed to have broken some invisible barrier that had always existed between them. As if all the recent chaos—Natasha's abduction, their confrontation on the night of the Crane Celebration, the threat from the Pines—had jiggled loose the stays on a Wall that Natasha had hardly known was there. Jeffrey seemed more comfortable around her, and more comfortable publicly sharing her company. Instead of lurking around the Office of Mercy after his shifts, he now would openly invite Natasha to spend the lunchhour or dinnerhour with him; and a few times, they even took an evening walk side-by-side in the Garden, something they had never done before.

The attention warmed Natasha's heart and overtook her thoughts to an almost unhealthy degree. She could forget the rest of her life when she was with Jeffrey. Her distress over what the Pines had done, how they had tricked her, how they had lied, drifted away in his presence. Her worry over how to get the Tribe a nova felt less urgent when he was there. At the same time, though, Natasha comprehended the danger of what she was doing. Here she was conspiring against the Office of Mercy, making deals with a Tribe, and breaking the most fundamental, Alpha-laid laws of the settlement, and who was she cozying up to? Who was she bringing closer and closer into her life? Jeffrey Montague. The Alpha favorite. The driving force in the Office of Mercy. The man who had singlehandedly swept more Tribespeople than any person in America-Five. Natasha could not waver in her duty to the Pines, and she could not stop seeing Jeffrey, and so she would walk with forced calm beside him in the Garden, listening while he talked about the abstract nature of the Ethical Code, her stomach clenched against the looming danger of her own deceptions.

"Old societies," Jeffrey was telling her one quiet evening, arriving at one of their usual subjects, "would talk for centuries and centuries— millennia even—about the possibility of eternity. They would write about it in stories and debate its availability for one type of person or another. Meanwhile, they were dying off in generational masses. For all their careful thoughts and complex considerations, for all their energy and imagination, they never seized wholeheartedly on the idea that the best place in which to herald in eternal life was within the realm of the living."

"Why didn't they?" Natasha asked, anxious to keep their conversation on these general, highly theoretical concepts. "Wasn't it obvious that the goals of society should be world peace and eternal life?"

"They didn't have their ethical priorities straight," Jeffrey said. "For instance, if you look more closely at Pre-Storm systems, it becomes clear that their most cherished ethical decrees served one of two purposes. The first was to maintain social order, and the second was to create a false sense of control over the natural world. Some ethical values served both purposes at once."

"Like what?" asked Natasha.

They had turned onto one of the narrow footpaths that dipped behind the row of trees, the high, latticed, and vine-covered wall rising on their right. Three little birds skipped away and took flight at their approach, and a large, bright green beetle flickered into the grass.

"Well, like sexual rules, for example," Jeffrey said. "It used to be that sexual relationships were sanctioned by whatever government or authority had power at the time."

"But that's private!" Natasha said. "That's only between the people involved."

Natasha glanced furtively at Jeffrey, expecting him to look as embarrassed as she felt; to her surprise, though, his expression was calm and his face retained its usual pallor.

"Now it is," he said, "because our government doesn't require any method of control beyond its own, self-evident logic. And we as citizens don't have to believe any illusions about our bodies. We control them. We control our own fate."

Jeffrey and Natasha reached the back wall of the Garden, and the floral sun that had been built for the Crane Celebration. They walked in silence until they reached the long, eastside wall and could slip behind a row of trees again. Casually, as though it were nothing, Jeffrey reached over and took Natasha's hand, lacing his fingers through hers.

In general, it was not such a meaningful gesture to take the hand of another person. Natasha and Raj had held hands in the woods, and Natasha had affectionately clasped hands with plenty of Epsilons over the years. But between her and Jeffrey, it was different. Natasha's heart beat hard, and she felt like time itself had become thick and slow. Even after they had reconciled, Natasha had not anticipated that Jeffrey would touch her like this, not after the disaster in his sleeproom. But here he was, squeezing her palm, gazing at her like there was nothing in America-Five that he cared about more.

As they continued down the path, Natasha's senses took in everything, startled by the surge of life in her veins. The call of birds through the branches, the delicate fall of two brown-fringed leaves, the measure of her steps next to Jeffrey's, the calm of the widening shadows as the diffuse light of evening died away—all of it touched with a fresh, vibrant aspect. She was acutely aware, too, of the tones and colors of her own feeling; how her happiness spread calm and bright like rippling waves over every surface, and also how, though she wished to deny it, a heavy sadness lay at the center of it all.

Sadness, yes, it was there, drawing in her joy with its pull. It had to be. Because Natasha had realized in this moment that Jeffrey might actually love her, and also that she might love him; and yet, in this near-perfect culmination of years of close friendship, their minds had never been so far apart.

She had lied to him, and she was lying to him now. And, worst of all, he did not in the very least suspect her. Her meetings with Neil Gershman were an act, and he believed it. Her regret for her actions during the mission and her acquiescence to his ethical views were manufactured, and he did not suspect a thing. How was it possible? Hadn't he always said that she was a terrible liar? He used to sense the most subtle upsets in her mood, her fears and her quiet desires. He had known when she was having a bad day in school or when her night-mares had kept her awake, however she might have denied it. Once she had grown up and taken the job in the Office of Mercy, he would notice—he and no one else—the certain times when she struggled to keep up the Wall.

At first, Natasha had been so proud of herself for fooling Jeffrey, but now that feeling was gone. She certainly did not wish Jeffrey would discover what she was hiding—but still, *but still*, it made her miserable. A whole other set of concerns existed in her head now, the concerns of the Tribe, and she could not share that with him. She hated that their minds had so diverged, and (though she knew she was being unfair) she was angry with Jeffrey, disappointed in him even, that he could not guess the truth.

They passed into a shadowy area enclosed by the long, delicate vines of a willow tree. A little bird chirped overhead, rotating its thick neck and showing a glimmer of blue-orange iridescence. It felt like they weren't in the settlement at all, in such a private and uncornered spot. A small, white tuft of pollen floated by Natasha's ear. Then a slight pressure on her arm made her stop. Jeffrey was looking at her, at all of her, with a focus that would have seemed more appropriate directed at a computer screen in the Office of Mercy. She did not real-ize what he was planning to do before he did it. His chin dipped and his lips met hers. It felt wonderful and strange, and so different, so much more deliberate and tender than the kiss in his sleeproom. His hands rubbed upward along her sides, but before their embrace could deepen, Natasha pulled back.

"Was that okay?" he said. He did not seem worried though; gladness and triumph lifted his voice.

"I think so," Natasha answered.

She reached out and took his hand and they started walking again. She was grateful the path was so dim; she felt sure that her face was flushed pink.

"This doesn't need to lead to any next steps," he said, after a pause, "if you don't want it to."

"I'm confused," she confessed.

The sadness that had been at Natasha's core was rising to the surface, but she watched the smooth dirt path at her feet, raked into lines by some fastidious worker that afternoon, and willed herself not to let her feelings show.

"I can understand that," Jeffrey said. "And there's so much going on right now, with the Pines out there and the Zetas coming." He held her hand tightly. "The last thing I want is to upset you."

"Okay," she said. But it was no good, the sadness was coming. "I really love you, you know," she burst out, as if those words alone had the power to make things right.

"Of course," he said. "And I love you."

In the following days, Natasha and Jeffrey continued to meet after the dinnerhour, only they did not keep to the usual public areas, and the intimacy between them did not stay hovering around handholding and kisses. They convened in Jeffrey's sleeproom, leaving the Dining Hall at discreet intervals, careful to signal each other with no more than a fleeting glance. Jeffrey would board the elephant first and Natasha would follow minutes later. He would greet her at the door, having listened for her footsteps in the hall, and then he would say, "Hello, beautiful," and draw her in with him, kicking the door closed on the vacant hall. Early on they kept the lamp off and stayed to the bed, clutching each other and speaking in quick whispers, as if they were two kids in a dormitory, afraid of getting caught by their teachers. And yet, as the nights passed without the faintest indication of rumor or recourse, they grew more reckless, and cared less about who might hear them. The walls were thin, yes, and people were nosy, but stranger things had happened than this.

Besides, the truth was that Natasha could not have stopped if she'd tried. It would have been impossible to stop. The more they possessed each other, the wilder her desire grew, as if they were passing through a finite dream of ultimate pleasure and happiness, a dream they could live out hungrily but could not save. Certainly the precariousness of Natasha's situation within the settlement prevented her from taking any kiss or touch for granted. But Jeffrey appeared to feel it too; the same looming knowledge seemed to energize them both. Natasha felt this desperation, this threat of disaster and future aloneness not yet come to pass, and she struggled against it with her whole body, she raged against it with ravenous force.

Jeffrey's sleeproom could not contain them, and they began to meet in other places: a latched stall in the level six shower room, the empty Office of Air and Energy during the noontime shift change. One evening they returned to the Garden, only this time they stayed past the first dimming of the overhead lights. In the shadowy recesses of the oak trees, several feet from the path and hidden from view, Jeffrey pressed her back against the rough trunk of a broad sycamore tree and took her there—their prote-pants kicked under the bare soles of their feet—with only the birds as witness.

When Natasha returned to her sleeproom that night, still brushing bits of leaves and bramble off her shirt, she found Min-he waiting for her, filled with anxious gossip about the New Wing.

"It's official," Min-he said, springing up from her wallcomputer as soon as Natasha had entered the room. "The Zetas have outgrown their phase-two incuvats. About half of them weigh over three pounds now, and if they're not transferred within the next fourteen days, the medworkers say they might experience developmental damage. The Alphas are mad, and Cameron Pacheco is an absolute wreck. I don't think he's slept in a week. They're saying they still need more workers. I heard from my Director that Cameron asked for a list of all nonessential personnel—people he could draft to make temporary construction teams. In the Archives, that's basically everyone, so I'm guessing I'm on the list. Did you hear anything like that from Arthur? I guess the Office of Mercy will have to hold some people back, but they might send the Epsilons first."

"Yeah," said Natasha.

"Oh, Arthur told you?"

"No. I mean, no. I hadn't heard anything."

"It would be fun, though, don't you think? I wouldn't mind if it's only a week or so. I think it's healthy to have a little workplace variety."

"Sure," Natasha said. "Well, I think I'm going to take a shower."

"You took one last night."

"I was in the Garden, though. I feel kind of dusty."

"You were with Jeffrey again, weren't you?" Min-he said with a smirk. "I knew it. You practically ran out of the Dining Hall when you saw him leave."

"We had plans to meet at nineteen hundred," Natasha said shortly.

"What's going on between you two? I never run into you during leisure hours anymore. Has he been sneaking you off to empty storagerooms or something? I bet he has access."

"No, nothing like that," Natasha objected, dismayed by how closely Min-he had guessed the truth. "Jeffrey's very conscious of what the Alphas advise."

"Except for starting romantic relationships with people outside his generation, for reasons possibly other than what the Alphas condone. I mean, honestly, Natasha, is your partnership truly based on fully empathetic grounds?"

"Of course."

"I'm just saying . . . you're an Epsilon and he's a Gamma. Your life experience is different, which makes it more difficult to create that sort of bond. There've been very few cross-generational partnerships, you know, for precisely that reason. You can look it up in the Archives, we keep track of the sleeproom assignments." Min-he raised her eyebrows. "Don't you think it's possible that he might be letting down his Wall, giving in to prerational instincts? Your body fits the ratios that people used to glorify in women during Pre-Storm times. Bust to waist to hips. It sends signals about sexual vitality, or something like that."

"Where do you come up with this stuff, Min-he?"

"You can read about it for yourself if you want. It's all in the Archives."

"I'm not going to read about it because that's not what's going on between me and Jeffrey," Natasha replied, her voice rising. "Age isn't always the most important thing. You're underestimating the power of empathy if you think so. Just because we don't have as many shared experiences as people of the same generation doesn't mean we can't form a deep connection. Look at our interests. How we both chose to work in the Office of Mercy. How we're interested in the Outside and how we like to discuss the Ethical Code."

"Okay, okay, I believe you!" Min-he said, putting her hands up. She plopped down on her pillow and gave a sudden, cheerful laugh. "Oh, Mother, I'm going to lose you, aren't I? I can see it already. They'll probably move in Hasmira or someone. Everyone knows that she snores."

"I'm not moving out."

"Aren't you going to apply for a couples' sleeproom?"

"No," Natasha said emphatically, turning her back on Min-he while she unfastened her shirt and her slightly wrinkled prote-pants and changed into her robe.

Min-he, who was usually good at backing off before the two of them got into any real arguments, only smirked in response, then returned to talking about the New Wing. Natasha was hardly listening, though, because she was still thinking of Jeffrey.

Truthfully, the idea of living in a couples' sleeproom with him had occurred to Natasha many times, and only the more pressing matter of the Tribe had kept her from plotting ways to suggest it. She thought she would like that. Lying beside him every night. Sharing a closeness that excluded all but their own two bodies. That would crush the distance her secrets continued to force between them. That would cure Natasha of her worries and confusion; after all, despite what the Alphas said, what were things like settlement rules and the Ethical Code compared with two people living as one? After the Pines, Natasha thought, her heart pounding and her fantasies loud in her head. After they figured out some way to get the novas to the ocean and after the Tribes were finally safe. She had to trust that Jeffrey would still love her then, no matter what she had done. She believed—she *had* to believe—that his loyalty to her would trump his loyalty to the settlement, that he would stand by her side.

By the time Natasha returned from the shower room, her damp hair tied up in a towel, Min-he was asleep. Natasha got into her own bed and huddled against the wall, the events of that evening still playing in her mind. A part of her remained shocked that she and Jeffrey were together at all. She would think, "Jeffrey loves me," and her mind would work to grasp such a strange occurrence as fact. It reminded Natasha of her contact with the Pines, how she struggled both in the moment of meeting them and afterward to convince herself that what had actually happened had happened. Her eyes closed and her breathing slowed. She could hardly tell the difference these days: the divide between real and pretend.

14

Because of Min-he's warning, Natasha was not as surprised as she might have been when she woke the next day to a flashing message on her wallcomputer: "Report to New Wing at 0800 for morning and afternoonshifts. Shifts in the Office of Mercy are canceled until further notice."

Min-he had the same instructions and, as they learned at breakfast, so did nearly every other Epsilon and a good portion of the older generations too. But not Jeffrey.

Natasha found him in the crowded Dome, on his way to the Department of the Exterior. The Alphas had assigned him double shifts in the Office of Mercy, putting his and Natasha's schedules into absolute conflict, and forcing their meet-ups, at least for now, to a halt.

"Just until we finish the wing," Jeffrey told her. He was being brave, but Natasha could hear the pain in his voice.

"Sure," said Natasha, matching his tone. "Small price to pay for the betterment of America-Five."

She smiled, though she had already felt it—the flicker of fear that what she had with Jeffrey was too precarious, that it would not survive a break.

"Shouldn't take too long," Jeffrey said. "And then we'll get our shifts together again in the Office of Mercy. I promise. You'll be sick of me, you'll see me so much."

Natasha laughed a little and they said a quick goodbye, both wanting to say more but unable. What they had together was private, and this was not the moment to change that.

He squeezed her wrist, pressing the veins under her skin with his thumb.

"Have fun in construction," he said.

Natasha flushed. "I will."

She watched him go. A trumpeting of new voices emerged from the elephant, and the bodies crossed the Dome before her. Finally she turned and joined the swelling crowd at the entrance to the New Wing.

The temporary airlock still separated the Dome from the construction area. The workers did not need full biosuits, as they would not be coming into direct contact with any natural elements; however, because they were still building the exterior walls, they did need masks and airfilters. Wires hung from the ceiling and the piping systems overhead cut off abruptly, needing their next fittings. The sound of zippy hammers and electron saws echoed in the massive chamber, and at the center of the room were eighty-three cylindrical and dome-topped vats, the incuvats for the third phase of the Zetas' prebirth development. The incuvats were empty of fluids now, and about ten citizens were fiddling with their electrical systems, installing small generators through open panels in the base. Other citizens were adjusting intricate webs of tubing that connected the clear, bubblelike interiors to the pipes on the ceiling. The bubbles were where the Zetas would go, and from where they would emerge to take their first breaths—if only the citizens could get this wing ready in time.

Cameron Pacheco did indeed look as if he had lost several pounds; his round, usually cheerful face was wan and tensed, and he was dashing from one area to another, determined to check every bolt and section of wire that went into the walls. He had all the labor he needed now. Though except for his core construction team and the Electricity and Piping crews (of which Raj was a member), everyone was under-trained and out of their depth, and required thorough and detailed instructions before they could even begin to help.

Natasha joined a team working ten feet off the ground on a long scaffold, bolting a row of metal panels into place. Originally, the open strip in the wall was supposed to receive a series of colored glass windows—each depicting a scene of everyday life in the settlement—though with the work so rushed, such extravagances would have to wait. It was one of the more difficult jobs; the panels were heavy and cumbersome, and required a person on each side to hold them in place while a third person (usually Natasha) drilled. Natasha worked hard, and she thought she was doing a pretty good job until Dalton Tulis, the construction worker in charge of this project, noticed she was using 3.5-centimeter bolts instead of the standard 6-centimeter and, nicely suppressing his own frustration, handed her a pair of zippy pliers to undo her work from the entire morning.

Natasha was down on the floor sorting through the supply bins (more carefully this time) when she noticed Raj. He was sitting on the lowest rung of a ladder, taking a break with several others. A group of three men from Electricity and Piping passed by.

"Hey, what's this?" one of them snapped at Raj. "Think you're too good to work for the Zetas?"

Raj did not answer, but sat calmly, looking straight ahead.

"He doesn't think he's too good for the Zetas, he thinks he's too good for Electricity and Piping," a second man said. "Had a bit of an attitude, haven't you? Ever since they sent you down from the Archives."

"I hate the Archives," the third man said. "I hate anyone who doesn't work to keep this place running."

(He'll get a course of reeducation for that, Natasha thought automatically. Every Office keeps the settlement running.)

Raj still would not respond, and so the third man, with a grunt of anger, kicked Raj's hardhat, which was resting near the foot of the ladder, so that it skidded across the floor.

Cameron Pacheco and Walker O'Reilly, who headed Electricity and Piping, descended upon the group in seconds.

"What's going on here?" Walker asked.

"This traitor is slacking off again," said the first man, pointing to Raj. "And the rest of us are getting sick of it."

"My group just finished installing the eighth yard of piping," said Raj, willing to speak at last. "We agreed to take a break before starting the next set." Raj was standing now, but he looked very alone. The other men and women on his team had returned to their task, and none were coming to his defense.

"Well, we can't have that," Cameron said. "Maybe you haven't noticed, but we're all working hard to get this thing done. Whatever views you hold against the collective goals of the settlement, please, this is not the time for a protest."

Natasha could not believe the injustice of it, especially because she had never known Cameron to be anything but kind and fair-minded. Now practically everyone in the New Wing was glaring at Raj, muttering in low voices to nearby citizens, their faces under their visors screwed into expressions of bitter disgust.

"But he was only taking a break!" Natasha said. "He's been working just like the rest of us."

The glares of the citizens shifted to her, and Natasha went silent. Raj, in his steadiness, in his own silence, was warning her not to continue; and, amid a group near the airlock, the eyes of Ben and Sarah jumped out at her, anxiously urging the same.

"We don't have time for this," Walker said. "My crew, I want you focused, now."

Heads turned back to the tasks at hand, and the clamor and movement of construction started again.

Only hours later did Natasha have the chance to talk to Raj, allowing him to intercept her at the supply bins.

"I'm sorry," Natasha said in a hushed voice. "I shouldn't have spoken up, it was stupid."

"They'll forget," Raj said. "It's you I'm worried about."

"Me?"

"It's going to get worse, Natasha, much worse, if we do what we're planning. I'm used to this, I honestly don't care how they treat me. But you need to understand how much things will change for you. Everyone, all your friends, they're going to turn against you. They're going to hate you."

Their eyes met briefly over the bin of silver washers, and then they both looked quickly down. Natasha wondered if Raj knew about Jeffrey. She considered assuring him that she had thought through all the possible repercussions already, personal and professional both, but decided against it. That was no one's business but her own.

"Nothing will change if we can't find a way out of this settlement," Natasha said instead.

"No breaks on your end, then?"

"I keep coming back to the same problem. I need to be in the Office of Mercy to shut off the alarms on the green. But then, even if I let you out of the settlement and stay back myself—"

"Someone will see us sneaking into the Office of Exit," Raj finished. "And we still can't get into the Strongroom. Well," he said, after a pause, "I'm working on something too. It's difficult, and it could only work once."

"We only need once."

"They'll kick me out if they catch me . . . if not worse. Honestly, I don't know what they'd do."

"If it's good, then it's worth it," Natasha said. "It's worth the risk."

"Later," Raj said, lowering his head. "People are looking."

Construction on the New Wing kept the days full, and Natasha did little else but eat, sleep, hammer, drill, and return to her sleeproom too exhausted to miss Jeffrey or worry about the Tribe. Several more times she witnessed Raj getting bullied by other members of Electricity and Piping, but she did not dare to speak up again. She noticed, too, when Sarah got snubbed by the other workers from Health during lunch, and when three Deltas deliberately turned their backs on Eduardo after he'd asked for help snapping one of the new incuvats into place. It will be worse, Raj had said, and Natasha believed it. If this was payback for holding "antisettlement" views, then she could hardly imagine the citizens' fury when she and the others betrayed America-Five and the Alphas outright.

As it turned out, the extra push did the trick. After eleven days of nearly nonstop labor, the New Wing—though it was not really complete—was at least in good enough shape for the transfer. Natasha stood in the crowd just inside the New Wing doors, waiting to get her first glimpse of the new generation. Raj, Mercedes, Eduardo, Sarah, and Ben were nowhere to be found, and Natasha wondered if they had skipped the event in an act of peaceful defiance. Part of her wished she could have skipped it too.

The Office of Reproduction scientists, all sporting long white lab coats and proud smiles, wheeled in the first tiny Zetas one by one. The new generation did not look like much—just pale, large-headed blobs floating in a slightly cloudy liquid. Their thin limbs curled against their bodies and a long, fleshy, purplish cord connected them to the base of their now too small, phase-two incuvats.

Zeta followed Zeta and everyone sighed in awe and applauded. Arthur whistled, eliciting cheerful admonishments from those around him. Min-he and two other women from the Archives were making a big show of themselves, holding their hands over their hearts and sighing long "*awww*s" every few minutes. Jeffrey, on the opposite side of the New Wing doors from Natasha, was more subdued, standing with his hands clasped behind his back, though he was certainly just as enthralled as the others. At one point near the middle of the long procession, Natasha glanced over at Eric, who stood next to her, and was surprised to see tears in his eyes.

"You're really excited about this!" she said, taken aback.

"Yeah, I am," Eric answered, wiping his face with the collar of his sleeve. "It's spectacular, bringing all these people into existence. Don't you feel it? Don't you feel how amazing it is?"

"I don't know," Natasha said. "I guess with everything going on I hadn't thought about it much. With the construction so rushed, and the Pines still out there . . ."

She trailed off, but Eric's posture stiffened. Up until now, Natasha had been careful to avoid making any references to Eric about the Tribes, except when absolutely necessary.

"Well, you can't help thinking about them," she whispered. "We have no right to be producing more generations with so many people suffering out there."

"Can I give you a piece of advice?" Eric asked, his voice dry. "Don't love anything on the Outside."

"Do you love them?" Natasha quickly countered. "The Zetas?"

"Not yet, but I'm starting to. Look at that little guy."

Eric pointed to the incuvat passing by, where inside a male Zeta, his eyes tightly closed and his minuscule hands balled into fists, was turning somersaults in the gently undulating fluid. Eric laughed, joining an amused chorus of several others. But it was impossible. The citizens' thoughts did not extend beyond the walls of the settlement; Natasha could not feel what they felt.

As the transfer continued, her thoughts drifted back to earlier that morning, when one of the Betas had posted the projected rankings for American settlement population growths. It was an act clearly motivated by prideful and competitive feelings, and Natasha was shocked that the Alphas had allowed it. Perhaps the old ones had thought the numbers would boost morale and, granted, for most people, they did. In two months, assuming the healthy birth of all eighty-three members of the Zeta generation, and the clean, successful sweep of the Pine Tribe, America-Five would soon lead the continent in both Tribespeople swept and settlement population. For Natasha, there was a terrible sickness in the symmetry of those numbers. Why can't we take in Tribespeople instead of making new generations? She had asked once and she would ask again; especially now that she felt sure, more sure than ever before, that no one—not Jeffrey or Arthur or even the Alphas—could give an acceptable answer.

Finally, the scientists declared the transfer complete. They stepped away to reveal four rows of Zetas, all floating lethargically in their new, slightly larger homes. Natasha watched them turn and bob. The Zetas had not asked to be created, or asked *not* to be created. A series of infinitely complex events had conspired to bring them into their present state of existence, and here they were—here and here and here—from airy possibility to flesh and blood and bone. Natasha's heart strained in their presence. She felt the pull toward them and the yearning to give them the unadulterated love that every innocent creature deserved—but Natasha felt distant from them too. She resented their luck, a luck they did not know they had, in coming to life in America-Five and not in the Outside.

Applause swelled from the crowd, and several speeches followed, but Natasha did not hear a word. She grabbed her own wrist at the place where, days ago, Jeffrey had touched her last. There was an anger growing within her, anger and resentment and a bitterness that she could not control. She knew something. She knew what she had never allowed herself to know. Her breaths came quick and shallow, and when she closed her eyes, she saw fire.

• • •

The smell of smoke wafted through the trees, rich and unmistakable. But it was wrong; it was not the comforting sensation it should have been, not the harbinger of warmth for the long night or a feast of meat about to fill their bellies. Instead the smoke was ominous, a sign of a danger too great and too big and too hot to control. The smell pervaded all. It saturated leaves and clothing and wrapped between the moving bodies. This smoke was a bad smoke; the smoke of a bad fire that would consume the trees and rabbits and deer and climb the hills and stop only when it hit the ocean.

Natasha cowered, clutching tightly around the neck of the man who carried her. She was small; gravity hardly pulled on her, and her sweaty, clumsy little fingers could not keep their hold on one another.

In a flicker of thought, Natasha knew it was really quite odd, her smallness. Only four or five times had Natasha ever experienced a simulation at an age different from her actual one—and never had she asked the computer to situate her perspective so far back in her youth. But this was Free Play. She had not directly asked for anything. She had come into the Pod with a mind of hot and jumbled emotions, and now the computer was reading her thoughts—thoughts too deep for Natasha to name. Though it was also true that Natasha knew these images and feelings, that she recognized them as *hers* as soon as they leapt into life before her wakeful senses.

She held on tight, squeezing her legs around the man's torso, her chin knocking against his hard shoulder as they moved. She tasted the smell, and yet she saw no flame lighting the brown-green mesh of forest from where they had come with such hurry.

A question sounded from her own self in a voice that was hers and yet not hers, because it had a highness and ungainliness that she must have shed long ago.

"Where is the fire?"

No one answered, though many people swarmed around her now: women with their lips stretched back in gummy shouts of fear, the babies strapped to their backs wailing and slipping by at eye level; hearing them cry made Natasha cry too.

The forest was quiet and then it was loud and then it was fast. They were running, running from the smell. Natasha's chin knocked hard, making her teeth crash together. From where they had come, there were others; fear made their faces long and tight and their legs weak so that sometimes a pair of eyes would be looking ahead and then the eyes would be down in the dirt. Others banged against their sides, crushing Natasha's legs.

She wanted to stop. She pushed around and saw the sharp gray-green cliffs that shot up to the sky. The people were trying to climb the cliffs, but that was silly, they had never climbed them before. Here in this valley, they slept on clear nights with the stars white pricklings in the black that shimmered *hello hello* if you looked for long and lay still.

She could taste the smoke in her throat; she coughed. She did not like the scrape of bodies climbing the cliffs and falling limp-limbed to the ground, and she did not like the screaming. The smoke arrived now, lazy and billowing black against the sky; and then she could see the bright orange, brighter than sky, winking at her through slats in the forest.

There. She pointed and spoke its presence without words. Two hands grabbed her around the middle, the familiar hands of a woman but not her mother—because her mother was gone with the other mothers and fathers to fight—these arms held her and rocked her back and forth.

But the fire was coming closer now and Natasha wanted to see; it was a bad fire to run around on its own, all the good fires stayed in one place and never wanted to eat the trees.

When the bodies pressed back, Natasha slipped out of the arms and landed on her open hands and knees. She scampered fast over the feet and legs that kicked and kept moving until she got away from them, but it was still hot.

The fire glared and the trees were torches. There was no place to go that would not be hot and then her body shook and shook and she coughed and she looked up to find the sky between the smoke. All she wanted was for the blue sky to reach down and lift her away. She raised her face to the blue, pleading for the white clouds to reach down and cradle her in their grasp.

And then the arms came, long and white from above. Arms like clouds; they grabbed her and she was flying over the tops of the flames. Her cheek pressed against something cool and soon the trees circled around her again; and she could breathe easily now, and she held on to run away from the fire.

The world faded to black. A bang sounded behind her. Natasha hung suspended in the quiet as the soft blue glow slowly illuminated the Pod. Three bangs now, muffled by the thick door, but insistent.

Natasha had just finished unbuckling herself from the harness when the door rose up and two people ducked inside.

"Sorry," Sarah said, in a breathless voice, closing the door behind her. "We couldn't wait any longer."

"I hope we didn't put your mind into shock," Eduardo said. "Did we?" he asked, examining her. "You look a little shaky."

"No—no, I'm fine," Natasha said. "I was out of the simulation already. What's the matter?"

Eduardo's face brightened. "Raj has a plan. He says he can get all of us out of the settlement."

"All of us?" Natasha repeated. "What about the sensors on the green?"

"Oh, they'll be off," Eduardo said.

"Everything will be off," added Sarah.

Natasha shook her head, not following their logic.

"Ever since we first met with you," Eduardo said, with giddy hurriedness, "Raj has been trying to figure out a way to use his position in E and P to override your Department's security. For a while, he thought it was impossible, because he didn't have access to half the systems and, anyway, he always worked in supervised teams. Even if he managed to cut the main power somehow, he'd get caught before he made it to the backup generator."

"The backup generator delivers power to essential systems," Sarah filled in, "including the Strongroom."

"So what changed?" Natasha asked.

"Raj got promoted," Sarah said. "It's really great. It got back to the Alphas how Walker treated him during the New Wing construction, and they transferred Walker and gave Raj his position. Now Raj has full access to every room on level nine, and he controls the shifts of the other workers."

"We're going right now to Mercedes's sleeproom," Eduardo said. "At midnight, Raj is going to cut the power, and the three of us and Ben and Mercedes—we're going to steal a nova and deliver it to the Pines. And then that's it. Don't you see? Once the Pines have the nova, no one will be able to stop them. The other citizens will have to do as we say and open the Strongroom, and then we can take our time getting the novas to the ocean."

"Hey," said Sarah, squinting her eyes at Natasha, "are you sure you're all right?"

Natasha bit her lip, forcing herself to calm down, to come back to this world.

"Fine," she told Sarah. "Better than ever."

15

The spark of consciousness is all, thought Raj as he walked down the deserted corridor of level three, passing sleeprooms on his left and right. Not the convoluted rules of the Ethical Code, or the too-convenient dogmas that we are meant to live by, but only the spark—that unisolatable ineffable something that makes cold matter leap awake into that strange reality we conscious beings ourselves can neither see nor smell nor touch nor taste nor hear but for the delicate music of our own thoughts, and not even then, not even tuned in to our own breadth of feeling and embedded knowledge, not even with our own familiar hand held before our own two eyes can we hope to say, *I am this*, to say, *I am.*

Raj pressed the command for the elephant. Arrow down.

Because here is the hand, he thought, blandly wrinkled and fleshed and tipped with nail, ordinary and yet wholly inexplicable because why should it be bland and usual, why this?—and there it is again, the mystery, and that is the spark, the spark that convinces without plea or argument that it, the spark, is all, and worth preserving.

With a final glance over his shoulder, Raj stepped into the tall box of the elephant, his lips moving soundlessly as the doors closed and he began to sink deeper and deeper into the earth. The dial over the door arced from five to six to seven to eight until, with a low grind of gears, the elephant settled on level nine, the absolute base of America-Five. The doors parted open, leading him into a short, wide hallway of low, water-stained and yellowish walls. Raj knew it well; this level had become his workplace ever since his transfer from the Archives. The familiar, pungent smell of mold and engine oil met above his lip as his boots marched, as if by their own accord, to the metal grate that blocked access to the backup generator and the main power cells.

He took a ring of small, tarnished keys from his pocket and, with the one sharply grooved in the middle, he opened the lock. He heaved the grate upward with the help of its system of pulleys and chains. Almost nothing ran on computer down here; it had, at one time, but the leaks and mold had caused too many shorts of simple systems and, in the end, the engineers had backed off and allowed level nine to lapse to the technologies outdated even tens of years before the Storm.

Gingerly, Raj stepped out onto a narrow, mesh metal balcony that ringed around a deep pit, the backup generator recessed at its center. He could hear the hum, or more, feel it, rising up through his feet, through his legs, through his groin while he stood holding the thin railing at the balcony's edge. He gazed downward: the backup genera-tor, the massive cylinder that allowed citizens to sleep fearlessly at night; the backup heart lodged deep, so deep, and ready to awaken into thumping life should the main solar and wind-powered cells fail—as they would, by Raj's own hand, tonight.

The spark is all, he thought, the spark of consciousness. Only the spark in this otherwise universe of rock and aimless molecule and distance.

He took a long breath into his gut, closing his eyes, focusing, seeing without seeing. This is how it had to be done. He had tried other meth-ods, more peaceful methods, but the citizens would not stop, they refused to stop, and he could not stand by and allow them to murder more people in the name of their cool rationality, their indefectible philosophy.

He would disable the backup generator first. He had learned how to do it during his initial training sessions, in case of a fire.

With precise steps, he descended the short ladder into the pit, and soon his fingers were moving nimbly over the wires. Emergency shut-off, then cross the T with the W thread so that the reset lever will short the system. He took a pair of clippers from his pocket and hacked off a bundle of multicolored connections that he knew would take weeks to repair.

He stepped back and wiped his forehead and the back of his neck. The humming had stopped, and the new quiet affected him deeply. Did that make him a sap? he wondered. That even a mechanical death roused a feeling of sadness within him?

He turned and climbed the short ladder back to the balcony. Another key. His hands shook, and Raj observed them shaking with a kind of bemused curiosity. In all his life, his body had never behaved like this before. The door opened and he was in a room of two-by-two-foot shining metal squares, forming the walls from ceiling to floor. These were the main power cells that held the charge from the solar panels and the wind turbines outside. He opened the control box, disconnected the holds, and slashed with fury at the wires until the world disappeared and no tension remained.

Raj cried out. He had never experienced this, the complete elimination of sight. But it had worked; if there was darkness, then it had worked.

Releasing his hold on the wall, he stepped forward, waving his hands, his eyes wide and useless. His head slammed into the still-open door. He fell to his knees and his fingers found the holes of the mesh balcony. He crawled forward—the metal flooring sharp on his legs—until he had managed to slip his arms around the railing that marked the balcony's rim. There were no lights, no sound within the dark. He tried to measure his movements, 180 degrees around to the grate from where he had entered, but he could not gauge it; and anyway, now, the immensity of what he had done was enveloping him with its own kind of blindness.

On the higher levels, up in the Dome, fear would come over the citizens now. As the moments of darkness lengthened, they would gradually realize that both power systems had failed. The older ones would guess a human agency behind it, and probably many independent minds would settle on him.

But the others—Natasha, Mercedes, Eduardo, Sarah, and Ben—if they had done it, if they had broken into the Strongroom and escaped from the settlement, then nothing else mattered. Because it was all darkness, all coldness and triviality except for the sparks of life on the globe, except for their own minds to imply that some other bend of physics existed along the untouched plane. Or no, not physics, Raj corrected himself, but the dimensionless world of pure emotion. Or no, not that, but self, selfless mind, pure timelessness and simultaneity. But here the mystery covered all and the muscles of human thought could push no further. Raj's long fingers gripped the railing, his weight shifted from his toes to his heels and back again, his forehead grazing cold metal as he swayed.

"God," he said, reaching for something, an ancient concept, a future idea, the amalgamation, the spark of sparks. "God. God. God. God."

It happened fast. A series of precise movements in the chaos. Down the dark hall of the Department of the Exterior and into the Strongroom. Then, once the door had closed, Ben and Eduardo, under Natasha's directions, maneuvered a small G3 nova into a canvas sling to carry between them. Mercedes and Sarah led the group to the Office of Exit, shoving confused, wandering citizens out of the way, a task which, in the absolute darkness, was as easy as it was anonymous. ("What's going on," the voices cried after them. "Who's there?") They passed swiftly through the airlock, through the supplyhouse and up the stone stairs that glowed a hazy white-gray in the moonlight.

"We're outside," Mercedes screamed. "Alpha believe it, we're outside!"

As they jogged in an uneven mass across the green, leaving the blacked-out Dome behind them, the others answered Mercedes with their own shouts. All but Natasha. She remained fixed on their destination, and she led them with quick, confident words and careful movements through the trees and over the gnarled forest ground, eastward to the shore.

They found the Tribe, finally, about four miles south of the Crane sweep site, the orange eruption of their fire like nothing else in the night. It was difficult to say who was more timid upon first seeing the others: the Pines, who darted out from the trees and then hastily back toward the fire; or Mercedes, Eduardo, Sarah, and Ben, who were cursing under their breath with amazement, and each of whom stopped several times during the long approach down the sand, until the person walking beside them nudged them on in encouragement. When the Pines saw the nova, though, and recognized it for what it was, the atmosphere changed. Suddenly there was no doubt, no fear. The pact they had offered this group of "god-people" became tightly sealed in their minds. Now the plans were all in place, now they had what they needed to force their way into the glasshouse; and soon it would be as fate had determined, the Birds of Fire destroyed at last, the fire swallowed up by the water, and the age of terror brought to an end.

Likewise, the excitement and trust evident in the Pines served to dispel the citizens' fear. Soon Ben and Eduardo had laid the nova carefully down on a patch of high, dry sand, brushed smooth by Tezo and Mattias. And once they were free of this burden, the introductions began. Each group was wide-eyed at the mere flesh-and-blood existence of the other, amazed that, despite a difference so strong they might have hailed from different planets, as opposed to the same strip of forest, each shared the same purpose, and would reach that purpose together or not at all.

Near the fire stood Axel, Sonlow, Tezo, and Raul. Natasha had worried about what her reception would be, considering the hysterical manner in which she had left them last. But Raul appeared calm, Sonlow had an aura of hopefulness, Axel grinned openly at her, and one look at Tezo was enough to put Natasha's trepidation to rest. As soon as Natasha reached them, Tezo held his arms open. Grasping his burly shoulders, she allowed him to wrap his thick, bare arms around her. The pungent stench of his body enveloped her too, at once high and sharp with sweat and deep with the echo of brine and muddy shore; and yet, far from being disgusted, Natasha felt comforted. For the first time in a long time, she remembered the smell of home.

They could have stayed like that, quietly side by side, but Axel interrupted them.

"I was afraid we'd lost you," Axel said. "Maybe we said too much. What happened was years ago. The more years that pass, the slower the telling should be."

"No," said Natasha, standing back. "I'm glad. I needed to know."

"You believe us then?" Tezo asked softly.

"Yes," Natasha said. "I didn't right away, but mostly because it was too much to face all at once. I've spent the last twenty-two years forcing myself to forget. But I never fully forgot. I dreamed about the Outside, I feared it and I loved it too. And it was there the whole time, my connection to you."

She looked at Tezo as she spoke these last words, and received in return a second embrace, more gentle than the first.

"Have they confessed at last?" Sonlow asked. "The people who took you? Did they tell you why?"

"They didn't tell me anything," Natasha said. "But I've seen things, certain images in the settlement. It's hard to explain. There's still a memory of what happened, a kind of a memory. I've seen enough to make me believe."

The vision of the white arms reaching down to clutch her overtook her mind, the feeling so vivid that it seemed momentarily unleashed from the past.

"You remember us?" Sonlow asked.

"Only a little," Natasha answered. Her eyelids flickered as a flush of heat passed over her. "I mostly remember the fire."

"You remember your brothers and sisters? You were with them, in the beginning. Did you see what happened to them?"

"I'm sorry," said Natasha, shaking her head. "I wish I could."

"But you lived," said Sonlow. "And I will always be grateful to God for that."

Natasha did not know how to respond, how to thank Sonlow and acknowledge her as her relation. She felt it would not show proper respect to hug Sonlow as Tezo had hugged her. So she took Sonlow's soft, grimy hand in hers, brought it to her lips, and kissed it. Out of the corner of her eye, she could see Ben watching her with amazement. Eduardo and Mercedes were whispering together; and Sarah regarded her with a mixture of curiosity, pity, and awe. They must be realizing now, by her actions, Natasha's true relationship to the Tribe; that what they had as a group so easily dismissed as a trick was not a trick at all.

She, Natasha—Nassia, as they called her—was one of the Tribe, not only by belief, but by blood. These voices were her voices. This Outside was her home. And if any in the Tribe still doubted the strength of her allegiance, well, they were wasting their worry. The memory in Free Play had changed her; it had stripped away the settlement's deceit and endless justifications. Once and for all, the hypocrisy of America-Five lay bare before her: the vast destruction and death they had caused. Never could Natasha go back to being the person she had been; she knew who she was now. She had found it out despite their lies. And, amazingly, the truth was burning bright within her, giving her strength and fusing her body into one powerful whole.

Natasha gently released Sonlow's hand, feeling the love present in the old woman's gaze. Her thoughts were swirling, because here in a moment was a taste of the life that Natasha should have lived. Her real life if not for the fire and arms like clouds reaching down to deliver her into the life that she *had* lived, the wrong one. The heat came over Natasha again. Jeffrey. She could not think about Jeffrey without wanting to scream. Her body trembled as though trying to throw the arms off her, the arms that were the Dome and the Office of Mercy and the person she had become in the settlement. And she *was* throwing them off, breaking free of their hold, because she was here in the Outside and they could not stop her. She was here with her family and *he* could not stop her.

"We will be together now," Axel said, heartily. "Once we destroy the Birds, once we put an end to the murders."

"Does that mean we can show them?" London asked, pushing through to stand by Axel's side. "Can we show them the guns?"

"Yes!" said Axel, his face growing brighter. "Our friends gave us a Bird, now let's show them how we will protect it."

Raul nodded; London gave a whoop of excitement. Mercedes, Eduardo, Sarah, and Ben looked questioningly at Natasha, but Natasha only shook her head, emerging from the fog of her own thoughts. She had no idea what was coming—what weapons they had to show.

Two men hurried over to the trees, to a place still within the glow of the fire. The land rose precipitously here and two slabs of high rock lay upright against it; the men began dragging the slabs away.

Inside, though Natasha could hardly believe it, was an armory, a very ancient armory. And not only that, but a room remarkably like their own supplyhouse in both its construction and arrangement of weapons. The metal shelves were lined with guns. The Tribe poured in with their torches aloft, pushing and shoving each other down the aisles. Their hands ran along the weapons: guns that resembled LUV-3s, only bulkier and caked with rust. They fingered the crumbling leather holsters and the rotted wooden boxes of ammunition, chattering excitedly to one another and looking to the citizens for their reaction.

"How is this possible?" Sarah asked in a low voice.

"It must be a Pre-Storm construction," said Ben. "The nearer you get to the settlements, the more structures survived. We learned a little about them in school."

"I don't remember that," said Mercedes.

"Probably because our teachers didn't make a big deal about it," Ben continued. "They definitely never implied that any of these structures might still be intact. I always assumed buildings like these were totally decomposed by now."

"There're other buildings too," Natasha said. "The night I left the settlement with Eric, they took me to one. I thought it was a regular cave at first, but it didn't make sense. The room I was in had windows, like it used to be above ground. I haven't even had time to think about it. But it was weird—I thought it was weird when I saw it. There must have been a whole city right in this area once, and whatever stayed standing got buried during the Storm."

"Still, why would the Alphas leave guns outside the settlement?" asked Eduardo, raising his eyebrows. "That wasn't too smart. They should have brought all the weapons inside before the Storm began."

"No," said Ben. "I bet whoever was fighting the Alphas left the guns here. There were still people around while the Alphas were converting the old Yang bunkers into settlements, and those people probably wanted in. The Alphas were stockpiling food and animals and a thousand other necessities—of course they must have had people attacking."

Around them, the Tribespeople were loading the guns with slow but accurate movements. A second entrance revealed itself at the opposite end of the armory—marked, like the cave at their old camp, by the red-brown print of a hand. They all pushed in that direction, the citizens with them. The Tribespeople had painted a series of targets on tree trunks, each target illuminated by torches. It appeared that they practiced their aim in a similar manner to what the citizens did in the Pretends.

"Our people have known since the tragedy in our youth," Axel said to the citizens, "that we could never succeed against your glasshouse with bows and arrows and knives." He began to load a gun, dropped the cartridge, but then succeeded on his second try with surprising skill. "I told you that we have been coming back here to spy on your people for twenty-two years, that for twenty-two years we have planned our return. We envisioned it in our minds and in our dreams. Gladly any one of us would have died for that purpose. Except that we knew better. It would do no good to march on the glasshouse again, not when our goal was to save our people—to get *inside* and destroy their Birds. Then, when the first frost was melting last year, Raul, Tezo, and I made a tent against this hill, and we discovered a hollow behind it." He laughed and gestured toward the guns. "Finally we had some of the god-people's power for ourselves. It was a gift from God, and we will use it well."

He thrust the gun into Eduardo's hands.

"Here," Axel continued, "we are all together. One moon from tonight, we will sneak through the woods with these guns and the Bird. We will go to the stone stairs and you will let us inside. They will be so afraid of us, the god-people! And while they are on their knees, pleading for our benevolence, we will steal their Birds away. The ocean will swallow the Birds whole, and then we will pass through this forest whenever we please. At last, only God will have the power to make us tremble. And the god-people will be people again."

The citizens heard this speech with silent accord, accepting the pats and handshakes of the Pines around them and betraying only slight unease at the thought of Tribespeople (even self-proclaimed peaceful Tribespeople) in possession of guns. A woman draped in green cloths tapped Natasha's shoulder and handed her a weapon. They wanted Natasha to shoot at the targets, the concentric circles of white on the bark. Natasha complied; she aimed for the farthest target, a tiny white dot in the knot of an oak, barely visible in the light of the torches. She exhaled a controlled breath and pulled the trigger.

The shot rang out, and a splinter of wood burst from the center of the knot. Now a black hole marked the target like the pupil of an eye.

"Whoa," breathed London. He aimed at the same spot with his own weapon and fired. The bullet disappeared in the dark beyond the trees.

"Let me try!" Another boy rushed forward, missed, and laughed wildly at himself. He drew up the sleeves of his tunic and missed again.

Mattias shot next and hit the oak, but well below the target. The other adults took up the challenge, accepting the citizens' help when required. Natasha shifted toward the back of the crowd.

"Are all your people as good as you?" asked Raul. He was the only one without a gun. "Because if they are, they may be less terrified than we need them to be."

Shots fired haphazardly into the dark, and Natasha felt the tug of doubt.

"If everything goes according to plan," she said quickly, "there won't be shooting on either side."

"It's a very delicate plan. Are you sure, little Nassia, that you are willing to risk your wonderful life for a family you don't even remember?"

"My life can't be wonderful in the settlement," she said, "now that I know the truth. Listen," she continued firmly, "I know who I am. I'm with you now. Of course I don't want anyone to get hurt on either side. But if something goes wrong, I'm willing to turn against the citizens."

"And fight them? Shoot at them and risk their lives, if they take up arms against us?"

"I won't let them hurt you," Natasha responded, her voice breaking. "I can promise you that. The citizens have done enough harm in the last three hundred years to last them their eternity."

Raul nodded; he believed her. And for some reason, his trust mattered greatly to Natasha. She liked Raul. He seemed like a good man. A man who had suffered. She wondered if, in the landscape of his thoughts, he would forever connect her to his family's death. She could understand if he did. Because if the Tribe had not abducted her, then the team would not have initiated the manual sweep. But there was no malice in him, no anger.

"I don't know any better than you why the settlement took me," Natasha continued. "Why they chose to save me after they'd killed all the others. But no matter what they've done for me, it can't change the fact that they tried to murder me first. And for that reason, they made themselves my enemy."

The moon rose large and bright. Raj had promised twelve hours of blackout, but Mercedes, Eduardo, Sarah, and Ben felt anxious and wanted to return to America-Five. They urged Natasha to come with them, but she was not ready to go; instead, she gave her word to meet them in the Office of Exit in the hour before dawn. The group said their farewells and started across the sand, but at the last second Sarah doubled back to hug Natasha goodbye.

"Is it true?" Sarah asked, before letting go. "Do you think you were really born out here?"

Natasha nodded. "Yes."

"I know they won't hurt you," Sarah whispered, after a pause. "But you still have to be careful. We're not used to Outside dangers."

"I will," Natasha assured. "And you be careful getting home."

The Tribe returned to the beach, and Natasha with them. The tide had come in and the waves rose high and crashed on the shore, drawing back into themselves and rising again. The planet seemed to breathe and speak through the ocean.

Tezo grabbed Natasha by the hand and pulled her down the beach to the water.

"You have to go in," he said, laughing. "You haven't lived until you've felt the ocean."

At his continued insistence, Natasha took off her boots and her socks and, for the first time she could remember, felt the coldness and give of real sand under her feet. The ocean spoke. The forward drift climaxed into the roil and churn of high waves, angry and beating against the earth as if wanting to burrow into the land. Natasha stepped closer, her body tight with anticipation. She watched the mountain of water approach, tall and unstoppable. A crash, the air exploded, and then the cold struck her and climbed her body. A white spray of salty iciness awakened her face with exhilarating pain. She screamed and Tezo caught her around the waist. Behind them, the rest of the Tribe howled with laughter.

The cold was stinging her legs, but Natasha held her ground, braced against Tezo. The water was rushing back now, hard, like it wanted to drag her with it. A piece of prickly, slimy seaweed caught around her left ankle and she kicked it off in horror.

Beyond the crests of the waves, which were sharpened by the brief reflections of moonlight, the ocean fanned out into black. Natasha and Tezo stood together, looking. Cold, white stars appeared, reflecting the ocean's vastness above. How beautiful and terrifying it was! And how the emptiness seemed to creep toward them, reaching out to engulf them! Tezo let go of her and Natasha wrapped her arms over her chest, her teeth chattering. She watched and cheered as Tezo chased the waves as they receded, then raced them back to the sand.

Higher up the shore, the fire burst alive as new wood was thrust into its center. The men beat their drums and sent hollow, rhythmic cries to the moon. Natasha smiled as she listened. A song swelled up from the group and Natasha went with Tezo to join them. The Tribe knelt together around the fire. They chanted while two drummers made a rhythm that pitted a chaotic, shattering rise and fall against an ordered thud like a heartbeat.

"God watching us from above," said Hesma. "We honor You and we pray for the strength to finish the work we began when we first marched on the god-people."

"Ah-men," answered the Tribe. The words beat like the drums and the power of this curious music merged the sounds into one voice.

"You have delivered to us the child we lost. She is ours now, we pray she will be ours forever."

"Ah-men."

"We hope you *will* stay with us," Axel said, once the song had ended. "We hope you'll live with us for good."

"Yes, I want to," said Natasha, looking around at them all, feeling the strength and vivacity of this life compared with her life Inside. For a moment, Natasha forgot Raj and the others, she forgot Min-he. And as for Jeffrey—Jeffrey whose very presence had for years deceptively promised this heat, this feeling of love and belonging—Natasha spit him from her thoughts. "Once we destroy the novas," she said, "there won't be anything left for me in the settlement. I want to leave with you. I want to come home."

They slept on the beach that night and, in fitful bursts, Natasha slept too. Tezo smoothed out a place for her beside him. He rolled up a blue tunic for them to use as a pillow. The sand dug into Natasha's hair. The dampness seeped through her clothes and through her flesh to chill her bones. The hard ground made her shoulder ache. Eventually this would be normal to her. One night soon it would seem the most usual thing in the world to sleep on a bed of earth, and then the strange thing would be beds and walls and ceilings and sheets. She looked at Tezo—his face ethereal and sweet in sleep—and imagined a future that might fulfill the wishes that, according to Axel, their two mothers had dreamt up long ago. Already, the settlement was receding from her. How far away it seemed, the long white hall of the Department of the Exterior; she never wished to see the Office of Mercy again. She understood now about the importance of living over all else, and the horror of ever stealing a life from the Earth and throwing it to the abyss. How could they? How could one human being do that to another? Like what Raj had said: The citizens of America-Five could build a body, they could build a person almost from scratch. But essentially, at the most basic level, they did not understand how life worked. They tinkered and pulled molecules apart and threw them together and thought their successes good enough to shove out the mystery, that embarrassing gulf of not-knowing that lay beneath their science. All of life was beautiful; all of life was mystery; to end it was the most horrible thing in the universe. Worse than suffering. Worse than pain.

She was awake when Axel came to her and said she should go back to the settlement. Raul stood beside him, his face drawn and tired; the rest of the Tribe lay sleeping. Natasha considered waking Tezo to say goodbye, but it was no matter, she would see him soon. She followed Axel and Raul, picking her way through the slumbering bodies.

"We'll walk with you through the forest," Axel said, "to where the trees end. You might know your way around the Eyes, but we know the way around bears."

They moved in silence through the woods and across the ridge. Natasha thought about the next full moon, when Axel and Raul would take this path again, that time with the nova. By their looks of consternation, Natasha guessed that their thoughts hovered around similar visions.

With the power out, America-Five became visible only when they reached the green. The Dome curved in the dark, silent and still, though Natasha knew it must harbor a world of movement and agitation inside.

"I'll see you soon," said Natasha. "I'll be waiting at the steps to lead you into the settlement."

"Be careful," said Raul.

"You too," said Natasha.

"We'll wait for you to get inside," Axel said.

Natasha moved swiftly over the dewy grass. She knew no one could see her, but still, crossing the open green gave her a tickling feeling on her neck. Once she had reached the supplyhouse, she relaxed. With the power off, getting back into the Dome would be easy. Even if someone caught her at the door of the Office of Exit, she could say that she was all turned around, that she couldn't tell what was what in the dark. Besides, either Mercedes, Eduardo, Sarah, or Ben should be there, keeping a lookout for her. Natasha passed through the two cubes of the airlock, prying the doors apart with her fingers. She still had plenty of time. Raj had given a full twelve hours and she had only used eight. She curled her fingers into the crease of the last door and pulled. Her mind registered the blue light just long enough to make her freeze in confusion, and then two strong hands reached out and grabbed her shoulders.

16

"What in the Father's name are you doing?"

Natasha felt herself being yanked violently out of the airlock.

"What are you thinking? Have you lost your mind?"

"Jeffrey."

Blue lights bathed his furious eyes. Backup power. The backup generator. They must have fixed it.

Jeffrey kept asking the same questions, shaking her shoulders, but she hardly heard the words.

"How did you know I was here?" she asked. Panic was overtaking her thoughts. She tried to push Jeffrey's arm away but he held on.

"The first team down to fix the power found Raj," Jeffrey said, his voice trembling with fury. "As soon as I heard, I came here. I caught Mercedes, Ben, Eduardo, and Sarah coming out of the airlock. Who orchestrated this? Was it you or Raj? I know it was one of you."

Natasha looked past him at the closed door of the Office.

"Do they all know?" she asked. "All the citizens?"

"Not yet. Not until the Alphas tell them!"

"But they can't—"

"What do you mean the Alphas can't? They can and they will. This is it, Natasha. Two months ago you looked me in the eye and told me that you'd never go to the Outside again. Not for the Pines, not for all eternity. How will I ever trust you now?"

"Yeah, well, what about me trusting you?" Jeffrey's indignation had suddenly reminded Natasha that she was in the right. That she had nothing to be sorry for. In a burst of anger, she wrestled free of his hold. "Half the people in this settlement have been lying to me my whole life!"

"What did they say to you? No, Natasha." He blocked her way out of the room. "You can't honestly be listening to the Tribes. How many times have I told you that?" His left hand hovered near his sleeve, as if he wanted to show her his burn.

"Forget it, Jeffrey. I've heard the whole story. I know about the attack. The Pines told me everything. About how you set the fire. You trapped those people, you killed them in the worst possible way. And I was there, wasn't I? I was one of *them*."

The life had withdrawn from Jeffrey's face; for a brief moment, he looked as old as an Alpha.

"No," he said.

"Yes," she answered viciously. "And it's not just the Pines who remember. I've seen it all in the Pretends. It's there, in Free Play, the computer has the whole attack. Raj told me how to find it. Your thoughts aren't as private as you think. You stole me. First you tried to kill me and then you stole me. But you never would have told me, if I hadn't found out on my own. You would have let me kill them!"

"Oh, Natasha."

He reached out and grabbed her roughly around the middle, and for some moments she did not have the will to pull away. She realized only now that some deep and quiet part of her had expected him to deny her accusations, to prove to her with a few simple but brilliant explanations that the Tribe *had* tricked her, that she had been born a citizen, and to assure her that everything could go back to normal now. But the seconds lengthened and he made no denial. It was all true; the past was fixed; no person on Earth could undo it.

"You have to forgive me for starting that fire. It drives me crazy when I think of those people. How easily you could have burned with them." He choked on his words.

"Tell me what happened," she said. "I've heard the truth, so you might as well tell me."

At first he was silent, and Natasha thought he was either too weak or too proud to confess. He pressed the back of his hand to his mouth, and for a terrible moment Natasha thought he was sick. But then he began to speak—to speak willingly and freely, as if he wanted very much to tell her everything.

"We tried so hard to avoid a second manual sweep," he said. "The sweep of the fighters was inevitable, of course. They had attacked us at our home. But we thought if we could drive the other ones north, away from the settlement, that we could nova them in the usual way. The Alphas put me in charge of the team. Claudia and Arthur were with me—this was before Arthur became Director—and also a Beta, Gaurav Gandhi. He moved to another department a long time ago. I was rushing. The settlement was under attack and I was distracted. I set off the fire bombs without checking the wind speed and direction, without consulting the weather log to get a good read on the forest humidity. We set off too many fires and we lost control almost immediately. The Tribe scattered in two directions. We followed the larger group toward the mountains, while the smaller group fled for the shoreline. We never caught up with them. That's as much as we know about those people. That part of the Tribe must have escaped the perimeter."

"And come back as the Pines."

Jeffrey nodded. "That's been the suspicion."

"We were always taught that the Palms started the fire," Natasha said with quiet fury. "You said so yourself."

"Yes," said Jeffrey, his eyes tearing up. "The Alphas did that for me. They thought it would help alleviate my suffering. My guilt."

"What happened to the larger group of Palms?" Natasha asked, moving on. She refused to feel sorry for Jeffrey right now.

"We realized pretty quickly that we had inadvertently cornered them. But there was nothing we could do. Nothing. They were up against the cliffs, and there was fire all around them. Our airfilters let us breathe through the smoke, and our biosuits gave us a limited degree of protection from the heat. But what good was that? There were over a hundred people, many of them passed out or nearly dead from the smoke already. We didn't have the means to save them. We couldn't ask the Office of Mercy for help. The fire retardants we have today only came later, as a result. And everyone else was fending off the attack on the green."

Jeffrey took a breath, briefly closing his eyes; clearly, this was difficult for him. But Natasha didn't care. She needed the truth.

"I heard you crying," he said. "You were trapped behind a wall of fire about as high as my waist. It was so hot, your face was bright red but you weren't burned at all. I saw you and I knew I had to save you. It was hard, I missed you twice. The ground was dry and the flames kept getting bigger. But then I lunged over the fire and I grabbed you. Once I had you in my arms, it was the best thing. The best moment of my life. Claudia couldn't stop me. She tried, but she wasn't strong enough. I managed to knock her down and hold on to you at the same time. Claudia and I, we've always had a complicated relationship, but she definitely hated me after that. And then, I left them all in the field. I took off in a sprint for the settlement. They tried to pry you away from me in the Office of Exit, and again in the Dome, but I wouldn't stop until I had you on a stretcher in the Department of Health, with a team of doctors swearing on the Mother and Father that they wouldn't harm a hair on your head."

"Your arm?"

"Yes, the burn. I got it reaching to get you. The biosuits were fire resistant, but they started to melt in direct flame."

"You said it was a trick."

"It was a trick. A good trick, a wonderful trick. You were so perfect and innocent. I would have thrown myself into the fire to save you."

Behind the door, the muffled voice from a loudspeaker rang out through the settlement, ordering the members of certain Offices to checkpoints in the Dome.

"So all the older generations have been lying to me," said Natasha. "They know I'm not a real Epsilon, they must."

"The Deltas don't know. They were only nine years old at the time. It wasn't hard to slip one more little baby under their noses. We said you'd been sick, tucked away by yourself in the medical wing. As for the Betas and Gammas—and the Alphas, of course—well, you couldn't really call it lying, after a while. You were still so young when you came here. Only about twenty-three months, according to the med-workers. The Epsilons had just turned two. It was perfect. You fit right in. Of course, early on, there was outrage over what I had done, but none of it was really directed at you. Then, as the years passed, people stopped thinking about it. You were here. That was what mattered." He shrugged, at a loss for words. "They loved you. We all loved you. As much as if we had made you ourselves." He looked her in the eyes, suddenly trying to impart to her a very important lesson. "You are just as much a citizen of this settlement as anyone else."

Natasha was silent. While Jeffrey had been speaking, the reality of her immediate situation had been slowly setting in. The citizens had managed to get the backup generator running. The Alphas had Raj and the others locked away in their private wing. What could she do now? Natasha wished that she had not returned, not now, not ever. She should have stayed with the Pines. She could have run away with them—she should have convinced them once and for all to run away.

"Will you remember that?" asked Jeffrey.

"Okay," said Natasha, unsure of what the question had been.

His smile was odd; he was forgiving her too easily.

"Good," he said. "Then go down to your sleeproom and clean yourself up and meet me in the Dome in one hour. Raj and the others have refused to talk to the Alphas, but I'm sure that will change soon, once they stop worrying about themselves and resume a more universal perspective. Don't be afraid. The Department of Government is a lovely place. Reeducation will be the best possible thing for you right now. I'll be sorry to lose you from the Office of Mercy, but I'm sure that, before too long, you'll come to a career that suits you even better."

"You're kicking me out of the Office of Mercy?"

"It's hardly a severe reaction, given what you've done."

"But I haven't done anything!" Natasha protested, reaching frantically for a lie. "I never even talked to them. Well, once before—when they took me—but that wasn't my fault. This time we only looked at them, from a distance. It didn't do any harm. The Pines never knew we were there!"

"That," Jeffrey said, undeterred, "you will need to discuss with the Alphas."

She was desperate. If they shut her away in reeducation, if they banned her from the Office of Mercy, then the Pines would not be able to get Inside. Everything depended on her silencing the alarms on the green.

"Please," she begged. "Give me one more day in the Office of Mercy. The chance to say goodbye. I love it there, and I love our team so much. Ever since I was a kid, it was my dream to work there. Let me say goodbye the right way."

He did not answer her immediately, but the hardness in his face was softening.

"Fine," he said. "One more day. The Alphas have enough to deal with at the moment. But tomorrow evening, you're coming with me to the Department of Government. No complaints."

"Yes, thank you, Jeffrey, thank you."

They walked out of the Office of Exit and into the eerie blue dim of the hall. Once the door had closed, Jeffrey touched the genetic code reader and began to reprogram the lock.

"So you're not tempted," he said.

The lock beeped three times fast; the change was complete. Jeffrey crossed the hall to the Office of Mercy without another word—confident, apparently, that Natasha was under his supervision. With a trembling hand, Natasha touched her finger to the reader. The light glowed red. She was trapped. Unless she took a nova to the lock, she no longer had any way into or out of the settlement. She looked to the yellow door of the Strongroom, actually wishing they had stolen a second nova for good measure. If only the settlement had more than one exit, if only they did not build the wings so solid . . .

But then, all of a sudden, Natasha knew what to do. And a moment later, she was racing into the Dome, darting inconspicuously between the hordes of citizens trying to find their checkpoints, and others who simply did not know where else to go. How long had it been since she had parted from Axel and Raul at the edge of the green? Five minutes? Ten at the most?

Natasha slipped swiftly through the door of the New Wing without looking back. Eighty-three incuvats glowed at the center of the room and, inside, the Zetas bobbed in the cloudy liquid; they were all thankfully unharmed by the blackout, as Raj had previously assured. As she moved around them, one tiny Zeta leg kicked in such a muscular flash of motion that it made Natasha jump.

The building tools lay scattered around the New Wing, abruptly abandoned when the power shut off. Natasha found a pair of pliers like the ones she had used on her first day of construction; she climbed the scaffold and began to work away with all her strength at one of the panels that she had installed just last week. For some seconds she thought it wouldn't give. But then, with a final pull, the panel dropped to the scaffold with a thunderous clang, and a rush of cool air met Natasha's face. There was no time to worry about the sound. No chance to check behind her. She stuck her whole body through the now-opened rectangular gap in the wall; and, holding the frame at the top, she jumped a half story to the cushiony grass below.

With her heart pounding, Natasha gathered herself to her feet and ran across the green and into the woods. Her calls found answer quickly, more quickly than she could have hoped. She reached Axel and Raul well before the river.

"They caught me," Natasha said before they could ask. "They were waiting for me at the door. They locked me out of the Exit and by the end of tomorrow, I'm going to lose access to the computers too—to the Eyes—they'll see you coming across the green."

They began to interrupt her with questions, but she didn't have time.

"Listen," she said. "The plan has to change. You'll have to get in through the New Wing. I'll mark the panel. It will look secure, but I'm going to leave it propped in its frame, without the bolts screwed in. Just pound on it a few times and it will give. I'll be waiting for you on the other side. On the scaffold. It's this thing like a raised platform. Well, it doesn't matter, you'll see. It will be harder for us to get to the Strong-room. We'll have to pass through the Dome. But I'll show you the way. That should be fine. The important thing is that you'll have the nova. Just show them the nova and they'll have to let us through."

"Not now, not tomorrow," Raul protested in disbelief. "We're not ready."

"Yes. Tomorrow. At noon, when the sun's the highest in the sky."

"But that's impossible," Axel said. "We need more practice."

"I'm sorry," said Natasha. "But if you wait any longer, I won't be able to turn off the alarms. They'll see you on the green and start a manual sweep before you've had a chance to talk to them. They could miss noticing the nova and start shooting and detonate it by accident."

"So let them," growled Raul. "Let them try to kill us all."

Axel shook his head and turned away from Natasha, toward the ocean, as if he were considering the fate of the people sleeping there on the sand. Something like anger stirred in Natasha. Didn't they realize how much she had risked for them? How far they had come with her help?

"I have to go back," said Natasha, "before they realize I'm gone. Will you do it, tomorrow at noon?"

"Yes," Axel said. He signaled Raul with a wave of his hand that they should go, but he pointedly did not look at Natasha or give any word of farewell. They began stepping away, disappearing into the dark.

"Wait!" said Natasha.

They stopped and turned.

"I'm still leaving with you, right?" she said. "After we destroy the novas—the Birds. You still want me, don't you?"

"Of course, little Nassia," Axel said. He returned to where she stood and touched his open hand to her cheek. "You are our sister."

When she nodded, they started away, but she called them again.

"And no one dies tomorrow," she said.

Axel turned, squinting at her in the dark. In a slow, measured voice, he answered, "No, no one dies."

The sun had yet to rise fully over the trees, and the Dome shimmered in the diffuse glow of the weak and early light. Why did it feel like the settlement was empty? The clock on the maincomputer read 0641 and a few early-rising citizens were spilling out from the elephant. But why did it feel so deserted, as if Natasha were alone?

No one had seen Natasha emerge from the New Wing. She took the elephant to level six and walked quickly down the hall with its familiar smell of dust and shower room water. The blue emergency lamps glowed overhead, and as Natasha entered her sleeproom, the open door threw a triangle of light across Min-he's bed.

"Where have you been?" she groaned. "Close the door, we still have ten minutes till wake-up."

"Sorry," Natasha whispered.

Natasha's hair was caked with sand and her hands were filthy. She grabbed a clean outfit from under her bed and went back down the hall to the shower room. She stripped off her clothes in the changing stall and dropped them down the damaged-clothing chute (let the Biotextile workers wonder all morning whose filthy clothes those were). She spent a long time in the shower, letting the hot water pound her face, washing the brown grime from around her nails and the flesh of her heels. She washed her hair twice through with soap. Did the Tribes have soap? It didn't seem so, considering how strong they smelled up close. They didn't have showers, certainly. Probably this would be the last shower of her life.

A few minutes later, as Natasha was leaving the shower room, there was a rumble and then a sudden illumination as all the lights turned on. She entered the hallway to the sound of people clapping and cheering and darting out of their sleeprooms to check that everything was, indeed, back up and running.

By the time Natasha returned to her own sleeproom, Min-he was gone and her bed was already made for the day. Panic came over Natasha in waves. It was happening too fast. She was letting things slip. Without even realizing it, she had missed her chance to say goodbye to Min-he.

Natasha had no appetite for breakfast, so she hid in her sleeproom until the 0800 alarm. She joined the line in the hallway with the other latecomers.

"Morning, Natasha." It was Sylvia Greene, a Delta, whose sleeproom was across the hall from her own.

"Morning."

Waiting for the elephant, the citizens chitchatted about the Electricity and Piping crews, wondering how the teams could have messed up badly enough to lose *both* the main power and backup generator for several hours. No one had told them. In front of her, Lee Davis and Lu Tang began discussing a game they had going in the Pretends: ". . . but I've been easy on you. Meet me after dinner tonight and I'll dissolve you to the marrow, I will. . . ." Natasha was sweating; her neck felt hot. Was it true they sensed nothing? It seemed impossible that no one else would know what was coming, that they could expect to be playing some frivolous game in the Pretends tonight. Elliot Beckman smiled at her and she looked away, though immediately regretted doing so. He was only saying good morning; she needed to get a grip.

As they rode up in the elephant, Natasha tried to force herself to assume the tired, bored expression of the other citizens. But by the time they had reached the ground level, she was sweating worse than before.

She tried to drink in everything: the grind of the elephant doors closing behind her, the sun glinting off the honeycomb windows, the clean air, a perfect 74 degrees Fahrenheit, the pleasant breeze blowing in from the vents. Her legs moved fast, too fast. But this was the speed that everyone moved; this was the quickness with which she walked every morning.

Jeffrey watched her as she entered the Office of Mercy. He waited at his desk until she had settled down at her computer. Then he walked over and knelt by her chair.

"I wasn't sure if you'd come," he said.

"Of course I would. I said I wanted one more day."

"I've been talking to Arthur about your transfer. Don't worry, though," he added quickly, "I told him it was your idea, for now. He doesn't suspect you of anything. He doesn't even know about the breach yet. I think the Alphas are planning to call him into their department this evening. Anyway, we were both thinking you'd do well in the Office of Neuroreplacement in the Department of Health. You've always excelled at three-dimensional conceptualization, and you have a nice blend of scientific skills and a capacity for human interest."

"Yeah," said Natasha. "That sounds fine."

"I've mentioned the transfer to a few others too. I hope you don't mind. I think it will make it easier for you, in the long run. You're perfectly at liberty to pretend the transfer was your idea." He dropped his voice lower. "The Alphas have decided to keep Raj's situation private. I'm sure they will extend the same kindness to you, and to the others."

"That's good. That will make our lives easier."

She tried to muster an appearance of relief. But it made no difference what the Alphas did. In a few hours, none of this would matter.

"Look, we can't talk much here, but have dinner with me tonight, after your shift. We can put off going to the Department of Government until after we eat. There're still things I want to tell you about—about your childhood. I've been agonizing over how to tell you these things for years. Twenty-two years, to be exact. Last night wasn't exactly what I'd imagined."

"Fine," she said. "Dinner tonight."

He gave her an unsure smile, confused, no doubt, by her conciliatory mood. Claudia glared at them, her hands hovering an inch over her keyboard. Natasha shivered, recognizing for the first time the true hatred in the other woman's eyes. Well, Natasha thought, at least that was one person who wouldn't be sorry to see her go. She tried to think of the Pines, and how exciting and different her life would be with them. And yet. Jeffrey's presence distracted her. Something was unsettling Natasha, a feeling dangerously close to regret. Would she ever speak to Jeffrey again? Would she even see him before she fled, amid the chaos of the Pines' arrival?

"I'm sorry," she burst out, in a whisper, as he rose to return to his desk. "I'm really, really sorry. For everything."

"There's no need to apologize," he told her, kneeling down again. "No one's mad at you. You don't have to be afraid of the Alphas—they only want what's best for you."

But he had no idea that the thing she was sorry for hadn't happened yet. She nodded; it hurt not being able to tell him.

"Maybe you should go back to your sleeproom. There's no reason for you to be on shift today. I shouldn't have let you come."

"No!" said Natasha. She returned her fingers to the feeler-cube and turned very suddenly back to the screen. "I've been at this desk for six years. I want to go out on a good note. I'll think about it forever if I don't."

"Okay," Jeffrey said, backing off. "I can understand that."

Natasha brought three different visuals up on the screen, all views of the far north deadzone perimeter; it was a place the Pines hadn't been in months. But no one in the Office knew that but her.

Jeffrey waited a moment, then he said softly, "Dinner later?"

"Eighteen hundred hours," Natasha said. "I'm there."

So that would be their last conversation, a lie.

The morning hours dragged on: the coffee dripped, the fans whirled and quieted, the computers hummed their electric hum, images flashed searchingly across the overhead screen, and the room became warm, as it always did, from the heat of bodies and machines. A woman named Bindi came to Natasha's desk to drop off some data reports from last week.

"There's a rumor you're leaving the Office," she said.

"Yes," said Natasha, "I think so."

"Was it just too much?" she asked in a hushed voice. "After the mission?"

"No," Natasha snapped. "To be honest, I'm bored with looking for

Tribes all the time. I'd rather do something with more day-to-day stimulation."

Bindi made some small remark and went away, clearly miffed by Natasha's answer.

The clock changed from 0958 to 0959 to 1000. Arthur sat hunched over his desk, visible through the glass window of his private office. He looked exhausted, overworked. His head drooped over his keyboard. How fast would he be able to respond to what was coming in only two hours? How unprepared would he be when the first alarms came not from the green, but from the Inside—when he found himself in the impossible role of protecting the settlement?

At 1039, William Donatello, a Beta, beckoned Natasha to the coffee machine, where he was pouring himself a cup. She had to comply, anything else would seem suspicious; apparently, the rumor about Natasha's transfer had made her suddenly popular.

"Heard you might be leaving us for Health," he said.

Natasha nodded.

"Did you know I worked in Bioreplacement for over thirty years?"

"I think you once told me."

"It was my first assignment, I kind of fell into it, I guess. I wasn't as mature at seventeen as you were. Well, I can't say I took to the job immediately. My stomach got all twisted watching them pump a person full of those fiber needles. My advisers thought I should take a year to watch them go through the procedure again and again, until my stomach got inured to it. But wouldn't you know? Seven months later, I had mastered the needles and was on to full organ replacements. You couldn't get the microknife away from me. I didn't trust anyone else to make the incisions as well as I could. Huh, those were some interesting years. Best job in the settlement, if you want my opinion." He wiggled his fingers. "It's all in the touch."

"What made you come here?" Natasha asked distractedly while

Claudia passed in front of Natasha's computer, on the way to Arthur's office. Had she glanced at the screen?

"Oh, I was anxious for a change, I guess. They say it's healthy to keep the mind active—give yourself fresh challenges. We've got the time, might as well learn something new."

Eric arrived early for the afternoonshift. He leaned back in his chair, his hands behind his head, his eyes roaming the room.

"And you know, Natasha," William continued, "you can always cycle back to the Department of the Exterior, if that's what you want. You young ones like to rush around, but you've got a near eternity before you. The way things are going in Research, potentially a true eternity."

"Yeah, definitely. I'm sorry, I think an error just came up on one of the sensors."

The minutes began to pass more quickly. It was all up to Axel now. People began to filter out of the Office for the lunchhour. Natasha pulled up the eight visuals of the green—sensors A1 through A8—and selected the north-facing sensor, the one positioned over the Department of the Exterior. She moved the control to rotate the camera up. The sky was a brilliant blue, and the sun burned high overhead. How precise would Axel be? The clock blinked from 1150 to 1151. All was still. Were they really coming? If the plans had changed, if Axel had rejected her instructions and decided he would break in when he wanted, without her help, she would have no way of knowing. Her eyes scanned the visuals, her heart thudding.

The figures flooded onto the screen so fast that Natasha started. Ten of them—no, nine. They raced across the top middle window. Sensor A1. Her hand silenced the alarm before it had hardly begun.

"What was that?" asked Jeffrey.

"Deer crossing the green," she answered dully. "I've got it."

A new window flashed up.

Do you want to override the alarm?

Yes.

Password.

Waverider4.

The Pines had found the unbolted panel of the New Wing—the one Natasha had marked some hours ago with a large, scratched *X*. They had the nova. Axel carried it alone. The others were stacking two stout logs against the wing's outer wall to use as steps.

Bindi got up to make a fresh pot of coffee, asking for a show of hands, who wanted more? Right now, two hundred meters away, the Tribe stood poised to enter the settlement, and no one knew. The rest of the group must be close, Natasha thought. And they were.

They poured across the A3 screen to A4 to A5 to A6. Four alarms flashed and Natasha silenced them one by one.

"Stupid deer," she said.

Eric stared blankly at her, then looked away.

She watched the larger group; they did not go around to the New Wing to meet Axel and the others as she'd expected. Instead they stopped at the exterior of the Garden and began climbing the walls. A pang of fear shot through Natasha. She had never told them anything about approaching the settlement in two places. They were supposed to come through the New Wing panel together. Hadn't they understood her? They were supposed to meet her on the scaffold, show the nova, and hold everyone calmly hostage while they emptied the Strongroom. Plus, what further disturbed Natasha was that the skylights in the Garden were the weakest part of the settlement. Debates sprang up every few years about replacing those windows with a solid roof and solar lamps. How had they known?

The Pines reached the top of the Garden, as quick and sure as insects. Some had guns slung over their backs and others carried bows and arrows. Natasha didn't know what they were doing, but there was no time to figure it out. She closed the visuals and pulled up the view of the northern deadzone, wondering distantly where Mercedes, Ben,

Eduardo, and Sarah were at this moment. How surprised would they be to hear that the Pines were on the green after all? Would the Alphas even allow them to know?

She pushed her chair back. She had to go; she had to meet Axel in the New Wing. Hopefully it wouldn't be too late to call the other group away from the Garden. Claudia and William were chatting near Natasha's desk, something about the satellite feeds.

Then, from all around came the scream of the manual alarm.

"What in the name of the Father is that?" a voice shouted from the front of the room.

"The alarm," Claudia answered, in shock.

"The alarm—what alarm?"

"It's coming from the Department of Agriculture," Eric said.

"Animals loose?" asked Jeffrey.

Claudia and William were back at their desks.

Arthur came bursting out of his office.

"Someone just typed the invasion code in the Garden."

"Impossible," Jeffrey said.

Arthur leaned over Jeffrey's computer, working fast. They seemed to realize at the same moment; Natasha saw their jaws go slack, heard their gasping curses. And then, suddenly, Jeffrey was on his feet, pushing Arthur out of the way.

"Natasha, did you—"

She could not move; her mind was screaming at her to run, now, to the New Wing, but Jeffrey's eyes had her trapped.

"What did you do?" he demanded.

The doors to the Office must have opened because the alarm blared louder now. Eric yelled out and put his hands over his ears. Lockers opened and slammed in the hall. Firm voices shouted commands, and the beat of footsteps sounded from those funneling into the hall.

"This has to be a mistake," Claudia said. But a second later, the image from Jeffrey's computer flashed on the overhead screen. The

Pines were scattered across the Garden skylights, beating at the glass with stones and the butts of their guns.

"Holy Father, holy," said Eric.

Natasha backed away a few steps at a time.

Jeffrey threw a furious look over his shoulder.

"Hey," he shouted, "you stay right there!"

But he could not decide whether to go after her or stay at his computer, and in his moment of hesitation, Natasha was gone.

17

Natasha slammed the Office door and crashed right into a formation of citizens marching down the hall in full biosuits, weapons drawn. She moved with them, pressing her way between their shoulders. As she was reaching the door, an explosion sent her down to her knees, the side of a LUV-3 jamming into her ribs and someone's helmet cracking against her head. Her first thought was of the nova, but no, if the nova had gone off in the New Wing, she would have been blown to ash by now, all of them would. A Gamma woman from the Office of Air and Energy began to sob. Natasha forced herself to her feet and ran ahead to the Dome.

Screams and gunfire sounded from the open doors of the Department of Agriculture. A giant tree had fallen across the lawn, blocking the entrance. People scurried in and out over the trunk and pushed between the dense leaves of the branches. The distant shatter of heavy glass panels striking the ground rippled the air. Two bodies lay bloodsplattered on the floor near the hub, while medworkers rushed toward them with stretchers. Natasha stepped quickly, maneuvering around citizens so stunned that they had tangled themselves up in their biosuits or dropped their guns.

The door to the New Wing called to her; Axel and the others must be inside by now. As for the Health workers who were monitoring the

Zetas this morning, well, Natasha had forgotten about them until this second. She guessed that the Pines must have silenced them because no one had set off alarms in there. It occurred to Natasha that she had also forgotten to tell Axel and Raul about the Zetas and, vaguely, amid a hundred other thoughts, she wondered what the Tribe would make of the naked little fetuses swimming around in their clear incuvats.

She had to go to the New Wing, but she didn't. The gunfire increased and the burst of another explosion reverberated through the Dome. This time Natasha stayed on her feet. What were they doing? This wasn't the plan. The whole point of the nova had been to prevent any fighting on their way to the Strongroom. And the guns were only supposed to be a last resort. A terrifying thought took hold of Natasha as she ran, pushing toward the Department of Agriculture. Had this been a spur-of-the-moment decision, or had they planned to attack the whole time and kept it from her? Had Axel lied to her in the woods? Either way, she had to make them stop. She would make them stop, and then she would go meet Axel in the New Wing.

Beyond the fallen tree at the Department entrance, the citizens stood with their guns raised, firing rounds at the shattered roof. The Garden itself was in devastation. The platform built for the Crane Ceremony had collapsed. The purple and yellow azalea heads were smashed to brown and trampled. The dirt of the paths had been kicked up all across the short, bright lawn. And there were bodies. Citizens still masked in their biosuits were sprawled across the ground. An explosion by the cherry trees sent two people onto their backs. Did the Pines have thermo-grenades too? Or had the citizens' weapons missed their target and fallen back too soon? Natasha could not see them at first, but then she did. There, at the sharp edges of the broken roof, the Tribespeople appeared as silhouettes against a violent sun, their own bullets and arrows pouring down on the Garden.

"No!" Natasha screamed. She ran toward the center of the room, waving her hands madly at the people above. She could recognize a blue tunic and, on another, a silver sling strapped across a muscular middle. "Stop it! Tezo! Mattias! What are you doing?"

"Get out of here! Why aren't you suited?" Someone pushed her roughly to the side, and she stumbled into the shade of the evergreens.

"Hey, help me with her," a second voice called.

"What?"

Nolan stomped over the brush and grabbed a person from under the arms. As he did, the head lolled back and the face became visible. It was Min-he. Her visor was cracked and a section of it had lodged into her cheek. Blood congealed around the cut and formed a thick red scab over her eye.

"Call anyone still in the Dome," a man shouted behind them. "Send Exterior teams to the roof—"

High above their heads, a coil of rope unleashed itself in the air. Then another, and another. The figures emerged; they were sliding down the ropes, coming inside. Mattias was laughing, whooping, he swung back and forth at the level of the treetops. His gun sprayed fire across the floor and his wild hair trailed behind him in the breeze of his own movement.

"Mattias!" Natasha abandoned Min-he to run back to the center of the lawn.

And now Tezo, swinging on a rope beside him, came into view. But he was different. His beautiful face was contorted with hatred. He raised his gun, shooting carelessly at the citizens beneath him.

"Stop!" Natasha screamed. Tezo saw her, and a look of confusion passed over his face. "Stop or I'll let them kill you!"

He stared, stunned out of the fight. She was supposed to be in the New Wing helping Axel and he knew it, but she didn't care.

"What are you doing?" she screamed.

He raised his gun. He was looking right at her.

A sharp pain erupted deep in Natasha's shoulder. The world hung strangely for a moment, as if it were resting on a sheet of ice and about to fall through. Then she fell, tripping forward, her hand rising to touch the pain. He had shot her; Tezo had shot her. The heat burned through her cells. She lay with her cheek on the cold grass, lines of green breaking her sight; her hand tightened over the fire in her skin while boots stamped by, near to her face. She must keep herself whole—suddenly that was her only purpose. Her mouth tasted sour and the room rocked above the green forest of grass.

The thought drifted through Natasha's mind that she needed to get to the New Wing. Axel and the others had a nova, and they were waiting for her. And if she failed to show up, she could not predict what they'd do. Now she had diverged from the plan, she realized, as much as they had. She wasn't on the scaffold to meet them and take them to the Strongroom. Boots trampled the orange-green beds of stargazing lilies and Natasha thought, with a kind of distant regret, that the Agriculture workers would not be able to replant those flowers until the following spring.

The sound and the colors swirled and moved, and then she really was moving. Past the guns, through the branches of the fallen tree, the rough leaves scratching her face. They had her on a stretcher; a gloved hand gripped the corner close to her eyes.

"The New Wing," she whispered, to remind herself.

Two citizens lowered her to the floor, and a new pair of hands gripped her, and then she was leaning against the curving wall of the Dome. A Health worker named Teresa injected something cold into Natasha's arm.

"Close your eyes and try to relax," said Teresa. "This will take the pain away. I'll come back to check on you soon."

Tiredness washed over Natasha from the top of her skull to her legs. They must have put more than pain relief in that syringe. She would only close her eyes for a minute. She could sleep, she could have fallen asleep at this moment, except—

A shot rang out inside the New Wing. In the clamor, no one had heard it. But it was there. She listened, but heard only silence. The New Wing did not have lockers yet, with biosuits and guns stashed away for the citizens. It must have been one of the Pines who fired the shot. Natasha held her injured shoulder with one hand and pushed herself up. Realization was spreading through her thoughts: The Tribe had lied. They were attacking full-force, attacking to kill.

"Last team!" a Delta leader shouted from his spot near the elephant doors. "One strong push and we've got them."

"There's a second group!" Natasha shouted. The floor swung and Natasha braced herself against the wall. A few people stared at her. "There's a second group of Pines and they're attacking in the New Wing!"

The Delta had heard her. His arm froze above his head. A Gamma clutching his thigh yelped and scooted away from the New Wing doors. The citizens turned in different directions, uncertain.

Then Arthur broke from the crowd. He was not wearing a biosuit, but he held a LUV-3 and had no visible injuries. He barreled toward the New Wing and kicked the doors open with a shout. The others fell into formation behind him. And as the citizens' cries of victory came from the Garden, the first rounds of gunfire erupted from the New Wing.

Natasha staggered forward, watching the battle through weary eyes. They carried out two Health workers on stretchers—each of them bleeding heavily. Natasha could see the Pines on the scaffold, the panel open to the Outside behind them, and she could see the citizens' fear and confusion when they realized the Tribe had a G3 nova. She watched with a still, distant gaze as a team of four citizens aimed their guns and shot Raul, without bringing any harm to themselves. The body fell from the scaffold and hit the floor face first, with a sickening limpness. The citizens had to be more careful now, because of the nova; but they shot Hesma, still wearing her red beads, so that she stumbled back against the wall, blood breaking out from under her arm with the force of water from a busted pipe.

Axel stood at the center of the scaffold, holding the nova in both arms, while Sonlow, London, and another young boy shot their weapons ineffectually into the room. Natasha realized how wrong she had been in thinking that the presence of a nova would force the citizens to hold their fire. The people of America-Five were not as timid as that. Like herself, they had honed their skills for years in the Pretends, and they took great pride in their marksmanship. The Tribe could never have advanced; they had no chance of descending the scaffold, much less of crossing the Dome and reaching the Strongroom. Axel was yelling to the others, his words lost to those below. But they were retreating, backing up toward the wall; and then, with Axel still yelling, first London, then the other boy, then Sonlow, old as she was, launched themselves through the open panel, back to the green.

The citizens did not fire directly at Axel; that would have been suicide. But they did their best to keep him afraid, and Axel did not seem to realize the difference. He abandoned the nova on the scaffold, near the edge of the grooved metal surface, rocking slightly on its side. A Dry Engineering team was already rushing in, climbing the ladders to the platform, even before Axel's sandaled foot had disappeared through the square of forest and blue sky.

The medworkers flooded the Dome. They wheeled out respirators and artificial heart machines and blood replacement stations. Other crews began clearing the incuvats from the New Wing, rushing the Zetas to the Office of Reproduction, where the scientists could check them for damage. A quickly assembled construction team fixed the fallen panel back into place; and the screech of electron saws sounded from the Garden. Gradually, more bangs and shouts added to the noise. They were sealing off the Garden roof, where the Pines had shattered the skylights. The fans kicked up to high speed, drawing out the dirty air and pumping in fresh, cold, purified air from the filters. Arthur wiped his eyes and laid his gun against the wall. One man—it was Jared Sullivan, an Epsilon—who had only joined the fight as the Pines were escaping, now shimmied the mask off his face.

"Whew," he said, shaking out his sweaty hair. "They have that thing under control?"

He was looking at the nova. The Dry Engineering team was stepping away, one female Delta brushing her hands on her pants—the prote-pants of a normal workday.

"I think so," said Natasha.

"Wish I had left my office when you did. I only suited up about forty seconds ago. Missed the whole thing. What happened to your shoulder?"

"I got shot in the Garden."

"You were in the Garden too? Mother."

Jared went away but Natasha hardly noticed, because Arthur was at her side now.

"You okay?" Arthur asked. "Do they need to bioreplace that?"

"No, it's not bad." The pins had come loose from the gauze and she had to hold the dressings firm to keep the bleeding thin.

"I left Claudia and Jeffrey running the Office," Arthur said, still catching his breath. "But I needed to be here. I couldn't let the rest of the settlement pay for my mistakes. If I could have known it would come to this . . ."

His mistakes? Natasha did not understand. Hadn't he seen Jeffrey yelling at her? Didn't he know this was all her fault? That if she had any sense of self-preservation, she would be making a run for it now?

Arthur looked at her, though, almost as if *he* were apologizing, asking *her* for forgiveness.

"Do you think anyone died?" he asked. He meant citizens, of course; plenty of Pines had died.

"I don't know." But as Natasha spoke, the image of Min-he's face, sliced by the shattered visor, rose up in her mind.

"Terrible," Arthur said. "I can't believe a Tribe got past us like that. All our checks and defenses."

The blood was seeping through the gauze—hot on Natasha's hand where she held the wound.

"You're bleeding," Arthur observed.

"Yes," said Natasha. "I guess I need this rewrapped."

Natasha returned to the Dome. The stretchers made a ring around the circular wall and the doctors and nurses ran from one to the next, tending to the wounded. The screams had mostly quieted to groans of pain. Two doctors quickly tended to Natasha's shoulder, making it numb and wrapping it tightly. Then they moved on to help others. But Min-he, thought Natasha, relaxing her arm. If Min-he was dead then she would never forgive herself. For all of them who had died, Natasha should die too. That would be the only justice; and Natasha did not believe in mercy anymore, only justice. Maybe not even that.

For several minutes, Natasha searched the beds for the long mop of glossy black hair. But before Natasha could find Min-he, Jeffrey found Natasha. She felt his hand on the small of her back and she froze.

"Keep walking," Jeffrey said near her ear. His voice was unsteady, as if an ocean of rage were convulsing beneath. "The Mother and Father are waiting for you."

He would not look at her. They reached the Department of Government entrance, and Jeffrey tapped his finger. The doors opened directly into a much smaller version of the elephant, this one paneled with thick, maroon fabric. As they sank down, the noise from the Dome disappeared. Jeffrey turned to face the doors on the opposite side. He was sweating; he kept taking off his glasses to rub his eyes. Natasha had never seen him look so pale; even his lips were white.

The little elevator eased to a slow stop, and the second set of doors opened. For her entire life, Natasha had wondered about the

Department of Government. All the Epsilons had. She had always imagined what a treat it would be to get to see it one day—but not like this, of course. She had not imagined this.

Terrified as she was, Natasha gasped in awe at the magnificent sight before her as she stepped into the wing. The space was big and airy like the Dome or the Garden. Little windowed rooms rose up on all sides, and the circular center of the wing was open to a frosted-glass ceiling above. But facing her was the thing that made this sight unlike anything Natasha had encountered before: thundering down from near the roof was a vertical river of blue and white water. A waterfall, Natasha thought, remembering the name. It was seven stories tall at least; and the cascading rush fed into a wide, deep pool, white with mist. The rest of the floor—if you could even call it a floor, the whole area seemed alive—consisted of the most beautiful garden that Natasha had ever seen, real life or Pretend. Little streams snaked off from the pool, winding under curved footbridges and through the vines of miniature trees. The grass was short and spongy, and the ground rose and fell in little hills dotted with subdued white flowers or intricate rock designs.

Natasha began to notice the Alphas then. They sat on benches or stood like statues amid the green. Many of them wore hoods that fell low over their faces, but Natasha could tell that they were looking at her. One man with a high brow and square chin shook his head sadly as Jeffrey led her along the path; they must know what she had done.

Natasha took in a breath and coughed.

"The atmosphere in this wing is different from what you're used to," Jeffrey said, his voice still shaky. "Try to take shallow breaths, otherwise you might faint. We're going to the fifth floor."

They rose up in a different elevator, this one glass and small like the first. It traveled alongside the edge of the waterfall and the two motions together combined to create a dizzying effect. Jeffrey led her into a bright room with white walls on the left and right. The back wall was not a wall of solid material, but the underside of the waterfall.

The Mother and Father sat with their backs to the water, on two tall white chairs that had a biological quality to them, like giant petals, the high tips of the chairs waving in the waterfall's breeze. Jeffrey led Natasha to a wide chair lined with controls that seemed like it belonged in the Department of Health, and which was separated from the Mother and Father by a narrow table of marble. Natasha thought that Raj or maybe a few of the others would be here—and her anxiety increased when she realized that she was alone.

The Mother pushed back her hood, revealing her bright hair, papery skin, and a pair of ice-blue eyes that were more stunning, even, than Jeffrey's.

"Thank you, Jeffrey," the Mother said, "for escorting Natasha here. Though I'm sure she would have come by her own volition, once she had checked her messages. Please relax, Natasha, I can't stand that shaking. Jeffrey, your expertise is now needed in the Office of Mercy. Kindly go to Arthur's aid. He is not as adept in emergencies as you are."

A hint of irony lit her last words, but Jeffrey did not seem to notice.

"I wanted to stay," he said loudly, with surprisingly little command over himself, as if he had suddenly forgotten where he was and to whom he was speaking. "This goes back to me. This began with me years ago. You can't blame Natasha. This is my doing. I take responsibility for what happened today."

"Responsibility is not yours to assign, Jeffrey," the Mother replied. "We'll get to you later. We're concerned with Natasha right now."

"Then I'll help," Jeffrey said quickly. "I'll explain myself. Just let me stay."

"No," said the Mother.

"Please." Jeffrey took off his glasses. "At least let me hear what you have to say to Natasha. I need to hear something. I can't understand how this happened."

From behind them, and in answer to a motion of the Father's hand, two male Betas entered the room. They stood on either side of Jeffrey, not quite touching his shoulders. Jeffrey began to speak again, but caught himself, his mouth hanging open. And with one long and terrified look at Natasha, he allowed the two Betas to lead him out of the room.

Her future must be hopeless, Natasha thought with growing panic as the door closed behind them. If Jeffrey was breaking down, then they must be banishing her. Jeffrey must already know.

"Well," said the Father, a man with a small, round face and shadowy eyes. "You've had a busy day. Romping through the forest, masterminding attacks, aligning yourself with a Tribe and then changing your mind. You're probably half-dead on your feet."

The Father's words injured her but, at the same time, they seemed far away. How long did she have? A day? Hours? How long until the airlock banged closed on her, and she was alone with the weather and the trees and the animals? Her best hope was that the surviving Pines would find her and, in their outrage, would kill her fast—that her death would not be slow.

"Please," said Natasha. She was not begging for forgiveness; it was too late for that. Her only wish was to make herself understood before they sent her away. "I never meant for anyone to get hurt. The Tribe lied to me. They weren't supposed to shoot anyone. They told me their only purpose was to destroy the novas. We were going to empty the Strongroom and bring the novas to the ocean. We were going to drop the novas in the water and that's all. After that we were going to disappear—"

"And you trusted them?" the Mother asked, cutting her off.

"Yes, yes," Natasha answered, frantic to explain everything, even though it was almost impossible to imagine that according to what she had thought before, at this moment she was supposed to be in the forest. "I had their word. I've been meeting with them, sneaking Outside. The chief, Axel, he promised me. He said they wanted to destroy the novas because they believe in life over death."

"And what, my dear child, do you think *we* believe in?" the Father asked. "Did we build this settlement because we thought it might look pretty? Do our citizens in the Department of Health and the Department of Research work sixteen-hour shifts perfecting new technologies because it makes for lively talk over dinner?" He raised a twisted, bony finger at her. "You have been spoiled into forgetting that your life and the life of your fellow citizens is something that we fight for every day. Yes, our daily workshifts may fail to provide the thrills of a Pre-Storm blood-and-guts war, we don't do it with guns or arrows, but we rise each morning in this settlement ready to do battle with death. The whole of America-Five is engineered toward that purpose!"

"I don't think that violence is exciting," Natasha protested. "Tezo, one of the Pines, he shot me. Do you think I planned that? He knew it was me. He saw I wasn't in the New Wing, and he probably assumed that I'd changed my mind. That I'd betrayed them. And he was right. I did betray them, because they betrayed me. They lied to me. I told you. They weren't supposed to shoot at people. If Min-he—if anything happens to Min-he or anyone—"

"Then you would only have your own choices to blame," said the Mother.

"I know," said Natasha. She was groaning now, a low, ugly, guttural noise. "Maybe this was inevitable," she said. "I could never have been a part of their Tribe. But I wasn't meant to be here either. I don't belong in the settlement. I don't belong anywhere. Because I am one of them. It's true. I know it's true. They told me, and I saw it in the Pretends. And when I asked Jeffrey, he admitted it. He said that he was the one to take me here, to make me a citizen. He shouldn't have. I didn't want it."

"The question of what a person wants or does not want holds no relevance here. What matters is the system that we have created and how each life factors into that system." The Mother shook her head. "You are very young, Natasha. And it is the special privilege of the young to live and breathe the present. To take the situation of the world you were born into largely for granted, with little interest in how it all came about."

"I don't take it for granted," Natasha said. "I wanted to change it!"

"Yes, you did, but not to anything new. We've been following your actions closely these last few months. We know that you and Eric left the settlement on the night of the Crane Celebration, and we know the basic content of your meetings with Raj and his Delta compatriots... though his antics down on level nine, I'll confess, did catch us by surprise, as did your breaking into the Strongroom. Indeed," the Mother conceded, "the methods were your own. But what you were trying to do, to destroy the control of the settlement and to spread the promise, the false promise, of life equally among the living is not a new idea in the least. If you had succeeded, you would have achieved nothing more or less than the destruction of three centuries of proven progress. You would have thrown us back into some of the darkest years of human existence, to the world before the Storm."

The Mother's face relaxed, but only in a pitying way.

"You have not lived in those times," she continued. "As I said, the young study the present. It is only when you are old, when the present is a little less captivating, that your mind can let go, and expand. We Alphas may not be as quick in the Bioreplacement rooms, or in the Research laboratories, but we do have that undervalued quality of unimpeachable memory. We remember. We remember what it was like before the Storm. When there were cities, and wars. When every single day was a struggle for power, and power was a thing that bounced around from one group to another, so that it was impossible to imagine how the fighting would end. For thousands of years, no one tried to stop it. It seemed *natural* to them, to compete for resources, to suffer and to die their noble little deaths. Instead of resisting, they said 'this is what makes us human,' and bore it, and were inexorably crushed beneath it. Generation after generation went like this. Advances in medicine, yes. Better living conditions in the richer nations, true. But those were small triumphs, little advances against a great darkness. Human society had no defined goal. It was a failing machine. It refused to throw off the laws of the animals."

"What about the Yangs?" Natasha challenged. She thought of the Alphas' vitriolic dismissal of that long-dead generation in the Ethical Code. "The Yangs wanted to make life good for everyone."

"Well, yes," said the Mother, a wistful smile touching her lips. "The Yangs were our intellectual forefathers, in a way. For many of us, they were our actual, biological parents. Edmund Yang was a gifted leader. And the group had great support in the early decades of their existence. They claimed that the divide between the very rich and very poor could be solved, not by sacrifice, as the wealthy class would have abhorred, but simply by better organization. That sounded good to everyone. Within thirty years, they had convinced a couple of billion people."

"And it would have worked," said Natasha, remembering what Mercedes had said once in the conference room, what seemed itself a hundred years ago. "If you had seen their project through, it would have worked."

"They had their chance, Natasha. No amount of time would have helped. You see, the Yangs' ideas made perfect sense on paper. In fact, we have many of their ideas in practice here in the settlement. Put people to work in agriculture, water purification, power production, teaching, scientific research, and medical science, and each citizen of the world should have enough to keep themselves alive and happy many times over. What we needed to eliminate, according to the Yangs, were the toys, the idleness, the wasted hours, the heaps of trash, from overvaried clothing to electronic knickknacks—to eliminate that great distraction called business, to replace the goal of making money with the goal of producing useful, life-preserving materials. But most of all, it was the Yangs' idea to give the trillions of hours of human labor that occurred each day a meaningful, clear, and concise direction."

"To extend human life."

They nodded.

"To end suffering."

"Yes," said the Mother. "Though they would have balked at the Office of Mercy. It wasn't their way."

"Why can't we be like the Yangs then?" demanded Natasha. "Why can't we stop the sweeps?"

"Because the Yangs failed," said the Mother. "We don't know exactly why. For a short time there was no fighting, no strife. People were still hungry, and in poor health, but there was hope. As I said, we hold the same ideals as the Yangs. Their collapse was really a great sadness to us. But they did fail, they did. Most believed the lessons of the Yangs in their minds, but not in their hearts. The upheavals came soon, and once they started, human beings found themselves in a terrible, terrible place. The population at that time numbered over fifty-nine billion. The structure of society—its equilibrium—was delicate. The Yangs had already disrupted it once. And once the dissolution process began, it could not be stopped."

"The Yang era," said the Father, "marked the last attempt to carry every living soul on earth into a peaceful future. And we Alphas were the first to put an end to those attempts and to take the necessary and merciful actions toward the world you live in today. It was difficult at first, to realize the extent of the sweeps that would be necessary to bring about this new society. But we can't be too hard on ourselves. The road to peace is always paved with corpses. Even in our most beautiful and fantastic dreams, human beings have accounted for that. The all-powerful God of the old religions was selective. Even heaven had gates. But if you get there in the end, if you create the earthly paradise at last—a paradise free of that threefold evil of physical pain, mental suffering, and death—then it's only logical to forgive yourself. As for the ones we had to leave behind, the ones we could not include as Alphas . . . Well, if they don't *know* they've been left behind, then where is the harm? The dead don't suffer. The dead feel no anguish or regret."

"So you started killing," Natasha said. "Whoever wasn't in your club of Alphas, you decided to kill."

"The first mercy sweep took place a few months before the demise of the Yang political group," the Father said, somewhat nostalgically. "One point three billion people in the heart of a country that has not existed by its former name since. There was a drought. The devastation it caused left the rest of the world with too many to help. Too many even to fathom. It was better than letting them thirst and starve."

"We Alphas had little choice," the Mother explained, as if wanting to soften this bluntly offered fact of the past. "We came alive in this mess of a world and we witnessed the failure of the Yangs for ourselves. We could not stand by. The centuries before us had dealt with suffering in two different ways: first, to ignore it, which we found cruel, and second, to end the causes of the suffering itself, which the Yangs' failure proved was impossible. Our generation was the first to commit itself to the only paradise possible on Earth: the one that allows for either a long, peaceful life, or else, for nothingness. We took over the old Yang bunkers and built these settlements with our paradise in mind, and three hundred and five years ago we launched simultaneous sweeps from our new homes to wipe the world clean of the unsavable human beings. Some managed to survive, and their descendants make up the Tribes. We are sorry that the Storm was not complete, but we try to atone for its failings the best we can."

"What about the Yangs? What happened to them? Were they in the settlements too?"

The Mother's eyes went suddenly cold, and she averted her gaze from Natasha's. "That is a moment in our history," she said, "that we do not need to revisit."

Natasha wondered if the Alphas were right, if life before had been so bad. But no, she stopped herself. No matter the terrible mistakes the

Pines had made, she could not begin trusting the Alphas now. She thought of Axel, of London, fleeing from the settlement, out in the forest somewhere. She knew that they probably despised her, and probably blamed her for their suffering. But that didn't matter. They were human beings and they had the right to live and be free without the interference of the strangers in America-Five.

"It's wrong," Natasha said, fighting against the dulling effects of the Alphas' logic. "You shouldn't kill, never kill."

"Do you remember the dog you encountered on your mission?" asked the Father.

"Yes," said Natasha, her heart filling with trepidation.

"You had the chance to end its life and you chose not to. You hesitated. The dog ran away, and before you could correct your mistake, you were captured. What if I told you, less than forty-nine hours after your encounter, that dog broke its leg chasing after a rabbit, was unable to return to its masters, and died of thirst in the woods?"

"Stop," said Natasha.

"Do you think the bit of life you gave that dog was worth it—forty-nine hours in exchange for a long, terrible death?"

But at this, Natasha screamed, she could not bear to hear them talk anymore. They were creating the Wall again, this time with their words. They used their words to make it right but what they said was not the truth, it wasn't real. She could feel the real thing but she couldn't say it. The real thing didn't fit within their language. She screamed and let the pain burn her from the inside out.

Only when the Mother and Father had been quiet a long time did Natasha speak.

"I feel empathy," she said.

"Misplaced Empathy."

"No," Natasha shouted, propelled to her feet by the force of her frustration. "It's not misplaced! You can't tell me that. I talked to them.

I understand them. Maybe I didn't know they'd lie about the attack. That they'd panic and shoot people instead of keeping their word. I hate them for hurting Min-he and everyone else. But you won't make me forget. You're the ones to blame for this. All these terrible things are your fault. Just like you say. The Storm, the settlements. You made it so that there was such a thing as the Tribes. And now look at what your Ethical Code has done to them. You Alphas didn't even realize that the Pines had passed down stories of the Storm. But I figured it out. I saw beyond your ethics and I can feel what they feel."

"And what do they feel?" the Mother asked, her voice thick with condescension.

"The same as us. They want to live. What if I came over there and put my hands around your neck and squeezed? You wouldn't think anything except that you wanted to live!"

"Sit down, Natasha. Now," said the Father.

She sank slowly to her seat. The Father had not raised his voice a decibel, but the sheer authority of a direct command made the muscles in her legs go soft.

"We are surprised at you," he continued. "We thought that witnessing the devastation you caused to this settlement, and to a great number of Tribespeople and citizens both, would be enough to make you reconsider your views. But it's no matter. We have other ways."

Natasha did not answer. Despite her fear, a sudden tiredness was coming over her. Because what good was it to fight? She was one person. Not even a real settlement-created citizen. Her arguments hit as severely as a fist against a concrete wall. The settlement was indomitable. If she had only understood that before, she never would have tried to bring it down.

"Please place your arms on the armrests, palms up. Kindly raise your head. That's it."

The frustration washed away, upward through her limbs, dissolving from her core. What was it about obeying that made that happen? Clamps came over her arms and legs. A helmet lowered from the ceiling fixed over her head. It fastened beneath her chin.

"Certain new technologies have emerged from the Department of Research in recent years," said the Mother. "This machine—but *machine* sounds too base a word—this *communicator* is a descendant of the Pretends you are familiar with."

The Mother rose and approached her with surprising gracefulness.

"You say that you feel empathy for the Tribes. Well, empathy is very important for ethics. Once upon a time, in fact, the only ethical systems available to the human race were glorified variations of the most common articulation of empathy, the Golden Rule. You remember learning about the Golden Rule, don't you, Natasha? Treat others as you would like to be treated. Love thy neighbor as thyself. Do unto others as you would have others do unto you. Laws depended on it, religion depended on it. But can you see the failure acknowledged within these formulations? Treat others as *you* would like to be treated. Love thy neighbor as *thyself.* Do unto others as you would have others do unto *you.* They made no bones about it. The statements themselves implicitly acknowledge that we can truly know nothing other than ourselves. It's the best we can do to project our minds onto others, and act accordingly. We Alphas, however, expect a bit more from the human race than portable solipsism. In order to make truly ethical decisions, we must holistically understand the minds involved. In the case of the sweeps, one must understand pain in order to understand the ethical purposes at work."

A surge of energy erupted in Natasha's head, and before she understood what was happening—that the Mother had touched some switch on the chair's controls—she plunged into a terror of feeling like she had never known. Her perceptions ripped away from her mind; her mind ripped away from her own self. What she had felt and thought a second ago—her anger at the Alphas, her outrage at their smugness, her fear for the future—had slipped into the farthest corners of awareness—gone. Pain splintered down the spine. Real, fiery pain. Nerves in the body that she had never felt before—the dead center of the brain, the full column of the neck, the guts through from flesh to bone—shook violently and screamed.

She looked around; the Department of Health. She recognized its sharp smell and high walls and ceiling that rained nets, tangles of clear thread thin as fishing lines and spiked with silver, *let me go, let go, oh, please let me go.*

Then she cowered because there were people: strangers with broad foreheads and white masks across their mouths. They held metal instruments in gloved hands, and she would not let them touch her. She needed to keep them away.

With a last burst of strength she threw herself at them. A hand, Natasha's hand but not Natasha's, lashed out at them and made contact, scratching across a woman's cheek. A last hatred. A last defiance. The masked faces scattered and screamed.

But she should not have done it, because as she fell back from them, the pain sliced through her. Deep in the chest. Natasha opened her mouth wide. Blood gurgled in the throat. She sucked at the air and flailed but her lips could not grasp it. Her hands reached for a burning pool of blood at her center, at the place of her lungs. Then a rush of feeling overwhelmed her and suddenly it was like her eyes had fallen into her head. She was hurtling toward a terrible darkness, with gathering speed, and there was no feeling but despair, because the others had gone, they had gone already. . . .

Natasha came alive again, suddenly, her mind bursting into the recognizable world like a deep-sea diver in the Pretends abruptly splashing through to the surface.

She gasped. Her hands went for her chest though the clamps restrained them. Her whole body trembled. Acid rose in her throat and stuck and she began to cough uncontrollably. The faces of the Mother and Father danced in her vision, stonelike and unconcerned.

"What was that?" Natasha asked finally, still struggling for air.

"Not what, *who*," answered the Mother. "As I said, there have been interesting developments in the Department of Research. Our earliest Pretends allowed us to stimulate the body's senses directly, making the player feel, touch, hear, smell, and see a reality that was not actually there. With Free Play, our technology allowed us to reverse the process—to draw out feelings and thoughts from the player's mind and project them in enhanced form. Now we have another breakthrough, one that combines these technologies. Our computers have learned to read the feelings and thoughts of one human being—the mental 'pattern' as the researchers call it—and enforce that pattern directly onto a second, entirely independent mind."

"You put someone's thoughts into my head?"

"Yes. That captures it well enough."

"Who was that then?"

"He calls himself 'Tezo.' He was one of five Tribespeople whom we recovered alive."

A chill went through Natasha. They knew; they were watching her closely for a reaction. Raj or Sarah must have told them that she and Tezo had been intended for each other all those years ago, that he was the focal point of the life she had not lived. Or else, perhaps the Alphas had more ways of knowing what went on outside the settlement than Natasha had guessed.

"Who else do you have?" she asked, afraid to hear the answer.

"We didn't get their names. But they have been granted mercy already. Tezo has done us the service of telling the Pines' story. The Palms' story, I should say. We expect his thoughts to be an invaluable resource for years to come."

"If that was him, then why is there pain? I thought you didn't believe in pain!"

"They administered the medicines several minutes ago. It takes some time to feel the effects, especially when the damage is great."

"He'll die?"

"Eventually, yes. We'll make it as easy as possible. But realize that what he endures in these moments will likely prevent other pain in the future. That is why it's allowed."

The Mother moved toward the controls on the chair and Natasha lunged against the restraints to stop her, the muscles in her body leaping instinctively into revolt.

"Don't!" she said. "Please!"

"We are not doing your body any actual damage," the Father assured from his chair. "Every organ, every molecule inside you is carrying happily along. It is only Pretend. Only a change in perception. Two minds merged together as one. You wanted real empathy, so here is your chance."

Again, Natasha plunged, this time deeper than before. Her nerves electrified, and the anguish that rolled over her drowned with its own tenor of horror. Natasha woke fully, with opened eyes. A whole universe of impossible memories battered every mote of this stranger's present—stranger and not stranger, because it and she, he and she, the separation did not hold.

The masked faces were huddled in the corner, one bleeding from the cheek. Good. Hatred for these people emanated in waves, a hatred that was always there, now unleashed. Their alien houses. Their alien clothes.

But as soon as the anger had fully taken hold, enough to nearly incite a second attack, the feeling cut off, suddenly, because now something else was happening. A crush inside the ribs, like three tons of weight had fallen, crushing them without relief. Their hands went to stop it—but too late. The room began to swirl and now the dizzying crush held the fleeting and impossible faces of Axel, Sonlow, London, and Raul. . . .

The air would not come, no matter how they demanded, and Tezo and Natasha and Natasha and Tezo began to fall. They howled a silent howl as they fell backward into oblivion. The abyss; a crash against a wall; and nothing to shout at, nothing to fight. The only action was arrival; the only distance, this; for nothing existed more absolute than the nothing, and so many had died, they had died already. And then the machine had nothing to grasp at, and the separation did come.

Natasha did not wake right away. Her body writhed, her lungs rising and falling forcefully, as if her mind feared that any cessation would be the final cessation, that breathing would not start again. When the Mother began to speak, her voice was far away.

"We understand how difficult this is for you, Natasha. Your life in this settlement has hardly prepared you for the pain of a broken finger, much less that of collapsed lungs and an agonizing death. However, this suffering occurred. It is real. It happened here, in America-Five, and as a direct result of your actions against us. We hope you understand the necessity of your feeling this pain for yourself. The necessity of confronting with your own body the evil thing that is the true enemy of this settlement."

Natasha trembled, her eyes opened to the bright, white room.

"We're also hoping you might comprehend better now," the Mother continued, "the difference between empathy and Misplaced Empathy. Would you have recognized that mind as Tezo's if we had not told you in advance?"

Natasha forced her lips to move. "No," she said.

"Is that a mind you could have loved?"

Natasha shuddered. "No."

As the Mother returned to her chair, she ran her fingers through the moving wall of water. The light glinted, dancing white ribbons of light.

"There is the chance for so much good in the world," she said. "But first, we must clean out the bad. Life without peace and eternity is terrible, and we must end it. We must clean it out. Nature couldn't do it. Faith couldn't. Only we can, man and woman. We are the only merciful intelligence in the universe."

The Mother and Father remained looking at her, and the only sounds were of rushing water and Natasha's sobs. The echo of Tezo's pain washed over her, again and again, making her cells tremble. Her legs jerked like they were trying to flee the suffering and the death that now had no vessel, no center, that hung like a low, threatening fog over the earth, clinging to the walls of the wings and the curve of the Dome. Anything was better than to let it in. If she could, she would run away from here and find a hidden cubby among the storagerooms on level eight. She would stay there forever and live on bread and water rather than face the pain again.

After some time, Natasha did not know how much, the Mother spoke, her voice calm and velvety.

"You think we're going to banish you from the settlement," she said. "But however much trouble you caused, we would never respond in that manner. We'll see what this meeting does for your thinking. If we find you still in need of illumination, there are other methods we might try. The process of reeducation varies with each individual, but a truthful ethics always triumphs in the end. We can guarantee that from three hundred years of experience. Believe it or not, you're not the first citizen in America-Five to question our way of life—though perhaps you came the closest to doing it real damage."

"Why did he save me?" Natasha asked. "I wish he hadn't. Why would he take me Inside?"

She did not know the question burned in her until she asked, but then she understood it as the crux, the origin of her unrest. Because it had all started with that, hadn't it? And now she could not begin to understand the losses of this day until she had finally made sense of her own position, until she had freed herself from the muddledness of her own imprisoning perspective.

"Ahhh," breathed the Mother. "Why did our most accomplished member of the Office of Mercy risk his life and throw away his beliefs to save a child he had set out to sweep? Well, have you asked him?"

"He told me that he didn't think. That I looked so perfect and inno-cent he couldn't help but take me."

"I'm sure that's true, but it's not the whole story. Over the years, your friend Jeffrey has experienced many of the same doubts that you yourself harbor. He's gone through countless sessions of reeducation, beginning when he was a very young man. He generally performed quite well at his job, but there have been hard times for him. Times when he regretted sweeping every human being whom he had saved from suffering. Before the Palms' attack, he was actually thinking about resigning from the Office of Mercy. We believe—and he believes too—that he saved you in an attempt to make up for the lives he had ended."

"It doesn't make up for it."

"No, of course not. One has nothing to do with the other."

"He shouldn't have taken me."

"It would have been fine if he hadn't. As it turns out, your suffering as a small child would not have equaled the suffering you caused to others as an adult. But Jeffrey did save you. He took you, and that's all that matters. Once you entered the settlement you became one of us. Your future was fixed. We named you immediately, within the first hour you came Inside. 'Natasha' was a variation of the name you called yourself—'Nassia.' We gave you 'Wiley' in honor of your cunning skill in so wholly altering the design of your life."

The clamps had fallen back from Natasha's wrists and the helmet had released its grip.

"Understand," said the Father, "we are not going to make this infor-mation public to the rest of the settlement, and neither should you. No one but Jeffrey—and eventually, Arthur—will know your full involve-ment in this incident. We have told your friends the same. Raj, Mer-cedes, Sarah, Ben, and Eduardo will each have their own program of reeducation. There is no danger that any of them will revisit the sub-ject of this treachery with you. Kindly pay them the same courtesy."

"What am I supposed to do now?" Natasha asked.

Two Betas had entered the room; they were helping her up from the chair.

The Father raised his eyebrows, as if the answer were obvious.

"You dedicate yourself to the betterment of the world," he said. "You preserve goodness and eliminate suffering. You labor to make your own life and the life of your fellow citizens peaceful and long."

"How will I?" Natasha said, pleading. "The suffering is so bad. I can't forget it. I'll never be able to think about anything else."

"Now you understand," the Mother said with a sigh, "just a tiny fraction of what it is to be an Alpha."

"How will I live though?" Natasha demanded, before the Betas could take her away. "How will I do anything without thinking about it?"

The Father looked down at her, the waterfall rushing behind him, and spoke his words slowly.

"You build a Wall," he said.

18

They let her sleep. The second round of medicine they administered for her wounded shoulder spread through her body, making her limbs feel numb and heavy and her thoughts groggy and slow. The Department of Government Betas took the job of escorting Natasha down to her sleeproom. Two Delta women rode the elephant with them, and despite the haziness of her mind, Natasha felt the sting of their every word.

"I heard it from Cameron Pacheco himself," the first woman said. "They're recycling the Zetas. With the New Wing so damaged, we can't possibly sustain them."

"No, it's too terrible," the other replied.

"But it's the only way," answered the first. "The future of the settlement depends on us obeying our own rules. We can't make a new generation unless we have triple the surplus to support them. And that's simply not the case at the moment. What with the Garden in ruins and Tom Doncaster trying to supervise twenty projects at once . . ."

Hours later, a heavy knocking at her sleeproom door roused Natasha awake. She threw back the covers and crossed the tiny space in the dark. Arthur stood in the hall. His grim and astonished look made Natasha sure that he knew, now, what she had done. The Alphas wanted Natasha in the Office of Mercy, Arthur told her; they had sent him down to collect her.

The Dome glowed mighty and sure, overwhelming the blank sky beyond its honeycomb windows. The floor was polished clean, and the injured citizens and medical supplies absorbed back into the Department of Health. At the end of the Department of the Exterior hall, the yellow door of the Strongroom glowed tall and impenetrable. Probably during the whole attack, no one had so much as touched it.

Inside the Office of Mercy, the computer stations were abandoned, the chairs tucked in and the screens blank, all except for Natasha's own. The room contained but three living souls: Jeffrey, the Mother, and the Father. They stood in a line beside her desk, and Arthur walked ahead to join them. Natasha had never seen an Alpha in the Office of Mercy before and, despite everything that had happened, she found their presence jarring.

"Your colleagues in the Office of Mercy worked all night to track the remaining members of the Pine Tribe," said the Mother. "They have been located on the shore, only seven miles north of the Crane sweep site. It appears that they are trying to return to the mountains where they came from. Many of them are seriously hurt, but they have been moving steadily, attempting to escape the perimeter. Do you understand what needs to be done?"

"Yes," said Natasha.

She sat down at her computer and touched the keys with clammy hands. The screen came alive, a black-and-white image of the surviving Pines scattered across the pale sand.

"The count is complete as far as we can tell," Jeffrey said. His face was turned to the screen, but Natasha could see that he looked somewhat ill. "We think they must have lost a few more during their escape. They left the green carrying at least two bodies with them."

She recognized them all, the figures on the screen. A head turned and Natasha saw the woman who had handed her a gun in the Pines'

cavelike armory, and then the man who had sung the prayers the loud-
est, in response to Hesma's calls. Two young boys lay side by side in
the shade of the trees, one with his head wrapped up in fabric. A
woman screamed in pain or in grief, while Sonlow attempted half-
heartedly to soothe her. A little outside the group, London sat doubled
over, looking out at the ocean, his long hair whipping across his face
in the wind. Axel walked over and crouched down beside him, rocking
on his heels, his face drawn and still.

Natasha made note of their coordinates. She opened the screen
marked "Sweep" and entered her username and password. Jeffrey gave
her the clearance code, and she typed it. She double-checked the coordinates and copied them to the command box.

Are you sure that you want to nova coordinates 1150 5918?
Yes.

In the background, Axel leaned over, speaking to London.

Weapon information?

A1, typed Natasha.

"I think size G will be sufficient, dear," came the Mother's voice
from over her shoulder. "There's no need to waste."

Natasha deleted her entry and typed in *G1*. It was not unfeeling, she
thought, it was only the practical implementation of ethics. Pain had
no place in a good universe, and it fell to men and women to eliminate
what pain did exist as efficiently as possible.

Please confirm command.

Natasha could have clicked the last button with her eyes closed, but
why shouldn't she watch?

The nova command box disappeared and the Pines returned to the
forefront. The wind blew, throwing London's hair all the way back
from his face. Axel placed a hand on the boy's neck, a gesture that at
once offered strength and also showed a deeper desperation. Natasha
thought that maybe the nova had malfunctioned, but then came a sudden burst and the whole visual went to static.

Jeffrey made a gagging sound in his throat. He turned and walked out of the room.

"Is that it?" asked Natasha.

"We can assume so," said the Mother. "In a few days, we'll send out a team to confirm it was clean. That was your first sweep, was it not?"

"Yes," said Natasha.

"And how do you feel?"

The static roared, empty and cold. The fight had left her, and the only answer beat in Natasha's mind like a truth so strong that it had its own heart.

"Relieved," she said.

The attack had scarred the settlement deeply, and cut wounds in some places—the New Wing, the Department of Agriculture, the citizens' general sense of security—that would take many years to heal. Min-he had one of the longest stays in the Department of Health; and she emerged from that wing only finally, with a certain sullenness of affect where once a sparkling vivaciousness had dwelled, and with a gash across her face, left from her visor, that Bioreplacement could not fully dissolve. Natasha noticed that her roommate did not sleep soundly anymore; and on some nights Min-he would actually leave their room and slip into the hall, the light catching the rough outline of her cheek and reminding Natasha—as she was often reminded—of what, for Min-he, had almost been.

A cleanup crew dismantled the incuvats and piping systems in the New Wing for reusable parts. For some time, the screeching of saws went on day and night; even six levels down they could hear it. The construction teams sealed off the New Wing doors to the Dome, abandoning eight years of work. Of course no one could disagree with the Alphas' decision to discontinue the Zetas. Though still, it was a sad, somber day when the official announcement came over the maincomputer: "We regret to inform you that the Tribe attack has forced us to postpone the creation of a Zeta generation indefinitely. . . ." As the citizens crossed through the Dome that week, many threw long, regretful looks toward the covered New Wing entrance. How terrible that they had named them, the citizens would say to one another. How sad that they had already begun to imagine who the Zetas would be and in what Office they would one day work.

The ethical principles were similar, perhaps, but destroying the Zetas had felt so different from a sweep. In a sweep, one put an end to inevitable suffering, but with this—well, these were lives that up until the attack would have been plentiful and peaceful and good.

"Horrible," the citizens would say, "and named already."

And yet. The Alphas encouraged the citizens to remember that it was not *too* overwhelmingly sad. Perhaps a new generation of Zetas would come along in the next decade or so, once America-Five had picked itself up and restored its equilibrium. The bioengineers had the Zetas' raw DNA safely stored in the labs, available for reuse; and though the next group would not be literally the *same*, it should be close enough to provide consolation.

"The funny thing is," Eric said loudly over dinner one night, largely repeating the Alphas' position, "once the new generation of Zetas comes, we won't feel badly about losing the first one at all. Because we'll know in the back of our minds that if the *old* Zetas hadn't been destroyed, these *new* ones could never have come into existence. And we'll love the *new* Zetas so much that all our loyalties will lie with them!"

As for Natasha, she did not dare test this logic with empathy— *Misplaced Empathy*—for the gone generation. Nor did she project onto the dead Pines, her blood family and her earliest companions on Earth, in foolish attempts to see the sweep from "their eyes"—eyes that were now molecules, dust. Her thoughts cowered in her head, not even needing a Wall to restrain them. Because how could she dare? Who was she to know, or to want to know, what lay beyond ordered life in the settlement?

Natasha could not tell how things were with the others. She saw Mercedes, Eduardo, Sarah, and Ben sometimes; but when she did, they never spoke to her. Like Natasha herself, they acted differently, timid and self-effacing. Once Natasha caught Sarah staring at her in the Dining Hall. But other than that, they showed no open curiosity about the extent of Natasha's additional involvement in the attack. Perhaps they could guess what she had done; or perhaps they assumed that the Pines had acted alone, and that Natasha was no more culpable in the attack than they were.

Raj looked different too, though not in the same way as the others. Where the others seemed guilty or remorseful, Raj was only hollow. Natasha wondered if he had experienced a simulation like what the Alphas had done to her—and if Raj, who had such an embracing mind, had learned suffering the way Natasha had learned it. They did speak once, despite the Mother and Father's prohibitions, finding themselves accidentally alone together in the elephant.

"We made a terrible mistake," said Raj, once the doors had closed behind two Gammas exiting on level two. His face had grown thin and sharp, and his flesh bluish around the eyes. "We're young and we did what young people do. We mistook passion for perception. I understand that now. I want to apologize for—" he stumbled. "For my part in contacting the Tribe."

"I'm sorry too," said Natasha, staring at the elephant doors.

"There is no in-between, is there?" asked Raj. "No good between nothingness and life in the settlements. And death like what happens Outside . . . it's a worse thing than I'd thought. To have all this ripped away from you. To watch as your life is stolen from you, and you unable to stop it. I love living. It made me realize how much I love being alive. I never want to die, do you?"

"No," said Natasha. "I never want to die. Never."

They parted ways in the Dome, and from then on Natasha tried her best not to come within several yards of Raj Radhakrishnan. For reasons she did not try to name, the mere sight of him—his erect and elegant posture, his wise face and sharp eyes—was enough to throw her into a frightening relapse of thought: Axel kneeling down beside his brother, the wind whipping their hair and the dead roar that followed, Tezo's mind, foreign and enraged—the memory of it would burst into Natasha's head, and the emptiness would try to swallow her too.

Meanwhile, the Betas who directed Natasha's reeducation made all sorts of promises. They claimed that her case was by no means hopeless; and they detected progress in her mode of thought even before Natasha herself could feel it. They constantly assured her that, with time and steady exertion, she would continue to improve. And in the weeks following the attack (she worked on a crew in the Garden, welding iron bars together that would serve to protect the new skylights in the roof), Natasha did her best to follow their instructions, and for whole mornings or afternoons would exercise blending her thoughts with the Ethical Code.

Often while Natasha worked, she found herself able to contemplate the Wall and the views of the Alphas with a newfound comprehension and ease. How the Alphas taught the younger generations to build Walls because they loved their children, and wished to protect them from a knowledge of the dreadful things Outside. And the danger too. The danger of throwing your mind too much at other people, as Natasha had done with the Tribe, so that you begin to lose your own self, and lose the beauty of your own life.

Natasha drew down her mask and guided a small blue flame along the juncture of an iron bar and its frame. A finished plate, this one circular and intended for the very center of the Garden roof, fell with a clang and she jumped, her heart racing.

Any sudden noise reminded her of the attack. The screams and the blood. How easily a place of calm and peace can shatter to reveal the hell at its foundation.

The heat of the flame rippled the air and, with practiced dexterity, Natasha rounded the flame to the opposite side of the bar.

The only hope was for places of peace to go on, she thought, and for places of horror to disappear. It would be difficult, of course, but they could make it happen if they tried. World Peace, Eternal Life, and All Suffering Ended. It helped Natasha to remember those aims, the bedrock of the settlement's ethics. And, in lengthening moments, she occasionally managed to stand on its plane, viewing the universe from that solid ground.

Even Natasha's own past had begun troubling her less than it had: the fact that, if Jeffrey had not rescued her twenty-two years ago, she would have numbered also among the nonexistent. Because there was another law, Natasha had found, a higher law, in which she could take comfort. The law of time. The past was past, as the Alphas had said. And Natasha's past could only have happened the way it had happened. The fire could only have rushed out of control and Jeffrey could never have chosen *not* to save her because if he had not saved her then he would not have been Jeffrey. It did not make sense to wonder, what if he had not reached over the fire and grabbed her, had not run until they reached the Dome? What if he had not held on until they had to pry her out of his arms? The law of time gave him only one chance to decide, and he had decided. It could not have happened differently. It could never be otherwise.

And he still loved her. Jeffrey. He was the only person in the settlement, excepting the Alphas and Arthur, who knew for sure the attack was her fault and, despite everything, he loved her still. Natasha hadn't expected it, given how much he'd changed in other respects. His fury toward her at the time of the invasion had dissipated almost impossibly fast, leaving behind a reservedness that, at least according to Natasha's experience, was completely unlike him. He refrained from speaking one word to her about what she had done or who she was, keeping instead to topics like how the cleanup was going or who was headed out next to work on the sensors. Even at mealtimes, he seemed nervous: once Natasha, Eric, and Min-he had noticed how his fork would shake on the way to his mouth. Gradually then, as the days passed and the citizens continued their repairs on the settlement, strange rumors began reaching Natasha from the Office of Mercy: that Jeffrey had moved to one of the front cubicles and worked exclusively on satellite watch, that Claudia had taken over what was left of his team, that she had become quite indispensable to Arthur, and, most bizarrely of all, that none of this seemed to upset Jeffrey or cause him the slightest concern.

On Natasha's last day doing cleanup in the Garden—a full ten weeks after the Pines' attack—she worked with a team high on the scaffolding, putting the final touches on the new roof. It was not pretty like the old one, because instead of pure sky, one looked up now to an iron grate. But it was safe and secure, and that was what mattered. When the dinnerhour came, Natasha gathered her supplies and climbed carefully down to the grass.

She was surprised to see Jeffrey at the edge of the lawn, though some seconds later she remembered that he had arranged to meet her here, and had said, in fact, that he had something very important to ask her. He sat on a bench beneath an oak tree, one of the only trees untouched by the attack. Two white butterflies flitted near him in the soft, evening light, and, invisible amid the branches, the birds called to one another in a curious but lazy way. He stood when he saw her and waited while she put her mask and welding tools away in the metal supply bins.

"Are you in a rush to get to dinner?" he asked.

She showed her hands, which were streaked with black, gritty oil.

"I'll need to shower first."

"Oh," he said.

"But I don't have to go right away."

She walked over to him and they sat together beneath the canopy of branches, slightly obscured from the view of the last cleanup crew members shuffling by. Tom Doncaster was the last to leave, securing the lids on the supply bins and sauntering across the grass with the flushed and satisfied expression of a citizen who has just put in a solid day's work.

Natasha waited for Jeffrey to speak, but he seemed unable. He rubbed his sleeve up and down his arm.

"I'm excited to start my new job," Natasha offered finally, to break the silence. "I met with Li Quin yesterday, and she's really nice. She just got appointed head of the Department of Health."

Jeffrey stopped rubbing his arm and folded his hands in his lap.

"You're not mad anymore that we transferred you out of the Office of Mercy?" he asked.

"No, Jeffrey, how could I be?"

He nodded and lapsed into silence again.

"They told me the origin of my surname," Natasha said, reaching for something to pique his interest. "The Alphas did."

"Wiley." He smiled nervously. "It turns out to suit you better than we could have imagined. It's funny how that happens sometimes. I'm one of those cases too. Do you know the origin of my surname?"

"Montague? That's Anglo-Saxon, right?"

"I'm eighty-one percent Anglo-Saxon, yes. So for me, they scoured the writings of a man who was probably the greatest thinker of my race, and plucked my name out of one of his plays. The character, Montague, is a young man who acts solely out of love, and destroys everything he touches. Especially the person he loves most of all."

Jeffrey laughed a short, weak laugh, but Natasha did not see what was amusing.

"What did you want to ask me, Jeffrey?"

He twitched, like she had startled him. Then he turned on the bench to face her.

"I'm going away," he said. "And I want you to come with me."

"You're leaving the Office of Mercy too?"

"Not just the Office," he said. "I'm leaving America-Five. I'm leaving the settlement. I don't belong here. I've tried to convince myself that I do, but I can't anymore."

"What are you talking about?" Natasha said incredulously, smiling at the sheer absurdity of what he was saying. "Since when have you had an idea like that?"

"Since a long time ago," he said. "Since before you were born. Since before I defied this whole society to save you."

"Be serious," Natasha demanded.

"I am," Jeffrey assured. "I'm absolutely serious. Look, I want you to understand, having the Palms return rattled something inside me. It didn't change me. It just forced me to stop hiding some very strong convictions."

"Well," Natasha answered swiftly. She felt disconcerted, despite herself, and she was annoyed at Jeffrey for saying such wild things. "Even if you wanted to leave, you can't. It's different than it was before the attack. We have all those new sensors. The Office of Mercy would locate you in two minutes and send out a team to bring you home."

"I won't be hurting anyone by going," Jeffrey replied, speaking softly, "and we're allowed to make our own decisions, as long as we cause no suffering to others. The Ethical Code tells us that much. It's a bit of a loophole, actually," he added with a small smile. "The Mother and Father were somewhat taken aback, I think, when I pointed that out during my reeducation. But they saw it too. A free and solitary man in the forest, a man who has knowingly chosen his own fate, poses no threat to the consistency of their ethical practices, while holding that same man against his will most certainly does." He glanced up at the roof, at the overlapping bars. "The Alphas aren't happy about it," he confessed, after a pause, "but they're going to let me leave. They had a vote last week in the Department of Government. I told them my plans and they gave their permission. There's nothing objectively bad about what I'm doing, everyone agrees."

He waited for her to respond, but Natasha only shook her head, stunned.

"I'm going south," he continued more slowly, "straight down longitude seventy-five, to the forest we have marked on our satellite maps. The place where the large animals migrated last year. I'll take my clothing and bedding. And tools. I've been talking to Nolan over in the labs. He's making me a freshwater filter and a tent for shelter. I'll have vitamin pills to supplement my diet."

"Enough for forever?"

"Not that long, no."

Natasha turned and looked at the lawn, her lips pressed in agitation.

"You can't come back, if you go," she said, her voice breaking slightly. "You have to be sure. I thought I was sure with the Pines and it turns out I wasn't. I was wrong and I can only thank the Alphas that I didn't give up my life to die out there."

Jeffrey nodded but did not reply. A robin swooped low over their heads, a small twig clutched in its beak; the cows groaned from adjacent pastures, anxious for milking.

"I always wondered if you remembered," Jeffrey said at length. "You were usually a cheerful child, but sometimes you would become so serious and silent. You'd stare up at the Dome windows in a kind of daze. There were times when I thought you knew everything."

"I didn't," Natasha said. "I never guessed I came from the Outside until the Pines told me."

"But the Office of Mercy," Jeffrey pushed. "You had such a precocious interest in the Tribes."

"Only because I found the Outside exciting. And because you worked there. You were so nice to me when I was a kid. I wanted to have the same job as you."

"Oh, Natasha, will you ever forgive me?" For a moment, Jeffrey was overcome, and he buried his face in his hands. "I needed you. I needed you so badly. Before I found you, I only felt like a murderer. They used to bring me in for reeducation but it didn't matter. They could try to reshape my mind all they wanted but that didn't change what I'd done. They used to follow me, all those people, after I killed them. The walls of the Dome couldn't keep them out. They would pass through a solid meter of concrete like it was air. And they'd pass through the floors to find me in my bed and they'd pass into my skull and stay there. But then I saved you. And when I showed them your face in my mind, it forced them back. You're special to me. Very, very special. Not only for your beauty or your intelligence, but because you're my warrior."

His knuckles grazed her chin and, gently, he kissed her lips.

"I can't," she said, pulling back. "I know we used to. But it's a distraction from our ethical goals."

"You'll come with me, though," he said, with passionate force. "You'll live with me in the forest. We don't have to leave right away. I swear I can wait as long as you need. Because think of how amazing it will be, once we're out there. No Office of Mercy, no endless rounds of bioreplacement. I'm so sick of being cooped up in this place. We'll walk as far south as our legs will carry us. We'll live in the forest and eat from the trees."

Natasha eyed him searchingly, looking to call his bluff, and wondering how a person who had seemed to understand the Ethical Code so thoroughly could believe that such an option existed within its bounds.

"They'll sweep you, you know," Natasha said finally, "if you ever go through with it."

Jeffrey did not answer, but his body subtly retreated from hers.

"They will," Natasha insisted. "Something tiny. A G4. You'd never see it coming."

"No," he said harshly, cutting her off. "I've thought about sweeps.

The Alphas won't do it. They wouldn't have lied. I've lived all my life in this settlement. Forty-three years. I've put in my time and they gave me permission."

"But it's different," Natasha replied, "once you're Outside. It won't matter what they said to you in the Department of Government." She shook her head. "Try, Jeffrey," she said, in a more intimate tone. "Try to think about this whole thing logically. The Ethical Code guarantees every person a life without suffering. Inside because there is no suffering, Outside because there is no life. Those are the only divisions that matter."

"You're forgetting to mention my suffering in this settlement," Jeffrey countered. "My guilt. My horror at the way we live. I can't believe anymore in a paradise that comes at the expense of so many, and I have no desire to continue my part in it. That's my feeling. And for once I'm going to trust my feeling." He looked at her, his anger suddenly vanishing. "You're not coming, are you?" he asked.

Natasha grimaced. "Not Outside, no."

He nodded. "I guess I knew that."

"I'm not coming because you'll die," Natasha said, thinking he must still be failing to comprehend this fact. "The Alphas will give the order to sweep as soon as you're far enough away for them to safely launch a nova."

"I don't care what they're planning."

"You do!"

"I mean that I'll accept the risk. I know the life I want to live. It will be up to the Alphas to take it away from me."

"Please, Jeffrey," Natasha cried, completely distraught, "stop acting like they're your enemy. The Alphas love you. I wish you could see that."

"But do *you* love me, Natasha?"

"Yes!"

Natasha reached out and clasped his hand to reassure him, but because she was distracted by the nightshift workers, who had just begun filtering into the wing, she missed the resigned disbelief that her answer had brought to Jeffrey's face.

The nightshift workers gathered their tools. They climbed the high ladders to the top of the scaffolding and, in the pooling light, they braced themselves against the railings as they began pounding the last iron bars into place.

For a long time, Natasha and Jeffrey sat on the bench, Natasha relentless in her efforts to persuade Jeffrey to stay. But her words were in vain. No threat of death or heartfelt plea could pull Jeffrey from the vision of open sky and raw, abundant earth that seemed to be taking shape, already, in the Garden air before him. Jeffrey would go. He would exit the settlement, leaving Natasha and all the citizens of America-Five to continue (as neither Natasha nor Jeffrey would dare to describe it) the deferment of that hovering hour when they, too, would face their reward or their punishment.

Acknowledgments

I am deeply grateful to Max Apple, Nicholas Delbanco, Peter Ho Davies, Laura Kasischke, Eileen Pollack, Nancy Reisman, Hendrik Meijer, Ron Carlson, Arlene Keizer, Celeste Ng, Marissa Perry, Anne Stameshkin, Sonia Djanikian, and Peter Bennett for their early and continued support. Thank you to Sally Wofford-Girand, Taylor Sperry, and all of the amazing people at Brick House Literary Agents and at Viking Penguin; and especially to my agent, Jenni Ferrari-Adler, and my editor, Allison Lorentzen, for their brilliant insights and crucial enthusiasm for this book. Thank you to Gregory Djanikian and Alysa Bennett for guiding the way; and (again) to Phil Sandick for everything.